MW00588206

WHEN THE SHADOWS FALL

Elise Noble

Published by Undercover Publishing Limited

Copyright © 2020 Elise Noble

v4

ISBN: 978-1-912888-28-3

Edited by Nikki Mentges, NAM Editorial

Cover design by Abigail Sins

www.undercover-publishing.com

www.elise-noble.com

All animals are equal, but some animals are more equal than others.
- *George Orwell*

let alone get access to his computer. His PA seems to deal with all his work-related communications. And if he has a second cell phone, it isn't registered in his name."

"Thanks, Mack." Emmy tossed her phone back onto a weight bench. "I hate this fucking job. Alaric's right. *Emerald*'s jinxed."

The emerald in question wasn't a gem but a stolen painting—*The Girl with the Emerald Ring*—and Alaric had been trying to retrieve her since his days as an FBI agent. Along with Blackwood, he'd recently recovered another painting stolen from the Becker Museum in the same heist—a rescue operation that had left four people dead and two more traumatised—but *Emerald* herself remained elusive, a malevolent presence hiding in the shadows. I'd seen a photo of her. A half-naked siren reclining on a bed of roses as her enigmatic smile lured men to their doom. I could understand her destructive attitude. The artist who painted her had been male, and if I'd had to lie there for all eternity with thorns stuck up my arse, then I'd want revenge on mankind too.

So far, she'd been responsible for Alaric and Emmy facing a hail of bullets when they tried to buy her from the thieves eight years ago, for Alaric losing his job when the pay-off vanished along with the painting, and for Emmy and Black's current marital problems. Why? Because I very much suspected Black was the one who'd disappeared the pay-off.

And where did Marshall come in? Well, he'd been the artnapper who showed up to collect the booty. Ten million bucks in cash and untraceable diamonds.

Which led us to our current predicament.

With the possibility of more booby traps plus

Emerald's curse hanging over our heads, nobody wanted to chance a raid on the property. Besides, we'd set up cameras to watch the place. Marshall had two armed guards stationed there at all times, twenty-three security lights, a plethora of motion sensors, and a groom who came morning, noon, and night to take care of his horses. He sponsored the sheriff's department's summer barbecue, which meant deputies did regular drive-bys. Oh, and he was an insomniac.

The conclusion? We'd have to target him away from the property, but that presented its own challenges because when he did venture out, he favoured events with crowds of people present. Nobody wanted to involve innocent bystanders in a shoot-out. A couple of weeks ago, we'd gathered in one of Riverley's conference rooms and brainstormed ideas to capture Marshall safely, but they were few and far between.

"Doesn't he eat at restaurants?" Black asked.

Dan, Black's number two in Blackwood's investigations division, shook her head. "He orders takeout, and one of his men collects it."

"What about visiting the mall? Where does he buy clothes?"

"Online, I guess. He gets a lot of packages delivered."

"So can't someone pose as a FedEx guy?"

"Nobody's allowed through the gates. A goon walks down the driveway to collect everything."

"Paranoid little fucker, isn't he?"

"Hardly surprising—the FBI's been after him for years."

"You give the FBI too much credit." Black glanced sideways at Alaric. "Sorry."

A "waiter" offered me a canapé from a silver tray, and I took a mini smoked salmon roll even though I wasn't hungry. I'd opted for non-alcoholic wine too, just to be on the safe side. Everything was ready. Killian Marshall would be receiving an Unsung Hero honour from the Blackwood Foundation at their inaugural awards dinner, along with Georgia, who volunteered at a nearby animal rescue centre and happened to be dating one of Emmy's exes, and Verity, an investigator from the LA branch who ran a literacy program for children on the weekends. The cash prizes would be real, and Bradley was already muttering about making it an annual event. Seemed he'd use any excuse for a party.

Rafael's hand on the small of my back made me jump, and he smirked again.

"It's not fucking funny, you asshole. In case you failed to notice, posh dinners aren't my usual scene."

"Shh. Your role in life is defined by your attitude. Believe you belong here, and you will."

I appreciated the sentiment, but I wasn't so sure I did belong. Yes, I'd bested Emmy once, but I seriously doubted I'd ever manage it again.

Back in London, I'd liked to think of myself as streetwise. Resourceful. But fuck, just look at this place. These people had laid on a black-tie dinner for two hundred people, and every detail was perfect. They even had a whole bunch of expensive cars parked outside and fake chauffeurs hanging out in a staff lounge attached to the old stables.

I was way, way out of my depth. Hell, I was just glad I'd put my shoes on the right feet. And did I mention that every muscle in me ached?

"What are you? My therapist?"

"No, Sunshine, I'm the *cabrón* who's gonna jump out of an airplane with you tomorrow morning."

"Wait. What?"

His smirk turned into a genuine grin, but it was cunning rather than joyful.

"Our guest of honour just drove through the gates."

"What do you mean, jump out of a plane?"

"It's time for dinner, Sky." He shepherded me towards a table near the stage. "Don't forget to smile."

you might freeze up at a critical time."

"I get that."

"What happened to you? Before the first episode, Alex was sitting on you, and this time, you tensed up when I touched your neck. I could take a guess, but..."

I knew what he was thinking. The horror and pity swirling in his charcoal eyes gave it away. All I could do was nod.

"Fuck."

Fuck indeed. But I knew if I wanted to keep my job, if I wanted to keep this life that made me feel like a part of something rather than a nuisance, a poor little street girl who'd never amount to much, then I had to spill my secrets. Only Lenny knew a version of the truth, but I'd left out the worst parts. When I cried, he'd given me a handful of loo roll and a hug, then offered to beat up whoever hurt me. I'd accepted the first two and declined the third. Even if Lenny managed to get near Brock Keaton without being flattened by his bodyguards, I couldn't afford bail money.

"It happened two and a half years ago." I couldn't look at Rafael as I spoke. I studied the painting on the wall opposite instead. An orchard with a horse hoovering up apples as birds perched on its back. "The ninth of January—I'll never forget that date. I was working at a nightclub near Brick Lane. The Academy, although the only thing I learned there was to stay the hell away from anyone with a dick." I glanced at Rafael's crotch without thinking, then immediately regretted it when he caught me looking. *Sky, you dumbass.* Maybe I could jump *through* the glass? "Sorry."

"Should I be wearing body armour?"

I choked out a laugh. "You're different."

Now *he* looked at his package. His rather substantial package. "I'm not sure whether to be relieved or disappointed by that comment."

Oh, hell, we were *not* having *that* conversation. "I'm sure you've got a perfectly adequate dick, but unlike some, it isn't possessed by the devil." I swallowed hard. "Do we have to do this? What about the party?"

"Keep talking."

We'd only been for a fancy dinner together once before, when Emmy told me she needed Rafael off the estate so she could do some crackpot experiment with her sister that involved a stunt plane, a skydive, and a bunch of bruises. Rafael had picked the restaurant—a Spanish place in downtown Richmond that boasted great food and great service. They hadn't been kidding. The tapas might have been my new favourite thing, but the dishes came quickly, far too quickly. When Emmy hadn't answered my texts requesting a status update, I feared I hadn't given her enough time, so I'd waited until we were almost back at Riverley, then pretended I'd left my wallet in the ladies' loo. *Idiot Sky, so forgetful.* Rafael had huffed and driven me all the way back again. At the time, I thought it was the most awkward evening ever, but clearly I'd been wrong.

"I was serving tables in the VIP section that night. Yes, I lied about my age to get the job, and I don't need a lecture for that, okay? If I didn't earn money, I'd have starved and so would Lenny." Or worse, I'd have been slung back into foster care, and guess where I'd first been sexually assaulted? "Anyhow, the place always attracted celebs. Not A-list, more like footballers' wives and twats from reality TV." And up-and-coming pop

CHAPTER 3 - SKY

PEOPLE WERE STARTING to take their seats when we walked into the ballroom, and Rafael must have known I wasn't in the mood for small talk because he steered me straight to our allocated table. We'd be sharing with Mack and her husband Luke, plus six others from various Blackwood branches. Black had offered plane tickets, two nights in a hotel, and an extra day of vacation to anyone volunteering to make the trip.

Who *wasn't* present? Emmy and Alaric. They were the only two people who'd come face to face with Marshall, and even though that had been eight years ago and Bradley offered to do full theatrical make-up, nobody wanted to take a chance on them being recognised. Sofia, my tutor in all things poisonous, had stepped in as Emmy's replacement, and Emmy had even lent Sofia her wedding rings. Black's face had clouded when he noticed her wearing them earlier, but he didn't say anything. Sofia's boyfriend was standing in as Hallie's other half at a different table.

Sort of like a swingers' party, Blackwood-style. All we needed was a pot to drop our car keys into.

Except for me, obviously. After the Brock incident, I'd embraced celibacy, and the only man at Riverley I'd even consider having a sleepover with was Bradley and that was solely because he was gay.

Ten minutes later, everybody was seated, and waiters began setting starters in front of us. Black hadn't skimped on the catering, that was for sure. We had goat's cheese soufflés with apple and walnut salad, complete with still-warm bread rolls and more non-alcoholic wine. Apparently, Killian Marshall would be getting the real deal.

Rafael chatted easily with the other guests, more talkative during tonight's charade than he ever was on a normal day. Apart from Luke, who really did own a software company, everyone was bullshitting. Mack claimed to be a housewife, and one of the other "wives" pretended she was a real estate agent. Cue an in-depth discussion on the benefits of Pottery Barn versus Crate and Barrel. Yawn. I actually preferred it when Mack talked about computers.

"Okay?" Rafael asked quietly.

As okay as I could be under the circumstances. Even though my stomach was churning, I'd managed to eat most of the starter, and my anxiety had subsided to a tolerable level. But I still wanted the evening to be over. Was everyone else genuinely enjoying themselves? They certainly seemed to be, but it probably beat paperwork and meetings and surveillance duty. And being shot at.

"I'm okay."

"Emmy'll be here late once they've got Marshall, so I'll walk you back to Little Riverley after dinner."

"You don't have to do that. This place is a fortress."

"Yes, I do."

The end. Trying to argue with a man like Rafael was basically impossible, and I knew it. Besides, I didn't totally despise the thought of him seeing me home. It was oddly sweet, and I was feeling a bit fragile after what had happened earlier.

I snuck a glance over at the top table. As well as Black and Sofia, Georgia was there with her boyfriend Xavier, Verity had borrowed Knox for the evening, and Dan was sitting next to Marshall. The remaining two places? A brunette I didn't recognise plus our secret weapon, Tripp Tolliver. Tripp had been selected for his undercover experience, his acting ability, and his physical appearance. While everyone ate dinner, he was studying Marshall, watching his mannerisms and memorising his voice because later, he'd become him for the journey back to Penngrove. Then he'd disappear.

And because he'd disappear from Marshall's home rather than from Riverley, Emmy and Alaric could spend as much time with Marshall as they needed.

The main course arrived, and I ate as much of the cumin-crusted lamb as I could manage. Butterflies fluttered in my belly, and I wasn't sure why. Worry about the panic attacks? Anticipation over what was to come? A general fear that I wasn't good enough?

Oh, here we go.

Black rose and climbed the steps to the stage with Sofia at his side.

"Ladies and gentlemen, thank you all for taking the time to join us tonight for the inaugural Blackwood Foundation Awards. We've always believed in supporting smaller charities, grassroots causes that might not get much attention on a national scale. These organisations can make a real difference at a local level, and we're proud to offer not only financial assistance to three such causes this evening but recognition for their valuable work as well. Firstly, I'd like to invite Georgia Rutherford from Hope for Hounds onto the stage."

Everyone applauded, and Georgia stepped forward to receive a giant cheque for fifty thousand bucks. As a senator's daughter, she'd once been used to the limelight, although I gathered she'd chosen to live a quieter life now. She gushed suitably, thanked everyone, and then it was Marshall's turn.

"Truthfully, it was a surprise to be asked here tonight," he said. "So often, the arts find themselves at the bottom of the pile when it comes to funding. Creativity has been devalued. But can you imagine a world without it? No books, no movies, no music, no museums. Our walls would be bare, sporting events would be played in silence, and the sounds of the radio would be a mere memory. Yet school budgets have been cut to the bare minimum, artists are expected to work 'for exposure,' and often, the only opportunity children have to access specialist tuition comes from the generosity of strangers. Not only will this grant help to secure the future of the Penngrove summer art camp, but it means we'll be able to expand the program by offering places to children from neighbouring towns as well. From the bottom of my heart, thank you for believing in what we're trying to do in our community. Art in all of its many forms helps to make the world more beautiful."

Listening to Marshall speak, I almost believed he was what he claimed to be—a caring old guy who just wanted to make the world a better place for generations to come. But Emmy and Alaric were both certain he was the asshole who'd ordered his henchmen to shoot at them plus a whole boatload of undercover agents.

One man had been seriously injured. Could a leopard change its spots? We were about to find out.

The third award winner did her thing, and a few minutes later, Black quietly led a group from the room —Sofia, Xavier, Dan, and Marshall. A moment later, Emmy's sister rose from her seat three tables away and headed in the same direction. Despite Marshall's crimes, I couldn't help feeling a tiny bit sorry for him.

"They're going to the gallery," Mack murmured. Like Rafael, she was wired for sound, her earpiece hidden under an elaborate sweep of red hair. "Marshall won't be coming back. Anyone know what's for dessert?"

And that was that. Our job was done. Days of planning, weeks of preparation, and the bad guy just disappeared quietly into the night.

Chapter 4 - Alaric

ALARIC MCLAIN PACED the half-decorated room beside the gallery, stepping around paint buckets and ladders as Emmy sat on a plastic-covered table and swung her legs.

"Chill, dude. It's usually me doing the pacing."

"Something's gonna go wrong."

"You don't know that."

"*Emerald*'s involved. I'm not even sure I want to find that damn painting anymore."

The last two months had been a roller-coaster ride. Alaric had met the second love of his life, then almost lost her along with the girl he considered his daughter. Over the years, *Emerald* had unleashed hell on the women he cared about. Emmy had borne the brunt of her wrath during the initial recovery attempt, then later Beth and Rune. Beth was still hobbling from an ankle injury. If so many people hadn't put so much effort into catching Marshall tonight, Alaric could quite happily have collected his family from the guest house out back and gotten the hell out of there.

But Beth herself had urged him to finish this, and he couldn't run, not again. All things happened for a reason, Rune told him, and she was right. That girl always had shown wisdom beyond her fifteen years. When Alaric left town after the initial *Emerald* fiasco, he'd ended up in the right place to rescue Rune, and his return to hunt for the painting a second time had led to him meeting Beth.

"While we wait for dessert, perhaps you'd like to take a look at our art collection?" Black suggested through Alaric's earpiece. "We have a few nice pieces here. A David Hockney, a Modigliani, a Mark Rothko, plus an Andy Warhol my wife bought at auction several years ago. An impulse buy, wasn't it, Diamond?"

Sofia giggled. "I went with a friend who wanted to buy a Marc Chagall, but something about the Warhol just spoke to me."

"Did your friend get the Chagall?" Marshall asked. Out of politeness? Or because it made a good target for his gang of thieves?

"No, she got outbid at the last minute." Sofia's English accent wasn't bad. "Bloody Russian oligarchs."

"A crying shame. Chagalls make a good investment."

Soft footsteps sounded in the carpeted hallway outside as Black's band of merry men walked past.

"After you," he said.

Alaric heard the clip of heels on a wooden floor. A quiet grunt. The rip of duct tape. Then silence followed by four sets of shackles ratcheting into place. Emmy pushed forward off the table.

"Sounds like we're on. Can't believe it took eight bloody years to catch this bastard." She echoed Black. "After you."

Killian Marshall sat on a lone chair in the middle of the gallery, blinking in the glare from two spotlights trained on him. Black's theatrics? Or Bradley's? Alaric guessed at the latter.

He saw the instant when recognition dawned. An infinitesimal widening of Marshall's eyes. A slight stiffening of his spine. He knew why he was there. Good. That saved an explanation. Alaric tore the duct tape away from his mouth, and the second it came unstuck, the idiot started yelling.

"Help! Help! I've been—"

Emmy stepped forward and backhanded him hard enough to loosen teeth. "That's for shooting at me, asshole. And yell all you want. This room's soundproofed, and everyone present tonight is in on the plan."

Marshall pondered that for a moment. "My men would never betray me."

"Perhaps not, but what makes you think they're still alive?"

That shook him. He paled a few more shades.

"You killed them? In cold blood?"

"We're asking the questions here. Let's start with the big one, shall we? Where's *The Girl with the Emerald Ring*?"

"I-I don't know."

"Oh, please. You offered her for sale eight years ago, and our research showed that you always delivered the goods. We wouldn't have played along otherwise."

"You didn't play along! You brought counterfeit money. Fake diamonds!"

"Did we? Or did you switch them as my friend here climbed on board the boat to make the handover?"

Marshall looked puzzled. Scared out of his mind, but genuinely perplexed. "What the hell are you talking about?"

"When he left FBI headquarters, there was real

Chapter 5 - Alaric

"I NEVER SET out to do anything illegal—you have to understand that," Marshall said with a pleading note in his voice. "At school, I used to paint, but one lesson a week wasn't enough, and my mom couldn't afford to pay for extra lessons or materials. So I never developed the skills to create my own masterpiece. But I studied hard and managed to land a scholarship to read art history at Cambridge University. And from there, I went to work at Sotheby's, and then for a small gallery in London."

"Pemberton Fine Arts."

There it was again—resignation, but this time with a hint of surprise. "You *have* done your homework."

"It's my job." Plus the Pemberton gallery was where the second phase of this perhaps not-so-wild goose chase had started off. Beth was employed there too. At least, she had been until she lost her job for being a little too suspicious over the history of some of the paintings being restored by Hugo Pemberton, the gallery's owner. "We also know you worked for Jago Rockingham."

"Yes. By then, I'd realised that my talents lay in matching buyers with sellers rather than in authentication or restoration work. And working with Jago took those skills to another level." Marshall broke eye contact for a moment. "Until the day I met you, I'd always prided myself on being able to spot a genuine purchaser from a fake, but you fooled me. I suppose I should offer my congratulations."

"It gives me no pleasure to accept them."

A nod of acknowledgement. "Jago was a real character."

"Until he got shot."

"A true tragedy."

"Perhaps he shouldn't have aggravated the wrong person."

"The police said it was a burglary gone wrong."

"Sure. And you're just a kind-hearted philanthropist. What did you do? Inherit his client list?"

Marshall sighed. For him, this was the point of no return, wasn't it?

"I knew where he hid his ledgers. Jago had always been suspicious of computers, and he kept everything written down. Once the police released the crime scene, I simply let myself into his home and picked them up. And I already knew Hugo Pemberton would restore stolen paintings, no questions asked. He believes he's doing the art world a service, that all great works should look their best, no matter their provenance."

"He does it for altruistic reasons? Not for the money?"

"Hugo's a terrible businessman. I once took him a torn Cézanne, and he fixed it for the price of dinner. A ruined masterpiece is worse than a stolen masterpiece, that's what he's always said."

"Good grief," Emmy muttered.

Alaric had to agree. Pemberton's ethics were

fucked. He'd happily handle stolen goods, yet he hadn't hesitated to fire Beth and leave her in dire straits financially.

"So you think it would be better for the paintings Hugo restores to continue deteriorating?" Marshall asked. "To be lost forever? At least this way, there's a chance they'll eventually resurface for the public to enjoy."

"How can you talk about public enjoyment?" Alaric asked. "You've had a hand in hiding hundreds of stolen paintings from view. *Emerald* was in a museum before you got involved. Anyone could walk in and see her."

"It was a dilemma I used to struggle with myself, but to quote Winston Churchill, never was so much owed by so many to so few. Except this time, the 'few' in question were works of art."

Was this asshole serious? They were talking about a criminal enterprise, not the Battle of Britain.

"Six months before Jago's death," Marshall continued, "the canning factory in Penngrove closed—the town's main employer. My mom lost her job along with hundreds of others. She sank into a depression, and the whole town fell into decline. So I sold a stolen Matisse and used my cut of the proceeds to open the Marshall Gallery. It offered four full-time positions plus a sales outlet for local artists, but more importantly, it gave the community back something they'd lost: hope. Every time I negotiated the sale of a piece for Jago, I was able to provide a little more hope to the town that helped to raise me after my father died. You might not condone what I did, but how else could a twenty-six-year-old earn enough money to save a neighbourhood?"

"You kept doing it for decades," Emmy pointed out.

"And I kept giving. Plus none of the marks I stole from were on the breadline."

Alaric took a deep breath. *Stay calm, McLain.* "You stole from the rich, but it was still theft, and we still want *Emerald* back. She's a national treasure. The Beckers wanted everyone to see her."

"Yes, yes, I understand that. But I don't know where she is. You might not have seen him, but there was another man on board the scalloper with us that day—a representative of the School of Shadows—and he left with me in the RIB while the rest of you were busy shooting. He took *Emerald* and the briefcase you gave me. Said he'd dispose of the evidence of our involvement."

"There was only one briefcase with you in the RIB?"

"Yes."

The School's man could have tossed one into the ocean, but a last-minute switch was seeming less and less likely in Alaric's eyes.

"Who was this man?"

Marshall tried to shrug, but the shackles meant his shoulders barely moved an inch. "I don't know his name. We'd only met once or twice before, and I didn't care for him much."

"You never saw him again?"

"After that day, I took a step back from the murky depths of the art world. I'm not nearly as involved as I used to be."

"But you still have contacts, right? And I bet you still hear things. Tell me more about the School of Shadows."

"In the beginning, it was an honourable enterprise.

The original Master's goal was to obtain works of art looted during the Holocaust and return them to their rightful owners, or to their heirs if that wasn't possible. Any other pieces taken were sold to fund the main objective. Five paintings were stolen in the Becker heist —tell me, which do you think was the true target?"

Fuck. How could so many people have missed that connection? For thirteen years, the FBI had believed *Emerald* was the main prize. She was the most valuable, after all.

"Boudin's *View Over Sainte-Anne-la-Palud*?"

The least admired painting of the five stolen and the only one with gaps in its provenance, taken from its spot beside *Emerald*. Everyone assumed the thieves had snatched it as an afterthought, Alaric included.

"Correct. It's back with the Steiner family now."

Focus on Emerald.

"You said the original Master. Does that mean there's a new Master?"

Marshall made a face. "Unfortunately, yes. He started to get more involved around the time of the *Emerald* debacle."

"You don't sound all that fond of him."

"He's not an easy man to work for. Too money-orientated. Always pushing, pushing, pushing on the timescales and quibbling over expenses. He puts profits ahead of justice."

So what had started as a dubiously admirable venture to return stolen art had turned into simple theft.

"And yet you *do* still work for him."

"As little as possible."

"You arranged the transfer of *Red After Dark* to

Irvine Carnes."

"Ah, the beautiful *Red*. I knew how much the senator wanted her."

Red After Dark had been stolen in the same heist as *Emerald*, and the subject of the painting had been Carnes's mistress. His true love. When Alaric met the former senator, by then affected by a stroke and most likely dementia too, he'd spent much of his time babbling away to her.

"And you facilitated the exchange out of the goodness of your heart?"

Marshall's brow creased. "Exchange? What exchange? It was a gift. The Master knew the senator was sick and wanted to make his final days happier."

"The new Master?"

"Yes. A rare glimpse of his altruistic side."

"Bullshit. He swapped Dominique for Carnes's endorsement of Kyla Devane."

"No way." Marshall's jaw dropped, and Alaric had to admit his denial was convincing. "That's interference in an election."

"Yeah, it is, and I'm sure the Master got paid handsomely for it."

"I only caught the tail end of the scandal, but Ms. Devane didn't seem to have the country's best interests at heart."

Understatement of the millennium.

"The man who visited Carnes to broker the exchange matches your description."

Late forties to early fifties with thinning medium-brown hair. Hardly conclusive, though. Millions of men fit that profile.

"No. No, no, no. That wasn't me. I made an initial

call, that's all. Four or five months ago. I was asked to contact Carnes to see if he was still interested in obtaining the painting. The Master claimed he wanted to show appreciation for Carnes's service to America."

"Well, you were involved, which means you were partly responsible for Devane's surge in the polls."

Marshall hung his head. "For years, I've been telling myself I should retire, but then the theatre roof springs a leak, or the after-school club can't afford supplies, or one of the seniors needs home help. That's why I was so keen to make the trip here tonight. I'd hoped that if we could attract outside funding, I could finally get out of the game for good."

Alaric had spent years imagining this meeting with Marshall. He'd dreamed of revenge, of making the man suffer just a fraction of the heartache he'd experienced. But Marshall wasn't at all the person he'd envisaged. Yes, he was a master criminal, but his motives hadn't been entirely selfish. From what Alaric had seen, Marshall lived comfortably but not ostentatiously, and there was no doubting that he'd done a lot for his community. Was he really that different from Emmy and Black? Alaric had long since learned to live with his ex's murderous tendencies. The good that she did outweighed the bad.

And although the aftermath of the botched *Emerald* job had hurt, in some ways, Alaric's life had actually become better for that pain. He'd lost Emmy but found Beth and Rune. He'd been fired from the FBI but gained a quarter-share of a growing company. He'd met Ravi, Judd, and Naz, his business partners at Sirius. And he'd seen the world during his wilderness years.

"So, here we are," he murmured, half to himself and half to Marshall.

"I've always been prepared to go to prison. My whole life has been one inevitable march towards a jail cell. But I've achieved what I set out to do—I've saved Penngrove—so I'm not sorry. If I had to do it all again, I would."

And Alaric couldn't honestly blame him for that.

"You're not going to prison."

"I'm not?"

"I've seen what you've done for Penngrove, so I'm going to offer you a choice. Help us to recover *Emerald*, and once she's safely back in the Becker Museum, you'll go back home and slip quietly into retirement. Decline, and you'll never see the town again."

Hell, he wouldn't even see the sky again. Emmy would see to that if necessary. Alaric glanced at her from the corner of his eye, and she gave the smallest of shrugs. Translation: she had his back, but Marshall's fate was Alaric's decision. Black didn't appear particularly happy with Alaric's offer, but he always had been a miserable fucker.

"Finding *Emerald* won't be easy."

"Finding you wasn't easy."

Marshall chuckled at that. "No, it wouldn't have been. Where did I slip up?"

"You arranged the videographer to record Irvine Carnes's endorsement speech, and you forgot to withhold your number."

"The speech? The videographer was for the speech?" Marshall closed his eyes and blew out a long breath. "I was told that Irvine wanted to record a message for his daughter. Something for her to

even held the door open for them as they left."

"So you don't carry out the thefts yourself? Who do you use?"

"Mr. Delray, that's a hard line in the sand for me. One that I won't cross. Punish me if you must, but I won't turn in the people I work with."

"Okay." Alaric had to admire the man's loyalty. "We won't go there. What's the target at the Medici?"

"They have a Botticelli there."

"I know the one. But there's no indication it was ever looted by the Nazis."

"No, it wasn't. Its provenance is perfect. But I suspect the Master has a buyer lined up for it, and he'll make a substantial amount from its sale."

"Did you get offered that job?"

"I did. But it wasn't one I felt I could accept, both for logistical reasons and for ethical ones."

"So where does that leave us?" Alaric muttered. "Why is nothing ever straightforward?"

"Oh, but it is," Emmy said. "Why are you being so negative?"

Fuck. That was her cunning smile. The one whose appearance usually led to chaos and destruction.

"I'm not sure I want to hear this."

"All we have to do is steal a painting."

"You?" Marshall asked. "*You* would steal a painting?"

"Short-term pain for long-term gain. Is the Master looking for anything in particular at the moment?"

Was it too late for Alaric to stuff cotton wool in his ears?

"There is one job that's been put out to tender recently."

"Fantastic. We'll do it."

"You don't even know what it is."

"I think between us, we're qualified to nick just about anything. Unless it's the *Mona* bloody *Lisa*."

"It's not the *Mona Lisa*, is it?" Alaric asked.

Marshall shook his head. "But what happens if I don't get chosen for the task? It's far from certain."

"Bid low, but not outrageously low," Emmy instructed. "And even if the Master picks someone else, who cares? We'll take the painting anyway. If he wants it, then he'll have to negotiate."

CHAPTER 6 - SKY

WHEN I STAGGERED into the kitchen on Sunday morning, I found Emmy sitting alone at the counter with a mug of coffee and an iPad. Still no sign of Black. I felt sorry for her because she seemed permanently down in the dumps. Black was gloomy too, but if he really had stolen money from Alaric, then it was all his own fault and he deserved the torment.

The two of them were still working together—their antics with a presidential parade and an airship had made the news last week—and Emmy put on a convincing facade in public, but boy did she know how to hold a grudge. Even more fun, another of her exes had shown up for that particular episode, and I'd thought Black's head was gonna explode.

"Good run?" she asked.

"Define 'good.'"

"Did you make it round without passing out or breaking anything?"

"Yes, but I was tempted to break Rafael when he made me run up yet another bloody hill."

Ten miles. Ten freaking miles of rocks and mud and branches that smacked you in the face if you didn't duck in time. What was wrong with a treadmill?

"It's character building."

"I'd rather sit and drink coffee."

"Like me, you mean? I already ran twelve miles with Kitty this morning. He's getting fat."

Of course she did, because Emmy was Superwoman. An impossible ideal to live up to. I bet she'd never had a panic attack in her life.

"What happened last night?" I asked, changing the subject away from my inadequacies. "Where's Killian Marshall?"

"At Riverley Hall."

"On ice?"

"Still breathing."

"A prisoner?"

"More of a guest with restricted privileges. He wasn't quite what I'd expected."

"In what way?"

"His motivations. He acted more out of altruism than greed."

"He stole paintings and shot at you out of altruism?"

"There's a bit more to it than that..."

While Emmy filled me in on what had happened with Marshall, I raided the breakfast buffet. Every morning, Mrs. Fairfax, the housekeeper, set out a selection that would rival that of any five-star hotel, or so I imagined. I'd only ever eaten breakfast at a three-star hotel before, and that was because one of my ex-housemates used to work there and snuck me in to snack on the leftovers. But at Riverley, there was everything. Fruit, bread, pastries, cereal, porridge, eggs and a pan for omelettes. Three kinds of juice, four kinds of coffee, and a whole variety of teas. And if you asked the day before, Mrs. Fairfax would cook you a proper English fry-up, although I never did that, no siree, because Toby—who was Emmy's nutritionist and now my nutritionist as well—would have hit the roof.

"You're going to steal a painting?" I asked Emmy when she got to the end of the story. "Like, seriously?"

"Yup."

"Not fake it?"

"Can't take that chance. It has to be real."

"Wow."

"We'll give it back afterwards. Think of it as a necessary evil."

"Where is it? In a museum?"

"At the moment, yes. It's part of the Stiller Collection in Miami."

"So you're going to Miami?"

"I'm not sure yet." Emmy glanced at her watch. "Security there's tighter than a gnat's arsehole. We've got a meeting today to discuss it. Want to sit in?"

Of course I did. I wanted to understand how Emmy's mind worked and see if she could possibly pull this off. But not only was I meant to be skydiving with Rafael, I also had a shooting session scheduled, plus my first scuba diving lesson in the pool. And after that, I needed to hit the books and boggle my brain with Spanish verbs.

"I'm supposed to be jumping out of a plane this morning."

"The meeting's not until this afternoon. It'll be a good learning experience." She pushed back her chair. "Two o'clock in the Windsor Room."

At least I could find my way around Riverley Hall

without a map now. The Windsor Room was the biggest of the three conference rooms on the ground floor, and when I walked in with Rafael, there were already a dozen people standing around drinking coffee. A few I didn't recognise turned to look at me, and I wished I'd had time to dry my hair after my shower.

"Have you met all these people?" I whispered to Rafael.

"Yes. Who don't you know?"

"Three o'clock. The man with dark hair and dimples."

"Nick. One of the other directors."

"Eleven o'clock. The preppy guy."

"Leander. Former FBI and also my sister's fiancé."

I swung back to Rafael and stared. "You have a sister? We've worked together every day for two months, and you never thought to tell me that?"

I'd mentioned his family once, soon after I arrived, and he'd quickly changed the subject. I always figured that apart from Black, they were dead or something.

"I don't broadcast information about my private life."

His words hurt more than any blow he'd delivered in training. I'd thought we trusted each other. Rafael knew my deepest secrets and my greatest fears, and this morning, I'd strapped my body to his and jumped out of a plane with him. Okay, so he'd had to unpeel my fingers from the edge of the door and push me out, but I'd still put on the harness in the first place. Yet he didn't feel able to tell me he had a sister who presumably lived somewhere nearby? That really fucking stung.

Screw him.

"I should go and say hello to Beth."

"Sunshine, wait."

But I didn't. I didn't want to hear his excuses or a half-hearted apology because he'd noticed the disappointment in my voice. I'd have left completely if Emmy hadn't been expecting to see me there. Thankfully, Beth greeted me with a smile.

"Sky! How are you?"

"Okay. Tired, the usual. Are you all right? After... you know?" Nearly dying in the wilds of Tennessee, that sort of thing.

"I have good days and bad days. Almost as if...as if everything's still sinking in. Two months ago, I was a divorcee working in an art gallery, and now I've cheated death and got a whole new family. It's a lot to absorb."

"How's Rune?"

"I've never met anyone as brave as her. Or as resilient. She's in the library if you want to say hello."

"I'd love to after this."

Beth giggled uncomfortably. "I can't believe I'm helping to plan an art theft. Honestly, I don't know how criminals manage to commit crimes without dying from nerves."

"Start small and work their way up, I guess."

"This is more like diving from the high board, don't you think?"

Yes, but what a fucking rush if we pulled it off.

"Just don't look down."

Rafael was hovering at my elbow. True to his word, he didn't touch me, but I could feel him there even without turning around. Didn't he understand when I needed space?

"Sky..."

Saved by Emmy. She walked in with Black and the biggest mug of coffee I'd ever seen.

"Everyone ready?" Black asked.

Nobody was going to say no, were they? Not to him. We all sat around the massive table, and unfortunately I got stuck next to Rafael. Brilliant.

"The rumours are true," Black told everyone. "Thanks to Mr. Marshall, we've got a lead on *The Girl with the Emerald Ring*, and in order to get her back, we need another painting to act as bait."

A picture flashed up on a screen at the far end of the room. The dark silhouette of a woman standing beside a lake, shadowed by overhanging trees. The water was a deep blue with ripples of white, while the foliage was every colour of the rainbow. It was joy and despair in one picture, the woman an enigma. Was she rejoicing in the beauty? Or wishing she could sink under the waves?

"This is *Spirit of the Lake*, painted in the late nineteenth century by Leonard Astinov and renowned for the artist's revolutionary use of colour. Three years ago, it sold at auction for eighteen million dollars. In twenty days, we're going to steal it. Dan?"

Dan stood up.

"The painting's currently displayed in a museum, and security there's top notch. But on August fifth, it'll be in Virginia as the big draw at an exhibition held by the Möller Foundation. *Spirit*'s current owner is a friend of Laurelin Möller, widow of Derek Möller, who sadly died from ALS three years ago. The exhibition will form the backdrop of a dinner set to raise funds in his memory. Although security will be tight, preliminary indications suggest that it'll be easier to take the painting from the exhibition than from its permanent home."

"This gets better and better," Nate muttered from the other side of Black. "We're going to raid a charity fundraiser?"

Emmy shrugged. "Don't worry; we'll wait until after dessert."

"And we'll make a donation too," Black added.

Oh, that was fine then. As long as they made a donation.

"Will we even get a table at this short notice?" Nate asked. "It's less than three weeks away, and these things are usually booked months out."

"It's full. But I once had some business interests with Derek, and when I called Laurelin and offered to lend a Picasso for the show, she promised to squeeze in an extra table for ten."

"Which ten?"

"We'll decide that once we've hammered out the other details. We'll also need an extended team inside and outside the hotel where the show's being held. It's part of a country-club complex near Roanoke. The Grove."

"I know it," Xavier volunteered. "We went there for dinner with Georgia's parents once."

"Which is one more time than I've been. I feel a weekend break coming on."

Emmy looked just thrilled about that idea.

"What's the place like?" she asked Xavier, and I knew she didn't mean the dinner menu or the spa treatments.

"Modern, but it's been built to resemble a mock-Tudor English mansion. Around fifty bedrooms, if I'm remembering right, plus a conference and banqueting suite in a separate wing. Security was nothing special—the usual cameras in the hallways and electronic locks you'd expect from a place of that size. Three storeys plus a basement, narrow hallways, and the windows are on the small side."

"Mack, can you try to find some sort of floor plan?" Black asked. "Preferably the architect's blueprint. We'll book a few rooms. Who wants to take a trip?"

It was a rhetorical question. I suspected everyone in the room, me excepted, would be staying at the Grove at some point during the next three weeks.

"How are we actually going to take the painting?" Logan asked. "Presumably there'll be additional security brought in for the event?"

"There will. Thankfully they haven't hired Blackwood because having to explain a significant breach to a client would be awkward. I'm minded to lift the painting during the event itself. A hundred guests milling around will add to the confusion, and nobody's going to risk shooting a VIP."

"So, what? We cause a distraction?"

"Exactly that. And then we remove *Spirit* from its frame and replace it with a replica. With any luck, nobody will notice the switch until after we've left."

"Wait, wait, wait." That was Beth. "We're talking about a masterpiece. Removing *Spirit* from her frame could cause significant damage."

Black trained his gaze on her. "Then your job will be to figure out the best way of doing it. Build a mock-up version and train the team in how to handle the painting."

"But how? Each canvas is mounted differently, and I've never seen *Spirit* in person."

"Laurelin mentioned the painting will be arriving on the Wednesday before the event. It's too late now to infiltrate the setup crew, but if we time it right, you can drop our Picasso off at the same time and take a look."

"But what if I can't take a look? What if I arrive at the wrong time?"

"Model various scenarios and come up with a solution for each. We'll adapt if we need to. And you'll need to go to London to pick up the Picasso first, of course."

Beth folded her arms and glowered at him. "You couldn't have lent a painting already in the US?"

"I looked through the online catalogue and felt this one would be a perfect fit for the event."

Alaric whispered in Beth's ear. First she sighed, and then she nodded.

"Okay. I'll do it."

As if she had a choice. If I'd learned one thing during my time in Virginia, it was that nobody argued with Black. Apart from Emmy, obviously.

"What about the reproduction?" Xavier asked. His tone said he already knew the answer to that question.

Emmy smiled at him. "Would you mind, honey?"

"It's not as straightforward as you think. The painting's oil on canvas. I might be able to imitate the style closely enough to fool a layperson, but I'd need several practice runs, and do you know how long oil paints take to dry?"

Xavier painted? I never knew that. And he must be good if Emmy was asking him to forge the Astinov.

Every new revelation about these people made me feel a little smaller. Apart from hustling, my only useful skill was mixing drinks.

"How long?" Emmy asked.

"Anything from two to twelve days to be dry enough for your purposes."

"So use the two-day ones."

"That's not how it works. Drying time is dependent on pigment. Prussian blue and the umbers take two days to dry, and at the other end of the scale, you've got anything with quinacridone, alizarin, or cadmium. Basically reds and yellows. And what colours are in those trees?"

"Shit."

Like Beth before him, Xavier sighed. "I can try, but we'll be cutting it fine." He turned to Black. "How do you plan to get the painting into the event? Is that picture life-sized?"

"It is. We'll need to roll it and strap it to Mack's leg under a dress."

Mack almost choked on her coffee. "Why me?"

"Because the painting's thirty inches by forty and out of all the women we could use for this job, you've got the longest legs."

"I'll be walking like my panties are bunched in my ass."

"We'll have the others follow closely behind to make it less noticeable. And nobody's going to be searching people on the way in."

"What about on the way out? If somebody notices the switch, how the heck do we get the painting out of the hotel?"

Black merely smiled the Machiavellian smile that

made me squirm in my seat. "Leave that to me."

CHAPTER 7 - SKY

I MADE IT out of the Windsor Room before anyone else, but Rafael was hot on my heels.

"Sky, wait."

"I need to fetch my guns."

"Right now, I'm not sure that's a great idea."

"Look, I get it, okay? We're not friends. We work together, that's all."

"I didn't mean it the way it came out." Some fancy footwork meant he got in front of me and stopped, blocking the hallway. "Don't do this, Sunshine."

"Don't you 'Sunshine' me."

He reached out, then seemed to remember his promise not to touch me and dropped his arm to his side. I used the opportunity to dart past him.

"*¡Carajo!*"

"Everything okay?" Emmy asked from behind us.

"Sure," I told her. "We're just heading out back for some target practice."

"Don't forget your waterproofs. It's pissing down."

Oh, brilliant. Just when I thought life couldn't possibly get any better.

"Sky could use more experience over shorter distances," Rafael said, using the distraction to get ahead of me again. Asshole. "We'll use the indoor range."

What indoor range?

"Good plan. I've got to run into the office, and then apparently, I'm off to pack for a romantic getaway." Emmy rolled her eyes. "I'll walk out to the garage with you."

The garage? Where were we driving to?

With more voices approaching from behind, I didn't have much choice but to follow. Why couldn't I just turn the clock back a few hours? Skydiving had been exhilarating—fun, even—once I'd got over my initial holy-fuck-I-just-jumped-out-of-a-plane shock. Rafael had let us free-fall for almost a minute before he deployed the chute, and then we'd spent another five minutes floating back to earth as he demonstrated how to swoop and turn. I was almost looking forward to doing it again.

But preferably not strapped to Mr. My-Private-Life-Is-None-Of-Your-Business this time.

"I don't have a gun with me," I said in a last-ditch attempt to escape.

But Rafael wasn't having it. "I have plenty of guns."

"It's good for you to practise with unfamiliar weapons," Emmy said. "Rafael, do you have any work scheduled for the next three weeks?"

"Besides training Sky and installing a bathroom? No."

"Fancy a trip to Roanoke?"

"I knew that question was coming."

"Well? Bradley can sort out the bathroom."

"We'll go. But Bradley is *not* allowed anywhere near my bathroom."

"Fair enough."

Hold on a second... *We'll* go?

"Do I get any say in this?"

Emmy gave me a curious look. "It's surveillance. Nothing too taxing. I thought you'd be glad for the respite."

"Yeah, clearly I am, but I've only been doing this shit for two months and it's an important job. What if I screw up?"

"Is she ready?" Emmy asked Rafael.

"Yes."

"There you go. I'll have Sloane send you an itinerary once she's made the arrangements."

By then, we were at the garage, which was in fact a row of converted coach houses beside the old stable yard, and my clothes were already soaked. Rafael bleeped open the doors of his Lincoln Navigator, and I had no option but to climb inside. I hoped his leather seats went wrinkly.

"So, where's this range?" I asked once he'd started the engine.

"My place."

"I'm sorry, for a moment I thought you said we were going to your place, Mr. I-Don't-Do-Personal?"

"We are. But first, we're gonna swing by and visit my grandma. That personal enough for you?"

"Your grandma? Now you're telling me you have a *grandma*?"

"Did you skip biology classes in school?"

"I skipped all of school, but you know perfectly well what I mean."

Rafael sighed. What was with all the sighing today? Had Toby put something in the smoothies?

"In my world, trust doesn't come easily. Too many people have spent too much time trying to kill me.

Staying quiet about my family is a defence mechanism, and I do it out of habit now. I didn't set out to keep secrets from you."

"Is that meant to be an apology?"

"Sky, I'm sorry I hurt you."

Well, that was...unexpected. Never in my life had a man said he was sorry and sounded as if he meant it. That left me at a bit of a loss.

"Fine." I folded my arms. "Go to your grandma's."

It turned out Nana da Silva lived in a palatial house on the edge of the Riverley estate. Rafael called it a cottage, but it was more like a mini-mansion, albeit laid out over one sprawling storey. The yard was still dotted with the telltale signs of building work—a stack of bricks, a dumpster, a pile of sand.

"Did she move in recently?" I asked, breaking my silence.

"Right before you arrived."

"Renovations?"

"New build. Bradley organised it. I've never seen a house go up so fast."

Rafael parked the Navigator haphazardly next to the front porch, then hopped out. Once or twice, he'd tried to open my car door for me, but that felt awkward so I'd told him I was perfectly capable of doing it myself. Now he left me to it.

I jogged to the porch and sheltered undercover while Rafael knocked on the front door.

"Does she live alone?" I whispered.

"No, with her boyfriend. That's why I always knock."

I gave an involuntary snort right before the door opened and I got my hundredth shock of the day. Given that this was Rafael's grandma and presumably Black's mother, and both men stood six and a half feet at least, I'd been expecting a tall Colombian lady because as Rafael had pointed out, genetics was a thing. I hadn't been prepared for the dark-haired woman staring up at me from a wheelchair. Fuck. She didn't even look Colombian.

Grandma gave Rafael a passing glance, and then her gaze locked onto me. Talk about intense.

"Who are you?"

Guess I knew now where Rafael's bluntness came from.

"Uh, I'm Sky."

Her expression softened. "Sky, *sí*. Rafael has told me about you." He had? "Forgive me if I don't get up."

"Sky, meet Marisol."

"Come in, come in. I've been baking *achiras*."

"A-whats?" I whispered to Rafael as Marisol spun her chair around and set off along the hallway.

"Cheesy biscuits."

The kitchen was quite spectacular. Bright, spacious, and clearly designed for Marisol because all the counters were at the perfect height. She picked up a saucepan, filled it with milk, and set it to boil on the stove.

"You like hot chocolate?" she asked me. Marisol spoke with a strange accent—mostly Spanish but with a hint of English underneath. "I can make something else if you'd prefer."

"I love hot chocolate."

"*Bueno*. Not so many people drink it here, at least, not the proper kind. But it's very popular in Colombia." Marisol wheeled herself to the table. "Sit, sit. So, you work with Rafael?"

"Yeah. Like, he helps me in the gym and stuff," I added, just in case she wasn't aware of her grandson's extracurricular activities. I mean, she was related to two assassins, but apart from that weird moment at the start, she seemed incredibly sweet. Maybe they kept her in the dark?

"He always did enjoy that sort of thing. I hear you're from London?"

"That's right."

"My parents were born in Salisbury. Do you know it?"

Marisol was English? Wow. "I've heard of it, but I've never been there."

"Neither have I, but maybe I'll visit someday."

"Black would take you tomorrow if you wanted to go," Rafael told her.

"Perhaps not tomorrow," I blurted, and they both stared at me.

Shit. *Think first, speak later, Sky.*

"Uh, Emmy said they were going for a romantic break."

"*Excelente.* He works too hard. And I want to get the house finished before I go anywhere. Bradley's been *maravilloso*, but if I leave him alone, he can be a little..."

"Insane?" Rafael suggested. "Pig-headed?"

"A little renegade, but his heart's in the right place. You're here to help Vicente to move the wardrobe?"

"*Sí.*"

"He's just taking a shower."

"We'll wait."

The milk boiled, and Marisol made four mugs of

hot chocolate with actual squares of chocolate and a whisk. Now that I'd tasted it, I'd never drink that overly sweet powdered stuff again. I also scoffed half a dozen *achiras*, and if I'd had a clue how to bake, I might have asked for the recipe. And also ended up really fat. Marisol asked me about life in London, and I tried not to make it sound too miserable.

Then Vicente appeared, and it was clear from his familiarity with Rafael that they were close. How long had he been dating Marisol? What had happened to Rafael's grandfather? Those questions would have to wait, because I was soon holding doors open while the two men hefted a giant Victorian-style armoire through the house. For an old guy, Vicente was surprisingly strong. Fifteen minutes later, the antique monstrosity was safely installed in one of the spare bedrooms, and that meant it was time to leave. In all honesty, I'd rather have stayed. Chatting with Marisol and drinking cocoa beat standing on a shooting range, and there was still some residual awkwardness between me and Rafael.

But alas, it wasn't to be. Rafael put our mugs into the dishwasher, and then he bent to kiss his grandma on the cheek.

"I'll see you tomorrow."

"You have plans this afternoon?"

"I'm going shooting with Sky."

"Close-range? Long-range?"

"Close-range."

"What gun do you usually shoot at twenty yards, Sky?" Marisol asked.

"Uh, a Walther P22."

"Borrowed from Emmy? She seems to favour

Walthers."

Well, this was a strange turn for the conversation to be taking.

"Yeah, but I don't have it with me today, so I'm going to borrow one of Rafael's."

Marisol reached under her seat, and my eyes bugged out of my head when she retrieved a suppressed .22 and held it out to me, grip first.

"Try this instead. It's a Smith & Wesson M&P22 Compact. With your smaller hands, you might find it more comfortable."

"Uh..." Holy fuck. She even had a laser mounted on the rail underneath the barrel. Was she planning to shoot in the dark? "Uh...thanks?"

"Look at the time—I'd better start dinner. Cora's coming over with Leander. Have a good afternoon."

I was left holding the gun limply in one hand as she turned away. Bloody hell. Who exactly was Marisol da Silva?

"Don't act so shocked, Sunshine," Rafael whispered.

"You and me, we need to have a serious talk about your communication skills."

"Later."

When I didn't move, his hand went to the nape of my neck again, and this time, I had so many thoughts churning through my mind that I barely flinched as he steered me out of the house.

CHAPTER 8 - SKY

"YOU DIDN'T THINK it might be a good idea to mention that your grandma's also an assassin?" I asked as Rafael drove. Not very far, as it turned out. He lived right next door to her.

"She's retired now, and it was up to Marisol whether she told you about her former profession." He turned and gifted me a half-smile. "She likes you."

"Really?"

"She wouldn't have given you her gun otherwise."

"Yeah, I was kind of surprised about that. I mean, what if she needs to shoot someone this afternoon?"

"She has plenty more guns."

Of course she did.

Rafael's house definitely wasn't a new build. It looked like an old farmhouse, complete with scattered outbuildings and paddocks all around. The grass was long. No livestock lived there. He seemed to be renovating, though, judging by the pile of lumber sticking out from under a tarpaulin and the cement mixer beside the double garage.

"It's a work in progress," he explained. "We've got it structurally sound, but the inside still needs a lot done."

"Where's the shooting range?"

"In a barn out the back."

I expected that we'd walk around the side of the house, but Rafael unlocked the front door, then held it open for me with his foot while he disarmed the security system. Yup, definitely a work in progress. The hall had been stripped back to plaster walls and plain floorboards, and the stairs had been sanded to bare wood as well. The windows didn't have any curtains, and a single bare bulb hung overhead.

"Is any of it finished?"

"The kitchen's mostly done, and the living room's getting there. Plus there's one habitable bedroom and a bathroom upstairs."

"You're doing it by yourself?"

"Vicente's helping. Cora too."

"What about Emmy's team? Bradley's super efficient."

"Yes, I know. He was involved to start with, but let's just say we had some creative differences. You want coffee before we start?"

"I wouldn't say no."

The kitchen... Well, it was stunning. Not as big as the one at Riverley, but still bigger than most of the flats I'd lived in back in London. Three months ago, I'd been squatting in a former pub with Lenny and a bunch of losers, and now I got to hang out in places like this. *Somebody pinch me.*

Shiny grey tiles on the floor, white cabinets with granite counters, stainless-steel fittings... A centre island held an extra sink and a breakfast bar with four grey leather stools lined up underneath. And Rafael's coffee machine rivalled Emmy's for complexity. Better still, he knew how to use it.

"What do you want? Espresso? Americano?

Cappuccino?"

"Americano." I stepped forward and took a closer look at the bottles lined up on the counter. "Is that syrup?"

"Yes, and if you tell anyone I take my coffee like a girl, I'll push you out of the plane without a parachute next time."

That afternoon, I saw a different side of Rafael. He wasn't chilled, far from it, but he was definitely less uptight than his usual swallow-coal-shit-diamonds. And I got yet another surprise when he led me out to his shooting barn. From the outside, it looked like one of those red-and-white Midwestern stereotypes with a high roof that sloped gently at the top and steeply at the sides. But inside...

"What the actual fuck?"

It wasn't a shooting range. It was a bowling alley. A four-lane freaking bowling alley with pin-setters, horseshoe seating at the top of each lane, even a handful of arcade games. Plus a scoreboard in case Rafael wanted to start his own league. And a rack of bowling shoes.

"Now do you see why I didn't want Bradley involved in my bathroom remodel? He'd probably put a water slide in the shower."

Rafael pushed a button, and the barriers between the lanes lowered into the floor, as did the seats. Four shooting booths dropped from the ceiling in front of the pins, and the wall opposite them slid to the side in sections to reveal four rotating targets.

"This is... It's... Wow."

"Three days. I went home to Colombia for three days, and he did this."

"Without asking?"

"He was rambling on about multifunctionality and style versus substance and modular design, but I was trying to focus on the job. So I just told him that as long as I could shoot in here, I didn't care what it looked like."

"Big mistake."

"Huge."

"It's a fucking bowling alley."

"*Sí*."

I started laughing. I couldn't help it. Rafael just stared at me, but honestly, this was too funny. There he was, one of the world's most feared assassins, and he had to practise his trade next to a claw machine filled with cuddly toys.

"It's not funny, *pequeña perra*."

"It's hilarious. Hey, at least you can brag that you've got the biggest balls."

I doubled up again, and Rafael only scowled harder.

"I didn't need this *mierda* to do that."

"Can we go bowling?"

"Not today."

"Hey, is that a popcorn machine?"

"We're here to shoot."

"I love popcorn."

"Load the gun and shoot the targets, Sky." He handed me a pair of fancy electronic earmuffs.

"Are you always this much fun?"

His gaze flicked to the ceiling. "Give me strength."

"Can we have popcorn next time?"

"Next time, we're practising outside at Riverley. I don't care how wet it is."

"Okay, okay. I'll shoot. Fine."

And I did. I shot, and I shot, and I shot. Standing up, sitting down, lying on my back. Marisol was right—the Smith & Wesson was good fun. Perhaps I even preferred it to the Walther. I practised drawing from my waistband, then Rafael found me a holster and I used that as well. I shot walking, running, and crouching. I hit the edges of the targets, then the outer rings, and finally the bullseyes. And then I caught the holster on one of the knobs on the fucking pinball machine, tripped over my feet, and put a round through the ceiling.

Ah, fuck.

"Sorry! I'm so sorry!" I stared in horror at the neat little bullet hole above my head.

Rafael merely shrugged. "You won't make that mistake again."

"I just shot your ceiling!"

"At least you didn't shoot me."

"But what if I did? What if I make another mistake?"

"You didn't. Shit happens. That's why it's called training."

"But—"

"Number-one rule: don't dwell on things you can't change. If you do that in the middle of a job, either you're in jail or you're dead."

Logically, I understood that. But there was still a hole in the damn ceiling. How could I forget that? I'd fucked up. If I'd tripped sideways, or if Rafael had been standing somewhere else…

"Sky. Snap out of it."

When I hesitated, Rafael huffed, then fired seven more shots with his own .22. *Pop pop pop pop pop pop*

pop. I looked up and saw a smiley face staring back at me.

"Now we don't even know which one was yours. Can we carry on?"

I just stared at him. "You shot your *own* ceiling?"

"Don't worry; I'm sure Bradley can fix it. Take a deep breath and reload your gun, Sunshine."

If there'd been any doubt in my mind as to how crazy Rafael was, it was completely erased after that little stunt. Not only because of the extra bullet holes or the grinning face, but because of how calm he'd been while he did it. And how accurate. I certainly wouldn't want to face him down a gun barrel.

Hating the tremble in my hands, I reloaded and lined up my sights. It took me half a dozen tries before I hit the bullseye again, but I got there. And sagged in relief.

"*Bueno*," Rafael said. "We'll end today's lesson there. Now it's time for scuba diving."

At that moment, simply drowning seemed like an attractive option. I was so exhausted I could barely lift my arms anymore.

"Hurrah."

Rafael studied me. "You're tired."

"Ten out of ten for observation."

"I have scuba kit here. We can do a short session and then have dinner."

"You have a pool?"

"On the other side of the house. I got involved with the plans for that, so Bradley had limited scope to run wild. How do you feel about Colombian food?"

"Are you offering to cook?"

"You wouldn't thank me for that."

"So...takeout?"

"Grandma. She always cooks twice as much food as she needs."

"I'd like to try Colombian food, but there's one tiny flaw in your plan."

Rafael raised an eyebrow.

"I didn't bring a swimsuit."

"You can use one of my sister's. Or I can lend you shorts and a T-shirt."

Despite the fact that I'd spent many, many nights in London wearing a glorified bikini top and a skirt that skimmed my ass, I suddenly felt self-conscious. Somehow, it was easier to deal with being gawped at by strangers than by a man I knew.

"Can I borrow both?"

"If that's what you want."

"Okay, then I'll stay for dinner. Thank you," I added. Not only for offering to feed me, but also for trusting me with his family secrets. I'd do my best not to let him down.

Thunk.

What the hell just happened? Where was I? Moonlight shone through the curtainless window and glinted off a mirror hanging on the wall opposite. It took a moment for my eyes to adjust to the gloom, and then I realised I was lying on a fluffy rug that still had the new-carpet smell.

Oh, crap.

I'd passed out on Rafael's sofa. Rather than waking me up and driving me home, he'd put a fleecy blanket over me and left me to sleep, which had worked out okay until I'd rolled over and hit the deck.

I sifted through hazy memories... A brief lesson on the basics of scuba, followed by learning how to put on all the kit and breathing underwater for a few minutes. The pool. *The fucking pool.* It was a work of art. Not the usual bright blue chlorinated rectangle, but a huge curved pond edged with weathered stone. Water lilies floated beside irises and flowering rushes in the shallow areas, and a pair of wooden steamer chairs sat on a weathered deck that overhung one side.

"This isn't a swimming pool," I'd said. "It's a lake."

"No, it's a pool."

"You designed this?"

He nodded. "A pump under the deck circulates the water, and the plants in the regeneration area clean it, so there's no need to use chemicals."

"It's beautiful."

Rafael shrugged. "I'm finally building the home I always wanted." Was it me, or did he give the tiniest smile too? "But enough stalling. Get in the water."

After scuba diving came a dinner of bandeja paisa—a massive platter of food with beans, rice, pork, chorizo, fried egg, avocado, arepa...the list went on. The whole evening was surprisingly pleasant. Comfortable. Perhaps I'd even been *happy.* Rafael put on a movie, him stretched out along one sofa and me on the other, and he was content to sit in silence rather than tiring me further with small talk the way some of my old flatmates used to.

Upstairs, I might have had a brief snoop around Rafael's bedroom when I went to use the only functioning bathroom, which happened to be his en suite. His style could best be described as utilitarian. No pictures, no knick-knacks, not a hint of untidiness anywhere. Just an enormous bed with a black-and-grey duvet cover, two nightstands, and a walk-in closet bigger than my last bedroom in London. And his shower *did* have room for a water slide.

Presumably, he was upstairs in his bed now. Either that or he'd gone on some sort of moonlit commando run, which knowing Rafael, was a definite possibility. I wasn't about to sneak into his lair to check, nor did I fancy traipsing back to Little Riverley in the middle of the night. So what did I do? I smiled to myself in the darkness, climbed back onto the sofa, and closed my eyes again.

CHAPTER 9 - ALARIC

"SO... THE TEAM?" Alaric said.

Monday morning, and planning was well underway. This afternoon, he'd fly to the UK with Bethany and Rune to pick up the Picasso and spend an hour or two with Chaucer, Beth's beloved horse. Perhaps it was overkill for all three of them to travel, but after the events of last month, Alaric didn't want either of his girls out of his sight for long. Time would heal—he had to believe that—but at this moment... Yeah, they'd be making the trip together.

In the meantime, Emmy and Black would carry on with the planning stateside as well as doing their regular jobs. Emmy had been sending out emails at one a.m. last night, and Alaric knew she'd got up to run at five. Black? He seemed kind of haggard too. Due to the workload? Or was something else eating at him? Maybe the humdinger of an argument he'd had with Emmy last month? In the fifteen years Alaric had known Black, he'd never looked anything less than put-together, but right now as he sipped his coffee? Rough.

"Me and Black will be on the team," Emmy said, stating the obvious. "Plus Mack and her legs. She'll need a date, and I was thinking Xav. He's sneaky as fuck, and he knows art."

"Agreed."

Emmy had let Alaric in on Xavier's secret after the meeting yesterday. That he'd adopted an alter ego to work as a relatively well-known artist for a few years until he'd conveniently died and been resurrected as Xavier Gray. Alaric had been wondering about the change of surname—the last time he'd seen the man was a decade ago, and he'd been Xavier Roth back then, also known as Smoke in the shadowy world of professional assassination. Now he was shacked up with a senator's daughter and they had a little girl. How things changed.

"And Ravi. He's good at stealing stuff, yes?"

An understatement. Ravi had grown up in the circus, but his parents' primary source of income had been cat burglary. They'd begun teaching Ravi the tricks of the trade as soon as he could walk, but his ethics had never jibed with theirs. When they went to prison, he'd quit that game and started hanging out on the same Thai beach as Alaric. Secretly, Alaric had always wondered whether the capture of Mr. and Mrs. Wells was quite the fluke it appeared to be. Certainly Ravi had never seemed too upset by their sentences.

"Yes, Ravi's good at stealing stuff."

"So Ravi with Dan."

"I figured she'd be in the mix somewhere."

"But of course."

"Who will I go with? Ana?"

Emmy shook her head. "Oh, no, no, no. Ana's with Quinn. You're not going."

Was she kidding? "Yes, I am. And don't give me some bullshit about being recognised by somebody from the Master's team. I was wearing a disguise for the operation on the boat." Coloured contact lenses.

Fake teeth. A ridiculous moustache. "The only person who saw me up close was Marshall. And don't forget, you were there too."

Still Emmy shook her head. "I was window dressing in a bikini. Trust me, nobody was paying attention to my face. And that's not why you're staying here. *Emerald*'s put you through enough shit already. If anything goes wrong and the place ends up crawling with cops, I want your name kept out of it. Don't jeopardise your future with Beth and Rune. This is non-negotiable, Prince."

Oh, now she was playing hardball with his old nickname.

"Cinders, I'm used to taking risks."

Although she did have a point. That cursed fucking painting had almost ruined his life twice now.

Black weighed in, and of course he agreed with his wife. "Emmy's right. This time, the risk is Blackwood's. You can listen on a live link."

"Ravi doesn't work for Blackwood."

"Dude, stop splitting hairs," Emmy said. "I'll put you in the holding cell with Marshall if I have to."

The holding cell in the basement was surprisingly comfortable now. They couldn't risk releasing Marshall until after they found *Emerald*, but he wasn't a typical prisoner either. They'd let him call his horses' groom—who also happened to be a neighbour—to say he'd taken an impromptu vacation, and Bradley had jazzed up his temporary accommodation with a rug and beanbag chairs. Every few hours, someone took him for a walk, like a dog on a leash. But even though Marshall had a TV and plenty of books, Alaric still didn't want to become his new roommate.

"Fine. But I want two-way comms."

Emmy nodded. "That we can do. And speaking of comms, if Mack's with us, we'll need Nate and Luke on the wider team. One in the hotel and another here."

Accommodation at the hotel had been scarce so close to the event, but they'd managed to book the honeymoon suite plus two more doubles for the weekend, plus a variety of rooms in the run-up. Cade, one of Emmy's guys, was already there with his fiancée and their kid, checking the layout under the guise of a family vacation.

"How many for the wider team?" Black asked. "We'll want a handful of people outside, plus more in the suite."

"A dozen should do it. Possibly a couple more depending on whether Marshall's bid for the job is accepted. If there's a rival team there, we'll need to intercept them."

"When will we know? Is the ad in place?"

"Mack submitted it online yesterday, and it showed up this morning," Alaric confirmed. He'd been checking every thirty minutes since dawn.

Dyson's House Clearance Services.
No job too big or too small.
Over 600 satisfied customers.
Call to arrange a quote.

Of course, the number in the ad was out of service, but it didn't matter. The key was the number of customers. Six hundred thousand bucks was Marshall's bid. *Spirit* might have sold for eighteen million dollars at auction, but she wouldn't achieve that on the black market. Hot paintings went for seven to ten percent of their worth, sometimes a little more if a private buyer was already lined up. Marshall had explained that he usually bid five percent, so the Master would be getting a discount.

"Let's just hope the postal service doesn't fuck up," Black grumbled. "What next? Drug dealers using carrier pigeons?"

Said the man who still insisted on writing his notes with a pen and paper when everyone else in the room used a tablet.

"We still have two spaces left at the table," Alaric reminded him.

"Rafael will take one of them. Emmy? Who do you want for the other?"

"Rafael's date needs to be on the younger side, but at the moment, I'm undecided between Sky and Hallie."

"Hallie's steadier. Sky looked uneasy on Saturday night."

"Any idea why?" Emmy questioned.

"I asked Rafael, and he said the setting intimidated her. I'm not sure taking her to another dinner is the best idea right now."

"She got through it, didn't she? And she has to learn. Plus she's working nicely with Rafael. Did you know she stayed at his house last night?"

"She did?"

"He called me at eleven to say she'd fallen asleep on the sofa and he was leaving her there. At least she seems comfortable with him now."

"She didn't before?"

Emmy rolled her eyes. "You haven't noticed that she's twitchy around men?"

Clearly not, and neither had Alaric. Sky Malone didn't seem the type to get intimidated, not by a man and certainly not by a banquet. Then again, Emmy had plucked her off the streets of London and transplanted her into another world, so was it any surprise if she was out of sorts?

"Hallie, then?"

"I don't have to decide yet. Let's see how Sky performs over the next two weeks."

Two weeks. A ripple of apprehension ran through Alaric. In two weeks, they'd be either a step closer to *Emerald* or a step closer to yet another disaster. Sometimes—most of the time—he really hated that green-ringed bitch.

CHAPTER 10 - SKY

WITH CARMEN IN Roanoke alongside Nate, Slater had taken over my sniping lessons. This sunny Tuesday morning found me lying in the grass behind Riverley Hall, focusing on a watermelon a thousand yards away. Until that point, we'd been shooting at paper targets, but Slater said watermelons were more fun. We had very different ideas of fun. Something was crawling under my T-shirt, and I was just waiting for it to bite me.

"See the nose?" Slater asked. He'd drawn a face on the watermelon with a Sharpie. "Aim right below it, at the philtrum. That way, the bullet's gonna go straight through and hit the apricot. Carmen told you about the apricot?"

In my first lesson. The apricot was the sniper's nickname for the medulla oblongata, the cone-shaped mass of neurons that connected the brain to the spinal cord. Sever that, and a person died instantly, and better still, they lost all motor function so there would be no residual twitches of a finger positioned over a trigger.

"Yeah, she told me about the apricot."

"Good. And if a person's side-on, aim for the bottom of the earlobe. Now take your shot."

I peered through my scope, remembering what I'd been taught. Apart from the distance, I needed to consider the wind—not just where I lay but at the target too—the temperature, the humidity. When I began tackling even longer distances, I'd have to think about the surface I was shooting over, the direction, and the rotation of the earth too. There was a ton of maths involved. I kind of wished I'd spent more time in school.

Holding my breath so I didn't accidentally move the barrel, I squeezed the trigger so, so slowly. The blast from the .50 calibre rifle hammered my eardrums, even with ear defenders on.

I missed.

Slater raised his head from his own scope. "Reload and try again."

Sniping was definitely not my favourite thing. Okay, so there was a modicum of satisfaction when I blasted the watermelon into smithereens, but it was basically just calculations, squinting, and a lot of scraping around in the dirt. Give me up close and personal any day.

"What's the longest shot you've made?" I asked Slater.

"Two thousand four hundred metres. It took me twenty-five minutes to set up for that one."

Yawn.

"Are we done yet?"

Even criminals got time off for good behaviour.

Slater checked his posh watch, which matched his posh clothes and his posh haircut, and stood. If he'd been British rather than American, we'd have called him a toff.

"It's about time we ate lunch."

Thank goodness. My stomach had been grumbling

for the last hour. I packed up my rifle and headed back to Riverley Hall, hoping there was pasta on offer. I needed carbs. Comfort food. It had been a long two weeks.

Tomorrow, I'd be heading to Roanoke too, with Rafael, and I wasn't sure whether to be elated or terrified. Elated because I'd made the team for the actual job itself—Emmy had told me this morning. Terrified because firstly, I might screw something up, and secondly, I'd have to spend three days sharing a confined space with Rafael before the day of the dinner itself.

On the bright side, at least I might get a lie-in. Waking up at five a.m. would only arouse suspicions in a ritzy hotel, wouldn't it? And maybe I could watch a movie? I missed movies. I never watched TV or listened to the radio just in case Brock Keaton came on, but movies, I liked, and I hadn't seen so much as a trailer since that night at Rafael's. And room service... There'd be room service, right? I'd never ordered room service before, not once, but if Blackwood was footing the bill, perhaps I could get dinner delivered on a cart instead of walking to the restaurant.

"Hey." Hallie waved from her seat at the table when I walked into the kitchen. "How are you?"

"I thought you were in Roanoke?"

"Just got back this morning. You're going tomorrow afternoon, aren't you?"

I nodded. "What's it like?"

"Busy. Everyone's getting ready for the paintings to arrive in the morning. Otto and I snuck into the ballroom to take a look around, and they're turning it into a fortress. Metal screens over the windows—for security and to control the light and heat—some of the doors sealed off, even a sniffer dog checking for explosives. The handler said it was just a precaution, but still... They're taking the protection of the paintings seriously."

"Terrified" was definitely winning. Did Emmy feel this way before a job? I couldn't imagine her being scared, ever.

"What about the rest of the hotel?"

"Quieter. We had the pool to ourselves, and the gym was almost empty too. There were a bunch of people on the golf course, but neither of us had a clue how to play golf, so we stayed away from there. Did you see the map Cade made with all the camera positions?"

"Yes." And I'd already memorised it.

"They added two more this week. One outside the ballroom and another above the first-floor fire exit. And if you need to sneak around, be careful—they're fond of gravel."

"Thanks."

"I might see you there at the weekend—Nate's hacked into the network so we can watch the camera feeds, and I'm meant to sneak back in and help to monitor things from the honeymoon suite. Bradley's gonna give me a makeover so I look totally different." Hallie gave a bright smile. "I love this job. What other career would give you free haircuts, a clothing allowance, and a gun?"

"I could live without the bruises that come with it. Is there any pasta for lunch?"

Hallie made a face. "Quinoa salad?"

Not quite what I'd had in mind, but it'd have to do. "Delicious."

"If you eat in the restaurant at the Grove, try the *vincisgrassi*."

"The what?"

"The pasta baked with Parma ham. It took me three tries to say the name, but the waiter helped me out."

"Pasta with Parma ham. Got it."

"If you like pasta, you should come to Il Tramonto with us when you come back. The lasagne's to die for, and Emmy's lawyer part-owns the restaurant so we get a discount."

"Who's 'we'?"

"Me, Cora, Mercy, and Izzy. We made a pact to have a girls' night out at least once a month."

"I'd like that, but I don't get much time off."

"You're training with Rafael, aren't you? He goes into Richmond in the evenings, so he can hardly criticise if you sneak out for a few hours."

"I can't imagine Rafael chilling in a restaurant."

Not when he could be doing something really exciting like tiling a shower stall.

"He goes to Black's."

"As in Black's, the nightclub? There's one in Richmond?"

Hallie nodded. "Emmy owns the chain. Can't you guess from the name?"

I'd always intended to apply to waitress at the London branch when I turned eighteen—not before because I'd heard they did worryingly thorough background checks. In all honesty, I never thought I'd land a job there, but at least I could have said I'd tried. How ironic that I'd ended up working for the head honcho.

"I suppose I never thought about it." Or my

mentor's social life. "Rafael dancing the night away? No, I can't picture it."

"He doesn't dance. He arrives, picks out the girl he wants to take home with him, and leaves with her. Mercy calls him the panty-whisperer, and Cora sticks her fingers in her ears every time we discuss it."

Hallie's words left me cold inside, and I felt just a little bit sick. I'd thought it was a big deal that Rafael took me to his half-finished house. His home. He said he didn't like getting personal, and yet he picked up random girls to do the horizontal tango? I realised it wasn't any of my business what he got up to in his spare time, but still... It was the hypocrisy of it all.

So screw him. Metaphorically, of course.

"Then sure, I'd love to go out with you guys."

"Great. We'll arrange a date when we get back."

If I'd pulled up outside the Grove three months ago, I'd have felt like royalty. Then I'd have stuffed every single complimentary toiletry from the bathroom into my suitcase along with all the free cookies and probably the coffee capsules too. But having spent time at Riverley, the five-star hotel felt rather...ordinary.

Rafael checked us in—as Rafael Sanchez and Sky Morley—and a uniformed bellhop wheeled our cases to the elevator. Rafael held my hand as we whooshed up to the second floor, which felt a bit odd considering that this morning, he'd had me in a headlock.

"First stay at the Grove, sir?" the bellhop asked.

"It is. But there are three of us in this elevator. My girlfriend hasn't been here before either."

The bellhop turned bright red. "Sorry, sir. I mean, ma'am. Both of you."

Rafael didn't say another word, although he did tip the man as he backed hurriedly out of our room.

"Was that really necessary?" I asked.

"Yes. Firstly, you deserve as much recognition as me, and secondly, I want the staff to give us a wide berth while we're here. So I'll be an asshole, but not too much of an asshole."

"I guess I can understand that."

"There are times when you want to get friendly with hotel employees, but this isn't one of them." He cracked open the door and hung the *Do Not Disturb* sign on the knob. "In this place, I don't trust anyone but our own team."

The room was nice enough—light, spacious, and with a view over the golf course. Tiny men in poncy trousers strolled from hole to hole while caddies lugged their stuff. Rafael stood behind me, looking over my shoulder.

"What kind of pussy doesn't carry his own bag?" he asked.

"Don't knock it. Students need summer jobs."

"True." Rafael's breath tickled my skin. His closeness didn't bother me anymore, not the way it used to. "I worked as a caddy once."

"You did?"

"For a month. I needed to kill a politician. I injected him with potassium chloride right after he got a hole-in-one, and everyone thought he had the heart attack out of excitement."

"Sometimes you scare me."

"I'd never hurt you, Sky. Not on purpose."

"I know. But... Fuck, I can't believe I went from pouring drinks to *this*."

"The thought of killing people bothers you?"

I'd spent plenty of nights considering precisely that question and come to the conclusion that no, it didn't. The logistics made me nervous, but not the outcome. Some people were monsters, and they didn't deserve the privilege of living. If a man—or a woman—spent their whole life hurting others, why should they get off scot-free? The punishment should fit the crime, and some people had no chance at redemption. They felt no remorse. I'd seen enough scrotes get away with shit on the streets of London to understand suffering, and once millionaires were involved, the amount of harm they could do went up by an order of magnitude. Somebody needed to police them, and there were times when the judicial system couldn't—or wouldn't—do its job.

"The thought of getting caught bothers me."

"So don't get caught." Rafael broke his rule, just for a second, and ran a finger over the back of my neck. "I'd break you out of jail, Sunshine."

"Aw, that's the sweetest thing anyone's ever said to me."

There he was, back to making me feel as if I mattered again. Rafael confused the hell out of me. I half wished Hallie hadn't mentioned his other women, but at the same time, I was glad I knew what I was dealing with. Forewarned was forearmed.

He stepped back. "Enough distractions; we need to get to work. Find your gun, your body camera, and appropriate footwear for walking outside."

"I need a gun? Here?"

"Unless you're wearing a bikini or going through a

metal detector, you should be carrying a weapon at all times. Let it become a part of you. That way, you won't fidget and give the game away because it's unfamiliar."

I picked out a loose linen jacket that would cover the subcompact Glock 43 holstered at the small of my back and found a pair of sandals. *Sandals.* I'd never worn sandals before I came to America. All I'd ever owned was stilettos for work and trainers for everything else. But now I had jewelled leather sandals courtesy of Bradley, the kind of thing Maximus Decimus Meridius might have worn if his final battle had been at Hobby Lobby rather than the Colosseum. On the bright side, I could run in them if I needed to. And probably sword fight too.

Behind me, Rafael grimaced as he unrolled a camping mattress on the floor at the foot of the bed. I felt guilty about that, but Emmy said Black had managed perfectly well on it, so I figured Rafael could cope too. I pinned the brooch with the camera in it onto my pink silk dress, Rafael checked the gun in his ankle holster and draped a sweater over his shoulders, and we were ready to go.

"Time to act like two trust fund babies," he said, offering me his arm.

"Don't mind if I do."

Chapter 11 - Sky

THREE DAYS LATER, the moment finally arrived. Preparations weren't perfect, but we'd done the best we could. Nate, Ravi, and an electronics specialist from Blackwood's LA office had done a little rewiring work, we knew the main building at the Grove like the backs of our hands, and both *Spirit* and the Picasso were temporarily ensconced in the ballroom—the Picasso on the wall, and *Spirit of the Lake* in pride of place on a stand on the stage. There were obvious gaps in our planning—we hadn't been able to have a full rehearsal, although the team had been practising with a replica layout at Riverley, and there were still question marks over the staff and guests. Tables were booked in the name of the host only, and the Grove seemed to use a lot of agency workers. Who would turn up for the gala was still something of a mystery.

On the bright side, Marshall had landed the job, so at least we didn't have another team of art thieves to worry about. The Master had thoughtfully sent his confirmation in a "Good Luck" card.

"Ready?" Rafael asked.

"Nearly. Can you help with my zipper?"

We'd all worn long dresses in solidarity with Mack, whose poufy number looked like one of those dolls grandmas put over the spare toilet roll. Except for

Rafael's grandma—she most probably kept a cattle prod in the middle of hers. My dress was made from teal satin, and it fit me like a second skin. Which was a slight problem when it came to underwear. I wasn't wearing any. And even Rafael had to concede there was nowhere for me to put a gun or even a knife.

"What do you want me to do?" I'd asked as he stood there studying me with a Benchmade Infidel in his hand. It was his favourite model of knife, and it certainly looked the part. A mini black dagger. "Stuff it up my—"

"Okay! Enough. I'll hold on to it, all right?"

I felt weirdly naked as he slid the zipper up. Vulnerable. I suppressed a shiver and told myself to knock it off. I was the baby of the team, the newbie, and I couldn't let Emmy or Rafael down. They'd both taken a chance on me.

"Now are you ready?" he asked.

"I just have to finish my make-up and sort out my earpiece."

Hallie was upstairs in the honeymoon suite, and she'd helped with my hair. Bradley had offered to come to the Grove and assist, but Emmy had vetoed that idea because we were undercover and Bradley didn't know how to do subtle. I also wondered whether there was an element of her protecting him too. The outcome of this job was far from certain, and although Emmy and Bradley bickered constantly, it was clear they cared about each other.

"In that case, I'll take one last look at the camera feeds before we head downstairs," Rafael said. "Back in five."

I applied lipstick, then put in my earpiece. For the

moment, we were in push-to-talk mode, both to save battery power and because it was less annoying. There was a button on my bracelet. Later, for the actual job, we'd run with open channels to give us one less thing to worry about.

Five minutes gone. I figured I'd head for the stairs and meet Rafael halfway. Anything was better than sitting alone with my butterflies.

Well, almost anything.

I was so busy trying to work out what to do with my room card because hello, no pockets, that I walked right into Brock fucking Keaton.

Right. Into. Him.

"Sorry, sorry," I muttered before I realised who it was. Before the stink of his aftershave burrowed its way into my lungs and choked me.

"No worries."

There wasn't the slightest flicker of recognition in his blue eyes. Why would there be? Last time he saw me, I'd been hawking shots in a London nightclub, and now I was on the other side of the world dressed up like a society girl. Besides, he hadn't exactly spent much time looking at my face.

Tonight, he must have mistaken my horror for awe because after a quick glance at my cleavage, he turned to the gorilla of a bodyguard walking behind him.

"Hey, Frank. Give the lady a signed postcard, would ya?"

The guy thrust a card at me, and the whole entourage carried on along the hallway as it fluttered to the carpet, leaving me clutching at the doorjamb for support. My knees buckled as an iron fist clamped around my chest, squeezing harder, harder, harder. I couldn't breathe. The air wouldn't go in. Stuck. *Stuck.*

What had Rafael told me to do? Think of five things I could see. I tried, but Brock Keaton's smug face stayed front and centre of my vision even after he'd gone.

Breathe, breathe, breathe.

I managed half a ragged lungful of air before my legs gave way completely, and then I was on the floor. Carpet. I could see carpet. Swirls of pink and cream, all fuzzy and blurry.

"What the fuck, Sky?"

Then I was in Rafael's arms. He snatched the room card out of my hand and bundled me back through the door. It slammed behind us, and then the tears came, a salty flood that did nothing to wash away the shame and anger and dismay inside me.

I clung to Rafael as he sat on the bed, and after a moment, his arms wrapped around me.

"Shh, it's okay."

"No, it's not."

I'd fucked up yet again.

"He can't get near you, Sunshine."

"But he *did*. He's here."

"What?"

That was the first time I'd ever heard Rafael sound shocked.

"He's right here in the hotel."

"Are you sure?"

"I didn't bloody imagine it."

"*Lo siento.* I should have known better than to ask."

A little more air trickled into my lungs, and along with it came Rafael's musky scent. I let it filter through me, let it push all the cloying fear away. He handed me another pocket square, and I wiped at the mess on my face. There would be no fixing it this time.

"I'm so sorry," I whispered.

Rafael blew out a long breath. "It's okay. Take a few minutes to calm down and fix your make-up. I'll let the others know we're running late."

"I can't go to the gala."

"Don't talk yourself down. You managed to get through Marshall's dinner."

"You don't understand. He was wearing black-tie. He's going to be there. When Emmy and the others get started, there'll be chaos, and if I bump into him in the middle of it..."

"Fuck. Fuck, fuck, fuck."

Rafael tore a hand through his hair, and I wished I'd never come to Virginia. Wished I'd never set eyes on him or Riverley because now that I'd had a taste of this life, leaving it would be so much harder. But how could I stay? I cracked under pressure like a rotten egg.

"Just go, okay? Get the job done."

"Stay in here. We'll talk about this later."

I didn't confirm that I would because there was a good chance I'd have been lying. Instead, I scrambled off Rafael's lap so he could do what he needed to. Never before had I felt like such a failure, and considering some of the places I'd woken up, that was a big statement to make.

"You're stronger than you think, Sunshine," he whispered right before the door clicked shut behind him.

No, I wasn't. He'd got that completely wrong. In London, I'd acted tough enough to fool Emmy and the rest of them, but in America? I'd been found wanting.

Chapter 12 - Emmy

"I LOOK LIKE I'm constipated," Mack complained.

She was right; she did. But it couldn't be helped. The problem was that we'd had to build a collapsible frame for the painting, and once it was all rolled up and stuffed between Mack's legs, it was kind of bulky.

"Most women would kill to have something that long and hard between their legs," Dan said.

"It's lumpy. Do most women want herpes?"

"Okay, I see your point."

"Bless your freaking heart."

"Just lean on Xav," I suggested. "Maybe shuffle along?"

"Next time, I'm staying with my computer and you can strap the painting to your leg."

"I'd have done it this time if I was four inches taller."

The door opened, and Rafael stomped in. Hadn't he just left? And why did he look as if he'd swallowed a wasp nest?

"Hallie, get your ass in a dress," he said.

What the...?

"Wait, wait, wait. Where's Sky?"

"Sick. Puking her guts up in the bathroom."

"Since when?"

"Since five minutes ago. She wasn't feeling great

earlier, but she thought she'd be okay, and now she isn't."

Oh, fuckety fuck. Still, this was why we had backup plans and backup people. "Hallie, find a damn dress. Dan, can you help with her hair?"

"Sure." She peered at Rafael's hand. "What's that? Why do you have a signed photo of Brock Keaton?"

"It's nothing. I found it on the floor downstairs."

"Throw it in the trash. Keaton's an asshole."

"Why do you say that?"

"His manager keeps asking Ethan to work with him, but one of Ethan's session singers says Keaton assaulted her backstage at a charity gig. Stuck his hand up her dress. So Ethan told the manager hell would have to freeze over first, and yet still he keeps calling."

"If he assaulted someone, he should face the consequences."

"That's what Ethan told his singer, but she said it would be her word against Keaton's and she didn't want her name dragged through the mud."

"Ethan believed her?"

"Yeah, he did. But why does that matter to you?"

"Just curious."

Now wasn't the time or the place for this conversation. "Be curious another time, okay? Does Sky need a doctor?"

"She says not. It's probably a virus."

"Well, let's hope it's not food poisoning since we're all about to eat dinner here."

Hallie was in the bathroom now, complete with half a dozen spare dresses. For once, I wanted to kiss Bradley for the ridiculous amount of clothes he'd made us bring. Something would fit her. And she was naturally pretty, especially now that she'd filled out a bit, so her make-up wouldn't take long.

"It's the curse," Alaric said in my ear. Nate had a live link to Riverley open so Alaric could hear everything we said. "Told you."

"Shut the fuck up, Negative Nelly." I didn't need that shit, not tonight. "I'm gonna head downstairs with Black to check things out. Ravi, Dan, Xav, Ana, and Quinn—you come next in a group around Mack. Rafael and Hallie can bring up the rear."

"I found a dress that works," Hallie called through the door.

"Great. If you need jewellery, there's plenty in my bag."

Come on, come on. This was the part of the job I hated most. The waiting. The lull between all the planning and preparation being done and the actual execution. Tonight's op wasn't difficult, per se, but there was so much that could go wrong. So many people, any one of whom could react in an unexpected way. I'd almost prefer to face a group of terrorists than try to second-guess what David and Madeleine Fullbright from Connecticut might do when the party turned into a crime scene. At least terrorists were predictable. They shot at you, usually somewhat wildly, and then they lost their heads.

Black held out his arm, and I linked mine through it. I was still really fucking pissed at him. The anger had been simmering away ever since I found out he'd switched *Emerald*'s pay-off eight years ago, and it wouldn't cool until he made amends. And by amends, I meant getting *Emerald* back into the Becker Museum and restoring Alaric's reputation as far as possible. Half of the intelligence community still thought he was a thief. Black had a ways to go with fixing things, but he was making an effort, so I'd play my part. And even though I didn't trust him the way I used to, he was the best team leader for the job tonight, of that I was confident.

Time to go.

I pasted on a smile as we walked through the hallways, nodding at the occasional person as we passed. I recognised a few from the fundraiser circuit. Usually, I found gala dinners tedious, but for a rare moment, I was glad we'd been to so many because it meant our presence here tonight wouldn't be considered at all unusual.

Our table was in the third row back, second from the left as we faced the stage. Being closer would have been handy, but Laurelin Möller had accommodated us as a favour so we could hardly ask to move. When we'd spoken to her earlier, she'd smiled and explained that she thought we might like to sit near the Picasso, forgetting that it was ours so we saw it all the time anyway.

Black and I took our seats, a waiter leapt forward to pour us wine we wouldn't drink, and I opened the gift bag left beside my chair. It contained a self-help book, a miniature bottle of gin, and a bottle of Chateau Miel's ZingZing eye cream among other things. I'd need all of it if I survived tonight. In the meantime, the bags just gave us something else to trip over.

Mack and co. appeared in the doorway, and when I saw the two guards stationed there start turning towards her, I pushed my water glass off the table. Oops.

The tactic worked. The pair—and the other half-dozen members of the security team dotted around the room—all swung their heads in my direction, and Mack made it to her seat without incident.

Objective one: achieved.

The waitstaff cleared up the mess and replaced my glass, and I forced a giggle.

"A thousand apologies. I'm such a butterfingers."

"Not a problem, ma'am. Accidents happen."

A band struck up on stage, and rather than the usual classical, Laurelin had gone for rock-slash-pop. As a "special last-minute treat," Brock Keaton got up and sang what I presumed were his greatest hits, but in my opinion, they weren't so great. Perhaps I was getting old? The younger guests seemed to be enjoying the performance. Maybe Sky would have too if she'd been there? At thirty-four, I was technically old enough to be her mother, which was a terrifying thought. Although not as terrifying as actually being a mother. I was fine with parachuting into hostile territory to assassinate a well-guarded despot, but the idea of having responsibility for a tiny person I couldn't communicate with scared the crap out of me.

Three, two, one, back in the room, bitch.

While Keaton sang or lip-synced or whatever, Mack extricated the rolled-up painting from under her skirt, and after we'd eaten our appetisers, we began the fiddly task of assembling the frame. Rune and Beth had designed it and spent the last week turning it into a reality—a wooden affair with tiny hidden clips that kept it rigid once they'd been slid into place. We'd spent half of Thursday practising with a dummy canvas under a table in the ballroom at Riverley, and now we knew how to assemble the thing with our eyes shut. The final step yesterday had been to attach the just-about-dry-enough forgery for one last run-through. As we went through the moves for real, the other guests were too busy watching Keaton and his hip thrusts to notice the slight movements of the tablecloth.

Objective two: achieved.

The waiters brought out the main course, slow-roasted lamb, which I didn't feel at all inclined to eat. At least the chef had gone for quality over quantity. For the most part, I didn't get nervous before jobs—I'd done too many of them now to consider wasting the energy—but this one mattered. Really mattered. I couldn't erase the bad parts of Alaric's past, but I wanted his future to be rosy.

That fucking painting.

We'd act after dessert was served. The guests would be preoccupied and tipsy, and hopefully the security team would have grown complacent, more concerned about an external threat than a bunch of slightly raucous partygoers. Black would make the final call, and I watched him as he watched the room.

"Could somebody pass the water?" Hallie asked.

"Still or sparkling?"

"Still."

Rafael topped off her glass as a waiter set dessert in front of me. Chocolate Surprise, according to the menu, and the surprise was that it nearly blew my fucking head off. Who thought it would be a good idea to add chilli to chocolate mousse? I swallowed a whole glass of water.

Not long now.

"One minute," Black murmured.

Nate began a countdown, and we switched to an open channel. Each of us wore a subvocal earpiece, small enough that it would pass a cursory inspection unnoticed. Ravi's hands moved in his lap, and I knew he was arranging his tools. He had the job of extracting *Spirit* from her ornate gilt frame and replacing her with Xav's version. Black was his bagman. The rest of us? We'd be running interference. I locked in on the nearest guard, memorised his position, calculated his likely path.

Ten, nine, eight...

I fished the smoke grenade out from between my legs and pulled the pin. Two faint metallic *ping*s told me Dan and Ana had done the same.

Seven, six, five...

Xav, Quinn, and Rafael? They had flashbangs. When the girls rolled the smoke canisters on zero, Nate would count us three more seconds, enough time to close our eyes and cover our ears. Then the men would let loose.

Four, three, two...

Fuck, a waiter was on the move. I cut my eyes in his direction, and Ana answered with a nod. She was on it.

One...

The lights went out. The metal screens installed for the event acted as blackout blinds. Thanks to Nate's activities during the week, the backup generators remained silent.

Zero...

I kicked my canister hard, and it skittered four tables away. The hiss of smoke was followed by gasps, then screams when the flashbangs went off. I leapt out of my seat and put myself on a course to intercept the guard. Felt rather than saw him ahead of me. Body-checked him hard enough that he landed on his ass.

"What the...?"

"Oh! I'm so sorry!"

If everything had gone according to plan, Ravi would be at the stage already. Beth had been unexpectedly brilliant in the run-up to tonight. When she delivered the Picasso to the hotel, she'd prattled on about her old job at the Pemberton gallery and talked up her art history degree, and the dude who'd brought *Spirit* was only too happy for her to take a closer look, front and back. Her body cam had recorded every detail of the painting and its frame, and she'd even managed to get her gloved hand in the picture for scale.

Black would be carrying the forgery across the room, holding it aloft so nobody walked into it by accident. At six feet seven, he was the tallest man at the gala apart from Rafael, and Rafael was busy bumping panicking guests out of Ravi's way.

Terror, confusion, horrified shouts—we had it all. Someone tried using a flashlight, but the beam bounced uselessly off the smoke.

"I have *Spirit*," Black announced.

Objective three: achieved.

"It's a tight fit," Ravi murmured.

I really didn't want to hear those words at that moment.

"Will it go in?" Nate asked.

"That's usually my line," Carmen quipped.

A groan. Was that Dan? "Too much information."

"It's done," Ravi said, and I let out the breath I'd been holding. Thank fuck for that.

"Places, everyone," Nate ordered.

We fought our way through the fray so we ended up somewhere in the vicinity of our table. We'd spied on the setup and replicated the layout at Riverley, learned the number of steps between each obstacle, and practised walking around the ballroom for days with our eyes closed. I reached my seat just as the lights came on again.

Holy hell. The banquet hall was a war zone. Stray shoes, smashed glass, blood because the latter didn't mix well with bare feet. Dazed diners stumbled around like zombies. On stage, *Spirit* looked untouched, and that was where the security team headed as soon as they found their feet. Would they notice the switch?

"The painting!" a woman shrieked. "It's gone!"

Ah, shit.

I spun to look at her, but she wasn't pointing at *Spirit*. No, her trembling finger was extended towards an empty spot on the side wall, three slots up from the Picasso.

To echo the guard's words from earlier: What the...?

"Which painting's gone?" a guard asked, and his voice held a hint of panic. Quite understandable, given the circumstances.

"*The Shepherd's Watch*."

"What's going on?" Alaric asked. "Somebody took a *different* painting?"

"Sure looks that way," I muttered under my breath.

"*The Shepherd's Watch*?" Bethany echoed. "Oh my goodness! I studied it at university, and... My gosh! It was rumoured to have been stolen during the Holocaust. The alleged owner lost a court battle to get it back."

Reality hit me like the proverbial freight train. Marshall had been used. *We'd* been used. The Master didn't want *Spirit*; he wanted *The Shepherd*. This gala had been the obvious place for an attempt to steal both *Spirit* and *The Shepherd*, and our team's efforts had been nothing but a distraction. A countermeasure. There *had* been a second crew here, and they'd got away with their prize.

That motherfucker had played us.

The hardening of Black's expression showed me he'd realised the truth at the same time as I did. A silent promise passed between us.

Whoever the Master was, when we caught up with him, he was a dead man.

Chapter 13 - Sky

STAY OR GO? Stay or go? Stay or go?

An hour after I'd run into my worst nightmare, and I'd scrubbed my face and changed into capri pants, golf shoes, and a pink polo shirt. Thanks, Bradley. All I wanted was a pair of jeans. And a cigarette. I *needed* a cigarette. Yes, I'd quit smoking when I moved to America, but if ever there was a time to start again, it was now.

Part of me wanted to call a cab and fade quietly into the night, but I owed it to Emmy to say goodbye. What had Rafael told her? Had he laid my secrets bare? I should have come clean three weeks ago, shouldn't I? Asked if it was possible for me to step down and perhaps help out at the office instead. Sat in the surveillance room or something. That way, I might have been able to salvage a fragment of my career at Blackwood.

My bag was packed, my dress back on its hanger. Just looking at it hurt. Right now, I should have been downstairs, keeping distressed guests away from Ravi. How was it going? I hadn't heard any alarms, but I didn't expect to—Nate had control of the entire system.

My fingers twitched as my body cried out for nicotine. While I'd been busy, I'd barely noticed the withdrawal symptoms, but now I wanted to stick

NiQuitin patches all over my body. A tribute to failure. One of the assholes downstairs would probably call it modern art and pay twenty thousand bucks for me to stand in a gallery. Hmm... A potential new vocation?

Oh, screw it, someone in this place must have a cigarette. Where was the smokers' corner? Every building had one—that little outdoor hidey-hole where like-minded addicts gathered to escape other people's disapproving glances.

Thankfully, I had somewhere to put my room card now. I slipped it into my pocket as the door closed behind me, then set off on my quest. At least I wouldn't bump into Brock Keaton again. Not only did I keep my wits about me this time, but he was undoubtedly being waited on hand and foot while women fawned over him in yet another example of injustice in the world.

A security guard was positioned by the side door, and he watched me as I approached.

"Any idea where the smoking area is?"

"No, ma'am."

Fat lot of good he was. I slipped outside and found myself in the side car park. For most of the week, it had been almost empty, but tonight it overflowed with Bentleys and Porsches and Ferraris and Range Rovers. Even an Aston Martin. And was that a Bugatti? A guy my age sat on a high stool behind the valet stand, and I headed in his direction.

"Hey."

He looked up, a key in his hand.

"You need your car?"

"I'm looking for the smoking area."

He glanced left and right. "It's over on the other side of the hotel, but you can smoke here. Nobody's around. They're all at the big party."

"So it's a bit awkward—I actually need to bum a cigarette because I'm meant to have given up smoking."

Another glance in each direction, and he fished around in his pocket and came up with a packet of Marlboros. My hero.

"Shh. I didn't give you this."

"I won't say a thing, I swear. Do you have a light?"

He did, and it was easier to breathe once I got my first hit of sweet, sweet nicotine. I inhaled deeply, coughed once because I'd been deprived for so long, then blew out a stream of smoke.

"Better."

"Rough night?" the valet asked.

"Something like that."

"Row with your parents?"

I figured I owed him a cover story. "My boyfriend. No offence, but men can be such jerks."

"I get it. My last boyfriend turned out to be a real asshole too."

"Sorry to hear that."

"Don't be—I met a much nicer guy."

"That gives me hope." Another lie—Rafael had been surprisingly understanding about my cock-ups so far, but not even he could brush tonight's incident under the carpet. "I was thinking of maybe getting out of here. Do you happen to have the number for a cab company?"

"Sure I do. You have your phone?"

I patted my pockets. Shit. "I left it in my room."

"It's okay, I can write it down for you."

The valet backed into the little hut behind him and came back with a piece of paper and a pen. Would I call for a ride? I still hadn't made up my mind.

"There you go."

"Thanks. Do you have to stay out here all night? Surely nobody'll arrive this late?"

"The boss says I have to stick around."

His tone said the boss was an idiot.

"Can't you sneak inside?"

"Nope, I need this job. Got one year of college left, and it won't pay for itself. And where else would I get paid to drive a Lamborghini? When I can find the key for it, that is." He held up a handful of keys, then dumped them onto the shelf in front of him. "This is a mess."

"There isn't a system?"

"Oh, sure there's a system. We write the registration number on a paper tag, tie it to the key, and drop it into the basket. Then at the end of the night, we spend fifteen minutes hunting through the pile and the guests get annoyed."

"What about using a numbered board? Or a secure cabinet?"

"You have no idea how many times I've suggested that, but the boss is old school." The valet put on a croaky voice. "'We've been doing it this way for years, son,' he always says. So I'm trying to separate the different makes. You know, all the Porsche keys together, that sort of thing."

"Good idea. I'll be looking for a new job soon. On balance, would you recommend valeting?"

At least I'd managed to get a driver's licence during my time at Riverley.

"It *can* be great. I'd suggest trying for an upscale restaurant when you're starting out. Fewer guests means lower tips, but it's a steady stream of customers through the evening rather than a crazy rush at the beginning and the end. Much easier."

"Thanks for the tip."

Movement behind the valet caught my eye. A man in a white shirt and black trousers had slipped out of the fire exit from the basement. Why? He wasn't one of our team. A waiter? He was wearing a tie rather than a bow tie, the same as all the staff. Yes, a waiter. When he turned, an outside light caught his face, and I recalled he'd served us breakfast the day before yesterday. But why was he leaving in the middle of the evening? And through an emergency exit? What was the package under his arm?

Something felt off about his movements.

"Are you working at the moment?" the valet asked.

"Right now?" A giggle bubbled out of me. "Of course not."

"I meant, like, when you're at home."

"Oh. I don't think so. My last job, I made a few mistakes, and it's either jump or be pushed."

"Things might not be as bad as you think."

The waiter avoided me and my new friend, making sure he put several vehicles between us as he flitted past in the gloom. But I watched him from the corner of my eye. He was carrying a handbag. A chunky leather ladies' handbag. Had he stolen it? From one of the party guests? If I had to guess, I'd say he probably had.

"No, things are pretty bad."

"Have you tried talking to your boss? Sometimes it helps. Not in my case, but my buddy Frederico..."

I tuned the valet out as the waiter crossed into the main car park, and a moment later, I heard a car door slam. An engine started. That fucker. He'd stolen some poor woman's handbag, and now he was doing a freaking runner.

I might have had one foot out of the door at Blackwood, but Emmy had still managed to instill some morals into me during my time there. Yes, I'd stolen from people myself in the past, but only wallets, never a whole bag. And on the odd occasion they'd contained personal items, I'd taken the cash and mailed the rest back to the owners. The people at the gala were all loaded. That bag most likely contained a stack of moolah.

What should I do? I only had a second or two to make up my mind. The waiter had already turned down the driveway. Soon, he'd be long gone.

"Look!" I pointed past the valet. "Is that a fox?"

He turned to see. "Where?"

"By the corner of the building."

I reached over the top of the stand and grabbed the first key that came to hand. Lucky dip.

"My mistake. I think it's just a shadow."

"Sometimes we do get foxes here. And one of the receptionists, she swears she saw a bear on the grounds."

"A bear? No way."

"That's what she said."

Wrap it up, Sky. "Thinking about your advice, I'm gonna take it. You're right. I *should* talk to my boss. Like, straight away."

"Now? On a Saturday night?"

"She works weird hours. Thanks for the cigarette. You're a lifesaver."

"Okay, nice talking with you."

I hurried back the way I'd come, and halfway to the door, I turned to check whether the valet was still watching me. He was. I gave him a little wave to let him know I'd caught him, and he looked away. Psychology 101. I cut left and crouched between two cars. What had I got?

A Ferrari key. I'd nicked a fucking Ferrari key.

Not ideal, but needs must, and before you give me a lecture, I was only planning to borrow the thing, not send it to a chop shop. And that waiter needed to be stopped. The way he'd moved, quickly yet confidently, made me think it wasn't the first time he'd pulled that trick. How many more people would he steal from if he got away? I might have screwed up everything else tonight, but perhaps I could redeem myself slightly if I tracked down a thief.

I duck-walked between rows, pressing the button on the fob until a shiny red car bleeped back at me. Hello, wheels. Whoever owned it must have been pretty tall because I could hardly reach the pedals, but I didn't have time to mess around with the seat position. Instead, I cringed as the engine started with a roar, then drove out of the car park as fast as I dared. How long did I have before the valet called the police? Surely he'd have noticed the Ferrari leaving?

At the end of the driveway, I glimpsed a pair of tail lights disappearing around a bend to my right and took off after them. If I'd had to pick the top ten worst vehicles for surveillance, this bloody car would definitely have made the top half of the list. There was absolutely nothing subtle about it. The only point in its favour was that I didn't look like a cop. The waiter was in a newish hatchback—a BMW, maybe, or an Audi.

Where was he going? I settled in at an appropriate distance to find out.

CHAPTER 14 - EMMY

NONE OF US had to fake our annoyance when the police questioned us. No, we hadn't seen anyone acting suspiciously near *The Shepherd*. No, we had no idea where the painting had gone. Yes, we were as shocked as everyone else by the theft. Laurelin was in tears, and Black offered a few words of comfort in between glaring at everyone else.

"If the police don't find the painting, I'll put a team on it," he promised.

"I just can't believe this is happening. This was meant to be a celebration of Derek's life."

If she'd known Derek had been shagging his secretary until he was no longer physically able to, she probably wouldn't have been quite so upset, but never mind.

"At least nobody got hurt."

Not badly, anyway. Half a dozen cut feet from the broken glass, some bruises from bumping into tables, and one woman had sprained an ankle when she fell out of her heels.

More cops arrived, including several female officers, and everyone got searched. Ravi's tools were split between my bra and Dan's, and nobody was confident enough to give us a really good grope. And Mack was in the clear now, the only evidence of her earlier subterfuge an overly complex garter belt whipped up by Bradley on his Janome.

Where the fuck was *The Shepherd*? The windows were all blocked off by the screens. The guards on the doors had secured the room as soon as the lights went out, and they swore nobody had gone past. Either they were dirty, or they were incompetent, or the painting was still in the room. Fuck, I hoped they didn't search too thoroughly, because *The Shepherd* wasn't the only hot painting located where it shouldn't have been.

"How big was the missing painting?" Dan asked. "Small, right? Like a foot square?"

"Eight inches," Beth said in our ears. "But it had quite an ornate frame."

"Eight inches?" I muttered. "Measured by a man or a woman?"

Dan jerked her head towards a pillar sticking out from the wall. "Small enough to fit through that AC duct?"

I followed her gaze and saw what she'd noticed. The grille was held in place by three screws.

She answered my unasked question. "Earlier, there were four screws."

And that was why Dan was the investigator and I was the assassin.

"Black." I nudged him, and he turned around. "Dan's worked out how they did it." We quickly explained. "Want to tell the police? Or keep quiet?"

"Might as well tell them. I can almost guarantee the School's people will have got away clean, and it might help us to get home at a reasonable hour."

He waved the nearest cop over. So far they'd been more concerned with the grenades than anything else, but that wouldn't help them. Even if they managed to trace them via their serial numbers, those serial numbers would show they'd disappeared somewhere in Russia. They were part of a stash we'd liberated from a Siberian army base a couple of years ago. And there would be no fingerprints. We'd kept the grenades wrapped in handkerchiefs until we rolled them across the floor.

"Will we get coffee?" a woman at the next table asked. "The menu said there'd be coffee."

For crying out loud, lady. Weren't there more important things to worry about?

"Perhaps the staff have other priorities right now?" I told her.

She pointed behind me. "That person has coffee."

The old dear at the table behind us didn't look in great shape, but when the medics diagnosed mild psychological shock and tried to take her to the hospital, she'd refused to go. A waiter had fetched her a hot drink instead.

In different company, I'd have made a crack about the whiner having her head stuck up her own arse, but today, I kept my mouth shut. Things were quite fraught enough in that room already. Black let the cop know who we were and explained our suspicions, and the pair of them went to inform his colleagues.

"Sky's not answering her phone," Rafael said.

"If she wasn't feeling well, she's probably taking a nap."

"In the middle of this?"

Why not? She probably figured we had it handled. There wasn't anything else she could do to help, and I'd instilled the importance of sleeping whenever she could.

"I doubt they've got around to searching every guest room yet."

Nate and co. would be packed up by now, just in case. His tools were long gone, and all he had left was laptops and the usual accoutrements a man brought with him on vacation.

A forensics team arrived and started taking fingerprints with a mobile scanner. If they wanted mine, they could fight my attorney. They were on a hiding to nothing anyway. Any thief worth his salt would have worn gloves the way Ravi did. His were stuffed into his underwear now, which didn't do his reputation with the ladies any harm. Unlike Brock Keaton. I'd noticed him trying to hide the damp patch on the front of his trousers.

Who had done this? If I had to guess, I'd say one of the waitstaff, but I wasn't ruling out a guest either. After all, we were guests and we'd pinched a painting too. Nate would have recorded everyone arriving and leaving, and tomorrow, Blackwood's investigative team would start the process of matching faces with names while I sharpened my claws.

Black came back half an hour later. The initial excitement had faded and people were starting to sober up by then. Getting tetchy.

"Any news?" I asked.

"Dan was right. They found an access panel unscrewed in the basement, and the fire door wasn't properly closed. It's meant to be alarmed, but the alarm hasn't worked for years, and apparently all the staff know that. Some of them use it as a shortcut to the parking lot."

Guess Laurelin's security team hadn't been quite as thorough as they thought—they should have spotted that.

"So the cops think it was a staff member?"

"One of the waiters is missing. Not one from the event; he was scheduled to work in the main restaurant this evening."

"He must have had an accomplice."

"They're going to keep the rest of the staff here for further questioning." Black beckoned to Laurelin, and she headed in our direction. "How are you holding up?"

She managed a nod that could have meant she was okay or it could have meant she was about to burst into tears.

"The police are going to start letting people go soon," Black told her. "I've got half a dozen of our own security people on their way, and they're going to watch the remaining paintings until they get packed up tomorrow. I've already cleared it with the police captain."

"Th-thank you."

"And we'd also like to donate an extra fifty thousand dollars to your foundation. The world is a poorer place for Derek's passing."

Now Laurelin did start crying, and Black passed her a handkerchief. Ironically, one I'd wrapped around a grenade earlier. He always had been creative about getting rid of evidence.

"You've got my number. Call if there's anything else we can do."

Finally, finally, they let us go, and we regrouped in the honeymoon suite. Black and I would head to a different hotel along with Xav, Dan, Mack, Hallie, and

Ravi as soon as we'd had a debrief. The first thing I did was neck the gin from my goody bag.

"What a shitshow."

"Be positive," Carmen said. "You got *Spirit*, and nobody's in jail."

Black took a seat on the sofa by the balcony. "But do we need *Spirit*? It's clear now that she wasn't the Master's main objective."

"You think he'll try to stiff us?" Dan asked.

"It wouldn't surprise me."

"Motherfucker," Nate cursed. My sentiments exactly. "At least we've got a definite pool of suspects. Nobody left the room during the drama, which means the accomplice was one of the people still inside at the end of it. We've got video of everyone. It'll take time, but we can narrow it down."

Nate still had one laptop open, and Alaric was on the screen. "I told you that painting's—"

"Don't say it!" Dan warned. "An inanimate object can't be cursed."

"At least we're further forward than we were before," I told him.

"This never ends."

"It'll end."

A knock sounded at the door, and Hallie got up to let Rafael in. He'd been pretty much expressionless downstairs, but now he looked...worried.

"What's up?"

"Sky's gone."

"Gone? Gone where?"

"I don't know."

"Have you tried calling her again?"

"Her phone's in the room. Along with the rest of her

belongings."

"Maybe she went to, I don't know, get a drink?"

"I checked the restaurant. She's not there. And the receptionist hasn't seen her."

Nate was a suspicious asshole, and of course his mind went from zero to conspiracy theory in two seconds flat.

"How well do you know this girl?"

"Forget it, Nate."

"She turned up out of the blue, and she had a stolen painting in the trunk of her car."

"*Beth's* car. Sky nicked it, remember? Beth put the painting in the boot."

"It was mighty convenient, that's all I'm saying."

"You're wrong," Rafael practically growled at him.

"Don't you accuse Beth of being a part of this," Alaric snapped.

Nate ignored Alaric and zeroed his gaze in on Rafael. "How can you be so sure?"

"Because I know why she left, and it was nothing to do with the damn painting."

"Why did she leave?" I asked softly. Somebody had to be the voice of reason.

"She thought she'd let us down."

"By skipping dinner?"

"Yes."

"You said she was sick," Black pointed out. "You lied?"

Pot. Kettle. Black. Seemed nobody in the whole fucking Blackwood ecosystem was capable of telling the truth.

"There's an issue. We were working through it. I didn't think she'd just leave, nor did I want to put her under additional pressure by having everyone ask questions."

"What issue?"

Rafael paused, and I thought for a minute that he wasn't going to tell me. Emotions swirled in his eyes, and when he saw me watching him, he closed them for a long moment. He was hurt, wasn't he? Hurt that Sky had run out on him without a word. But he finally gave me a version of what might have been the truth.

"Some time ago, Sky had a run-in with a guest at tonight's gala. She didn't want to risk causing a scene that might jeopardise the operation."

"Why didn't you just say that?"

"Her past isn't something she likes to discuss."

"Fine." A sigh slipped between my lips. "So now we have two problems. We need to track down yet another bloody painting, and we also need to find Sky."

"Sky's resourceful," Alaric said. "She'll show up eventually."

Having done a runner once myself when things got too much for me, I understood that sometimes a person needed space. But seeing somebody she once knew at dinner was hardly a crisis, was it? I liked Sky. She reminded me of myself fifteen years ago. But now I had concerns. Could she handle the pressure of the job we wanted her to do? Or were we all wasting a hell of a lot of time and effort in training her?

CHAPTER 15 - SKY

HOW FAR WAS this sodding waiter planning to drive? We'd been going for almost a hundred miles already, first on I-81 and then on I-64, and now I was about to have a problem. The Ferrari might have been a dream to drive, but fuel economy wasn't one of its strong points. I was almost out of petrol. And if that wasn't bad enough, I had no money and no phone either. While I drove, I'd checked every nook and cranny of the passenger compartment, and there wasn't so much as a stray dollar bill.

The satnav built into the dash told me we were heading for Charlottesville. Was that our final destination? I sure hoped so. Did I mention that I also needed to pee? This *fucking* job. How long did I have left? I guessed twenty miles max, which meant I had a choice to make. Should I carry on following the Audi—and it definitely was an Audi, although the driver had carefully dirtied up the licence plate so I couldn't read it—and hope that we got to wherever we were going before the Ferrari sputtered to a halt? Or should I try to stop somewhere for gas?

I zoomed out on the map and traced my way along the next stretch of I-64. The nearest gas station would come up in ten miles, assuming we didn't turn off first. But if I stopped, the waiter would be long gone by the time I filled up. Unless... What if I took a chance? How many exits were there between us and the gas station? Only one, it looked like. If I assumed that my prey would carry on along I-64 until the gas station at least, then I could go on ahead. He wouldn't need to stop, of that I was certain. Because I knew now that he hadn't just stolen a handbag. He'd nicked another bloody painting. I'd turned on the radio, and the host had been talking about a daring heist at the Grove Hotel and Country Club for the last half hour. It seemed that Team Blackwood hadn't been the only ones planning a theft tonight. I bet Emmy was pissed. Really pissed.

Fuck it. I pressed the loud pedal to the floor and sped past the Audi like my wheels were on fire. If there was a cop on this stretch of highway, I was buggered, but with any luck, they were all back at the Grove, trying to work out what the hell happened. Good luck with that. I still hadn't put all the pieces together, and my jigsaw had come partially assembled.

The Audi's headlights faded into the distance as the speedometer passed a hundred. One-ten. One-twenty. The waiter had been doing a steady sixty-five the whole way, and soon he was left in the dust. The Ferrari ate up the miles, and it was running on fumes when I finally reached the rickety gas station. A floodlight blinked on and off overhead as I pulled up behind a decrepit Ford. My plan was to fill the Ferrari up, speed off, then mail the cash to the manager once I got back to civilisation. Except when I climbed out, I realised I wasn't the first person to have that idea, and probably the other assholes hadn't sent the money either.

A handwritten sign was taped to the pump: *Pay first, gas second.*

Shit.

I couldn't even beg the driver of the Ford for a loan because he was already in the kiosk, talking to the guy behind the counter. Fuck. And if I went inside and tried to negotiate, the waiter would vanish into the night. I glanced across at the Ford in case a miracle happened and the driver had left a fifty on the passenger seat. No such luck.

But he'd gone one better.

The window was open and the keys were in the ignition. I didn't hesitate. I couldn't, not when the owner was halfway to the door. I jumped into the driver's seat and turned the key. The engine coughed and died. I tried again, and the owner suddenly realised what was happening and started running towards me. Brilliant. *Start, you piece of crap!* The engine caught on the fourth attempt, just as the driver reached for the door handle.

"Enjoy the Ferrari," I shouted and lobbed the key at him. It hit him square in the chest, which made him pause long enough for me to floor it off the forecourt. And in a masterpiece of timing, the waiter had just gone past.

In the rear-view mirror, I saw the owner of the Ford pick up the Ferrari key and stare at it. Then he got smaller, smaller, smaller until he disappeared.

I followed the Audi into the night.

The Ford clunked along for another forty miles before we turned off somewhere past Culpeper. The roads grew narrower and bumpier, the signs of life sparser.

The radio faded into a hiss of static so I turned it off. Then the rain started—the perfect end to a perfect evening. The windscreen wipers screeched across the glass as the blurry tail lights of the Audi faded in and out of sight. Surely we had to be reaching the end of the road, both literally and metaphorically?

A moment later, the lights disappeared. One second they were there, and the next they were gone. Had I been spotted? What if the waiter had pulled over to hide? I turned off the Ford's headlights and proceeded with caution. Should I get out and walk? I didn't have a weapon. Nothing. Not even a pen. Emmy once told me that if I trained hard enough, I would become the weapon, but I was pretty sure I wasn't there yet.

I crept forward with the engine on tick-over, my heart thumping so loudly I could hear it over the rain. Where was my quarry? Then I saw it. A driveway, half-hidden by the trees. Their boughs met overhead, leading to a beyond-creepy tunnel effect. The moon shone off wet tarmac, shadows chasing across the pitted surface as leaves blew in the wind. A wooden sign was fixed to one of the imposing stone pillars that held a pair of chunky wrought-iron gates. I risked flicking the headlights back on.

And when I saw what the sign said, I laughed and I laughed and I laughed.

Chapter 16 - Emmy

"EMMY? I KNOW you're marked as 'do not disturb' this evening, but I have a caller who won't take no for an answer."

I paused halfway to the door of the hotel suite. Tiredness had sapped my resolve, and when Black's arm crept around my waist, I'd given in and left it there. The Blackwood switchboard operator who'd phoned me sounded nervous, and understandably so. I counted to five before I answered so I didn't bite her head off.

"Who is it?"

"A Sky Malone? She says you know her."

Sky? Relief flooded through me, but why the hell was she calling the switchboard? Oh, who was I kidding? This was Sky. Anything but predictable.

"Put her through."

"I'll do it right away."

A second passed, and I put the phone on speaker.

"Emmy?"

"Where are you?"

"Eddie's Roadhouse."

"Elaborate."

"It's a dive bar in Culpeper. Can someone pick me up?"

"What the hell are you doing in Culpeper?"

"You won't believe the answer."

This was Sky. A fucking piñata of surprises. "Try me."

"I found the School of Shadows."

"You're joking?"

"I'm not."

"How do you know?"

"Because according to the sign outside, it's an actual bloody school. Shadow Falls Academy."

"Come again?"

"It has to be the place, right? I mean, I followed the guy right there."

"What guy?"

"A waiter from the Grove. I went outside to get some air, and he came out of the basement fire exit with a bag under his arm. A woman's handbag. I thought he was just a dirty thief, but then the car radio said someone nicked another painting. A shepherd?" Sky laughed. "Bet you didn't see that one coming, eh?"

That brat. I didn't know whether to hug her or shake her. As usual, she'd broken every rule, but in doing so, she'd also broken the case. I loved that girl, and yes, I felt a little bit smug for bringing her to Virginia at that moment.

Black was already tapping away at his phone screen. "Shadow Falls Academy, providing a first-class education to boys and girls from grades nine through twelve. A selective school for gifted pupils, specialising in the arts."

Bloody hell. A school? A real school? That was... insane. And audacious. And possibly the work of a genius. I mean, who would ever suspect that a school was the front for a ring of art thieves?

I had a million questions. "Somebody needs to pick Sky up."

"I'll go," Rafael said, already heading for the door. "Send me the address."

"How did you get to Culpeper?" I asked her.

"Borrowed a Ferrari from the parking lot. And when that ran out of petrol, I swapped it for a Ford Fiesta with a guy near Charlottesville."

"When you say 'swapped'...?"

"Okay, so I just drove the Fiesta away while he paid for his fuel."

"Did you wipe your prints?"

"Uh..."

"Don't worry," Mack said. "I'll clean it up."

She meant that if Sky's prints popped up in a police database, she'd get rid of them. It wouldn't be the first time she'd pulled that trick.

"Are you safe?" I asked Sky. "We'll get there as soon as we can."

"Yeah, I'm fine. This place is open all night." A door opened in the background, and I heard voices. "But I gotta go."

She hung up, and I blew out a breath. Once again, the whole case had been flipped on its head.

"Get Sky and drive straight back to Riverley," Black instructed Rafael. "Emmy and I will join you as soon as we've picked the Picasso up tomorrow morning."

Today had been a roller coaster. The nerve-racking ride up the incline followed by the adrenaline rush of the *Spirit* theft. Then the crushing realisation that we'd been tricked by the Master. But now? We'd hit one final loop and come out on top. Tomorrow, we'd regroup and start planning for the next ride.

A trip to Shadow Falls Academy.
The funhouse.

CHAPTER 17 - SKY

"BYE, GUYS."

STUD, one of my new buddies from the Venom Motorcycle Club, crushed me in a hug, and Rafael glared at him. Stud glared right back.

"Look after our girl."

"She's not your girl."

"Boys, boys, it's three a.m. Can we avoid getting into a punch-up? Rafael, these gents have been taking care of me all evening. Stud, my brother can get a teensy bit overprotective sometimes."

Finally, Stud nodded and held out a hand. "Good. He should be."

After a moment, Rafael offered his hand too, and I breathed a sigh of relief. Massacre averted. Phew. I was too tired to play referee, too tired to panic at Stud's touch, too tired to think.

Rafael opened the passenger door of the Navigator, and a quick glance into the back told me he'd packed up all my stuff from the hotel room. My case was there with the beautiful, tear-stained dress draped over the top of it.

The night could have been worse, I suppose. After I'd followed the waiter to the school in Shadow Falls— population 1,027 according to the sign at the town limits—I backtracked to Culpeper and abandoned the

Ford outside a strip mall with the key in the footwell. Someone would find it. Hopefully the right someone. Then I schlepped up the road to Eddie's Roadhouse, a bar with bad decor and good music. The place had been packed, and when I'd offered to help out behind the bar for an hour in return for use of the phone and a couple of drinks, the bartender's eyebrows had shot into his hairline, but he'd agreed.

I fit in there better than at the Grove, despite my stupid outfit, and when trade dropped off after midnight, the bikers had invited me to play pool. Mostly so they could stare at my ass, I suspected, but when a slimy little cowboy patted it, they picked him up and dumped him in the parking lot.

But now Rafael was here, and we were back to awkwardness.

He drove the first five miles in silence, and since I didn't know what to say either, I just stared out the window. Finally, he spoke.

"I thought you'd gone."

To lie or not to lie, that was the question.

"I considered leaving," I admitted.

Silence.

"What did you tell Emmy?"

"That you were sick. And then later, I had to admit that you weren't, and she wasn't impressed that I'd lied."

"Sorry."

"She knows there was someone from your past at the event who you didn't want to run into, but I didn't go into the details."

"Thank you."

"Can't guarantee she's not going to ask you about

it."

I'd have to deal with that when the time came. "Did the job go okay? I mean, I heard what happened with the other painting. It was on the radio."

"We got away clean. After *The Shepherd* vanished, nobody was looking at *Spirit*."

"What about the Ferrari I took? Is the owner pissed?"

"When I left the party, nobody had even noticed the car was missing." Wow, really? Perhaps I was a better thief than I thought. "Most likely the owner's staying at the hotel."

"Oops. Somewhere out there, a kid's having the night of his life."

Rafael barked out a laugh. "At least somebody's happy."

"What'll happen to the valet? I nicked the keys when he wasn't looking, but I don't want him to lose his job."

"If he let a customer's car get stolen, he deserves to be fired."

Shit. Although that was sort of true, I didn't need an extra helping of guilt with my transgression. "It was his boss's fault. He insists on keeping all the keys in a bloody basket."

"Fine. I'll ask Black to put in a word." A pause. "So, the thief really went to a school?"

Rafael still didn't look happy. Should I apologise again? Probably, but what was the point? Even if I grovelled every day for the rest of my life, it wouldn't make up for completely losing my head the way I had earlier.

"Yup. It's in the middle of nowhere. Creepy as

fuck."

"Creepy isn't a problem. A school—that's the problem."

I saw his point. Casing a school would be almost impossible. Send the men from Blackwood to take a peek, and they'd get arrested. Although I couldn't imagine the pupils being too upset if they showed up, especially if they took their shirts off.

"Speaking of problems... What about me?"

"Get some sleep. We've got a meeting about the School of Shadows at eleven o'clock, and then we're going climbing."

"But Emmy—"

"I'll handle Emmy. Sleep."

Everyone stared at me when I walked into the Windsor Room the next morning, and I wished I'd stayed in Eddie's Roadhouse. Being the centre of attention because I had tits and ass was something I could handle. The whole of Blackwood knowing I fucked up? Not so much.

"Here she is," Nate said. "The hero of the hour."

Huh?

"Heroine," Carmen corrected.

They weren't mad at me?

Bradley came in with a tray of pastries, followed by Mrs. Fairfax with fruit, juice, and coffee on a cart. I realised how hungry I was. Bar snacks from Eddie's had been a poor substitute for a three-course dinner. Since it seemed I still had a job, at least until my next faux pas, I took a croissant and helped myself to a mug of black coffee, then found a seat.

Xavier appeared with a toddler in his arms—his daughter, I presumed—followed by Ana and Quinn with their little girl. Was it "take your kid to work" day? Yes, it seemed, because Emmy was followed in by Beth with Rune, and after them came Alaric and Black carrying a slim wooden crate between them. Plus Rafael had let Marshall out of the basement. Hallie and Dan came next with Caleb, Dan's son, then Mack and Luke appeared too, plus half a dozen people I'd never seen before. Wow. This was one big meeting.

"First things first," Black announced, prying the front off the crate with a nasty-looking knife. "Let's get this hung up."

The Picasso was none the worse for its adventure, thank goodness. I'll admit I didn't quite understand the appeal of a portrait with all the bits of face in the wrong place, but the colours were pretty. Still vivid, and with the climate control in the gallery downstairs, hopefully they always would be. But for now, Black hung it on a spare hook next to the whiteboard, and everyone leaned forward in their seats as he swung open the front of the specially modified frame.

There she was, sandwiched between the Picasso and a false canvas back. *Spirit of the Lake.*

"Exquisite," Alaric murmured.

"I've never been so terrified as I was when I picked her up," Beth said.

Understandable. The last time Beth had transported stolen goods, she'd been totally oblivious to what she was doing. Now? We'd corrupted her completely.

"Any problems?" Emmy asked.

"Apart from me almost passing out? No. Two of the policemen even helped me to carry the box to the car."

"We'll make an agent of you yet."

Alaric scowled at Emmy. "No, you won't."

I pushed my chair back and stepped forward to take a closer look at the painting. On balance, I preferred *Spirit* to the Picasso. The lone woman reminded me of myself, one girl against the world. Or was I? Right now, I wasn't sure.

But I didn't want to be alone anymore.

"Sky, while you're standing up, can you talk us through what happened last night?" Black asked. "From the beginning, please."

I told the story for the third time. The version I'd given Emmy over the phone from the back room at Eddie's had been somewhat garbled, the tale I'd told Rafael tempered by tiredness. Now I went through everything. And then went through it again. And afterwards, Black and Emmy and Dan and Alaric and Hallie asked me enough questions that my brain turned to mush and left me second-guessing myself. Had I definitely been following the right car? Could I have imagined him turning into the driveway? Perhaps he'd simply gone around a bend farther ahead?

But no, it would have been too much of a coincidence, right? The School of fucking Shadows. Shadow Falls Academy. Talk about thumbing their noses at people.

Mack thought so too.

"While you lightweights were sleeping, Luke and I did some preliminary research. Shadow Falls Academy was founded seventy years ago by Phineas and Golda Rosenberg out of concern that the arts were being neglected in the public school system. A few pupils live nearby and go home each day, but ninety percent of them board. There's an emphasis on painting, sculpture, music, dance, and drama. Their former students have won two Oscars, three Golden Globes, four Tony Awards, an Emmy, one regular GRAMMY, and nineteen classical GRAMMYs. We lost count of the number of art and dance prizes. The school is basically the creative industries' best-kept secret. But they're no slouches when it comes to academia either. Over half of their students go on to attend Ivy League schools. Care to take a guess who one of their past pupils was? I'll give you a clue—after she got married, her surname rhymed with 'insane.'"

"Fuck," Emmy muttered. "Kyla Devane's mother?"

"Got it in one. The Devane family endowed a scholarship at the Shadow Falls Academy, and Kyla presented a prize there two years ago. I found a picture of the ceremony on a cached version of the school's website. And we can't be sure it was connected, but President Harrison is pushing for legislation to charge property taxes on private schools, and one of the items on Kyla's manifesto was a promise to block that."

At least now we knew how Kyla had gotten hold of the painting she'd used to bribe Irvine Carnes for his endorsement in the senatorial election. I'd been curious about that. And thankfully, she was last month's problem.

"Oh, it would have been connected," Emmy said.

"So we can assume that the Rosenbergs are involved, and we sure as heck know they're rich. As well as obscene fees and alumni donations, they'll have income from their sideline."

"So we'll have to tread very, very carefully. Who runs the place now? Presumably Phineas and Golda are dead and buried?"

"In the family mausoleum. Their son, Sandor, took over as principal, but he retired a decade ago with heart problems. There was a celebratory dinner." Mack flashed a photo up on the screen. "Recognise anybody?"

"Congressman Lewis," Black said. "And Governor Leclerc."

Alaric pointed at a woman with impossibly red hair. "Nerissa Fremantle. Married to Paul Sterling."

The Hollywood director? Wow.

"Front right. That guy's a professor at the Holborn School," Sofia said. I hadn't noticed her sneak in at the back.

"What's the Holborn School?" I asked.

"A first-rate place where genius musicians go."

The list went on. Basically, if you attended Shadow Falls Academy, you were more or less guaranteed an easy ride through life, unlike at Greenfields Comprehensive. Which was a misnomer if there ever was one. It wasn't near any fields, and the only greenery was the forest of cannabis plants some enterprising sod had grown on the roof. The police helicopter spotted them on a flyover, and they raided the school in the middle of one of the few lessons I'd bothered to go to. Biology, I recalled. Because everyone needed to know the anatomy of a goldfish.

"Sandor passed away the year before last, I believe," Mack said. "No fanfare, but I found a death certificate. And after Sandor came Ezra. He's the current principal. Look familiar to anyone?"

Another picture appeared, this time of a man in his

late forties with wispy brown hair and glasses. Emmy cursed under her breath.

"He was sitting behind me at dinner last night, except he wasn't wearing the glasses then. Contacts, probably."

"And here's the family photo. Sandor and his wife, Tovah, in the back row, their kids in front. Ezra, Saul, and Mina."

"They were all there except Sandor and Mina." Tovah had been the grey-haired lady feigning shock. "Sandor had an excuse for skipping the party—he's dead—but where was the daughter?"

"Could she have been the accomplice in the basement?"

I shook my head. "It was definitely a guy. The body shape, the way he moved... A guy."

"Do you know anything about this?" Alaric asked Marshall.

Marshall held both hands up. "Not me. A school? I'm as surprised as anyone. Who risks involving children in a criminal enterprise?" He glanced around the room and realised who was present. "Not that this is a criminal enterprise," he added hastily. "More of a rescue mission."

"It's summer break," Dan told him. "You try finding last-minute childcare."

"Of course, of course. I suppose the letters from the Master could have been written by a teacher. They were always grammatically correct."

"You'll need to contact him about *Spirit*."

"I've already drafted the wording. Unless you'd care to give me access to the internet, one of your people will have to place the ad."

"Understood," Black said. "But in the meantime, we need to take a closer look at this school, which is going to be a challenge. Do we know if they're recruiting staff at the moment?"

Mack answered, but it wasn't good news. "No current vacancies according to the careers page on their website."

"Start researching the staff they do have: teachers, the back-office team, cleaners, groundsmen. Find someone who's short of cash. They may be willing to sell information."

"Too slow," Emmy said. "If *The Shepherd* was stolen to order, they'll be moving it on sooner rather than later. How long does a handover take to arrange? A week? A month?"

"Possibly longer if they're using the USPS. And there is one obvious solution. As Mr. Marshall here so helpfully pointed out, we have several children on summer break. One of them can pose as a potential pupil and ask for a tour."

"Me!" Caleb volunteered. "I'll go."

"You're too young, honey," Dan told him. "Maybe in a couple of years."

"I'll do it," Rune said.

Alaric was shaking his head before she finished the sentence. "No, you won't."

"But I love school."

"I think you've had enough excitement in the last month, don't you?"

Rune harrumphed and folded her arms, but she didn't argue. Wait. Why was everyone looking at me?

"Uh, I'm not the best person for this."

"It's only an interview," Emmy said. "A little chat."

"I failed everything except PE."

"Not because you're stupid. You just didn't go to class, did you?"

"I had better things to do."

"Yes, like learning how to hustle, which is why you'll be perfect for this job. And you won't be alone. You'll have your parents with you."

"My parents?"

My birth mother had pissed off into the sunset when I was two, and I hadn't seen my father since I was ten. No great loss. At least the physical scars had faded now, even if the mental ones hadn't.

"Yeah, you'll need parents. I'm out because the Rosenbergs have seen my face. Ditto for everyone else at the gala, which leaves one obvious candidate. Sky McLain—it has a nice ring to it."

"Sky McLain?"

"Alaric was lamenting his lack of involvement before. Now he can walk right into the hornets' nest. Right, Prince?"

"Right. But only if Sky agrees."

Talk about déjà vu. The first day I met Alaric, I'd been thrust into the role of his daughter as a punishment for stealing Bethany's car. That surveillance operation was what landed me the job at Blackwood in the first place. How could I say no?

I fluttered my eyelids. "Should I call you Daddy?"

"No."

Emmy snorted, then quickly got back to business. "Alaric, you'll need a wife. Who do we have left? Sofia? Or I could bring Mimi over from Australia, but she's kind of a bitch."

"She's also half-Vietnamese," Black pointed out.

"So she'd have to be a stepmom. What about Cora?"

"Cora's only five years older than Sky."

"Trophy wife? Dammit, we need to hire more women."

"I'll do it," Beth said.

Alaric's mouth set in a hard line. "A thousand times no."

"Why not? As Emmy said, it's just a simple interview. And I went to a private school. I'll know the right questions to ask."

"You almost died last month."

"And yet I'm still here. Don't you dare write me off as a helpless female."

"Good luck arguing with that," Emmy whispered.

Alaric knew when he was beaten. Smart man. "Fine. *Fine.* But we'll need new identities. And a cover story. Plus Sky should have some sort of transcript or she won't get an interview at all."

"What if the school's full?" I asked hopefully.

Black merely smiled. "Walk in with enough money, and a place like that will always find space."

Chapter 18 - Alaric

MEET THE MILBURNS...

Alaric straightened his tie in the hallway mirror at Riverley, adjusted his glasses, then took one last look around.

"Camera feed still okay?" he asked in the British accent he'd be using today.

"Perfect," Mack said into his ear. "The truck won't be far away."

Alaric, Beth, and Sky all wore cameras and microphones. Everything they saw and heard at Shadow Falls Academy would transmit to a Blackwood unit parked on the road outside, which would then boost the signal back to Riverley. Since there wasn't much cover around, two men dressed as forestry guys would hang around in the trees looking busy while a technician hid in the back of the van.

As Black had predicted, the school was happy to grant an interview when presented with appropriate credentials. Alaric was a senior manager for HC Systems, a UK-based cybersecurity company with a branch in Richmond, and he'd been transferred at the last minute to head a new project. Mack's husband owned the company, and he'd back up the claim if necessary.

His "daughter's" story had been trickier. But thanks

to some smooth negotiation from Judd, seventeen-year-old Sky Milburn had a glowing transcript from Abbington Grammar School in Berkshire, England. Abbington Grammar was currently in the process of planning their new library, which would now come with a full audio-visual system and a staff lounge funded by the Blackwood Foundation. The headmaster had struck a hard bargain.

"I look stupid," Sky complained.

"You don't look stupid," Beth said. "Just different."

"Do people really wear this stuff every day? Teenagers?"

"In my old world, they do."

Bradley had dressed Sky in a pale-pink pleated skirt, a cream blouse with a bow at the neck, and kitten heels. The brooch in the middle of the bow held a GPS tracker, her glasses came with a miniature camera in the bridge, and her slim gold watch had a built-in microphone. Beth had gone for a knee-length summer dress with plenty of frills. The outfit shouldn't have turned Alaric on, but it most definitely did. Something about the way the primness hid the filthy side he knew lurked underneath made his blood run hot. He looked forward to stripping her out of that frock later.

"We need to go," he said to the girls. "If Ezra Rosenberg's anything like the principals at my old schools, he won't tolerate lateness."

The drive from Richmond to Shadow Falls took an hour and a half in their borrowed Mercedes, and Sky barely spoke the whole way. A fish out of water. Alaric hadn't quite worked her out yet. In London, she'd been streetwise and confident, but now? She seemed somehow more fragile. Hard on the outside, soft on the inside, and now a few cracks were showing. Would she make the final grade? Only time would tell.

Today would be the first time Alaric saw Shadow Falls Academy in person. He'd snooped around the small town with Beth the day before yesterday— nothing much to write home about there—and of course he'd studied satellite maps. The campus was spread over four hundred acres, much of it woodland, which had at first given them hope for surveillance. But then they realised one of the groundsmen kept dogs. Noisy ones, and he liked to bring them to work with him. Emmy and Ana had gone for a scout around and been forced to climb a tree. They'd been stuck up there for three hours, hiding high among the foliage while the groundsman complained about "those darn squirrels."

The main school building rivalled Riverley Hall in both size and ugliness. According to the town's website, it had been built in the late nineteenth century by an eccentric English nobleman convinced the end of the world was nigh and that northern Virginia was the best place to ride out the apocalypse. He'd died from a bear attack in 1893.

There were also a number of other buildings—some large, which appeared from the school's website to be accommodation, and others smaller, possibly storage— plus the usual facilities one found with a private school. Tennis courts, two sports pitches, a swimming pool, a running track, that sort of thing. If all went according to plan, their trip today would include a tour of the campus.

Nearly there.

Even with the sun high in the sky, the driveway was dark, shadowed by the spreading boughs of oaks either side. And steep. The car dropped down a gear as Alaric steered around the bends.

"This place had the same architect as Riverley," Sky muttered as the main building came into view.

Not true, but they'd certainly shared a love of gargoyles.

Alaric parked near the front entrance, and as they approached, the right-hand door swung open to reveal a girl in school uniform. A white blouse, a navy-blue blazer, and a tartan kilt.

"Yeuch," Sky muttered.

The uniform was worn to instill discipline and to promote a sense of equality, so said the school's website. Not necessarily a bad thing. The number of people who didn't know how to tie a tie nowadays was disappointing.

"Mr. Milburn?" the girl asked.

"That's right."

"I'm Marigold. I'm to show you to Mr. Rosenberg's office."

Marigold set off at a fast clip, but when Alaric lagged behind, she had no choice but to slow down. He wanted to get a feel for the place and let the team back at Riverley take a good look too. Gloomy wood-panelled hallways were brightened up by paintings, presumably done by pupils past and present. Classrooms held rows of old-fashioned wooden desks with starkly modern interactive whiteboards at the front. Small groups of silent teenagers watched them as they walked past. It reminded Alaric of the boarding school he'd attended in Surrey, England, when his father spent two years working at the US Embassy in London. Woodbury College had been his mother's alma mater. Which was possibly why his parents had been so upset when he got threatened with expulsion for corrupting the math teacher's daughter. But money talked, the math teacher had moved on, and Alaric learned a valuable lesson: if you're going to break the rules, don't get caught.

Rosenberg stood from behind his desk and offered a hand when they walked in. Marigold melted away along the hallway.

"Ezra Rosenberg. It's good to meet you."

"Alan Milburn. My wife, Bethan, and Sky, my daughter."

"Please, take a seat."

Three high-backed wooden chairs were lined up opposite, and Alaric nudged Sky into the middle one. This chat was to focus on her. Emmy's interrogation team had been drilling her with questions all week, and despite her discomfort, she hadn't cracked. Today should be a walk in the park.

"This is an unusually late application, Mr. Milburn," Rosenberg said. "Our fall term started today. We like to begin early so students can have a longer Christmas break with their families."

"I understand it's far from ideal, but I got a job offer that was too good to pass up."

"You didn't consider a British boarding school?"

"Considered it, but we're hoping to stay in the US for a number of years, so we want to get Sky settled here as soon as possible. It's never too early to start making connections."

"Indeed, indeed. Where do you see yourself in five years' time, Sky?"

"I'll have completed my biology degree and be

getting ready to attend Harvard Medical School."

"You want to be a doctor?"

"My mum died when I was young. I want to help others like her."

"Bethan's my second wife," Alaric explained.

"Yes, yes, I see. A noble goal, Sky." As they'd hoped, he moved on to a different subject. "What made you apply to our school?"

"I heard it was the best. You've turned out pioneers in their fields and even a Nobel Prize winner. Plus I'd be near to my parents but not *too* near."

Everyone laughed at that, and Alaric knew they had Ezra on-side. Sky was an obstreperous little bitch sometimes, but she could also be charming when she wanted to be. As could the Milburn family's money. After another fifteen minutes of small talk and softball questions, Rosenberg leaned forward with his chin on his hands.

"It seems to me that Sky will fit in perfectly here at Shadow Falls Academy. I suspected from her transcript and the glowing letter of recommendation from Mr. Bell at Abbington that she would, and since the fall term is already in progress, I took the liberty of preparing our entrance exam so you wouldn't have to make another trip. She can sit it right now."

Sky didn't have to speak for Alaric to hear her internal monologue. *Oh, no. No way. I did* not *sign up for this.*

And the website clearly stated that applicants who proved successful at the first stage of application would be invited back at a later date to sit the test. They hadn't intended to return. All they'd wanted was a damn tour.

Emmy spoke up from Riverley. "Chill, Sky. You can do this. We've got a whole bunch of people who can help you. All you need to do is write the answers down." Then in the background, "Someone find Mack. And Nate. And Black. Why? Because I don't know the first fucking thing about algebra, that's why."

"Sure," Sky said weakly. "I'd love to."

"Excellent. And in the meantime, your parents can begin filling out the paperwork."

Sky shuffled off behind Marigold like a condemned woman, but Alaric couldn't afford to lose focus.

"Where do we need to do the paperwork? In here?"

"I'll take you through to the admissions office. Mrs. Prendergast will help you."

"Is there a bathroom I could use first? We had a long drive here."

"Turn left out the door, follow the hallway around to the right, and it's the third door after the bust of Abraham Lincoln. You'll see the sign."

"Turn left out the door, follow the hallway forever, open all the doors," Emmy said in Alaric's ear. "That bust's never Abraham Lincoln. The hair's wrong. It looks more like Julius Caesar."

"Get Rune," Alaric muttered. "To help Sky."

Rune could do algebra in her sleep. In fact, she sometimes did. Alaric heard her muttering about variables and coefficients as she tossed and turned in the dark. But rather that than her reliving all the horrors she'd had to endure in her short life.

"Rune? I guess that makes sense. Hey, can someone find Rune as well?"

Alaric tried a door. Locked. Opened the next one and found himself in a stairwell. Up or down? The basement seemed like a better bet if somebody wanted to hide stolen art, but all he saw was stacks of dusty chairs and a bunch of old desks. And the second floor looked just the same as the first—dark hallways filled with paintings and the occasional noticeboard. Every so often, he came across a classroom filled with pupils, and he hurried past those. There didn't seem to be any security cameras, which was both a good and a bad thing. Good because nobody was watching him. Bad because it meant Mack couldn't do her tech-wizard magic and hack into the system. Their only option was to map the place manually.

And it was a maze. If *Emerald* were hanging on a wall in plain view, he could walk around the building forever and never find her. Hell, he wasn't sure he'd find Ezra Rosenberg's office again. How long had he been gone? Ten minutes. Even if he'd been taking a shit, that was a long time for a bathroom break. Time to head back.

"Who are you?" a man asked from behind.

"Oh, hello."

Alaric held out a hand, leaving the guy a choice of shaking it or being rude. After a moment's hesitation, he opted for the former. Presumably the man was left-handed because he wore a watch on his right wrist, a gold OMEGA De Ville remarkably similar to the timepiece Alaric's father favoured. Understated yet expensive. How many schoolteachers could afford a ten-thousand-dollar watch on their regular salary? His brogues didn't look cheap either.

"I'm Alan Milburn. My daughter's here for an entrance interview, and I got lost on the way to the bathroom." Alaric forced a laugh. "Ezra Rosenberg said to take the third door after the bust of Abe Lincoln, but I only saw a bust of Julius Caesar, and then I got hopelessly lost."

The man's expression softened. "I'm Saul. Ezra's brother. This place does have a labyrinthine quality to it. I'll take you back to his office."

"I'd appreciate it."

Saul led the way, this time down a different staircase via what appeared to be a more direct route. How was Sky getting on? Emmy had gone quiet. All Alaric could hear was the echo of his footsteps on the polished wooden floors, the soft murmur of voices as they passed yet more classrooms. Nice small class sizes, though. And the kids respected the teachers. Overall, he preferred Rune's school because it wasn't so dark and depressing, but he understood why the pupils at Shadow Falls got good grades.

"Ah, you're back," Emmy said. "The feed broke up, and you disappeared for a while." Probably due to the building's construction. The place was put together like a castle with thick stone walls and small windows. "Sky's doing okay. Rune's got people researching Latin phrases, but apart from that, she's basically taken over."

"Is your daughter looking for a place this year?" Saul asked.

"Yes. Short notice, I know, but it was a sudden move to Virginia for us."

"How old is she?"

"She'd be a senior. Do you teach here?"

"I'm head of the art department. Does your daughter paint?"

The art department, huh?

"Sky's more into drama."

"Well, we also have a first-class drama department." They arrived back at the elder Rosenberg brother's office. "Ezra, I found your guest. We really ought to get some maps printed."

"Ah, Mr. Milburn, we were wondering where you'd got to. Thank you, Saul. Maps... Yes, I'll investigate the possibility."

"And I keep telling you that bust looks like Julius Caesar. It confuses people." Saul turned back to Alaric. "It was one of Kirsten Briard's first attempts at sculpture. Thankfully she improved. Even had her own show in New York last year."

"Very impressive."

"We're proud of our alumni," Ezra said. "Nothing gives me more satisfaction as principal than seeing a young person whose talents I've helped to nurture go on to do great things."

Alaric knew that feeling. Rune scored ninety-four percent on Sky's test, which meant they got granted the all-important tour. Although that didn't help as much as he'd hoped. They only covered a fraction of the main building and skipped one wing entirely.

"And this is one of our dorms," Ezra said, stopping outside a large brick building. "Marigold, would you please show Sky and her mother around? We have rules about men walking into the girls' houses, I'm afraid. We don't want anyone to feel uncomfortable."

"That's understandable."

"Each bedroom is roughly the same, shared between two girls or boys. We're not a hotel. Parents can't pay extra for more desirable accommodation. Our pupils are treated as equals. A rising tide floats all boats, as the saying goes."

"An admirable attitude."

Although since it came from a man who quite possibly made millions running a global art-theft ring, Alaric found it just a tiny bit hypocritical.

"We find the connections made here at Shadow Falls will serve students and staff alike for the rest of their lives. Parents too. We have regular recitals and exhibitions for family and friends. Now, shall we head to the dining hall? We'll have lunch before you leave."

Outside, Sky gave the school a wave goodbye as they trundled down the driveway.

"Well, that was perfectly horrible. Do people really pay money to go there?"

"Boarding school can be a very rewarding experience," Beth told her.

"It's basically a prison with tests."

"You did well with your entrance exam."

"Rune's scary. How does she know all that stuff?"

Alaric chuckled. "Because she goes to a good school. She'll be kicking herself for getting some of the questions wrong, though."

"Oh, she knew the right answers. But she said that if I scored a hundred percent, it'd look suspicious, so she made me mess a few up."

Of course she did. That was Alaric's girl.

Rune never ceased to amaze him, and although becoming a father had been the farthest thing from his mind when he set off on that fateful trip to Thailand, he thanked fate every day for allowing their paths to cross. Any other kid would have fallen apart after what Rune had been through—first in the Phuket brothel Alaric had rescued her from, and then during her recent kidnap ordeal—but Rune was a survivor. More than that, she was a fighter.

There were still lingering problems from the latest torment—insomnia was one of them, Alaric had noticed —but she'd bounce back, he was confident of that. Rune had even managed to charm Emmy when they'd met properly for the first time last month, and by "properly," Alaric meant Rune hadn't been at death's door and Emmy wasn't dressed up like a commando. His ex had come over for dinner, and the initial stilted conversation had turned into a female bonding session over Beth's home-made chocolate fudge cake. Alaric wasn't too keen on Rune taking up Emmy's offer of shooting lessons, though.

Yes, things were finally slotting into place in his life. Family, friends, work... The only thing missing was that damn painting.

CHAPTER 19 - SKY

ON TUESDAY MORNING, we all got together and had another meeting. Emmy and Mack and the rest of the bigwigs had analysed the footage me, Alaric, and Beth got from walking around the academy and come to the conclusion that we were screwed. Various suggestions were put forward, everything from Emmy dressing up as a schoolgirl, which was vetoed because she really was too old—although I noticed Black did look kind of interested when somebody mentioned the uniform—to Nate flying a remote-controlled cockroach around the hallways. Again, that was ruled out because apparently there'd been glitches in the feed yesterday, and if the signal disappeared, several thousand bucks' worth of gadget would either get stomped under someone's foot or swept up by the janitor.

"You're forgetting the other obvious option," Emmy said.

Black raised an eyebrow.

"Sky aced her entrance exam. There's a good chance she'll be offered a place at the school. We can have her wander around with a camera for a few weeks."

What? No way.

"Are you kidding? I'd go crazy in that place. You said it was just an interview. A little chat. And the only reason I passed the test was because Rune was telling me the answers. I didn't even understand most of the questions."

"Fall term at Shadow Falls has already started. Rune, when do you go back to school?"

"September twelfth."

"So you could coach Sky for almost four weeks?"

"Sure."

"Emmy, Rune's meant to be on vacation," Alaric pointed out. "You know, rest and relaxation?"

"I don't mind helping. Learning's fun."

Emmy grinned. "There we go."

No, no we didn't go. Not if I could help it. "Don't I get any say in this? I'm only three months into my training. I'm still on probation. What about all the other stuff I have to do? Shooting? Running? Climbing?"

"You can pick that up afterwards. Right, Rafael?"

He hesitated for the longest moment. Part of me wanted him to tell Emmy that I wasn't ready. That she shouldn't send me out on my own to spend weeks undercover. But I also wanted him to think that I was good enough to hold my own in this team. I'd already let him down twice and somehow got away with it. I wouldn't get a third chance.

"Can we run through the alternatives once more?"

He *didn't* think I was good enough, and that felt like a knife to the heart.

"Nothing we've spoken about so far is viable, but if you've got a new idea, I'm all ears."

"We should wait for a support staff vacancy."

"And draw this out for even longer?"

Alaric's phone rang.

"It's the school."

Everyone sucked in a collective breath.

"What are we doing?" he asked.

Emmy turned to me. "Sky?"

Shit. I was stuck between a rock and a bigger rock. But when it came down to it, I wanted to prove to Rafael that I could do a job without screwing up more than I didn't want to spend a month in academic jail.

"I'll go."

"Super. Alaric, would you do the honours?"

And there it was... The portal to hell had opened up, and I had no choice but to step through.

When Blackwood moved, they moved fast. By six a.m. on Thursday, I not only had a school uniform that fit me, but I also had a full complement of electronic widgets, all disguised to look like something they weren't. Basically, I had two jobs at Shadow Falls. Well, three if you counted not getting expelled. I was to map out as much of the buildings and grounds as possible, and also install recording devices all around the academy, focusing on the staff offices and any areas off limits to students.

Nate had built bugs into everything—air fresheners, plug adaptors, lightbulbs, pens... I only hoped nobody checked my suitcase because they might wonder why I was carrying five wall clocks. Claiming I had a fetish for punctuality probably wouldn't cut it. And then there were the three smoke alarms. He'd also designed a box of tricks to amplify the signals, and the fake forestry guys had hidden it in a pile of fake logs near the school's entrance.

A shadow darkened my bedroom doorway. Rafael.

"So..." he said.

"So."

We'd barely spoken on our run yesterday morning. I'd apologised—again—and he'd told me I'd been slow on the last mile and I needed to speed up. And then when we got back, he'd vanished while I was taking off my trainers. Perhaps I should have gone to find him, but I had too much to do. I'd needed to call Lenny to explain I'd be busy for the next few weeks, then meet with Rune and Beth for a briefing on boarding school etiquette.

"Be careful, Sky."

"It's a school, Rafael. Hundreds of people my age manage to survive there every day."

"That's not what I meant."

"Then what? You think I'm going to melt down every other day? I'll be staying in an all-girls dormitory. There are actual rules if we want to have a boy over to visit." I'd studied the welcome pack yesterday evening. The school handbook ran to almost two hundred pages. "Bedroom doors have to remain open, and at least three feet must remain on the floor at all times."

Rafael's eyes darkened. "There's plenty a man and a woman can do together with three feet on the floor."

"For fuck's sake! I'm not going to be doing any of it."

"Good. We still have desensitisation to work on. But that wasn't what I meant when I said to be careful, Sunshine. You're going to be snooping around, and these aren't nice people."

"There's literally a whole team who'll be listening to my every move. They've rented a house three freaking miles away."

"A lot could go wrong in the time it takes to drive three miles."

"I'll be careful, okay? I promise."

Rafael ran a finger over the back of my neck, and I shivered. Which was better than having a panic attack, at least.

"I'm gonna hold you to that, *mi pequeño rayo de sol*."

CHAPTER 20 - SKY

AT SEVEN THIRTY on that rainy Thursday morning, we pulled up outside Shadow Falls Academy for the second time. Today, I had on a perfectly tailored uniform, and the boot of the car was filled with three suitcases of clothes, toiletries, stationery, and assorted surveillance gear. If I needed more, one of my minions would deliver it to the gates within the hour.

Alaric helped me to get my luggage out. "Thanks for doing this, Sky. I know this isn't your battle to fight."

"Hey, at least I get a few weeks off combat training."

The bruises might even have faded by the time I got back to Riverley. In the meantime, I'd just have to be careful around the showers. I didn't want to face awkward questions about where the marks came from.

A lady with pink hair walked down the steps at the front of the main building and headed in our direction. A teacher? She didn't look that old. Maybe thirty-five?

"You must be the Milburns? I'm Miss Potter. I teach in the art department, but I'm also one of the house leaders over at New Hall. It's not often we have a student start late, so I'll quickly show you to your room, and you can meet your roommate after today's classes. Do your parents want to walk with us?"

"Why not?"

Every bit of surveillance counted. The faster Blackwood managed to put together an operation to find the stolen paintings, the faster I could get the hell out of there.

New Hall, it turned out, was something of a misnomer. According to the plaque over the front doors, it had been built in 1947. I could only guess that it was less old than the other buildings. Outside, I hugged my "parents" goodbye because it would have been weird not to. When I got to Alaric, I whispered, "Hurry up and do your stuff."

"Rest assured, we're trying."

Then they were gone, and I was on my own. Well, this wasn't quite what I'd envisaged when I moved to Virginia. On balance, I'd rather have been in rehab with Lenny. His group therapy sessions were probably easier than socio-emotional learning, whatever the hell that was. According to my schedule, I had a class on it every Wednesday afternoon. In all honesty, I'd rather have had a detention. The rest of the timetable was the stuff of nightmares—four eighty-minute classes per day, Monday through Saturday, with the final class each day being part of the school's Afternoon Enrichment Program. Something sporty or arty or social, basically. And the first session each Monday was an assembly that everyone was expected to attend, usually with a guest speaker or a performance by a group of students.

Classes ran from eight o'clock until three, and most students signed up for club activities after that. Not me. That would be my snooping time.

Marigold had shown Beth and me around a different dorm when we came to visit, but New Hall was much the same. A bunch of bedrooms, each with two single beds, two desks, two chairs, two closets, and two corkboards. Basic but functional. Some of the doors were open, and I saw the girls had personalised their spaces with posters and keepsakes and... Oh, yuck. One of them had a duvet cover with Brock Keaton's face on it. I suppressed a shudder and hurried past.

My room was at the back of the building with a view over the forest—kind of pretty, I had to admit. Downstairs, there was a communal sitting room with a kitchenette. There didn't seem to be a stove, but that didn't matter because we all ate our meals in the dining hall, which was in the east wing of the main building and resembled a scene from Harry Potter. Hmm. Was the art teacher a relative of the boy wizard?

"I'm afraid there's no time to look around," Miss Potter said. "You'll need to grab your textbooks and pencil case. Which class do you have first?"

"Creative writing in room A7."

Creative writing was just making stuff up, right? I could manage that. Especially since Emmy had seen my timetable and arranged to have Sapphire freaking Duvall on the other end of the phone. I used to buy her books from charity shops back in London. They'd given me hope that good men did exist, that one day I'd find a white knight who'd sweep me off my feet, but then I'd met Brock Keaton and I hadn't read a romance novel since.

"All the 'A' rooms are over in the main building. I'll show you the way."

There was one wooden desk left, right at the front of the classroom, and all eyes followed me as I took my seat. Eleven others shared the class, eight girls and three boys. It felt weirdly intimate. On the rare occasions I'd been to school in England, there had been almost forty people in each lesson, three to a textbook. How would life have turned out if I'd attended a school like this for real? I might even have learned something. As it was, I made sure to film every corner of the room as Sapphire dictated my essay. She was funny. Every so often, she'd accidentally say something dirty, then gasp and tell me to "scratch that, scratch that."

After creative writing, it was time for chemistry. Since I'd stupidly said I wanted to be a doctor, I'd been put down for biology, chemistry, and physics as well as drama, English, and maths. Or math, as the Americans called it because they couldn't bloody spell. Plus there was "art enrichment," which was the class that scared me the most. Nobody else could do the work for me, and the closest I'd got to painting was spraying graffiti tags all over Whitechapel. I wasn't particularly proud of it, but Squelch, the de facto leader of that little gang, always had food and he was willing to share. But then the Keaton episode had happened, and the guy who'd scooped me out of the gutter that night ran a parkour club. They'd sort of adopted me, and I'd been only too happy to toss my spray cans straight into the nearest dumpster.

The science lab at Shadow Falls Academy was state of the art, filled with white benches and fume cupboards and gas burners and glass flasks. It was also in the centre of the main building, or A-block as people seemed to call it, and there I discovered a fatal flaw in our plan. Until I got to the door, I had the comforting chatter of the team back at Blackwood. Rune for the most part, but occasionally one of the others would chip in. Then I walked inside and...nothing.

Silence.

Ah, crap.

Every atom in me wanted to turn around and leave, but the entire class was staring at me, and the teacher too. Only pride and the thought of a three-hundred-grand payday made me keep going to the nearest empty space. Each bench had room for two people, and the other half was already occupied.

"Is this seat taken?"

The girl turned to me, and I felt my eyes widen. *Dammit, Sky. Don't stare.* The girl was beautiful with smooth chestnut skin, but she had an odd white patch that sliced across her left cheek. Her hair was tied up in a topknot, and when she smiled, I saw she had braces. Proper train tracks, the kind I could never afford even with the NHS subsidy. I'd just learned to live with slightly wonky front teeth. Her glasses were metal-rimmed, much finer than my clear-lensed chunky-framed pair.

"No, it's free."

"Uh, I'm Sky. It's my first day here."

"Vanessa. It's vitiligo. Don't worry; you can't catch it."

"I didn't..."

"Class, settle down," said the teacher, a gnarly old guy whose lab coat came almost to his feet. "For the benefit of those just joining us, I'm Dr. Merritt, and today, we're going to talk about the transition metals. Who can name those for me?"

A bunch of coloured boxes appeared on the SMART Board, and a distant memory told me it was the periodic table. Gases at the top, metals at the bottom, something like that?

Vanessa spoke first. "Manganese."

Another voice piped up. "Palladium."

Wasn't that a theatre in London?

"Iron."

"Platinum."

"Gold."

"Sky?" Who told Dr. Merritt my name? "Would you like to have a try?"

Not in the slightest. My mind went blank as I prayed for a signal to somehow wiggle its way through the wall, but my earpiece remained silent. Was Rune freaking out as much as me?

"Uh..."

"Sorry I'm late."

Oh, thank goodness—an interruption. The newcomer looked as if he'd only just climbed out of bed, and he hadn't bothered to comb his hair either. Or knot his tie. Or tuck his shirt in.

"Asher Martinez, if you were sorry, you wouldn't be late every single time."

Asher merely shrugged.

"Now that you're here, perhaps you'd like to tell everyone the definition of a transition metal?"

"The ones in the middle part of the periodic table."

Thank you.

"And can you name some?"

Asher turned to the back and flashed a smile. "Ladies, you want to help me out here?"

Before Dr. Merritt could cut in, four blondes at the back called what sounded like all of the answers, and the teacher let out a long sigh. I got the impression that this was the start of a typical day for Asher. But since he'd saved me from a world of embarrassment, I couldn't complain.

Dr. Merritt tried to get us back on track. "For today's practical, we're going to compare the colour changes demonstrated by transition metal ions in solution. I'll pass out instruction sheets and answer grids. Asher, you can turn around to work with Vanessa and Sky."

"Great," Vanessa muttered. "Asher's a bum."

Asher didn't look like a bum. He looked like the sort of boy your mother warned you about. Not my mother, obviously, but most mothers. Messy dark-blond hair, vivid blue eyes, and a mouth that did bad, bad things. Such as talking in class.

"You're new here?" he asked.

"Just arrived this morning."

"Where from? You're English?"

The teacher tutted. "Asher, this is a classroom, not a bar."

"Yeah, sorry."

No, he wasn't. Asher Martinez was boy-next-door meets juvie. The blondes at the back seemed to like that, though.

The teacher talked us through the experiment, but most of it went right over my head. Cobalt chloride, ammonium ferrous sulphate, sodium hydroxide, deionised water... The colours were pretty. Blues and greens and pinks and violets. Vanessa did most of the work, and I felt kind of guilty about that.

"Can one of you take notes if you're not going to help?" she asked.

"Sure, I'll do it."

What was I meant to be writing?

I must've looked like a deer in headlights because Asher took pity on me. "Just write down what colour the stuff goes. Whether there's a precipitate or whatever."

A precipitate... That was lumps, right? I'd been to a couple of chemistry lessons about five years ago—they liked to start us on the hard stuff young in England—but those had in no way prepared me for this. I bumbled my way through the notes. Next time, I'd pretend I was sick if the lesson was in the same lab. Or Nate would have to find me an earpiece with a better signal.

At least I only had drama and PE left today. I stood a chance of surviving those, especially since Dan had promised to have a friend of hers coach me for the acting parts. I had no idea who he was, but he had a nice voice. Thanks to his advice, I made it through to lunch break, which allowed me enough time to gulp down an individual chicken pot pie—no mass-produced slop here—and get back to my room to change.

Except when I walked in, I found Vanessa standing there, staring at my suitcases.

"Uh, hi."

"Guess I've got a new roommate, then."

She turned and walked out.

I'd done my best to block my schooldays from my mind, but every interaction I had at Shadow Falls reminded me why I'd hated them. The cliques. The pressure. The sniping. The awkwardness. The feeling that I was dumber than everybody else.

You're getting paid to be here, Sky.

Yeah, but I'd rather have been pummelled in the gym.

At least I had Rune. "Wow, she sounds friendly."

"That was Vanessa."

"The girl from chemistry class? Yikes."

"I'm skipping it next time."

"You can't. Not so soon after you've arrived. You'll get sent to the principal's office."

"Good. I can bug it while I'm there."

"No. Not good. We're getting a copy of the exam syllabus. That'll tell us what you need to study, and I can run through everything with you before class in case the feed cuts out again."

"You sound as though you're enjoying this a little too much."

"I don't get to do this sort of thing every day. It's awesome. Like, I'm studying all my favourite subjects and getting to be a spy at the same time."

"Awesome? That's not the word I'd use."

"And I suppose it helps to keep my mind off...you know, the other stuff."

I did. The "nearly dying" stuff. In a way, it was strange. A quirk of fate had seen Rune land in the middle of my world, and now here I was, stuck in hers.

"Perhaps you could ask Rafael to teach you self-defence? He's good at that."

"Rafael's scary."

"Yeah, but he won't hurt you."

"Maybe, but I can't ask him anyway because he took off."

"Took off? What do you mean, he took off?"

"Emmy was complaining about it earlier. Black said Rafael took some personal time, and Emmy said Black should have stopped him because we're in the middle of a job, and Black said he wasn't Rafael's keeper, and then Emmy slammed the door on her way out and I haven't seen her since."

Rafael had abandoned me?

That hurt, but in a way, I was also relieved. Rafael's absence meant he wouldn't see me flailing around at Shadow Falls like a duck out of water. As long as he was back in time for me to continue my training at Riverley, what did it matter where he went in the meantime?

"I need to get out to the sports field."

"Good luck. That's something I can't help you with."

Didn't matter. If there was one thing I could do, it was run. Apparently, I was only two-tenths of a second off the school record in the hundred metres, and suddenly, the blonde girls wanted to be friends with me. Tiffany, Meaghan, Carlie, and Deandra. Four clones. I hoped somebody back at base would write their names down because I'd forgotten them already. In my head, I christened them the Britneys because their skirts were too short and they'd hiked up their boobs like in the "Baby One More Time" video.

"Hey, do you want to eat dinner with us?" Britney number one asked. "It's Sky, right?"

"I need to unpack this evening."

"Tomorrow?"

"Maybe."

If I couldn't think up a plausible excuse not to. They weren't my kind of people at all. Too false. Too plastic. Fake hair, fake nails, fake eyelashes. I didn't have any of those. Emmy hadn't put a limit on my expense account for this job, but I still didn't want to spend my free Sunday wandering around the mall in Culpeper in an attempt to fit in, which was apparently an option according to the brochure. The school ran a shuttle bus service there every weekend.

Asher Martinez wasn't my kind of person either. Too lazy, too cocky, too damn slick. But I still caught him watching me as I walked back to New Hall at the end of the afternoon.

CHAPTER 21 - SKY

THANKS TO RUNE, plus Xav who helped me out with art advice, and the gods of technology who smiled down on me, I survived Friday's classes. I also had a snoop around the staff offices and bugged three of them, although I had a hairy moment when one of the janitors decided to start cleaning early. Those three had been reasonably straightforward—unlocked doors and enough mess that nobody would notice one of Nate's special two-way adapters in an electrical socket. If they did, then the janitors would hopefully get the blame. Nate's adapters worked just the way regular adapters did, with the added bonus that their built-in bugs could draw power from the mains. No pesky batteries to change.

The other offices would be a bit trickier because their owners kept them locked. I'd learned to pick simple locks in London, plus Ravi had spent some time instructing me on more complicated ones during quiet moments in the run-up to the operation at the Grove. But opening locks took time. I'd go for the easy wins first.

After dinner, I went for a meander around the grounds. Technically, we were meant to go in pairs, but nobody noticed when I slipped into the woods. And I had Dan with me in spirit if not in body.

"Mack's started making a 3D model of the campus," she told me. "We've got rough footprints of most of the buildings from satellite photos, but tree cover's made some of the edges unclear. Could you walk around the tennis pavilion? And there're several small buildings behind the gym we need to take a closer look at."

"A 3D model? Like with bits of cardboard?"

Dan burst out laughing. "No, like a hologram."

Oh.

Her giggles subsided, but my embarrassment didn't. Just for five minutes, could I manage to not say something dumb? I headed along a gravel path in the direction of the tennis courts, hidden away behind another dormitory.

"When I first started at Blackwood, we only had basic computer programs and they were a real pain to set up, so sometimes we did use cardboard and glue," Dan said. "I remember spending evenings building crime scene mock-ups with Black, and he'd always curse because his fingers were too big to do the fiddly bits."

"Did the models help?"

"It's always useful to get a visual. And now with the improvements in technology, we can take Mack's simulation, feed it into VR goggles, and use it to practise walking around the campus. Plus we might be able to find a possible location for the paintings. Those old buildings sometimes have hidden rooms."

"Really? Does Riverley?"

"It might have one or two."

"Can I see them when I get back?"

"Ask Emmy."

"I've got a question for you as well. Who was the

guy who talked me through my drama class yesterday?"

"You don't want to know."

Why not? It didn't exactly matter, but it bugged me when I didn't know who I was speaking to. He hadn't introduced himself, and I could hardly ask in front of everyone.

"I do."

"Are you sure?"

"Yeah."

Dan gave a soft "fine, you asked for it" snort. "Armand Taylor."

I'd met a bunch of actors when I served drinks in various clubs, and my run-in with Brock Keaton had put me off celebs for good. But there were still limits to my composure.

"Armand Taylor? No way. You're joking."

He was A-list. Arguably Hollywood's number-one heart-throb. And now that I thought about it, the voice on the phone had sounded kind of familiar. My knees went weird, and I sat down on an old tree stump.

"I did not spend eighty minutes being told how to act by Armand Taylor."

Another peal of laughter was all the answer I needed.

"Sometimes I hate you."

"So you don't want to meet him when you get back?"

"No, I... Really?" More bloody laughter. "Shut up. I'm going to walk around the tennis pavilion now."

The freaking tennis pavilion. I'd never picked up a racquet in my life. Good thing tennis wasn't on the schedule until the summer term or that would be yet another thing I needed to learn. Who would Dan find to teach me? A Wimbledon finalist?

I stayed outside until the nine o'clock curfew. Why bother going back early? Blondes one through four were doing their nails in the living room when I walked into New Hall, and Vanessa was stretched out on her bed, reading a book.

"Hi."

She ignored me.

"Did you have a nice evening?"

"You don't need to pretend to be my friend, you know."

"Just being civil."

Was it really that difficult to say "hello" back? Even when I'd lived in squats with virtual strangers, we'd said "good morning" and made an effort to get along.

"Whatever."

"Okay, fine. You win. I don't want to be here any more than you do, so let's just keep out of each other's way and try to make it bearable, okay?"

Her answer was to turn over and tuck the quilt tighter around herself.

"Goodnight, Sky," Dan whispered in my ear. "Talk to you tomorrow."

Saturday afternoon found me lined up on the sports field for a cross-country run. I'd had the choice of more running, a dance workshop, or horse riding. Twerking probably wouldn't go down so well at Shadow Falls, and Emmy's horse had gnashed his teeth at me when I met him last week, so the choice was a no-brainer. We only had to do three miles—two laps of a winding woodland circuit—and without Alex chasing me on a dirt bike or Rafael making me stop to do push-ups every five minutes, it would be a walk in the park. I could cruise it.

Or maybe not.

"Afternoon," Emmy said in my ear. "I hope you're not thinking of slacking."

"Of course not. The thought never entered my mind."

A pause.

"Liar. Your pulse just increased. Honey, you need to get better at fibbing."

I glared at my traitorous watch. As well as two-way comms, it came with a heart-rate monitor and a GPS tracker. And, it appeared, a race simulator. Two blobs appeared on the screen, labelled S and E. Emmy was running too?

"The top six finishers will get the chance to represent Shadow Falls in the Independent Schools Athletics League in two weeks' time," the coach announced. "The first heats will be held at the Kennedy Academy in Maryland."

Who cared? I was more concerned about staying within spitting distance of my boss. The whistle blew, and I took off as if a pack of rabid wolves was chasing me. Then remembered I needed to pace myself and slowed down a bit as I ran over the first hillock. Was I ahead? Only just, and I had a massive bloody hill to go up. If Emmy had started off from Riverley, she'd still be on the flat. The first slope there started two hundred yards from the terrace, and it was a gentle incline, not like the climb I was facing.

"You're slowing," Emmy warned a couple of minutes later.

I glanced over my shoulder and saw I'd opened up a big enough gap from my fellow students to choke out a response.

"I'm on a fucking mountain."

"Bullshit. You're on a hill."

"It's steeper than the ones near Riverley."

"I'm in Zermatt."

"Where?"

"In the fucking Alps, Sky. On an actual mountain. We should've enrolled you in geography lessons."

Ah, crap. I ran faster.

By halfway through the second lap, I'd opened up a comfortable lead over everyone but Emmy. We were still jostling back and forth for position, and she'd cursed a number of times because apparently there were boulders in Zermatt and she had to jump over them.

Hold on, who was that ahead? I was fast, but I shouldn't have been able to lap anyone, not in that space of time. As I got closer, I realised it was Vanessa.

"My roommate's ahead, and she's limping," I muttered to Emmy.

"Go do what you need to. We can pick this up tomorrow."

"Oh, brilliant. I can't wait."

Vanessa pivoted as I closed the distance, but she didn't look particularly happy to see me.

"Are you okay?"

"I just twisted my ankle. It's fine."

"It's obviously not. Why don't you wait here while I fetch someone to help?"

"The last thing I need is a fuss. I can walk back."

Even as the words left her mouth, her face screwed up in pain as she stumbled over a tree root. Instinct made me grab her around the waist to stop her from hitting the deck.

"We can walk back together."

"But you're in the lead. If you keep going, you'll score a place on the cross-country team."

"Who cares about that? You need ice on that ankle."

The girl in second place whizzed past and turned to do a double take. She tripped too, but thankfully she saved herself and kept going. The last thing I needed was two injuries to deal with. My feet itched to catch her up and overtake because I hated to lose, but Vanessa and her leg were more important.

"Lean on me, okay?" I arranged Vanessa's arm over my shoulders and put my own arm around her waist again. "We'll take it slowly."

"You ladies okay?" a voice asked from behind, then Asher appeared beside us. He hadn't even broken a sweat.

"Fine," Vanessa practically growled at him.

"Suit yourselves."

He ambled off, but instead of carrying on along the path, he cut left into the trees.

"Where's he going?" I asked.

"He takes a shortcut."

A...shortcut? In training? No, no, no. You pushed hard in training so you could take shortcuts in battle. What was the point in cheating yourself? And more importantly, how did he get away with it?

"The coach doesn't notice?"

"He probably does, but it doesn't matter. Asher's the principal's nephew. He can do whatever he wants."

Asher Martinez was related to the Rosenbergs? Well, that certainly explained his attitude. It also meant I'd have to watch my step around him.

"Thanks for the heads-up."

"No problem."

Was that a hint of civility from Vanessa? Wonders would never cease.

Back at the sports field, the coach glanced up from his stopwatch, looked back down again, then raised his head to stare.

"What happened?"

"Vanessa twisted her ankle. Nobody else mentioned it?"

Because they'd all run past us except Asher, and despite him bypassing half of the route, he was just emerging from the treeline at a slow jog.

"No, they didn't. If they had, we could have brought a stretcher."

Vanessa rolled her eyes. "I don't need a stretcher."

"We don't take any chances with our students' well-being. Perhaps I should call the nurse?"

"No! I just need to sit down, that's all."

Why so vehement? Did Vanessa have a phobia of nurses? I couldn't say I was fond of them myself, based on past experience. *Where did that bruise come from? Where do you live? Where are your parents?* And that was just when I'd taken an acquaintance to A&E.

"She *did* manage to walk back by herself," I told the coach. "An ice pack would probably do the trick."

"I'm not sure…"

But Vanessa was already hobbling towards New Hall.

"I'll take care of her. If somebody could just bring a bag of ice...?"

I didn't wait for an answer. What were they gonna do, tell me off for helping? Our room was on the second floor—third floor in American—and since there was no elevator, Vanessa needed assistance to get up the stairs.

"I'll be back in a minute," I said once she'd settled herself on her bed.

Silence.

Thankfully, the coach was already halfway up the path with a fancy blue gel pack. When he got to the front door, he knocked. I liked that about this place. People were respectful.

"Ta. I mean, thank you." I reached out to take the ice pack, and he held on to it for a moment before he handed it over.

"Call the nurse if the swelling gets any worse. Vanessa won't do it herself."

"Why not?"

"I can't discuss a fellow student's personal affairs. But understand that we only want to help her."

Weird comment, but okay.

"Can I bring her dinner over here tonight? I know we're not supposed to take the plates out of the dining room, but..."

The coach smiled and nodded. "I'll let the catering staff know."

CHAPTER 22 - SKY

"HEY, SKY. NICE outfit."

In the kitchenette, I glanced up from making coffee —instant, unfortunately—to find the four Britneys in front of me. Was that sarcasm? Or did they genuinely like my clothes? Normally, I'd have assumed the former, but Bradley had packed my suitcase, and the jeans probably cost more than I used to make in a week serving drinks. And my pink shirt was by Ralph Lauren. Even *I'd* heard of him. At first, I'd wondered how Bradley always picked out clothes that fitted perfectly, not just for me but for everybody else too, but the day before I left Riverley, I'd found out his secret. He had a sewing room in the attic, and in the sewing room was a creepy army of dressmakers' mannequins, each with a name badge. He simply bought clothes based on our widest measurements, then tailored them based on our body doubles so they fitted everywhere else as well. Genius.

"Thanks."

"Where did you get the jeans?"

"Uh, I don't know. My assistant bought them."

The four of them looked at each other.

"You have an assistant?"

Inside, I grinned, but outside I stayed casual.

"You don't?"

"Wanna come to the mall with us today?" the tallest blonde asked. Tiffany? Meaghan? "We're gonna visit a few stores and then catch a movie."

Going shopping with that crowd was the absolute last thing I wanted to do.

"No, thanks, uh..."

"Carlie," a voice supplied in my ear. Since it was Sunday and I didn't have any classes, Rune was taking a break and I had Ryder helping me out.

"...Carlie," I finished. "I'll pass."

"You ran fast yesterday," another of the blondes said. "At least until you stopped to help Vanessa. Were you on the track team at your old school?"

Why not? "Yes."

"You should run with Tiffany next time." She nodded towards Britney number three. "She made the championships last year."

"I prefer to run alone."

"Right." The four of them stepped back as one, clearly unaccustomed to being turned down. "Well, see ya."

The microwave pinged, and I took out the jug of boiling water and poured it into two mugs, one for me and one for Vanessa. Why didn't Americans have electric kettles? Or egg cups? Or use the word "fortnight"? Their chocolate was peculiar too. And their selection of swear words was woefully inadequate. When I'd called Ryder a tosser for waking me up at six a.m. on a Sunday, he hadn't a clue what I was talking about, but eventually he got the gist and told me he'd acted on Emmy's orders. When I texted at five past six to call her a thundercunt, she'd understood exactly what I meant. And then she'd informed me we'd be running at eight thirty sharp.

"Here you go." I put the mug on Vanessa's nightstand. "I couldn't find any teabags, so we're stuck with coffee."

"You drink hot tea in summer?"

Good grief. "Of course. Cold tea is an abomination."

"You don't have to make me drinks. I'm sure you've got better things to do, like going to the mall."

"You heard what Carlie said?"

Vanessa looked away sheepishly. "The acoustics are weird in here. And Carlie's voice could cut through steel."

Noted. I'd have to be careful when I talked, especially to Blackwood. And Vanessa was right about Carlie.

"I'm happy to make you drinks. How's your ankle this morning?"

"The swelling's gone down."

"Great. So why don't *we* go to the mall together later?"

I didn't think for a moment that Vanessa would accept, but I wanted to push her into talking to me. To understand her. We'd be sharing this space for weeks, and despite what I'd said before, life would be more pleasant if we could hold a conversation.

"I don't go to the mall."

"And yet you tried to make me go?"

"You can afford to go."

"You can't?"

"I get financial aid, okay? I'm not like most of the others here." Vanessa's gaze fixed on the floor. "Someone's gonna tell you sooner or later, so you might as well hear it from me."

"That's it? That's your big secret? You're not rich? Who cares?"

"Around here? Almost everyone. The only thing worse than being poor is having money and then losing it. And then there's my skin colour. I stick out in all the wrong ways."

Now I understood. Vanessa used her prickliness as a defence mechanism. A spiky suit of armour. She wasn't nasty underneath, but if she didn't let anyone in, then nobody could hurt her.

"I thought Shadow Falls Academy was all about equality?"

"To paraphrase George Orwell, everyone's equal, but some people are more equal than others. *Animal Farm*?" she added when she saw my blank look. "You haven't read it?"

Only the first dozen pages, and then I gave up. The English teacher at Greenfields Comprehensive hadn't given a shit.

"Nah, we mostly did Shakespeare. But I get an allowance. If you want to go to the movies, I can pay."

And honestly, I'd like to. I'd spent so long not having money that it would be nice to help somebody else out for a change. But Vanessa just scowled.

"I'm not a charity case."

"I wasn't suggesting for a minute that you were."

"You should go to the mall with Carlie." I got the cold shoulder again. "Hang with me, and you can kiss your social standing goodbye."

"If you don't like it here, then why do you stay?" I asked.

"If it weren't for the Rosenbergs, I'd have to live with my mother. I owe them everything. And at least here, I get a good education." She showed me her back. "Go to the mall, Sky."

I didn't. Instead, I pulled on my running gear and took a fresh camera and earpiece from the wireless charging mat I'd stashed in the drawer of my nightstand. Nate had built me several sets of comms equipment, and today's was disguised as regular AirPods, an Apple watch, and another pair of glasses. Nothing that would look out of place if anyone happened to glance in the drawer and see them charging there. I also had a box of single-use contact lenses so I had an excuse for not wearing the glasses all the time. Bradley had thought of everything.

"You doing okay?" Emmy asked once I was on the trail in the woods.

"Just peachy. How's Zermatt?"

"I'm in Chamonix now. Don't worry; there's still plenty of mountains."

"Why Chamonix?"

"Our client thought one of his people might have been selling company secrets, but we're ninety percent sure he's just screwing his mistress. I'll probably fly home in a day or two. Anything new at Shadow Falls?"

I told her about the Britneys' invitation and Vanessa's confession. "I'm not sure what to do. Honestly, I hate all the cliquishness. I don't want to act like a complete loner either, but Vanessa seems to be on Team Rosenberg."

"If you were genuinely attending that school, what would you do?"

"Probably hang out with Vanessa. She seems nice under the hard shell, plus she's my lab partner in chemistry and I can learn from her."

"So do that."

"You're not worried where her loyalties might lie?"

"There's an old saying—keep your friends close, but keep your enemies closer."

"Vanessa isn't my enemy."

"But the same principle applies. You're on a hill again, aren't you?"

Had I slowed up? I checked the stats on my watch and found that I had. Shit. I sucked in a breath, put my head down, and pushed harder. Right into...*bam*. Right into Asher Martinez.

"I'm so sorry!"

I'd knocked him right on his ass, which was reasonably impressive because he was five or six inches taller than me and wider as well. Should I help him up? I held out a hand, but he was already on his knees. Emmy must have had access to a video feed because she was laughing her head off. But she'd screwed up too because I heard her talking to some guy in Chamonix.

"No, no, I'm fine, thanks. Just listening to a comedy podcast, and it's hilarious." Pause. "Which one? Uh, it's called *My Dad Wrote a Porno*." Pause. "Yeah, you should give it a listen." Pause. "Sorry, dude. Married."

So she wasn't drafting the divorce papers yet. Interesting. I was in two minds over whether I wanted her and Black to make up. Yes, they were miserable without each other, but he'd done a really, really shitty thing and he needed to suffer.

"Guess that'll teach me to look where I'm going, Chemistry Girl."

"Sky. My name's Sky."

"Sky. I knew that."

"Did you, Shortcut Boy? I'm surprised to see you

out running considering the lengths you went to yesterday to avoid it."

"I had my reasons."

"Which were?"

"Are you always this nosy?"

I shrugged. "Pretty much."

Asher just laughed. "Bye, Chem Girl."

"Bye, Shortcut."

"Who was that?" Emmy asked.

"My other chemistry lab partner," I whispered once Asher had vanished into the distance. "Ezra and Saul Rosenberg's nephew. He doesn't seem to do much work."

"There's a nephew? Are you sure?"

"Vanessa told me yesterday. I presume whoever was monitoring me added it to the notes."

"I'll make sure it's followed up."

"Is there any more news on the paintings?"

"Nothing in Marshall's PO box, but he recognised a groundsman in your video footage as a courier he handed a painting to three years ago. So it appears the Rosenbergs have quite the enterprise going at Shadow Falls. We've tapped the school's phones, but I'm not expecting to get much from that. The Rosenbergs will speak to their team in person, and they'll most likely use burners if they need to call clients. Why are you standing around, slacker? You should be running."

"You can be a real bitch."

"Yes. Yes, I can. Now get going."

Chapter 23 - Sky

AT GREENFIELDS COMPREHENSIVE, assembly meant fidgeting in a cold hall for fifteen minutes while the headmaster bollocked us for smoking behind the bike sheds, lamented our poor grades, begged us not to swear during next week's Ofsted inspection, and reminded us that students weren't allowed in the stationery cupboard, with or without a teacher. Especially *with* a teacher. Everyone knew where Channel in year twelve had got caught doing a practical with the biology teacher the previous Friday night. They hadn't exactly been subtle about it. And yes, her name really was Channel. Pronounced Chanel, like the perfume, but her mum copied the spelling from her handbag and it was a knock-off.

At Shadow Falls, Mr. Rosenberg welcomed us to the start of a new week and encouraged us to sign up for the annual ski trip to Whistler if we hadn't already, and then we were treated to a performance from the woodwind ensemble plus a motivational talk from a former pupil who'd clerked for a Supreme Court justice before starting her own law firm. I wasn't worthy. And I was also beginning to see why the fees at Shadow Falls were so high.

"Monday morning blues, Chem Girl?"

"Huh?"

Asher put two fingertips to the corners of his mouth and pulled them down in an exaggerated sad face.

"Maybe I'm dreading the thought of spending the next eighty minutes sitting with you."

That and the fact that my comms would most likely cut out again. Rune had started talking at six this morning, guessing what might come up in my chemistry lesson while I brushed my teeth and combed my hair.

"And there I was thinking you just weren't impressed by my uncle's line in self-righteous bullshit."

Wait a second. Asher didn't get along with his uncle? I'd assumed the whole family was tight. They lived and worked together, after all. The research was trickling in. Grandma Rosenberg—Tovah—lived in an annexe to the family home, which was set back in the woods to the east of the main school building. Officially, it was known as the Lodge, but it was the size of a mansion. Saul had the largest portion of the house. Until recently, his wife and daughter had shared it with him, but they'd moved out after a divorce— irreconcilable differences, apparently. According to the court documents, Ayda, the daughter, visited every other weekend, but I hadn't seen her yet. Ezra appeared to live in a wing attached at a right angle beside the quadruple garage. I hadn't yet worked out how Asher fitted into the accommodation arrangements.

Could he be testing me? Seeing where my loyalties lay? Or was the old Blackwood cynicism rubbing off on yours truly? They all had it. Emmy, Black, Rafael... Nate was the worst. Sometimes, he struck me as being one step away from full-blown paranoia.

"Mr. Rosenberg seems quite genuine to me."

Asher rolled his eyes. "You've got chemistry now?"

"Yup."

"Know where you're going?"

Before I could answer in the affirmative, a high-pitched voice called out from behind us.

"Asher!"

I didn't need to turn around to know it was one of the Britneys. Nor did it surprise me when Asher peeled away to talk to her. They seemed like each other's type. Pretty to look at and vaguely annoying. I carried on to the chemistry lab.

"Good luck," Rune whispered. "Sofia's going to cover biology for me. I need to..." She trailed off. "Alaric wants me to speak to a therapist about what happened. I haven't been sleeping well."

Moments like that were the worst part of my situation. I wanted to reach out and give Rune a hug, but I couldn't even offer a word of sympathy.

"I'll talk to you this evening," she said, and then she was gone.

Vanessa was already in the lab, and... Oh, crap. There was equipment out on the bench. Beakers, thermometers, little dishes with powder in them.

"We're measuring enthalpy changes," she said. "What did you think of this morning's talk?"

"Inspiring."

"Another one who's been drinking the Kool-Aid," Asher said from behind me.

"Don't you ever have anything nice to say?" Vanessa asked.

"About this place?" He shrugged. "What are we meant to be doing today?"

Dr. Merritt went over the instructions, and Asher decided he was helping Vanessa with the practical parts. That left me to write everything down, which was the easiest job. I could manage to draw a graph, just about. The lesson was almost fun.

Unlike biology.

I sat on my own at the front, only for Asher to walk in at the last minute and sit next to me. The lab was already too hot, possibly to keep the tankful of tropical frogs living on a shelf at the back happy, and his arrival made the back of my neck tingle. He didn't have the same pheromone-laced aura as Rafael, but the vibes he gave off made me uncomfortable for a whole variety of reasons.

"Are you always late?" I asked.

"Ideally. If I get here any earlier, some girl sits next to me."

I pointed at my boobs. "Hello? You sat next to *me*."

"You don't count."

Was that a compliment or an insult? I wasn't sure.

"I'm sorry?"

"You're different."

"In what way?"

Sofia was supposed to be an adult, and yet she was snickering away in my ear. I was one big joke to them, wasn't I?

"You just are."

Gee, that was helpful. "You seemed happy enough to speak to the Barbie dolls earlier."

"If I don't stop right away, they follow me around until I do. Trust me, it's easier to get it over with."

Asher had been reasonably bearable in chemistry. He'd taken some of the load off Vanessa and participated. Not so in biology. He scribbled a few sentences in unreadable handwriting and then leaned back in his seat, arms folded as the teacher covered the basics of human reproduction.

The mechanics, I could cope with—shove part A into slot B—just as long as I didn't think about the actual experience. A bead of sweat rolled down my back, and I focused on writing. As long as ink was flowing across the page, I couldn't seize up completely. Did I look normal? My spine prickled with ice crystals, little needles that jabbed into my back and reminded me that I was damaged inside.

And the final straw? When I was drawing an *ahem* diagram, Asher peered at it and smirked.

"Is that drawn from experience? Because you can do better than that, Chem."

"Shut up. Aren't you even going to take notes?"

"No need, babe. I already know all this stuff."

"I'm not your babe, asshole."

The teacher cleared his throat. "Sky, would you care to recap that last part?"

Why me? Why not Asher? Because he was a Rosenberg and I wasn't? Vanessa was right—they paid lip service to equality here. My cheeks burned as I read out what I'd written. At that moment, I hated Asher Martinez and his whole damn family.

"What a dick," Sofia said in my ear. "Chill, sweetie. Revenge comes later. Do you have gloves with you? I saw a clump of poison oak in one of your videos of the grounds."

I wrote a reply on the edge of my paper. *Yes, I have gloves.*

"It's a shame those are leopard frogs in that tank in

the corner. If they were *Phyllobates terribilis*, we could have some fun with them. The golden poison frog. One can kill ten men, did you know that? When I lived in Peru, I kept half a dozen as pets. I'm thinking of getting more, but Leo isn't keen on the idea."

Poor guy. I pitied any man who lived with Sofia. She was certifiable. Emmy's moral compass was wobbly, but Sofia's pointed in the wrong direction entirely from what I'd seen of her.

I scrawled *NO* in the margin.

"It was just an idea. Okay, something more subtle. I saw what might have been *Coprinopsis atramentaria* over by the tennis pavilion. The common ink cap mushroom. Eaten on its own, it won't do much harm, but mix it with alcohol, and *boom*. He'll be puking for days."

STILL NO.

"You're the life and soul of the fucking party, aren't you?"

What were the frogs for, anyway? I had an awful feeling we were meant to dissect them. At Greenfields Comprehensive, they'd made us cut up mice and Johnny Mowlem threw the insides at me. That had been my last ever biology lesson. Until today, clearly.

When the teacher gave us a set of questions to read through and answer, I leaned closer to Asher.

"Do we have to dissect frogs?"

"Today?"

"Any day."

"Yeah, why? You're not gonna puke, are you?"

Maybe. "I don't want to kill an animal."

"How about a human?"

Did he know? How could he? I felt the colour drain

out of my face.

"It's getting more tempting by the second," I said through gritted teeth.

"Chill, Chem. I'm joking. You seemed pretty pissed with me earlier, that's all. And we don't dissect real frogs. The girls freaked out last year, and the school ended up keeping them as pets. We have fake frogs now. They look just like the real thing, but they're made of rubber."

Phew. Rubber frogs I could deal with. Did Emmy get squeamish? Probably not.

I managed to ignore Asher for the rest of the lesson, and he made little effort to participate. Was this what it was like to be rich? The guy was squandering an education that cost more than most people's salary each year.

His privilege made me angry. I might not have had much to show for my time in London, but I'd kept Lenny and myself out of jail, and everything I *did* have, I'd worked damn hard for. Vanessa had been right. Asher *was* a bum.

"You going swimming this afternoon?" he asked after class.

It was that or yoga, and swimming had its plus points. My training bruises had faded enough for me to wear a bathing suit now.

"Probably. You?"

"Nah."

"You prefer downward-facing dog?"

He shook his head. "Not my thing. But watch out for Freddie Thornberg. He'll offer to help with your stroke, but he just wants to cop a feel."

Asher seemed genuine in his warning. I didn't

understand him. One moment he was a prick, and the next, he was...sort of nice.

"Thanks. Are you going running instead?"

"No."

"But you like running, right?"

"It's okay."

"Just 'okay'? Why did you cheat on Saturday and then get up early to run on Sunday?"

"Because one time when I got around the course too fast, they tried to put me on a team. And I'm not representing those assholes." He jerked his head east, in the direction of the Rosenbergs' house. "So I told them I cheated when I got my best times. And now I have to keep up the pretence."

Interesting logic.

"And the swimming?"

"I'll swim on my own later. Unless you want to join me?"

"Er, no."

Asher somehow managed to smirk and laugh at the same time. "Take care of yourself, Chem Girl."

Of course, I still had Sofia with me when I headed for the pool. And she was still acting like a psycho.

"So, Freddie Thornberg, huh? I've got his bio here. The apple doesn't fall far from the tree with that one—his daddy got accused of rape by his former secretary. The charges went away, though. Guess there was a pay-off."

"Is it too late to switch to yoga?" I muttered.

"Don't worry; you're trained for this. If he gets handsy, grab his balls and twist. Or we can get creative. Pools are fun—they use chlorine-based disinfectant to destroy pathogens and acid to control pH. Mix the two, and voila! Chlorine gas. If you do it the right way, the pulmonary oedema looks like a total accident."

I had a horrible feeling she was speaking from experience, and I really didn't want to hear it.

"Is this earpiece waterproof?" I whispered.

"Uh, no. I don't think so. I'll check with Nate."

"Shame. Guess I'd better take it out then."

Peace at last. Thank goodness.

Of course, all good things come to an end, and Emmy was waiting for me when I plugged myself back in. Vanessa was nowhere to be seen, and I made sure to close the bedroom door before I started talking.

"Don't bullshit me," Emmy said. "You knew that earpiece wasn't waterproof when you picked swimming."

"If you'd spent the entire day with Sofia explaining a thousand ways to kill people, you'd have done the same."

"She's dedicated."

"She's insane. And she wouldn't shut up."

"There's a possibility she might have forgotten to take her meds this morning," Emmy conceded.

"Next time, give me Ryder if I can't have Rune. At least he's quiet."

"I'll see what I can do. But first, an update. We've hit a slight snag with the backup plan."

My stomach dropped.

"What snag?"

"Marshall got a letter from the Master. Seems he doesn't believe we managed to steal *Spirit*, so we won't be able to catch one of his people in the act at a handover. Xav's copy was too damn good."

"So what happens next?"

"If *Spirit* was our only connection to the School of Shadows, perhaps we'd alert the authorities to the theft. But thanks to you, we don't need to do that."

"Which means...?"

"Which means all the eggs are in your basket at the moment."

Great. No pressure. Just me, a four-hundred-acre campus, and a stolen painting to find.

"Sky?"

"I'm here."

"You're doing fine. We don't need to solve this tomorrow. Slow and steady wins the game, so keep mapping out the campus, carry on listening, and we'll narrow down the areas where a painting could be hidden. We put a tracker on Ezra's car while he was in town this afternoon."

"What about Saul's?"

"We're working on it. He doesn't seem to go out much."

I lay on the bed and closed my eyes. "A den of thieves, and I'm stuck right in the middle of it."

"Look on the bright side—Shadow Falls is meant to be pretty in the autumn."

Chapter 24 - Sky

"WHO WERE YOU talking to?"

My head snapped around, and I found Vanessa standing in the bedroom doorway. Sometimes, she was sneakier than Emmy, and it seemed the maintenance team had oiled every hinge in the place. Tuesday morning was off to a great start.

Had Vanessa heard my words? Or just my voice? Rune had gone silent in my ear.

"Uh, nobody."

"I definitely heard you speaking."

Think, Sky. Think!

"It's a visualisation technique. If I tell myself what I want to achieve, it gets me closer to my goals."

Vanessa seemed dubious, and I couldn't blame her. Visualisation technique? Was that even a thing?

"My therapist told me to do it."

"You have a therapist?"

"Doesn't everybody? Mine's in England, so I have to do phone consults at the moment, and I guess I should find a new one, but... Anyhow, at first I tried just thinking about my goals, but that didn't keep me accountable. So now I say them out loud, like a pep talk." I forced a giggle. "Half the time, I forget I'm even doing it."

"And it really works?"

"Yup. You should try it. It works best if you start in front of a mirror, but once you get used to it, you can do it anywhere."

Might as well cover myself for any future slip-ups.

Vanessa stepped fully inside the room and closed the door. "I'm not sure it would work for me. I'm just not that lucky."

"We make our own luck, and how will you know unless you try it?" I put my hands on her shoulders and steered her over to the mirror on the wall. "What's your goal for today? Tell yourself."

Fuck, I felt like such a fraud. But when the alternative was admitting I was an undercover investigator, the guilt was a small price to pay.

"Okay." Vanessa gave a nervous giggle. "Today, I want to hit every high note in 'Dove Sono.'"

"In what?"

"It's a Mozart aria from *The Marriage of Figaro*. We have auditions this morning. The winner gets to represent Shadow Falls Academy at an interscholastic singing competition in Florida, all expenses paid."

"Right. Well, don't say you *want* to hit the high notes. Say you're *going* to hit them."

Vanessa grinned at me, the first genuine smile I'd got from her. Maybe this visualisation mumbo jumbo had some benefits after all?

"I'm *going* to hit them."

"Don't tell me. Tell yourself."

She looked back in the mirror. "I'm *going* to hit them."

"Brilliant. Off you go and sing."

Once she'd disappeared—and I listened carefully for her footsteps to make sure she truly had gone downstairs—I sighed and fell backwards onto the bed. The springs squeaked beneath my weight.

"Nice save," Rune whispered.

"You don't need to whisper anymore. She's gone." But I still talked bloody quietly. "Do therapists seriously say that shit?"

"Mine doesn't. She just asks loads of questions."

"Does it help?"

"I've only had one session so far, and it was horribly uncomfortable, but I slept better last night, so I suppose it did."

"That's good. Really. I'm glad you're getting help. What happened to you... You never should have had to..."

"If I hadn't done what I did, Beth and I would both be dead. I guess... I guess when the chips are down, we both do whatever's necessary, don't we?" I heard Rune swallow, and there was a long pause before she came back, this time sounding overly cheerful. "Which means you have to visualise your goal for the day. Go on, talk to the mirror."

I heard crunching, and I suspected Rune was scoffing carrot sticks for breakfast. She ate a lot of them, which was probably how she managed to stay rail-thin, although stress undoubtedly helped with that too. She'd been through so much lately.

"Mirror, mirror on the wall..." Despite the situation, I struggled to take Rune's order seriously. "I can't."

"No, you have to do it."

"Fine. I'm going to not embarrass myself in maths, drama, or physics, and then I'm gonna run a good time for the four-hundred metres in track practice later."

But not too good, because like Asher, I definitely

didn't want to make it onto the athletics team.

A week had passed since my arrival at Shadow Falls, and I was beginning to settle. Get into a routine. Wake up, blag my way through lessons I barely understood, then snoop around in the evenings. Rune had focused her late-night tutoring sessions on chemistry seeing as that was where I struggled the most. And when I stopped worrying about paintings twenty-four seven, when I compartmentalised and listened to the teachers, I found I even learned something.

I began to feel as if I belonged at Shadow Falls, just a tiny bit.

Vanessa was waiting for me outside the chemistry lab on Thursday, textbooks in hand, but before I got to her, one of the teachers stopped to say a few words.

"Congratulations, Vanessa. A well-deserved prize."

"What did you win?" I asked her once we got inside.

"Remember that singing audition? I got selected."

"Really? That's great! See? Visualisation totally works."

If the whole investigation/assassination thing didn't pan out, maybe I could become a life coach?

"I suppose. But I didn't think for a minute that I'd actually get picked. I just didn't want to screw up the song."

"You smashed it, and now you get a free trip to Florida. Win-win."

"Win-lose."

"What am I missing?"

Vanessa slumped onto her stool. "Deandra was

meant to get the place. She's got an amazing voice, and she always goes to the contests."

"You beat her fair and square."

"Yes, but..." Vanessa lowered her voice as the Britneys walked in, and I didn't miss the way Deandra narrowed her eyes. "But now I'll have to pay for that. She hates losing."

"She can't expect to come first in everything. That's not how life works."

Vanessa just shrugged. "You don't know Deandra."

No, I didn't, but perhaps I should get to know her. What had Emmy said? *Keep your friends close, but keep your enemies closer.*

Hmm...

Asher strolled over to the bench in front of us three seconds before Dr. Merritt arrived. How did he fit in with that philosophy? I wouldn't have described Asher Martinez as a friend, but nor was he an enemy. He belonged in some hitherto unknown third category, one that fucked with my brain and sent sparks shooting to all the wrong places. A frenemesis.

"Hey, Chem," he said. "Vanessa."

"Are you gonna do any work today?" I asked.

"Why break the habit of a lifetime?"

"Because we're meant to be a team here? What are you bringing to the party?"

"My sparkling personality and killer looks."

"Killer looks? You mean like Jason Voorhees?"

"You wound me, Chem Girl."

"And humility. You forgot to mention humility."

The teacher cleared his throat, and Asher turned around. My gaze dropped. He brought a nice ass. But I wasn't going to mention that, not in a million years.

"What happened?"

Vanessa limped towards me between two football players—American football players, all shoulder pads and tight trousers—and I ran out of New Hall to meet them on the path.

"She tripped," one of them said.

"Over what?" I asked as the two beefcakes deposited Vanessa into my arms.

"Over Deandra's hockey stick," she muttered. "Told you she'd get me."

What a bitch. "She did it on purpose?"

"We weren't even near the ball. I was jogging, and she stuck the stick out for no reason."

Vanessa was favouring the same ankle that she'd injured the other day, only this time it was swollen twice as big.

"Have you seen the nurse?"

"No, and I'm not going to."

"But—"

"I can't. If I see the nurse, she'll make me go to the hospital for X-rays as a precaution. The school doesn't want to take the risk of being sued, so they send you just in case. And I don't have medical insurance."

"But if you're hurt…"

"I need ice, that's all."

"If it's about the cost, I can pay."

Might as well use that expense account for something, eh?

"Like I said before, I don't need pity."

Damned if you do, damned if you don't. Mind you,

I'd been guilty of the same thing. When I'd bolloxed my ankle doing parkour in London, the lads I ran with had offered to have a whip-round so I could take a couple of days off work, but I figured it was my own stupid fault I'd fallen off the wall, and pride meant I'd hobbled into the club with an elastic band around my shoe because the strap wouldn't do up.

"Fine, go sit down, and I'll get the ice."

And I'd also think up a nice surprise for Deandra. Nobody hurt my roommate and got away with it.

Not only did I find an ice pack, but I also wheedled and cajoled and got Ryder to drive over with a care package and meet me at the bottom of the school driveway.

"Emmy's gonna kick my ass," he complained.

"It's for medicinal purposes."

"The Advil's for medicinal purposes. The vodka's for getting drunk."

"I'm a student. It's practically mandatory for us to bend the rules."

"Just don't get caught."

I didn't intend to.

Vanessa's eyes bugged out when I pulled the bottle out of the book bag Ryder had brought it in. What? Hadn't she ever seen alcohol before?

"You're not supposed to have that," she hissed.

"I won't tell if you don't."

"But..." She trailed off. But nothing.

I grabbed two tumblers from the shelf near my desk, tipped our toothbrushes out, then poured a generous measure for Vanessa and a smaller shot for me. I had work to do first thing in the morning, and a hangover would only make things uncomfortable. Trying to pick a lock with blurred vision wasn't the easiest thing in the world.

"Bottoms up."

"I can't drink that."

"Why not? You need something to wash down your painkillers."

"Are you crazy?"

"You'll feel better. Trust me. Do you need a mixer? I'm sure there's a carton of orange juice downstairs."

"Where did you get the vodka?"

"From a friend. Shh."

"I guess... I guess maybe I could just have a small sip."

An hour later, Vanessa lay on the bed giggling, her arms and legs spread out like a starfish. Water dripped onto the floor from the melting ice. The good news was that the swelling didn't look any worse, but the bad news was that her eyes were staring in two different directions. I had a sneaking suspicion she didn't drink very often.

"Deandra's such a bitch. I mean, all the Britneys are bitches..." She dissolved into laughter again. "I can't believe you call them Britneys, but you're sooooo right."

"I'm guessing theirs is the clique I want to avoid?"

"One of them. There's a worse one, but they live in Lower Hall and they mostly hang out with the football team. You should be safe. Anyhooos, out of the Britneys, Deandra's the worst. Always mean, and nasty, and trying to impress the others... She's basically my mom but younger."

"You don't get on with your mother?"

"Not even a little bit. She ruined my life. One day, everything seemed fine, and the next day, she left my dad and moved in with her boyfriend. Her *boyfriend*. She'd been seeing him secretly for a year, *a freaking year*, and she just expected me to be fine with it."

"She wanted you to move in with them?"

"Yeah, and I didn't have a choice. Because the divorce got nasty and there was a paternity test, and it turned out my dad wasn't even my dad."

"Wow. I'm sorry."

"So was my mom. The boyfriend dumped her after eight months, and she started a new relationship with alcohol instead." Vanessa stared at the vodka bottle. "I don't even know why I'm drinking this. Oh my gosh, I'm turning into her."

"I'm sure that's not true."

Even so, I pushed the bottle to the other side of the desk, out of Vanessa's reach.

"I guess at least I haven't hit on Mr. Rosenberg yet."

I almost choked on my water. "Your mother did that? She really hit on Ezra Rosenberg?"

"Not Ezra. Saul."

"What did he do?"

"Looked kind of shocked as he peeled her hand off his arm, then called Mrs. Hannigan over to help. I mean, it was obvious Mom had been drinking. She *reeked* of wine. Now I don't tell her about any school events, and she stays in California. It's for the best."

"Do you go home for the holidays?"

"Not if I can help it. She's shacked up with some dot-com tech geek who's barely out of college. She keeps saying he's going to be the next big thing. The guy can't even wear matching socks."

"I knew a guy who wore odd socks once. He said it was lucky."

But he'd also died in a drive-by when a drug deal went wrong, so maybe not.

"He also wears the socks with sandals."

"Yeuch. That's unforgivable."

"Exactly. But the Rosenbergs are good about letting me stay here. The kitchen's always open because the staff work over the break periods. I swim, I read, I catch up on studying. At least my grades are good."

If I'd really been the girl I claimed to be, I could have invited Vanessa to Casa Milburn for Thanksgiving. But fingers crossed, I'd be long gone by that time. This was perhaps the hardest part of the job. Gaining people's trust, only to have to break it later on.

"Are you planning to go to college?"

"Hopefully. As long as I can get a scholarship. Pass the vodka?"

"I think you've had enough for tonight."

"Sky!" Vanessa melted into giggles, then winced when her bad ankle clonked the chair. "You're sooo unadventurous."

Oh, if only she knew.

I bent closer and squinted through the glass of the oversized aquarium.

"Ribbet."

The frog staring back at me didn't answer. He seemed to be the strong, silent type. It was so, so tempting to scoop him up and take him with me, but I wasn't that cruel. I wouldn't wish Deandra on anyone, not even that slimy little sucker. Now, where the hell were those fake amphibians?

I opened one cupboard after another. Spare textbooks, a plastic model of the human torso, little dishes and vials and a whole bunch of microscopes. Hey, was this them? SynFrogs. Yup. I opened one of the boxes and found that Asher was right. They *were* realistic. I shoved Kermit into my bag alongside my set of lock picks, rearranged the boxes so it didn't look as if anything had been disturbed, and retraced my steps out of the lab.

"What were you doing in there?"

"Fuck, you nearly gave me a heart attack."

At least I didn't have Blackwood listening in this morning. I'd woken up early and gone out without my earpiece. They didn't need to know about my extracurricular activities.

"Well?" Asher raised an eyebrow.

"I lost an earring yesterday. I thought it might be in the lab, so I went to check."

"But you didn't have biology yesterday."

"Uh, I think maybe I actually lost the earring on Wednesday. I just noticed yesterday."

Since when had Asher been monitoring my schedule?

"The lab wasn't locked?"

"No. Why? Should it have been?"

"It usually is."

"Then I guess I got lucky." And I wasn't even wearing odd socks.

"Did you find it?"

"The earring? No."

"So you weren't *that* lucky."

"You really know how to cheer a girl up on a Friday morning, don't you?"

His lips quirked at the corners. "I could buy you breakfast."

"All the food here is free."

The asshole just laughed and sauntered off. "Don't say I didn't offer."

Chapter 25 - Sky

A SHRILL SCREAM cut through the air in my art enrichment class, and everyone froze. Everyone except me, anyway. I just kept gluing jelly beans to my masterpiece while I tried not to smile. Why jelly beans, you ask? Because we were meant to be using mixed media, and the teacher told us to get creative. And I was hungry. When I begged packets of candy from the kitchen to use in my project, the teacher beamed with delight at my originality, my "inspired vision," so it was a win-win situation. One sweet for me, one for the canvas, one sweet for me, one for the canvas.

Then I thought that perhaps keeping my composure would appear suspicious, so I put down my glue gun and plastered on a horrified expression—hands to my cheeks and everything—as Deandra danced around her bag, shrieking.

"Get it out! Get it out!"

Meaghan peered into the bag and squealed too. "OMG! Is it alive?"

Not unless it had been fucking possessed.

"It moved! It just moved!"

For pity's sake... Talk about being melodramatic. Deandra carried on squealing as a couple of guys downed tools and shuffled forward to take a better look.

"It's a toad," one of them said.

Close, but not quite.

Asher was on the other side of the room, standing in front of his own painting. He definitely had a dark side. A child sat cross-legged in the middle of a filthy sidewalk, his back to crowds of pedestrians that parted as they walked around him. The embodiment of loneliness. Did that come from within? Or had he seen the idea somewhere and copied it? Asher didn't seem unhappy. In fact, he smirked as he caught my eye. Did he know?

Oh, who was I kidding? Of course he knew. The question was, would he tell anyone?

He abandoned his brush on a palette filled with dark blobs of oil paint and moseyed over to Deandra. Was it my imagination, or did she pause her hysteria for a moment to preen?

"Asher, can you help? I think I'm gonna be sick."

Not only did Asher laugh, but he also flapped his arms and made chicken noises before he scooped the fake frog into his closed hands.

"Don't be such a drama queen. The poor little guy's escaped from the biology lab, that's all."

Her fear turned to dismay. "How can you hold it? It's a *toad*."

"It's a frog. It won't kill you."

"Some frogs are poisonous."

"Not this one."

How was he keeping a straight face? It was made of freaking rubber.

Deandra folded her arms. "Well, it's slimy."

"Go back to your coop, Dea."

Her bottom lip quivered as Asher left the room, and

a bunch of her so-called friends snickered too. I didn't laugh, but I did feel a sense of satisfaction that at least she'd been brought down a peg or two. After her nastiness towards Vanessa, she deserved it.

"Did you find your earring?" Asher asked nonchalantly on Saturday. But quietly, so the people sitting at the bench behind us couldn't hear.

"Did you put the frog back?"

"It took me ages to find the empty box."

"Perseverance is an admirable quality."

"Why'd you do it?"

"Do what?" I played innocent. "Why were you such a dick to Deandra?"

"I'm a dick to everyone. Here at Shadow Falls, we place great importance on equality, remember?"

I just stared at him.

"Don't look at me like that, Chem. I saw what Dea did to Vanessa on the hockey pitch, and it was shitty. Is she okay?"

"The swelling's going down, but her foot still won't fit in anything but flip-flops."

"What about..." Asher tapped his head. "Up there?"

"She's upset, and understandably so. Deandra's a nasty piece of work."

"Yeah, I know."

"Then why don't you tell your uncle? He could fix the problem."

"I'm not getting involved in school politics."

"It's hardly political. Deandra's a bully, and you're in a better position than most people to do something about it."

"I *was* doing something about it. Why do you think I was outside the lab yesterday morning?" He broke into an unexpected grin. "Great minds think alike."

It took a moment for his words to sink in.

"Wait, you mean..."

"The difference between you and me, Chem Girl?" He leaned in closer, and his breath puffed over my ear. "I was tempted to use a real frog."

Rune sighed in my ear. "I think I like him."

That was worrying. And you know what was more worrying? I thought I might like Asher too.

Deandra wasn't in our biology class, thank goodness, but Tiffany was, and when Professor Eastman announced we needed to work in pairs for a project over the weekend, Tiffany sidled up to the bench me and Asher were sharing.

"Want to work with me, Asher?"

"I already said I'd work with Sky."

He'd done nothing of the sort, but I found I didn't mind. Who else would I pair up with? Apart from Asher and Vanessa, I'd basically been avoiding my fellow pupils. I had no desire to make friends with people who might expect me to forgo my precious snooping time to go shopping or play extra sports.

But I didn't miss the anger that blazed in Tiffany's eyes. I was the new girl, and whether I'd intended to or not, I was treading on her toes. Well, she'd just have to get over herself. In a week or two, I'd be gone, and I wasn't about to compromise my work to keep her happy.

"Each pair needs to prepare a slide from plant cells using the squash method, then calculate the mitotic index," Professor Eastman instructed. "And I'd also like you to design a poster showing the stages of mitosis along with a brief explanation of each. Most of the work can be done in class, but you'll need to finish off in private study time by Monday."

Ugh. Homework. We hadn't had too much of it yet, but Vanessa said the teachers broke us in gently at the start of each school year. And once again, I didn't understand the questions. *Rune, help.*

"Mitosis is the way most cells divide," she told me. "Each division produces two cells that are genetically identical to the parent cell. In any given cell sample, some cells will be in the process of dividing. The mitotic index is the number of dividing cells over the total number of cells. And there are four phases of division: prophase, metaphase, anaphase, and telophase."

What language was she speaking? And what the hell was the squash method?

Thankfully, Asher knew, so he prepped our slides and then talked me through how to set up the microscope and what to look for. I counted the cells and wrote the numbers down, while Rune helped me out by calculating the mitotic index.

"Do my own cells look like that?" I asked Asher as I peered into the microscope again.

"Not quite. They divide in the same way, but animal cells don't have walls the way plant cells do. I thought you'd studied biology in England?"

Oops. "I might have skipped a few lessons."

"And yet you still managed to pass your entrance exam?"

Shit. I didn't like the way this conversation was going. But before I could steer it in a different direction, Asher shrugged.

"Hey, who am I to judge? I didn't even take the entrance exam."

Phew. "So, what do you want to do about finishing off this project? Work on it tonight and get it over with?"

"I can't tonight."

"Tomorrow?" Not that we had a lot of choice since the paper was due in on Monday.

"I've got shit to do in the morning. Gimme your number and I'll call you."

"What if I've got shit to do in the afternoon?"

"That leaves the evening." He treated me to another of those stellar grins as he packed up his stuff to go. "I'll buy you dinner."

"Dinner's also free, you dick."

"See you tomorrow, Chem."

If I hadn't dropped my pen, I might have missed it —the open-mouthed shock on the faces of the two girls sitting behind me.

"What?" I asked.

"Asher Martinez offered to buy you dinner. He never buys anybody dinner."

"It was a joke."

"Asher doesn't joke either."

"Well, I guess he does now."

On Sunday, late afternoon found me sitting in an empty classroom with Asher, my laptop, a giant poster-board, and a selection of pens. I didn't mind being inside for the evening. My feet ached from walking around the campus all day, and it was raining again. Plus I'd snuck some of my art-project jelly beans into my bag, so I had snacks.

I'd arrived first and typed up the results of the experiment, but when I asked Asher if he wanted to read my work over, he said he trusted me. Flattering perhaps, but in reality, I suspected he just couldn't be bothered. Although he wasn't bad company. He told me more about Shadow Falls—the town, not the school— and I came to the conclusion that I wasn't missing much by being stuck up in the hills.

"A one-horse town," he said. "There's even a hitching post outside the grocery store."

"Did you grow up around here?"

"No, in San Diego. Not many horses, but a whole lot of beaches."

"I know which I'd prefer."

"Do you surf?"

The only time I'd seen the ocean was when I jetted over it on my way to America, but I could hardly admit that in present company.

"Never tried it. I think I'd fall off the board."

"Nah, I think you'd do okay. You're sporty. I saw you out running again this morning. You know you're not meant to go alone, right?"

"Are you going to tell on me?"

"Do I look like that kind of guy?"

Hmm, good question. What did a tattletale look like, anyway? I'd come across plenty of police informants, slimy little snakes that'd sell out their friends for cash, but I imagined these things worked differently in a private school.

"You're a Rosenberg."

"I'm *not* a fucking Rosenberg."

Asher's words were forceful. Angry, even. He definitely didn't seem fond of his family. Could I use that to my advantage in any way? Possibly, but I felt like a traitor for even considering it. This job was *hard*.

"Okay, okay. Fine, you're not a Rosenberg."

Asher blew out a long breath. "Sorry, I shouldn't have flown off the handle. But they're not my family."

"But you're related. What's the saying? That blood is thicker than water?"

"'The blood of the covenant is thicker than the water of the womb.' It means the opposite—that the family you choose comes first. Did I tell anyone about the frog?"

"I guess not."

"Then I'm not going to tell anyone about your illicit sporting activities. But I will offer to run with you next weekend if you want company."

Was that a good idea? I wouldn't be able to talk to anyone at Blackwood, but Asher's presence would give me a good cover story while I videoed the grounds. I could run with him for an hour and catch up with Emmy and the others in private later. The mapping project was going well. My main task at the moment was sneaking into the private areas to plant bugs, but I could only do one or two rooms a night. I needed to get some sleep too.

"As long as you promise to keep up. And no shortcuts."

I was starting to like those smiles a little too much.

"Deal."

By dusk, Asher had drawn four pictures of cell division, and he wasn't a bad artist, I'd give him that.

But he couldn't bloody spell.

"Prophase has a 'ph' in the middle, not an 'f,'" Rune informed me, and I relayed that little titbit to Asher. He gritted his teeth and grabbed a bottle of Tipp-Ex—or Wite-Out as they called it in America, which was slightly ironic because it seemed the manufacturers of that couldn't spell either.

"He's spelled 'nucleus' wrong too," Rune said. "The c's in the wrong place." So it was. *Nulecus.* "And protein is 'e' before 'i.'"

Benign errors, or so I thought, but when I pointed them out to Asher, his reaction was anything but. His pen clattered to the floor.

"If you can do better, then go right ahead."

"It's not a problem. I'm just saying…"

"They're mistakes, that's all. Work on a Sunday—it's bullshit." He shoved his chair back. "I've had enough of this."

The door bounced off the wall and crashed shut behind him, and Rune sounded as shocked as I felt.

"Whoa. Somebody needs a Snickers."

"What did I say?"

I'd obviously touched a nerve, but which one?

"I have no idea. I mean, you were even polite for once."

"Is it weird to study on a Sunday? Do you have to at your school?"

"Most people do, unless they work extra in the evenings instead."

"Should I go after him?"

"Uh, I don't know. I probably wouldn't."

I didn't want to either, but I couldn't allow Asher's ire to fester. We still needed to work together, and I had chemistry and then biology after assembly tomorrow. But whatever I did, I had to decide fast. The sound of slamming doors was fading.

"Sod it, I have to find him."

"Good luck."

CHAPTER 26 - SKY

THE VIBRATIONS FROM the slam of the last door reverberated down the hallway, but as I paused outside the room, wondering whether to go inside or just say "fuck it" and head to bed, the echoing crash was replaced by the notes of a piano. I couldn't name the tune, but I'd heard it before. Something low and dark and angry, emotions tangled with the music as it rose and fell.

Was *Asher* playing? He'd never once mentioned any musical abilities.

I cracked the door open and peered through the gap. Sure enough, he was sitting side-on at a grand piano, eyes shut, lost in the song.

"Asher?"

His eyes flew open. "What are you doing here?"

"You walked out on me. I came to check you're okay."

"I'm fine. Do me a favour and close the door on your way out."

"You can close it yourself when we leave."

Rune came back. "Hold on a second. Dan's here, and she wants a word."

Oh, brilliant. More people sticking their oar in. Exactly what I needed. Didn't they realise I had enough on my plate already this evening?

"I caught the end of your discussion, and Asher's blow-up. The transposition of letters, the phonetic errors... I think he might have dyslexia. One of Caleb's friends does, and he makes the same kind of mistakes. Just be careful what you say to Asher."

Dyslexia? I didn't know a whole lot about it, but it might explain a few things. Asher barely took notes in class. He palmed that off on me or Vanessa, and while he generally listened to the teacher, he didn't pay much attention to anything written on the board. I'd assumed he had a lazy streak, but could I have got that badly wrong?

"I'm sorry if I upset you."

He stopped playing.

"I didn't want for you to think that I was mocking you or anything. If you want to stay here, I can finish the poster and bring your pens and stuff back tomorrow."

Asher muttered something under his breath that was probably a curse. Aimed at me or the situation?

"I shouldn't have snapped at you, Chem. It's me who should be apologising."

"Forget it."

He got up and walked towards me. Changed his mind and switched direction, heading towards the darkened window instead.

"Have you always had trouble with words?" I asked softly.

That stopped him in his tracks, and he raked a hand through his already messy hair.

"I'm just tired."

All or nothing. Either I'd be right, or I'd end up calling him a liar. Brock Keaton aside, I wasn't bad at reading people, so I decided to take a gamble. Asher's defensiveness reminded me of Lenny when he'd been doing something he didn't want me to find out about, usually illegal substances.

"I don't think so."

"Think what you like."

"Do the Rosenbergs know?"

I almost said "your family" instead, but that wouldn't have gone down well.

"Will you drop this bullshit?" Asher growled.

"No, because I'm a tenacious little bitch. I've been told it's one of my worst qualities."

He began pacing in jerky steps. "No, they don't know, okay? Nobody fucking knows. Now will you leave me alone?"

I took a seat on the piano stool. When I pressed the keys, it sounded as if the thing was being run over by a dump truck.

"Where I come from, we don't abandon our friends."

And I guessed Asher had sort of become a friend. I didn't mind hanging out with him, and we'd spent enough time together for me to know he was no Brock Keaton. To start with, I'd felt slightly edgy in his presence, but I'd been secure in the knowledge that I could kick his ass thanks to Rafael and his gruelling gym sessions. But fast-forward to today? Today I felt safe enough to be alone with Asher in this music room without my chest going tight.

"Where I come from, we don't have friends."

That... That was super sad. Even in London, I'd had Lenny and the parkour crowd.

"People don't have friends in San Diego?"

"In the circles I ran in, you were only worth what you could do for people."

"And now?"

"Now I'm my grandma's pity project. Don't turn me into yours too. I see the same look in your eyes."

"That's not pity." A little guilt, maybe, because I'd been working out how I could use him. "I just want to pass chemistry and biology, and since we're working together... My motives are purely selfish." When he didn't say anything, I pivoted to a different subject. "Are your parents still in San Diego?"

"Side by side in Mount Hope Cemetery."

Oh. Shit.

"I'm so sorry. You must miss them."

"In some ways."

"Ask if he wants to talk about it," Rune whispered. "That's what my therapist does."

Shit, I'd almost forgotten she was there. This was one hell of a violation of trust. I wanted to turn off my comms system, but I could hardly stick my finger in my ear without Asher thinking I was a right weirdo.

"Uh, do you want to talk about it?"

The silence stretched for so long I thought he wasn't going to answer, but finally, he spoke.

"Do you know, you're the first person who's ever asked me that."

My heart ached for him. I was beginning to understand that Asher Martinez wasn't the man I'd thought. Most of the time, he wore a better mask than Emmy.

"What's the answer?"

"I'm not sure where I'd start," he admitted. "I guess... I once told my mom I had trouble reading and writing, but she said that it didn't matter, that I had an artist's soul."

Asher sat down next to me, nudging me over so we each had half of the stool. Then he began to play again, this time a depressingly beautiful melody that made the hairs on my arms stand on end. He might have had trouble writing, but the music spoke for him. His pain was all too obvious. When he finished the piece, he let out the longest sigh.

"Come on, Chem. Guess we should finish this poster. You'll help with the words?"

I nodded, the lump in my throat making it hard to speak.

"Promise I won't fly off the handle at you again. I just didn't want you to think I was stupid."

"So you'd rather I thought you were a prizewinning prick?"

"I didn't say I'd thought it through." His fingers brushed my arm, the lightest of touches. It felt as if he'd seared me with a Bunsen burner. "Thanks for putting up with me."

"Hurry up and get back to work, Shortcut. I need some sleep tonight."

"What the hell happened?"

Vanessa kicked the door to our room shut behind herself and leaned against it, her breath coming in pants. Blood ran down both of her knees, and when she raised a hand to swipe at her eyes, I saw grazes on her palm too.

"I fell."

"Over Deandra's hockey stick again?"

"This time it was her foot."

Oh, that did it. Hadn't the frog been enough? Or was Deandra stupid enough to believe it really had escaped from the lab as Asher suggested?

"She tripped you intentionally?" I asked, just to confirm.

"I walked around the corner, then someone pushed me from behind and I fell right over her."

"Who pushed you?"

"I didn't see."

Three guesses. Literally three. Tiffany, Meaghan, or Carlie. Why couldn't they act like the adults they were about to become? I might have worked for a group of assassins, but they were so much more civilised than these high school brats.

In my ear, Emmy sighed. "I know what you're thinking, and I agree. Fucking playground bullies. Deal with the one you know and leave the other three. Separate her from the pack and go in hard, but don't leave any marks."

I nodded my agreement, then realised she couldn't see me. Thankfully Vanessa didn't notice either, probably because she was wiping her eyes with a blood-streaked tissue. Deandra could wait. First, I needed to take care of my roommate. My friend.

"We need to wash the grit out of these cuts and clean them."

"I-I-I don't have any antiseptic."

"I do."

Bradley had helped me to pack, so I practically had my own ambulance. Bathrooms in New Hall were shared—each floor had five individual toilet stalls and five individual showers—so I helped Vanessa along to the nearest shower and had her stand barefoot while I rinsed her hands and knees with the handheld sprayer. Ouch. Deandra had done a good job. The grazes crisscrossed Vanessa's skin and the blood kept seeping out for a good ten minutes after I finished cleaning them, and with every drop that dripped into the damp shower tray and spread out to a pale pink, my anger grew until it ran hot in my veins. Vanessa winced when I finally dabbed antiseptic cream onto the broken skin.

"Any idea why Deandra did this?"

"The singing teacher said she wanted to put me forward for another contest. I should have stuck to art."

"Never give up on your dreams, especially because of one spiteful little witch."

"Easy for you to say. It's not you that she hates."

Give it a couple of hours. I'd soon change that.

"You should probably lie down for the rest of the evening. Any movement's going to make your knees start bleeding again."

I helped her back to our room, and she walked stiff-legged like a wooden doll. Even getting onto the bed was difficult for her. I had to haul her backwards by her armpits.

"Where are you going?" she asked when I went to leave.

"We've got a biology test on Saturday, and I promised Asher I'd study with him this evening. I'll stop at the dining hall on the way back and sneak some food out for you. Any requests?"

"Chocolate. I need chocolate."

"I'll do my best."

My best involved skulking around the school for

almost an hour before I found the four Britneys holding court in an empty practice room in A-block. Tiffany and Meaghan were sitting on top of a grand piano, swinging their legs, while Deandra shared the stool with Carlie. A gaggle of adoring freshmen were clustered around them, hanging on their every word, and they'd brought drinks and snacks, which weren't allowed in any of the classrooms. I was tempted to report them, but that would be letting those bitches off too easy.

Carve Deandra away from the pack, Emmy had said. How the hell did I do that? I didn't have her phone number, so I couldn't lure her out with a text, and if I set off the fire alarm, they'd all rush outside. I was puzzling over the conundrum when Deandra gave me the answer herself. She left the room, turning right into the hallway and heading for the nearest loo.

At Greenfields Comprehensive, a common punishment for lesser mortals was to have your head flushed down the toilet. How did I know? Because when I was twelve, it had happened to me after I bumped into a sixth-former and spilled her Fanta. My lips curved up in a smile as I fell into step behind Deandra. She was so self-absorbed that she didn't even notice me following.

But she sure as hell noticed when I shoved her into the bathroom with one arm twisted up behind her back. I used a leg to sweep her feet out from underneath her, and she practically fell into the toilet bowl. Perfect. The glorious sound of her choking as I flushed was music to my ears.

"That was for Vanessa," I hissed, just to make sure she got the message this time.

Then I was gone. No marks.

"Nice job," Emmy said in my ear.

It was, wasn't it? And since I'd kept Deandra's back to me, she couldn't even be certain who had done it, although I was sure she'd be able to make an educated guess.

Now, where was that chocolate?

CHAPTER 27 - SKY

ONCE I EXPLAINED to the staff in the dining hall that Vanessa had accidentally tripped and hurt herself, they packaged her dinner onto a tray to go, including a slice of chocolate cake.

"Hungry this evening?" Asher asked, falling into step beside me as I hurried out the door.

"It's for Vanessa," I explained. "She fell over earlier and—"

I didn't get to finish the sentence before Ezra Rosenberg blocked my way. "A word, please, Sky."

"Can't it wait?" Asher asked. "She's taking dinner to her roommate."

I'd never seen Asher interact with one of the Rosenbergs before, and it was clear there was no love lost between them. Ezra's jaw clenched, but he didn't chastise Asher for speaking to him in that manner.

"No, it can't wait. A few minutes ago, I had a very serious incident reported to me, and the complainant alleged that Sky was involved."

"Involved with what? We haven't heard about any incident." Asher shrugged. "Although we've been studying together in the library this evening, and the gossip doesn't always get that far."

"*You've* been with Sky this evening?"

"Didn't I just say that?"

"All evening?"

"Since five o'clock. We're lab partners, and we have a biology test on Saturday."

When Rosenberg stood there, unmoving as he processed that little snippet of news, Asher took another jab.

"What? You keep telling me to make friends and study harder, and now that I am, you're complaining about it?"

Uncle Ezra gave his head a little shake. "Not at all. I see now that there's been some kind of a mistake. Sky, I apologise for interrupting your evening."

I almost sagged with relief. My heart had begun racing, but I didn't realise quite how fast until Ezra strode off towards A-block, and in the remaining silence, I heard the *thump-thump-thump* in my ears. And Emmy. She was there too.

"Interesting exchange. Why did Asher cover for you?"

I had no idea.

"Thanks," I mumbled.

"Did you do it?" Asher asked.

"Do what?"

He just stared, his gaze locked onto mine, and those big blue eyes dragged the truth out of me.

"Of course I did."

His laughter was...unexpected. But nice.

"Come on, you'd better take that food to Vanessa before it gets cold. Did Deandra hurt her badly this time?"

"Scraped up her hands and knees. Were you really in the library?"

Asher snorted. "Of course not."

"Then where were you?" I asked before I could stop myself. What Asher Martinez did in his spare time was none of my business. But at that moment, I realised I kind of *wanted* it to be my business. The revelation hit me like a punch to the gut, and I would have walked into the door of New Hall if Asher hadn't opened it for me.

"I snuck out to buy cigarettes. Don't worry; nobody saw me."

Cigarettes? He had cigarettes? I really, really needed a puff right now. "Can I bum one?"

"You smoke too?" Asher asked.

Ah, shit. Emmy was still listening, wasn't she?

"Not often. I mean, not at school."

"I'll wait here for you. We've both broken enough rules tonight without me sneaking into a girls' dorm."

True. I jogged up two flights of stairs, careful not to drop Vanessa's food. The last thing I needed was a bigger mess. This should have been such a simple job—get in, record some video, plant some bugs, get out—but it was turning out to be more complicated than I ever imagined. Why? Because of people. People turned even the best-laid plans into mayhem.

"Here you go. Mac and cheese with triple chocolate fudge cake. How are you feeling?"

"You brought cake? Now I'm feeling *much* better. Wait, you're not staying?"

"Haven't finished that study session. Mitosis is a bitch."

I slipped out the door before she could ask any more questions. I was all out of answers tonight. But before I went downstairs, I locked myself in one of the toilet stalls and sat on the closed lid.

"Emmy?"

"What are you doing, Sky?"

"I have no idea. Isn't that obvious?"

"I'm not your mother. I'm not going to give you a lecture. But just remember you'll be leaving Shadow Falls in a few weeks. I don't want anyone to get hurt, especially you."

"I don't want anyone to get hurt either, but I need to stay on good terms with Asher. If he hadn't stepped in tonight, I'd be in Ezra Rosenberg's office right now, getting a bollocking."

"I understand that."

"And do you know how awkward it feels, having to have these conversations with people, trying to form bonds and cultivate relationships with somebody from Blackwood listening in the whole time?"

"Yes."

"So what do you do in that situation?"

"Simple. I turn my microphone off when things get heavy."

"I didn't realise that was an option."

"Trust goes both ways. If we're asking you to trust us, then we have to trust you as well. If you feel it's safe to go dark, just let whoever's monitoring you know there'll be radio silence for a while."

"Okay." I hesitated for a moment. "Aren't you going to scold me for smoking?"

"If I told you off for having a cheeky cigarette, I'd be the biggest hypocrite on the planet."

"You smoke?"

"*Very* occasionally. Don't you dare tell Black."

"My lips are sealed."

"Asher's waiting for you."

"Uh, so I guess I'm going quiet for a while."

"Just check in with me later, all right?"

I removed the earpiece and turned the tiny dial to switch off the microphone, but I left the speaker on. That way, I could still hear Blackwood, but they couldn't hear me. Then I jogged downstairs to Asher.

"Hey." With the radio turned off, I'd expected things to feel less awkward, but it turned out the opposite was true. "Where are we going?"

He put a finger to his lips and headed for a running trail that led into the woods. When the lights from the dorms had faded away, he turned on a small torch.

"I can't smoke in my apartment. One of the housekeeping staff would smell it and report me."

"You have an apartment?"

"One of the few perks of being related to the Rosenbergs. Ezra was going to put me in a regular room, but Grandma overruled him and gave me a staff apartment. Officially, I'm meant to be the student liaison for Linton Hall, but things run pretty smoothly over there. It's geek city."

The ground was slippery after today's rainfall, and when Asher cut right onto a smaller path that climbed steeply uphill, he offered me a hand. I took it. It would have been rude not to, right? And then we found ourselves in a small clearing with a tumbledown wooden shack at the far end.

"What is this place?" I asked.

"Not sure. It might have been a toolshed once, but now it's full of old junk." The door hung off rusted hinges, and he led me inside. "I don't think anyone comes here now except me."

No one but spiders, anyway. A cobweb tickled my

face, and I knocked it out of the way only for another to take its place. Yeuch. The moonlight that filtered through the filthy window cast creepy shadows over the inside of the shed, and Asher's torch lit up half a dozen broken chairs, a rusted spade, and a pile of old newspapers. The place smelled damp and musty with an underlying hint of what could have been a dead mouse.

"Do you bring all the girls here?" I asked.

"Can you imagine Tiffany or Meaghan in a place like this? They'd both have run screaming by now." He grew more serious. "No, you're the first girl I've ever brought here."

"You really know how to make me feel special."

He studied the collection of chairs, dragged out the two that looked the most intact, and wiped them with his sleeve. A cloud of dust billowed into the murky light.

"Take a seat. Don't say I never spoil you."

I forgave him when he offered me a Lucky Strike from the packet in his pocket. "Thanks. Do you smoke a lot?"

"Not often. Only when I'm stressed."

"Why are you stressed? Is it the test on Saturday?"

"Partly."

"Partly? What's the other part?"

He didn't speak. Avoiding the question? Or just considering his answer?

"Asher?"

"I'm deciding whether or not to be honest."

"Why wouldn't you be?"

A match flared in the darkness, and Asher lit my cigarette and then his own. I inhaled deeply and quickly regretted it when I began coughing.

"I don't smoke much either," I explained. "Only when I need to take the edge off."

"Why do *you* need to take the edge off?"

"It's not every day you flush a tart's head down the toilet and nearly get caught."

"You did *what*?"

"I thought you already knew?"

"I saw Deandra coming out of Ezra's office with one of the other Dingbat Barbies, and Deandra's MO is to weaponise the teachers against her enemies. When Ezra wanted to talk to you, I knew she'd reported you for something. But giving her a swirly? She's had that coming for a long time. Chem, you deserve a medal."

"So do you, because that was a nice deflection. C'mon, Shortcut—what's eating at you?"

"Are you always this perceptive?"

"There you go again."

"Don't you ever quit?"

"I—"

He held up a hand to silence me. "On second thought, I don't want to know the answer. I'll talk, okay? Have you ever considered working at Guantanamo Bay? I hear the CIA's interrogation team has openings."

The wall of the shed creaked alarmingly when Asher stood and leaned against it, and I had visions of being buried under a pile of rotting wood. Perhaps I should have left my microphone on after all? Emmy could send Ryder and his merry men to rescue me because no way was I explaining that predicament to the fire brigade.

"Being around you makes me stressed," Asher said.

Well, shit. I hadn't been expecting that.

"Sorry. I don't mean to make you feel that way."

"I know. But you...you see me in a way nobody else does, not even my family. All the things I try to hide, you either notice them on your own..." He waved the glowing end of the cigarette. "Or I blurt them out when you ask. I feel as if I'm losing control of my life."

"I'm not planning to tell anyone your secrets, if that's what you're worried about." I rose to face him. "You know one of mine too. Why *did* you cover for me?"

"I already told you—Deandra deserved to be taken down a peg or two." He chuckled. "Or ten. And Ezra's a whiny asshole."

"Why do you hate the Rosenbergs so much?"

"Because of the way they treated my mother. They disowned her after she went to college." He sighed. "She grew up here, but she broke with family tradition and chose California College of the Arts instead of Harvard."

"They disowned her for picking a different school?"

"No, they disowned her because she fell in love with my dad. His father was a janitor at CCA."

"Oh."

"Yeah. His family was the wrong colour, and from the wrong social class. But my mom said to hell with it and married him anyway."

"Wow. That's...that's disgusting. What they did to her," I hastened to add. "Not what she did."

"The joke was on them because my Californian grandparents worked their asses off so Dad could be the first person in their family to go to college, and he graduated from Stanford with distinction. And then he went to law school. I had a good life as a kid, at least until Mom died."

"I'm so sorry." I squeezed his free hand with mine. It seemed like an appropriate thing to do. "But I still don't understand how you ended up here."

"It's a long, long story."

"If you want to talk, I'm here to listen. But if you don't, that's okay too."

He flicked his cigarette butt onto the cracked concrete floor and ground it out with his heel, then bent to pick it up and drop it into a battered metal watering can. I followed suit and saw the little pile of dog-ends already in there. Perhaps Asher got more stressed than he cared to admit.

"Mom died suddenly. Her aorta ruptured in the middle of a yoga lesson, and by the time the ambulance got there, she was gone. Do me a favour and skip the yoga lessons, Sky. I hate the thought of you..." Popping my clogs the same way? "Never mind."

"I'll avoid yoga."

He squeezed my hand back.

"I was twelve. And the bottom dropped out of my world. Dad always made sure we had family time at the weekend, but during the week, he worked long hours, so it was just me and Mom. She picked me up from school, helped with my homework, ate dinner with me. Then suddenly she was gone. I couldn't handle it. From the outside, I looked okay, but inside, it felt as if a wrecking ball had gone through my ribs. I fucked up my first year of junior high and had to repeat it."

Grief. I'd barely experienced it, not really, but Lenny had almost died three months ago and the numbness I'd felt in those few minutes...

"That's completely understandable."

"Not to my dad. He had this crazy work ethic, and he couldn't figure out why I didn't share it. Plus he fell apart after Mom died too. He'd already buried both of his parents, and after Mom's funeral, he stopped coming home, stopped eating, developed this distance in his eyes. She was his soulmate, and without her, he was never the same. After one of our many, many arguments, he told me he couldn't bear to look at me because I reminded him of what he'd lost."

What a cruel thing to tell a child. If what I saw in Asher's eyes was any indication, then words hurt far more than fists ever could. For once, I was grateful my father had chosen the latter.

"I wish I could go back in time and flush *his* head down the toilet."

That got me the tiniest smile. "What's done is done. We drifted apart after that. Dad spent most of his time in the office, and I spent most of mine getting into trouble. Lucky I knew a good lawyer."

"Did you ever get arrested?"

"A few times. Mostly, I hightailed it before the cops came. Ever driven a modified Mustang along a freeway with the sound of sirens in the background? It's a fuckin' rush."

Asher had been a street racer? I got a rush too, all my blood heading south to places it definitely shouldn't have gone. But those guys had balls.

"Do you still have the Mustang?"

"Not that one, but a different one. I had to hide it from my dad. Our relationship had broken down completely by that point, and he'd have crushed the car if he'd found out about it. I guess I couldn't have blamed him. He'd sent me to three good schools, two of which I got expelled from, and I'd failed everything and quit. I turned eighteen, got a job where I earned good money, and messed around with cars in my spare time. Only went home to sleep. Figured I'd do that for the rest of my life, but then Dad had a heart attack at his desk one night. His PA didn't find him until the next morning."

Any words would have been totally inadequate. There wasn't enough sympathy in the world for what had happened to Asher. So I did the only thing I could think of and wrapped my arms around him in a slightly awkward hug. We stood in silence long enough for a spider to drop from the roof, crawl all the way across my shoulder, and start creeping down my arm. I wasn't arachnophobic or anything, but it took willpower I didn't know I possessed to keep from flicking it away. I tried shifting to the side, but it tippy-toed over my wrist and took up residence on my hand.

"So after that, what, you decided to reconnect with your mother's side of the family?"

"Not exactly, not by choice anyway. By then, Dad and I had clashed so many times that he'd added a clause to his will. If I want to inherit a cent, I have to get my high school diploma."

My eyes widened. "Oh, shit."

"As I said, I can't blame him. If I'd had a kid like me, I'd probably have done the same thing. And maybe I'd have stayed in California if I hadn't lost my job, but..." He paused for a moment. Swallowed. "Anyhow, Grandma Rosenberg heard what had happened and reached out. Mom had partially reconciled with her over the years—not Ezra or Saul and definitely not her father, but she spoke to Grandma. We even visited a time or two. Which left me with two choices—going to public school in San Diego and scraping by on my own, or coming here and doing the bare minimum. Both shitty options, but this place seemed like the lesser of two evils. So that's my story, Chem. Told you it was long."

"How are you finding Shadow Falls?"

"So far, it's met with my expectations, but the future seems a little brighter." Asher smiled at me. "You can take your hand off my ass now. Or leave it there. I don't care."

Oops. Damn spider. I shifted my arm to a more appropriate position, and the eight-legged freak floated to the floor and scuttled away.

"Sorry. Uh, if you need to graduate, then perhaps we really should do some studying this evening?"

He made a face.

"Oh, don't give me that look. I can help you with reading or whatever. Honestly, I don't mind."

"Have you eaten dinner?"

I shook my head. "But it's fine. I have a stash of jelly beans in my room."

In forty-seven different flavours, no less. That was practically a meal in itself. But Asher didn't seem to think so. He pushed away from the wall, forcing me to take a step backwards.

"It's not fine. You need to eat." He held out a hand, and this time, I didn't think twice before I took it. "I have a kitchen. You'll have to sneak into Linton Hall, but I'll make you dinner."

"You can cook?"

"I can microwave."

"That's good enough for me."

Chapter 28 - Sky

IF LENNY'S THERAPY sessions *were* anything like socio-emotional learning, then I sure felt sorry for him. Wednesday afternoon, and twelve of us were sitting around in a circle on the floor, waiting for the teacher to arrive. At Shadow Falls Academy, they liked to mix things up a bit for this session, and none of these people were in any of my other classes. The guy with the coloured bracelets, I wasn't even sure he was on the same planet. He'd brought his own freaking cushion.

Eventually, the teacher arrived. Normally, she taught pottery, but today she was stuck with us lot.

"Apologies for being late. A freshman had a crisis of confidence and locked herself in a bathroom stall, but that's all sorted out now. Just a reminder: if one of your peers seems troubled, be the friend they need. Working together makes each one of us stronger. That's synergy."

"She means symbiosis," the guy next to me muttered.

"Today," the teacher continued, "is all about problem-solving. Who can finish the saying for me? A problem shared is..."

"A problem halved," everyone answered in chorus.

Although she should have added a disclaimer. If I shared most of my problems with the people here, they'd turn into even bigger problems.

"Each of you take a card from the pile and pass it on. I want you to write down an issue that's bothering you—anonymously, of course—and we'll share ideas as a group and see if we can come up with a solution."

What a waste of time. For me, anyway. Perhaps the others might find it helpful. But all I could think of was that I'd be wasting eighty minutes, and I could have spent those eighty minutes doing something that actually mattered. Such as brainstorming with the team at Blackwood to work out how the hell we were going to find these damn paintings. *Emerald* and *The Shepherd* were ghosts. I'd been at Shadow Falls for almost two weeks, and although I'd made progress with the bugs and whatnot, none of the players were actually talking about the game. *That* was my problem.

I also had to watch my back as well as Vanessa's because I'd pissed off the Britneys. Only a fool would have missed the glares they gave me every time we passed in the hallways, and I liked to think I was no fool.

And then there was my latest issue. Asher. He'd walked me back to New Hall yesterday evening, and I couldn't get his final words out of my head. The ones he'd leaned in close and whispered right before I went inside.

"You want to know the real reason I covered for you with Deandra? Because I like you, Chem."

What was a girl supposed to say to that?

I liked him too—I just wasn't sure I was meant to, not in that way. Emmy was right—I'd be gone soon, and I'd already gotten in deep enough with Asher that I knew he'd be hurt when I left.

But I could hardly write any of those problems down on my piece of card, could I now?

Instead, when the time was almost up, I scribbled five words that bore a resemblance to the truth.

I feel like an imposter.

In a way, being assigned to this group was a blessing. These people weren't my tribe. It didn't matter what they thought of me.

"Feeling vulnerable in a new position is natural," one girl said. "People aspire to attend this school. I think it's natural for a person to feel that they don't deserve to be here. But remember—you got here on merit, and that means it's your home."

I hadn't come to Shadow Falls on merit, not by any stretch of the imagination, but what about my job at Blackwood? There'd been no interview. There'd been no bullshit test. Emmy had picked me based on my performance in a couple of awkward situations.

"We all make mistakes," another girl said. "What defines us is how we act afterwards."

I'd almost run after my fuck-up at the Grove, but I hadn't. Surely that counted for something?

"Everybody feels like an imposter at some time or another," a boy said. He'd played on stage with the woodwind ensemble on Monday, so presumably he knew what he was talking about. "Once you realise that, it's easier to build up your confidence."

What they said... It actually helped. Okay, so the cushion guy told me to listen to my cosmic influences, whatever those were, but everyone else helped. I wasn't expecting them to, but they did. Perhaps it wasn't such a waste of eighty minutes, after all.

But I still had bugs to plant.

After classes, I stuck to the deal I'd made last night with Asher and spent an hour studying with him, in the library this time since a bunch of his dorm buddies were lounging around in the communal living room at Linton Hall and I didn't fancy walking through the middle of them. Gossip was rife on campus. I tried to stay out of it, but I still heard the rumours, mainly via Vanessa.

*Chet Somerville got seen leaving Emily Morten's room, and before that the door was closed for at least five minutes. *shocked face.**

Janie Beardsley caught a ride home on Hunter Shaw's parents' private jet at the end of last term, and they were meant to be sworn enemies. Can you believe that?

Melody Raine found a pair of boxers stuffed down the back of a couch in one of the practice rooms, and Tim Stevens said they belonged to Mike Hamburg. Mike Hamburg. *He was meant to be dating Jenny Stewart, and* she *wore a purity ring. Gasp.*

Asher's apartment was on the second floor, and the fire escape was alarmed, unlike the one at the Grove. Asher knew that because one of his responsibilities as student liaison was to test the system once a month. Which meant I couldn't sneak in that way. Nor did I want to become the subject of school scuttlebutt myself, not when I was supposed to be keeping a low profile and definitely not when I had no idea what, if anything, was going on between me and Asher Martinez.

So we'd shared a table in the reference section, and even better, Ezra Rosenberg happened to walk past, which lent weight to my alibi for the Deandra incident. Asher seemed relaxed. Chilled. Less bothered about the test than I was, which was kind of surprising because now that he'd confided in me, I saw the true extent of his struggles to read and write. If a book came in electronic format, he had his phone read it to him, but words on paper? A whole other story. Typing was fine—he said spellcheck was his best friend—but give him a pen and he'd dither. And then there was his mind. It was sharper than he'd ever let on, and his memory was phenomenal.

I could easily have talked to Asher all night, but I still had work to do, so at half past six, I told him I needed some girl time and went to eat dinner with Vanessa. Afterwards, I planned to slink out and sneak into a staff office or two. I still had half of the rooms in that area left to bug, including Saul and Ezra Rosenberg's. Their offices were down a separate hallway, their own little enclave, and they both spent way too much time working in them.

Luckily, Vanessa assumed I was going to see Asher again.

"You're going out? Where? Wait—don't tell me, don't tell me... I still think he's a bum, but if he makes you happy, then I guess that makes him an okay bum."

"An okay bum? What do you call people you *don't* like?"

Vanessa giggled. "Go, go! Or you'll be late for your hook-up."

I didn't bother to correct her, not about the hook-up—or rather, the lack of one—or about her perception of Asher's laziness. I'd promised to keep his secrets, and I would. Plus it was better for her to think I was a wannabe slut than a wannabe spy.

Tonight, I planned to get into two more offices. We knew from Marshall's information that staff at the school were involved, but finding out who was tricky. I decided that on this occasion, I'd go for the pottery teacher because Marshall said he'd once been hired to move an expensive vase and I figured she might know a thing or two about that, plus Professor Eastman—the biology teacher—because I'd seen him hobnobbing with Saul Rosenberg on several occasions.

I didn't need to take much with me—just a pair of gloves, a set of lock picks, the bugs themselves, and a multitool. I'd gotten the process down to a fine art over the past two weeks, and I could install a bug in an electrical socket in under five minutes. At first, Nate had been on hand to help me, but I was confident doing them alone now. Ryder was listening in, but he didn't say much. The sound of a TV in the background suggested he was multitasking.

The pottery teacher's office looked more like a gift shop. Every surface was covered in trinkets, mostly pots and dishes but also paintings and beaded thingamajigs and bizarrely, several dozen pairs of chopsticks. I resisted the urge to poke around and focused on my goal instead. *Remove the front plate. Find the right wires. Clip the bug in. Screw everything back where it should be.*

Another one down. What was behind door number two?

A painfully tidy office, it turned out. Everything on Professor Eastman's desk was lined up precisely, perfectly parallel. Nothing was out of place. Even the potted plant on the windowsill had been pruned to within an inch of its life. I crouched behind the desk and started work on the socket, stifling a yawn as I tinkered. The late nights were catching up with me. Five more minutes, and I could go to bed.

At least, that was the plan.

I so, so nearly made it out of there. I'd attached the bug and screwed the front plate back on when the sound of footsteps in the hallway made my heart seize. *Go past, go past, go past.* The steps were soft but steady, no hesitation, and karma obviously had it in for me because they stopped right outside the door. The sound of scraping came from the lock, then I heard a quiet exclamation.

"Huh?"

The doorknob began to turn. Shit. All I could do was squash myself as far under the desk as I could get and pray whoever was out there didn't come right into the room.

No such luck.

My heart was thumping so loudly that I thought it would give me away, but the visitor didn't seem interested in the desk. Instead, he—and it was a "he" judging by the size of his feet—headed for the filing cabinets that lined the far wall. They were all locked. I'd checked. But that pesky inconvenience didn't stop the guy. Did he have a set of lock picks too? He definitely had a torch. Every so often, the beam bounced in my direction.

"What's happening?" Ryder asked. "Is everything

okay?"

A drawer opened and papers rustled. Then the footsteps came towards me.

There was nowhere I could go. Nothing I could do except smile and... What the...?

"Fancy seeing you here," I said.

I wasn't sure who was more surprised—me, Asher, or possibly Ryder.

"What the hell are you doing down there?" Asher hissed.

"Uh..."

"Tell him it was a prank," Ryder said. "A dare. One of the other girls dared you to break into the office."

Sweat beaded on the back of my neck as I scrambled to my feet. "Uh, a bunch of us were playing truth or dare, and guess what my dare was?"

"To hide under the desk in Professor Eastman's office?"

I went for sheepish. "I was meant to take a selfie sitting on his desk, but then I heard you coming."

"How did you get in here? Wasn't the door locked?"

Busted. "I thought it would be, but... Wait—what are *you* doing in here?" And what was that look in Asher's eyes? Shame? He glanced downwards, and I followed his gaze to the thin booklet in his hand. "Is that a test paper? Is that *Saturday's* test paper?"

Asher slumped into Professor Eastman's swivel chair, eyes cast down at the floor. Guilty as charged. *This* was his strategy for getting his high school diploma? To cheat? I wasn't sure whether to be sad or horrified or impressed.

"I'll never pass otherwise," he mumbled. "I can't even read the questions in the time allowed, let alone write the answers too."

"But what will you do in a year? After you graduate? You can't steal the answers to life."

"I'll get a job where I don't need to read papers all day. I want to work with cars, racing them or customising them, but I can't even get an interview at an auto shop without my diploma."

Plus if Asher graduated, he'd have his father's money to fall back on. What was I meant to do? Cheating was wrong, but I wasn't about to march into Ezra Rosenberg's office and tell tales. Not only would it draw attention to what I'd been doing, but the Rosenbergs were a bunch of dishonest bastards who deserved to get a dose of their own medicine anyway.

"Is there anything I can do to persuade you not to report this?" Asher asked.

Oh, for fuck's sake. "Now you're offering to bribe me?"

My morals might have been questionable, but I took offence at that.

Asher sucked in a breath. "Uh, no?"

Ryder chuckled in my ear. "This was *not* how I saw tonight going."

I needed a timeout to ask for advice, but unfortunately, that wasn't an option. I'd have to handle this by myself. In truth, I was the last person who should be giving Asher a lecture on ethics—how could I when Rune helped me to cheat my ass off in every class?—but turning a blind eye didn't feel right either.

"You have to study, Shortcut."

"I did study this evening."

"I mean more than once. Every day."

Asher put his head in his hands, but then he peeped

out from between his fingers. It was oddly cute. "With you?"

"With me." At least for the next week. "And maybe with Vanessa too."

If I could convince him to confide in her as well, perhaps she'd change her stance on him being a bum and help. We might have got off to a rocky start, but now that she'd thawed out, I saw she had a good heart.

"Okay." He held out his little finger. "Pinky swear."

What age was Asher? Sometimes he acted like a kid, and sometimes he seemed old beyond his years. Jaded. Weary, even. If he'd repeated a year of junior high and then sat out a year of high school, he had to be at least nineteen.

I sighed and linked my pinky with his. "Don't make me regret this. What do you do, photograph the test papers?"

He nodded.

"Hurry up. I'll hold the torch. The flashlight."

"You're my kind of girl, Chem. Gutsy and morally grey."

"Don't forget to take your selfie," Ryder reminded me.

"Wait a second." I sat on the desk and snapped a photo of myself, making a mental note to destroy the evidence later. "Okay, now hurry up."

CHAPTER 29 - SKY

"SKY, CAN I borrow your highlighter?" Vanessa asked.

"Borrow anything of mine you want. What are roommates for?"

I'd spent the past three days settling into the new normal. Since I caught Asher on Wednesday night, he'd kept his word and studied with me and Vanessa before dinner each day, although he hadn't let Vanessa in on his secret. I'd covered for him a little. Read the odd sentence out loud, leaned over and corrected a word or two when she wasn't looking, that sort of thing. Yes, he'd cheated his way through the biology test yesterday, but so had I, just in a different way. Asher was trying.

He was easy to get along with too. The three of us had taken to studying in his apartment. I figured that with Vanessa there, the rumours wouldn't start to fly, although one of Asher's dorm buddies had made a crack about a threesome. Asher glared at him until he held his hands up, apologised, and backed away.

Those evenings were oddly pleasant. They made me realise what my teenage years should have been like if my father hadn't been an abusive arsehole and I hadn't been forced onto the streets to survive. But what was the point in dwelling on the past? I couldn't change it. And now Emmy had given me a second chance. I was getting paid to glue jelly beans onto canvas and run around a sports field and learn about chemistry. Perhaps even more than one kind of chemistry.

If only I'd known that this was the calm before the storm.

The wind began whipping up the next day. Labor Day. Also known as a day off to celebrate work. How ironic. Half of my fellow students had gone to the mall to take advantage of the discounts, and the other half were lying around on the lawn, making the most of the bumper picnic the catering staff had prepared. At that point, the sun was still shining.

And we were still studying. The workload was getting heavier, and we had another test on Thursday. Chemistry this time. I'd spent the afternoon studying alcohol, but the boring kind you couldn't drink. Vanessa was making little notecards for us all, hence needing the highlighter, but Asher had already looked alarmed when she waved one in his face and asked him what he thought. Yes, he'd praised her efforts, but I knew he wouldn't use them. And after dinner, when he said he needed a few hours to himself, I knew exactly what he planned to do.

"No," I whispered, and Vanessa gave me a curious look.

"I need to."

"Need to what?" Vanessa asked.

I was gonna go to hell for lying. "Asher sometimes has a sneaky beer in the evenings. He's meant to be quitting." I swivelled to face him, arms folded. "Aren't you?"

"I'm cutting down."

Vanessa's hesitant smile was at odds with Asher's glower. "You have beer here?"

"Sure, you want one?"

"No!" I said. "No beer for either of you."

"Aw, Sky, don't be such a stick-in-the-mud. I really need a beer today."

"Why? What happened?"

Vanessa quickly back-pedalled. "Nothing. Forget I said a word."

Asher tried too. "Vanessa, just tell us."

"Honestly, it's no big deal. Deandra elbowed me in the ribs, that's all. It might even have been an accident."

An accident. Right. "Did she say anything?"

"Not a word. But I think maybe... Maybe it was a reminder that she hasn't forgotten about the toilet incident. *Was* that you? She told people it was, but then Tiffany said Deandra didn't see the person's face, just said that they were really strong, so I guess it could've been a guy."

I shrugged. "It's a mystery."

Beside her, Asher rolled his eyes, and I kicked him under the table. We'd finish discussing this later.

"Later" turned out to be just after ten. Past curfew, and definitely way too late for an argument over the wisdom of breaking into Dr. Merritt's office. I caught Asher creeping up to the side door of the main building.

"Boo."

"Fuck!" He clapped a hand over his chest. "You scared the shit out of me."

"You should be more aware of your surroundings."

Gah. Now I sounded like Rafael.

"Hey, it's not as if I do this for a living."

No, that was me.

"You'd be terrible at it."

Emmy was on duty tonight, and she agreed with me. "Bloody hopeless."

"Agreed," Asher conceded. "But if you've come to stop me, then don't bother."

"I haven't come to stop you from pilfering another bloody test paper. I've come to stop you from getting caught."

Asher's expression softened, and he brushed a stray lock of hair away from my face. That one touch made my skin tingle all over.

"That's the sweetest thing anyone's ever done for me. But I'll be fine."

Maybe, maybe not. I didn't like taking chances. And although I'd never admit it, I wanted that chemistry paper too. It was the one subject Rune couldn't help me with in real time, and half of Vanessa's notecards appeared to be written in Swahili.

"Dr. Merritt's office is at the end of a hallway. You need a lookout."

Asher tilted his head to one side. "How do you know that?"

Oops. "Mr. Rosenberg introduced us on my interview day. Get a move on—we can't stand out here all night."

I didn't have to tell him twice. He swiped his pass card, and a quiet *beep* let us know the door was open. Mack had already investigated the locking system, and it was basic. Each entry and exit was recorded as an event, but user names weren't registered. And the internal doors still used old-fashioned keys, the staff offices included. What else would we expect from a gang of thieves whose primary method of communication was the US Postal Service?

Asher caught my hand in his as we stole through the hallways. Enough lights were on that we didn't trip, and we both knew the way in any case. *Left, right, left, left, right.* It didn't take long for us to reach the door we needed, and Asher produced a slim leather wallet from his back pocket. Lock picks. Nice.

When he saw me looking, that brilliant smile came back. "Told you I was good with my hands."

Just for a second, the twinkle in his eye turned to something altogether more intense, and I wondered what else those hands could do. Then I gave myself a mental slap. *Wrong time, wrong place, Sky.*

A quiet *click*, and the door swung open. Asher had managed that even faster than I would have. Nobody would ever beat Ravi, but nonetheless, I was impressed.

Although I was playing lookout, I needed a few seconds inside. Why? Because I had an ulterior motive. I hadn't yet managed to bug Dr. Merritt's office, so I figured I'd kill two birds with one stone. Using a mains-powered widget was out of the question, but Nate had supplied me with smaller ones too, tiny dots that I could attach anywhere. The batteries would only last a couple of weeks, but if this job took any longer than that, we'd have bigger problems than a lack of power. The number of staff Blackwood had committed to the operation wasn't sustainable indefinitely.

While Asher headed to the filing cabinet, I took a quick look around, used a fingernail to activate the bug via its tiny switch, peeled the backing off the adhesive pad, and stuck the thing under the desk.

"I'll wait at the end of the corridor," I whispered.

"Five minutes."

It turned out we only had two.

Footsteps sounded, the distinctive clip of leather-soled Oxfords on wood. I waited a moment, listening for the direction. Shit! Someone was heading towards us, a man, and one who belonged there. No hesitation in his steps. I scooted back to Asher.

"We have to go."

"I need another minute."

"We don't have another minute. Somebody's coming *right now*."

"Just two more pages."

"Sky, get out," Emmy ordered.

But I couldn't. I couldn't leave Asher.

"Hurry up!"

Time seemed to slow, and every tick of the clock squeezed a metal band around my chest tighter, tighter, tighter as Asher stuffed the test paper back into the filing cabinet and eased the drawer shut. We made it out of the office and got the door closed, but it was too late. Whoever was coming, they were right there. Five more steps and they'd walk around the corner.

My brain went into overdrive. We needed an excuse. An excuse for being where we shouldn't have been, doing things we shouldn't have been doing. Hmm... Things we shouldn't have been doing... It was worth a shot. Truth be told, we didn't have much choice.

"Kiss me," I hissed.

"What?" Asher's eyes saucered.

I didn't bother to explain, just flung an arm around his neck and stood on tiptoes. A lightbulb pinged on as he finally understood, and the scoundrel actually had the presence of mind to squeeze my ass. He'd pay for that later. But for now, his gaze met mine, then his lips, and as Ezra Rosenberg appeared, Asher's tongue joined the party. I might have sighed if I hadn't been holding my breath.

"What's going on here?"

The overhead light flickered on, and I blinked a few times, but otherwise my body was frozen. Asher and I both slowly turned our heads, but he didn't let go of me. If anything, the arm around my waist tightened. I didn't have to fake my trepidation. Emmy started laughing, the bitch.

"What are you doing in here?" Ezra asked.

"What does it look like?" Asher countered.

"This area is off limits, and so are the other students. We spoke about this. And you, Sky... I'm disappointed. This isn't how we behave at Shadow Falls Academy."

"Sorry," I mumbled, relief flooding through me that he seemed to have bought our act.

"Go back to your rooms, both of you. We'll deal with this in the morning."

CHAPTER 30 - ALARIC

"IS THIS WHAT it's like to be a parent?" Beth asked Alaric. "Feeling sick while you wait to get called into the principal's office?"

An admin assistant had left them waiting on two hard wooden chairs in an anteroom. Neither of them had seen Sky yet, but she'd explained what happened over the phone. Give the kid points for quick thinking.

"Guess I've been lucky so far. Rune never gets into trouble. The one time I got called into the headmistress's office, she spent half an hour talking to me about the benefits of their advanced math program over coffee and then ran her foot up my leg."

Beth spluttered out a laugh. "And what did you do?"

"Pretended I didn't notice and moved my chair back."

"Do you think it was an accident?"

Absolutely not. The woman had kicked her shoe off, and her toes had practically been in his crotch.

"Rune said Mrs. Penlington never normally wears perfume, lipstick, and mascara all on the same day."

"Gosh. I bet that made the next parents' evening awkward."

"For Mrs. Penlington, not me. I took Ravi along and introduced him as my fiancé. She was speechless for a good twenty seconds. Of course, at that point I didn't think I was actually going to get married, so explaining your presence in my life might be interesting."

"Perhaps she'll be speechless for thirty seconds this time?"

Alaric loved that about Beth. The way she took all the little difficulties in her stride. The big ones too. For the first few weeks after the Devane episode, she'd insisted on sleeping with a light on, but she could cope with the dark now. Her ankle was fully healed, and last week, she'd got behind the wheel of a car again. They'd only driven around the Riverley estate, but it was progress. Plus she'd been surprisingly understanding when she found out Alaric really did have a fling with Ravi.

He hadn't asked Beth to marry him yet, but he would. Soon.

In one week, four days, and ten hours.

He was tempted to lean over and kiss her, but he heard voices outside the door, and one of them belonged to Ezra Rosenberg. The man had a way of sounding both authoritative and whiny at the same time.

Maybe Alaric *should* have gone for an inappropriate smooch. Like father, like daughter.

"Mr. and Mrs. Milburn." Rosenberg shook both of their hands. "Perhaps you'd like to take a seat in my office? Thank you for coming at such short notice."

"What else would we do? You said there was a problem with our daughter?"

"Coffee? Tea?"

"I don't need a drink; I need an explanation."

"Yes, yes, I understand. There was a small incident involving Sky last night, and while it was relatively minor, I believe in nipping these things in the bud before they escalate. Tell me, has Sky shown much interest in boys before?"

Beth did a great job of looking shocked. "Boys? No, never. What happened?"

"I came across your daughter with a boy in the staff area. They were..." Rosenberg cleared his throat. "They were kissing."

"I see," Alaric said, taking the opportunity to slip a bug under the desk while Rosenberg fidgeted with his handkerchief. The guy was so uncomfortable, it was amusing.

"I spoke to Sky this morning, and she told me it was she who'd instigated the kiss. It can't be allowed to happen again."

"We'll talk to her."

Tell her not to get caught next time.

"I'm afraid it's not quite as simple as that. The boy involved also claimed he was the instigator, and I'm inclined to believe him. I'm afraid..." Rosenberg inhaled, held the breath for a beat, then slowly let it out. "I'm afraid the boy is my nephew. We've had a few problems with him, and I can only apologise for him corrupting your daughter. Here at Shadow Falls, we take discipline very seriously, and honesty is one of our core values."

Alaric almost laughed out loud. Honour among thieves, right?

"I appreciate your candour."

"Last night, I sent them to their respective rooms, but we need to take steps to avoid a repeat of the issue."

"They're teenagers, Mr. Rosenberg. Telling them not to do something usually has the opposite effect."

A lesson Alaric had learned first-hand. When his parents banned him from bringing girls home, he'd lost his virginity in the back of a diplomatic limousine.

"We'll put measures in place. Additional monitoring to keep them apart out of hours, that sort of thing."

Additional monitoring? This might be a problem.

"Is that really necessary?"

"Where my nephew is involved? I'm afraid so."

"I'll have a talk with Sky," Beth said. "She never normally behaves like this. I think the move's unsettled her. Having to leave her previous school and her friends with so little notice wasn't easy, but the promotion was an opportunity Alan couldn't afford to pass up."

"We've had many students in the same situation. I'm sure you're right and this is just a temporary blip. Her teachers report she's getting excellent grades, plus she excels in sports. And her mixed media portrait of a young President Clinton was something to behold."

Bill Clinton? The jelly bean thing? Sky said that was Tom Cruise.

"Good to hear."

"We don't want to disrupt her schooling, but I wanted you to be aware that she shares some classes with my nephew. Scheduling difficulties mean it won't be easy for her to change groups, but if you want us to look at alternate solutions…"

"They'll be fine. How much trouble can they get up to with a teacher in the room?"

"I hoped you'd say that. Thank you for your understanding."

"We've all got Sky's best interests at heart."

And speaking of Sky, Alaric needed to find her and give her the latest piece of news.

"How'd it go?" Sky asked.

Alaric embraced her in a slightly awkward one-armed hug and slipped a new comms system into her pocket. Nate had made this one to look like a pair of silver earrings and a matching watch. And Beth had brought a new batch of bugs in her purse, each one individually wrapped in gold foil and nestled in what looked like a box of expensive chocolates. Nate had even included a bunch of real candies for effect.

"New boyfriend?"

"New cover story."

Was that a hint of defensiveness in Sky's tone? Cute.

"Sure," Alaric said agreeably. "Whatever you say."

"It's true!" Then she looked away. "Sorry I fucked up again."

"Oh, but you didn't. The bug you planted last night picked up another clue. At least, we hope so. This morning, somebody in that office mentioned *The Count of San Trior.*"

"It's a painting," Beth filled in. "Quite a famous one, and it's been missing for three decades. It was stolen from the Malermo Gallery in Turin."

"Was it Dr. Merritt speaking? What did he say?"

"Dr. Merritt's your chemistry teacher, right? Because we don't have a transmission of your classes with him. Can you do a basic recording on your phone and email it afterwards? Then we can compare voiceprints."

"Not until tomorrow. I don't have chemistry today. But Asher records all the classes—I could ask him for one of the files. I'll tell him I need to fill in some gaps in my notes."

"That's not a good idea at the moment."

"What? Why?" Sky sagged, and her too-short tie swung forward. "Rosenberg?"

"He's putting extra monitoring in place to keep you two apart."

"Extra monitoring? What the hell is that supposed to mean?"

"He didn't elaborate, and I didn't feel it was the right moment to ask. He considered moving you to different classes, but we all agreed things can stay as they are. Apparently you both took the blame?"

"We did? Why? It was my fault."

"Asher was trying to protect you." And if he'd done that, he probably wasn't a bad sort. "Beth and I are meant to be warning you off him."

"And are you?"

"As your father, I'm going to give you this..." Alaric slid a condom into her pocket alongside the spare comms set. "And tell you to be careful. If you have any more questions, ask your mother."

Beth elbowed Alaric in the side, her cheeks reddening nicely. He'd pay for that later, but you know what? He didn't even care. In the last few weeks, he'd discovered that under her oh-so-English upper-class exterior, Beth hid a filthy side most people would never even guess at. If she wanted to spank him, he'd willingly bend over.

Thankfully, Sky changed the subject. "Who else was

in Dr. Merritt's office? Or was he talking on the phone?"

"We believe it was Saul Rosenberg."

"Did they say anything more?"

"Not much. The unsub—unknown subject—said the people with *The Count of San Trior* had been in touch, and Saul said they'd talk about it at the meeting."

"What meeting?"

"That's a question we don't yet know the answer to."

"Is Saul the Master?"

"We don't know that either."

Sky harrumphed, frustrated, but at least things were moving in the right direction. They had leads now. It was just a question of slowly unravelling them. Alaric's current hypothesis did indeed have Saul as the Master, a position he might well have inherited from his father. The timeline fit. Sandor Rosenberg would have needed an heir, and who better than one of his sons?

"So what do I do now?" Sky asked.

"Right now? I believe you solve quadratic equations and then go running."

"Haha, very funny."

"Just carry on exactly as you've been doing. Plant bugs when you can, but watch out for extra eyes. We're getting closer. I can feel it."

"Are you staying nearby?"

"For tonight. Tomorrow, I need to travel to Ohio with Emmy to follow up a lead on another case, but call if you need me. You'll be okay?"

"I don't have a lot of choice, do I?"

He gave her another dad-hug. "Thank you for doing

this."

"Hey, somebody's paying me."

"You know what I mean."

Beth handed over her goodies. "Thank you from me too."

"Figure I still owe you for nicking your car."

As Alaric walked back to his vehicle with Beth, he felt eyes following. Ezra Rosenberg? He knelt to retie a shoelace that wasn't undone and cut his eyes sideways. A man stood watching him from the shade of an old oak tree, half-hidden in the shadows. An inch or two shorter than Alaric, arms loose by his sides, wearing a school uniform. He glanced back at Sky for a second, and in profile, Alaric recognised him as Asher Martinez. Olive skin, tousled dark-blond hair. He'd inherited his father's skin tone and his mother's hair colour. Emmy had done a background check, of course, and they'd worked out where the third Rosenberg sibling had ended up. Asher's life was one of tragedy. Losing not one parent but two would screw with anybody's mind. How far gone was he? Research showed he'd veered off the rails and hung with the wrong crowd in San Diego, but he'd escaped charges thanks to some skilful negotiating by his father. After the final incident, he'd dropped off the radar for a year. Poof. Gone. No record of employment, he hadn't paid any taxes, and he hadn't gone to school. Then he'd shown up here for the last term of his junior year. Not the behaviour of your average nineteen-year-old.

When Alaric stood, he raised a hand in greeting so Asher would know he'd been spotted. A smile curled at Alaric's lips when Asher tentatively waved back. Not a complete asshole, then. Alaric only hoped Sky knew what she was doing.

The next morning, Alaric paused with one hand on his fly. He should have been zipping it up and buckling his belt, but all he wanted to do was shuck his pants and climb back into bed with Beth. It was too early for a road trip with Emmy, let alone a seven-hour drive to fucking Ohio, and he also felt like an asshole for lying to the love of his life about the purpose of the trip. He'd stuck to the story he'd told Sky, but there was no lead. There wasn't even a case.

It would be okay, he kept telling himself. If things worked out the way he hoped, Beth would forgive him, and if they didn't work out... Well, Emmy knew how to keep her mouth shut.

CHAPTER 31 - SKY

WHY DID THINGS always have to fall apart? Every time a chink of light shone onto my life, some asshole had to go and flip the switch. Again and again it had happened, ever since I was a little girl. When I finally got taken away from my dad and put into foster care, my first foster sister had hated me. I got moved from that place and met Lenny, only for us to be split up. My third foster mom said I had bad juju, but I'm pretty sure she was into voodoo. I wasn't with her for long. She accidentally burned her flat to ashes when one of her spells went wrong.

That streak of luck had followed me across the Atlantic, it appeared. I'd begun to enjoy my life, and then the events at the Grove had brought it crashing down around my ears. I'd picked up the pieces as best I could, only for Rafael, the guy I'd come to trust, to pull away from me completely. He'd ghosted me. Every time I tried to call him, I got voicemail.

And I'd met Asher and Vanessa, only for fate or karma or whatever to step in once more. I'd been banned from talking to Asher outside of class, and now Vanessa was in tears. Again. It was only nine thirty a.m., and I'd found her like that when I came back to our room after a biology lesson in which Asher and I were made to sit at opposite ends of the lab. Halfway through class, someone passed me a note from him. Ezra had confiscated his phone.

"What did she do?" I asked.

It had to be Deandra again, right? Vanessa had just had a music lesson with the bitch.

She pointed at her desk, and I saw the mangled remains of her glasses sitting on her composition book. She didn't wear them all the time, but she needed them for close-up work. One of the lenses was mostly intact, but the other was covered in a spiderweb of cracks and the arms were twisted.

"She knocked them off my desk and stepped on them."

"Deandra?"

Vanessa nodded, and a tear rolled down her cheek and plopped from her chin.

"Let me guess—another accident?"

"That's what she said."

Was the girl dense? Was getting her hair washed in eau de toilet once not enough? Good grief. What was it my parkour teacher used to tell me every time an idiot got in our way?

"You can't fix stupid, even with zip ties and duct tape," I muttered.

"You can't fix it, but you can knock it out with ketamine," said the voice in my ear. Yup, Sofia was back on duty. She seemed slightly calmer today. Perhaps Emmy hadn't been kidding about the meds?

"I just want her to leave me alone. Even the others looked shocked by what she did. Carlie apologised before she ran out after her."

Had I contributed to the problem? I'd only been trying to help, but what if I'd pushed Deandra over the edge? A cornered dog always fought the hardest.

"I'm so sorry." I seemed to be apologising a lot too lately, mostly on other people's behalf. "Can you get new glasses? We could go to the mall on Sunday."

"Maybe. I don't have the money, but I can call my mom."

"I can pay."

"That's not fair."

But it was right. "I'm paying."

"Don't wait until the weekend," Sofia told me. "Ryder's on his way. Meet him at the gates and give him what's left of the glasses, and Bradley can get another pair for you by this evening."

I couldn't answer, but it didn't matter because Sofia wasn't asking a question. She was telling me how it was going to be. For once, I didn't mind her pushiness. Vanessa needed glasses, and perhaps the sweetest revenge on Deandra would be for Vanessa to turn up with a new pair first thing tomorrow morning.

"Can you manage for today?" I asked Vanessa.

"I don't have much choice. We've got chemistry next—will you help me if I can't see the textbook?"

"Sure. I'll meet you in the chemistry lab, okay?"

"Ooh, the chemistry lab," Sofia said. "I love chemistry labs. Here's what we're going to do..."

That evening, I found out what Ezra Rosenberg meant when he said they'd be putting extra monitoring in place. Ryder texted to say he had Vanessa's new glasses plus a spare phone for Asher, but when I put on a pair of shoes to go and meet him, I only made it halfway across the living room before a voice stopped me.

"Where are you going?"

I turned to see Miss Brooks sitting on the couch by the fireplace, a novel splayed out across one thigh. She taught cello and violin, so I hadn't had much interaction with her, but I knew her by reputation. Rumour said she'd been a dominatrix in a previous life.

"For a walk."

"I don't think that's a good idea."

She stared at me. I stared at her. I knew I wasn't going to win this one, so I shrugged and walked back upstairs. Then I opened the window and shinned down the sturdy tree outside. Rafael had taught me that head-on confrontation wasn't always the best policy. Sometimes, a little out-of-the-box thinking was required.

The wind whipped through the trees and made their branches twist and bend as I jogged down the driveway. I didn't mind the weather. I'd worn a dark tracksuit with a hood, and the dancing shadows helped me to blend in with the scenery. Ryder too. If I hadn't known exactly where he'd be waiting, I'd never have found him. A hand flashed out from the undergrowth, I got a quick smile and a wave, and then he melted away into the darkness. I'd heard he was former special forces, and it showed.

But I'd learned a few tricks myself, and I stuck to the treeline, keeping my footsteps quiet out of habit even though there was nobody to hear them.

Or was there?

I was halfway up the driveway when I saw a silhouette heading towards me. Ah, shit. Had I been spotted? Or did other students make unauthorised

pickups from their Man Friday late at night too? I
ducked among the trees to wait for the interloper to
pass, only to do a double take when I realised who it
was.

"Asher?"

"Sky? Where are you?"

I quickly stepped out of the bushes and pulled him
closer, keeping us both out of sight.

"What are you doing here?"

"I wanted to talk to you, but when I got close to
New Hall, I saw you climb down a tree and vanish in
this direction. What are you? A ghost?"

"You got out? Don't you have a babysitter?"

"Yeah, but it's Dr. Pearson. He's got bowel
problems. He went to take a dump, which means I've
got at least twenty minutes."

"Here, take this." I pressed the phone into his hand.
"It should be charged."

"A phone? Where did you get it?"

"My parents live nearby. Did you hear Deandra
broke Vanessa's glasses this morning? I wanted to get
her a spare pair as a surprise, and I asked for a phone
at the same time."

"You're too damn sweet, Sky Milburn."

Malone. My name was Sky Malone, and I wished I
could tell him. Mind you, he usually called me Chem
Girl, so I figured I should celebrate the small wins.

"I'm sorry about last night."

"Why are you sorry? I'm the one who should've
been faster."

"Because I caused even more problems. Now they
think we need chaperones."

Asher ran his fingertips down my arm, leaving a

trail of fire in their wake. When his hand reached mine, he twined our fingers together.

"Are they wrong?"

My heart went from tortoise to hare in half a second. What was he saying? Not... Not... I waited for the familiar tightness to grip my chest, for the air to stick in my lungs. But the panic didn't come. And when I realised I was okay, I felt more confusion than relief.

"What did your parents say?" he asked. "I saw them here yesterday."

"About us getting caught together? They're fine with it."

"They are? I thought the Rosenbergs were gonna shit bricks. I got the whole 'how dare you risk the reputation of this school?' lecture from Ezra, then Saul showed up, and he only stopped yelling when Grandma appeared and banged her cane on the floor. Ezra was ready to send me to public school until she stepped in. If he'd caught me with the test paper, I'd probably be on a plane back to San Diego right now."

"I'm glad you're not."

"Me too."

Asher watched me in the moonlight. What was he thinking? Trying to decide whether I was worth the trouble?

"Do you need to get back?" I asked.

"Yeah, I do."

Then he kissed me. And it wasn't a rabid, sloppy disaster like fourteen-year-old me's first mistake with a boy, nor the nasty show of dominance I'd got from Brock Keaton. It definitely wasn't a chaste peck on the cheek either. No, it was more like a continuation of our first fumbled attempt in the hallway outside Dr.

Merrit's office, except this time Asher's tongue got farther and my toes curled in my trainers.

Wow. I never knew it could be like that.

"Neither did I," he whispered.

Oops. Had I said that out loud? Thank goodness I'd left my comms unit charging or it would have been even more awkward.

"How long do you have left?" I could do that all over again.

He checked his watch. "I really have to go. I wish I could stay."

"I'll call you, Shortcut."

"Don't fall out of your tree, Chem."

"I won't."

But I did have trouble climbing it. The strength had gone from my legs, and I had to haul myself up with arms and willpower. Asher had kissed me. And I'd survived to tell the tale. Wow. I slithered through the window and crawled over to my bed.

"Asher?" Vanessa asked from the other side of the room.

"Who else?" I pulled her glasses out of my pocket. "Here, I got you a present. Happy Christmas."

"Huh?"

I was too tired to explain any further. No, not tired. Dazed. "Dazed" was the right word. I crawled under the covers and closed my eyes.

CHAPTER 32 - SKY

"WHAT'S THAT SMELL?" Vanessa whispered.

"I have no idea," I lied, careful to keep my hands on the desk where everyone could see them.

I knew precisely what the smell was. Carbon disulphide, but to most people it smelled like a really bad fart. Childish, perhaps, but I'd tried scaring Deandra, and I'd tried having a quiet word in private, and neither of them had worked. So I figured I might as well try public embarrassment. Sofia had told me exactly what to do.

Yesterday in chemistry class, I'd pilfered a glass bottle of carbon disulphide and snuck it back to my room. According to Sofia, it was a boring but stinky organic solvent. Then, during today's morning break, I'd tipped the ginseng capsules Bradley had packed for me out of their little brown plastic pill bottle, paid a visit to the bathroom, and poured an ounce or two of the liquid in. Timing was key, Sofia said. I had twenty minutes. So I'd hurried to today's chemistry class early and taped the bottle under Deandra's lab bench, ditched my gloves, then taken my own place near the front. Now, ten minutes in, the solvent had begun eating through the polycarbonate bottle and drip-drip-dripping onto the floor underneath.

And everyone was wrinkling their noses, even Dr.

Merritt, the thieving bastard.

The stench grew stronger, and nobody was looking at the whiteboard anymore. Yeuch, that stuff really did reek. The only thing worse was Lenny the night after a curry.

Follow your noses, people. Come on, you can do it.

"Why is everyone looking at me?" Deandra shrieked.

Nobody answered, but nobody looked away either. How strong was the smell at the back? Tiffany was gagging, and Meaghan had gone a peculiar shade of green.

"Stop staring!" Deandra ordered, standing up to emphasise her point.

The problem was, I'd sprinkled a little dry tempera paint on her stool, a fetching shade of brown that didn't show up against the dark wood. And she'd tied a non-regulation cream cardigan around her waist, the same way as she always did. Carlie saw the skid mark first, and her eyes bugged out of her head.

"Uh, Dea?" Carlie pointed one trembling finger.

"What? *What?*"

Deandra spun around, and everyone saw it. Whispers turned to laughter, and not even kidding, Deandra went scarlet as she twisted to see what everyone was looking at.

"That isn't... I didn't..."

"Sure, we believe you," Asher said. He was sitting at the back with a ridiculous grin on his face. I couldn't meet his eyes. I didn't dare. Not just because I'd burst into a fit of giggles, but because we'd freaking kissed last night and I hadn't got the faintest clue what to do about it. He'd texted me earlier to say good morning, and I'd done the same back. But now? Muggins here was clueless. I had no idea of flirting etiquette because I'd never had to do it before. Smiling at assholes in the club when they smacked my ass didn't count. *Was* this even flirting? I wasn't sure.

Deandra ran out of the classroom like her swanky designer heels were on fire, and Dr. Merritt gaped after her. Was the Wicked Witch dead yet? Perhaps not, but I sure hoped she was flailing.

My phone buzzed, and I snuck a peek under the table. Asher had sent me a row of clapping emojis. I sent back a face with a finger to its lips.

Asher: Chemistry's more fun than I thought.

Me: Sometimes listening in class pays off.

Asher: Maybe, but I keep getting distracted by the view.

What view? I focused on a framed diagram of an ethanol molecule hanging beside Dr. Merritt, and the reflection in the glass showed Asher watching me.

Me: Pervert.

Asher: Guilty as charged.

It turned out that talking to Asher by text wasn't as difficult as I'd thought. He was happy to joke around, and the little messages he sent me throughout the day made me smile. But I still missed the real thing. That was one big drawback to school—people telling me what to do all the time. Where to go and how to act. Yes, I got ordered around at Blackwood, but it was different. Their rules had a point to them, and they were also negotiable. I liked to think of them more as guidelines.

So what did I do? I did what I always did, of course. Looked for a way to break Shadow Falls Academy's stupid damn rules.

I could get out of my room, but Dr. Pearson had apparently taken up residence on the sofa at Linton Hall. Apparently he'd even fallen asleep there last night. I eyed up the outside of the dorm during my afternoon cross-country session. Unfortunately, Asher's room didn't have a handy tree outside, but it did have a wall nearby. About six feet high and six feet from the building, presumably built to stop busybodies from looking into the living room because Dr. Pearson needed his privacy, didn't he? Hmm...

Me: Leave your window open tonight. And your light on.

Asher: Why? What are you planning?

Me: Just do it.

Asher: Yes, ma'am.

After dinner, I left Vanessa in our room sketching the outline of a castle—with dragons, because every castle needed dragons—and climbed down my new favourite tree. Vanessa knew where I was going, but she wouldn't say anything. She'd even become friends with Asher, sort of—they had a music class together this term, and he actually worked in that, so she'd upgraded his status to "half-bum."

Nobody else was around as I skirted the back lawn and jogged towards Linton Hall. As I got closer, I built up speed, ran up the wall, balanced on the top for a split second, tipped my weight forward, and leapt. It wasn't the most elegant of manoeuvres, but I made it through the window and used a forward roll to scrub off the rest of my momentum.

"Holy fuck. Are you okay?" Asher asked, offering me a hand.

"Fine, perfectly fine."

"Are you *insane*?"

"That's a definite possibility."

"Where the hell did you learn to do that?"

"In London. I got bored and joined a parkour club. We met every Monday and Saturday to practise."

"Bet that takes some skill."

"It's about fifty percent skill and fifty percent balls, that's what my instructor always said. Except I don't have any balls, so he figured I was just crazy."

"I can agree with that assessment." He shook his head, still incredulous. "Wow. So, what do you want to do? I thought maybe we'd study, but you haven't brought any books."

"I..." There was the flaw in my plan. I hadn't entirely thought this through. "I just wanted to see you. To talk to you. To hang out, I guess. Being forced apart sucks."

"To hang out..." He sighed. "Have you eaten dinner?"

I nodded. "With Vanessa."

"Saw she got the new glasses."

"You both had a music class earlier, didn't you?"

"Yeah. We're working together at the moment— she's singing, and I'm playing the piano."

"For credit?"

"Yeah. Mrs. Keele's latest project. We have to compose a song based on either a happy or a sad event in our lives. It's fuckin' miserable."

"Whose life are you basing it on? Yours or hers?"

"Hers. No way am I talking about mine. Or even singing about it. Want a beer?"

When I hesitated, he said, "I'm not trying to get you drunk or anything. I'm not that kind of guy."

"What kind of guy are you?"

Might as well get that question out of the way at the beginning. Asher wouldn't force himself on me the way Brock had, of that I was sure, but yesterday's kiss had left me worried. Yes, it had been weirdly pleasant, and yes, I liked spending time with Asher, but I didn't want to spend time with him naked.

"The kind of guy who surprised himself last night."

I trailed Asher into his tiny kitchen. He wasn't the tidiest of people, but his apartment wasn't dirty. He just didn't put things away. There was a box of cereal on the counter, papers all over the desk-slash-dining table, a sweater slung over the back of the couch... The place had a lived-in feel about it. I didn't mind that.

"Surprised yourself in what way?"

"By kissing you. Cards on the table, Sky. I have no desire to sleep my way through the entire senior year, no matter what my uncles think. I don't have a desire to sleep with *any* girls in the senior year. Or the school. Or anywhere else."

Now I was even more confused. "So you're...gay?"

"No, I'm not gay."

"I don't get it."

"I just don't like sex. And when every other girl in this school says they want to hang out, that's what they expect."

"You don't like sex?" A wave of relief crashed over me. Asher was my fucking soulmate. But unfortunately, that relief made itself known in the form of a high-pitched giggle, and I saw Asher's eyes shutter.

"No! I didn't mean it that way. It's not funny, not at all."

"I've never told anyone that before. I thought you were different."

How could things have gone from awesome to awful so fast? Now Asher was hurt, and I... I was so far off balance that I kind of wished I'd missed the damn window.

"I *am* different."

Uh-oh. Asher's folded arms weren't a good sign. I panicked. I didn't want to lose his friendship, and I reacted without thinking things through.

"You want my cards on the table too? Okay, fine. I lost my virginity to a rapist when I was fifteen. The thought of sex makes me want to puke, and I really do just want to hang out."

I'd never forget the look of absolute horror on his face. The widening of his eyes. The way his jaw dropped. The bob of his Adam's apple as he swallowed. But I blathered on regardless.

"You're the first person I've kissed since then. And it was nicer than I expected. Usually, I have a panic attack if a man touches me funny, but I didn't, and I was pretty happy when I managed to stay standing. You know, I thought of becoming a nun, but they wear those ugly dresses and pray all day, and—"

"Sky, shut up."

"Maybe I should leave."

"No, don't leave." He scraped a hand through his hair. "Fuck. I don't know whether to hug you or swear I'll never touch you again."

"How about you just get me that beer?"

"A beer? Right, a beer."

Asher opened a cupboard, gave his head a confused shake, then opened the refrigerator. Now *he* was off balance, and I'd never meant for him to end up that way.

"Hey, it's okay."

"Okay? *Okay?* No, Sky, it's not okay. Who was it? A boyfriend? A stranger?"

"Just some guy I met in a club. Please don't get stressed."

"Fuck. Fuck!"

He stopped rummaging and leaned against the counter.

"Please?" I put a hand on his arm, and he stared at it, frozen. "It was two and a half years ago. I've learned to live with it."

"Did they catch the guy? Tell me he's in prison."

"I never told the police. It would have been my word against his."

"What about DNA?"

"He used a condom." A tear leaked out and trickled down my cheek. "Can we please stop talking about this?"

I desperately needed that beer. I grabbed a bottle from the fridge myself, then opened the drawers until I found a bottle opener. In truth, I'd have preferred something stronger, but Vanessa had finished the vodka and the only other place I could get alcohol on campus was the chemistry lab. And I wanted to drown my sorrows, not preserve my insides for eternity.

"What should I do, Sky? I don't know what to do."

"Don't do anything different. If you want to kiss me again, then fine. If you don't, that's okay too. We can just be two friends who hang out and don't have sex."

Asher's turn with the nervous laughter. "Sounds good to me."

"Great."

"Uh, you wanna watch a movie?"

"Do you have popcorn?"

"No, but I have chips."

Tendrils of tension still crackled between us when we sat on the sofa—me at one end, Asher at the other, and a bowl of potato crisps in the middle—and I wondered what I'd do if I could turn the clock back to a point where I had a fully functioning set of brain cells. Would I still have told Asher about my past? If everything between us was real, then the answer was unquestionably yes. I really could be friends with this guy, but I was a liar, and in a few short weeks I'd disappear out of his life for good. Perhaps it would have been more sensible to use his confession as an excuse to back away?

"What kind of movies do you like?" he asked.

Too late now.

"Anything without subtitles." Shit. I smacked my head. "Sorry."

Could I get any more insensitive?

"Forget it. I actually speak Spanish too. Learned it from my dad."

"I'm learning Spanish."

"Really? Where?"

Engage your damn brain, Sky.

"Uh, I mean I was. In England. We had a Spanish club on Monday evenings. *Mi nombre es Sky y tengo diecisiete anos.*"

Asher burst out laughing, a proper belly laugh this

time.

"What?"

"Your name is Sky and you have seventeen anuses? You mean *an-yos*, not *a-nos*."

"Ah, shit. *Años*. I always forget about that little accent thing."

"So I guess we'll be watching a movie in English?"

"That might be best."

We picked out an action movie, which turned out to be possibly the worst action movie ever made. You could still see the stuntman's wires. And the love affair between a Navy SEAL who could barely swim and a grocery store cashier who looked like a catwalk model wasn't particularly realistic either.

Or was it? The idea of falling in love had always seemed weird to me. Two people start by exchanging messages on a dating website, and suddenly they want to get an apartment and a cat? They share a bottle of wine, the guy sticks unmentionable parts of himself into the girl, and before you know it, they're off on a minibreak to Butlins? I didn't get it. Had Asher ever dated? What made him decide he hated sex?

"Sky?"

"Huh?"

"What are you thinking about?"

"Uh, the movie?"

"You haven't been watching the movie for at least fifteen minutes."

Busted. "Which means you've been watching me for at least fifteen minutes."

He didn't try to deny it. "What's eating at you?"

"Curiosity."

Asher raised one dark eyebrow. How come his

eyebrows were almost black and his hair was blond? Genetics, I guess. Maybe a touch of bleach. Overall, I had to concede he hadn't done badly in the looks department.

"What are you curious about?"

"You."

"What about me?"

"The thing you said earlier... Why do you hate sex? Presumably you've tried it?"

"In every possible way you can imagine."

Instead of elaborating, he went to the kitchen, and when he came back, he had a bottle of Jack Daniels in his hand.

"I suppose I owe you an explanation, but I'm gonna need this. It ain't pretty."

He took a long swallow, and I held out my hand. After a brief hesitation, he passed me the bottle, and I relished the burn as I poured a good measure down my throat. Better. I hugged a cushion on my lap as Asher began his tale, a pointless move if ever there was one because from the look of dread on his face, there would be no soft landing for either of us.

"I was seventeen when my dad cut off my allowance. No grades, no gas money, that's what he said. And driving was the only thing that kept me sane back then. Still is, if I'm truthful. So I got a job. Weekend pool cleaner at the Oakwood Estates Country Club, with plenty of overtime on offer as well. And it was great. I got to work on my tan and look at women in bathing suits all day, plus the boss paid cash in hand every Friday. Sure beat school."

Beat serving drinks in a nightclub too. "What did your dad say?"

"He wasn't happy, but by that point, I didn't care. And then I turned eighteen, and the woman who ran the spa, Lillian, she heard I was thinking of quitting school altogether and told me I'd make a great massage therapist. Said I had nice hands and offered me a trainee position."

I took one of his hands in mine and uncurled his fingers. They were longer than mine. He didn't wear any jewellery, but he obviously spent time with a nail file.

"You *do* have nice hands." Elegant hands. Probably came from playing the piano. "Did you take the new job?"

"The pay was better. Plus Lillian said they were always busy so I could work as many hours as I wanted. They sent me on a course. It was only six weeks—not really long enough to learn everything, but it turned out that didn't matter."

"What do you mean?"

"The first day, they threw me in at the deep end. Six clients. I quickly worked out what the women liked and what they didn't like. I'd left school to take the course, but I was still sleeping at home, and I earned enough to keep my car running. Then one day—three weeks in, maybe four—one of the regular clients asked for a seated Indian head massage. No problem, I was good at those. I was working the pressure points on her face when she unzipped my fly, and before I knew what the fuck was going on, she was on her knees with my cock in her mouth."

My gasp of shock drowned out several movie gunshots. "Are you serious?"

He was. Deadly. There was no humour in his

expression. In fact, he looked quite sick.

"She gave me a two-hundred-dollar tip. Cash. She dropped it on the table when she left. But she came back three days later."

"She did the same again?"

"That time, she wanted more. So I gave it to her. Judge me if you want, but I was a horny eighteen-year-old and four hundred dollars bought a heck of a lot of gas."

I'd never slept with anyone for money, but serving shots in a bikini top and a miniskirt so short it showed my ass cheeks meant I was no choirgirl.

"I'm not judging."

Asher brushed the hair away from my face and studied me. "No, I don't believe you are." He took another swig of whiskey. "Turns out that when one of those women gets her claws into you, it's just the beginning. She passed me around her friends like a party favour."

"Holy shit."

"At first, it wasn't that bad. I mean, these trophy wives look after themselves. Everything's nipped and tucked and frozen into place. But fuck, are they entitled. After a few months, the novelty of boning women all day, every day wore off and I realised I was nothing more than a trained monkey. But I was making more money than I'd ever had in my life, so I kept going. I hated myself, but I kept going."

"Didn't your boss say anything? Lillian?"

"I soon learned Lillian was more of a pimp than a beauty therapist. She had me tag-teaming with the other guys, and she was banging half of the husbands herself. I used to dream of going home and putting my feet up with a mug of fucking cocoa. By the end, I was swallowing little blue pills like candy to get it up and downing bourbon so I could face myself in the mornings."

"By the end? You quit?"

"Not exactly. First, my dad died, and as soon as the funeral was over, the Rosenbergs started sniffing around. Then the FBI raided the country club, and the owner got arrested."

"For running a brothel?"

"For money laundering. When the special agents arrived, I was stripping at Edwina Cunningham's daughter's bachelorette party, so I missed all the fun." Asher mock-pouted and then spread his arms. "So here I am. Tired, jaded, and definitely not in the market for a hook-up. Those bitches literally wore out my dick."

Perhaps it was the alcohol, and perhaps it was the situation, but I looked at Asher, and he looked at me, and then we both began to laugh. And laugh and laugh and laugh.

"We're such a pair of fuck-ups," I choked out.

"I can still give you a massage if you want. I'm not bad at those."

Tears were streaming down my face. "You're my perfect man. Is there anything left in that bottle?"

"A mouthful." He handed it over, then slung an arm over my shoulders. "C'mon. Let's watch another movie and not have sex."

"Horror or romance?"

"In our world, they're the same thing, Chem."

I snuggled against his side. It felt nice. No pressure whatsoever, just warmth and friendship.

"Homance it is, Shortcut."

CHAPTER 33 - SKY

OH, NO.

WHAT time was it?

Late enough, or rather, early enough that I could make out the pair of bluebirds sitting on Asher's windowsill, although they still looked grey and black instead of red and blue in the gloom. Asher's chest rose and fell under my cheek, and he'd draped one arm loosely over my back, possibly to keep me from falling off the sofa.

"Asher, wake up." I poked his shoulder. "It's morning."

"Wha..." He looked dorkily adorable as he rubbed sleep from his eyes. "Shit."

"I've got to go." I rolled off him and looked for my shoes. There they were, next to the table. "Talk to you later."

"Wait." He sat up, eyelids still at half mast. "We fell asleep?"

"Sure looks that way. See you in biology. Don't forget your textbook today."

I moved towards the window, but he caught my hand to hold me in place as he stood.

"Sorry, I'm not good at mornings."

"No kidding. It's Friday, just in case you've forgotten. You've got music theory first period."

Asher pressed his lips to my temple in a soft kiss, catching me by surprise.

"Friday. Right. Thanks, Chem."

Then he slumped back onto the sofa and closed his eyes while I climbed out the window, twisted, and lowered myself off the sill by my fingertips. Once I was hanging straight, I let go, remembering to bend my knees when I landed.

Had anyone seen me? Didn't look like it. Phew. I was soon jogging through the woods, taking the long way back to New Hall. I only saw one person awake, a freshman doing what looked like Pilates on a stone terrace near Lower Hall. Some people were a little too keen.

The window to my room was open, just the way I'd left it, and I swarmed up the tree like a hung-over monkey, slithered along an outstretched branch, and plopped onto the floor by my desk.

The sight that greeted me was worse than any horror movie. Worse even than a romance movie. I froze, staring up at Vanessa as a million expletives jammed in my throat.

"I don't understand—Sky, what are these things?"

Bugs. They were bugs. Eight or nine of them, nestled in coloured foil and little paper cases beside the box of "chocolates" Bethany had handed me on Tuesday.

"What are you doing?" I rasped.

"I got hungry. I didn't think you'd mind. But these... They're not candy. They look like something out of a spy movie."

"I can explain."

No, actually I couldn't. Where did I even start? Had

she managed to turn one on? It didn't appear so. The switches were really tiny and hidden away on the sides.

"They... I..."

"Oh my gosh! *Are* you a spy?"

"Yes. No. Sort of." This was actually more uncomfortable than last night's conversation with Asher, and I hadn't thought anything would ever top that. "I work for a team of investigators."

"And you're investigating...what? Is it something to do with cheating? Because I heard a rumour that somebody stole a test paper."

"It's got nothing to do with the students."

Her eyes ballooned. "Then who? A *teacher*? No way! Is it a sex scandal? Mr. Teller looks at the freshmen real funny, but I don't think he actually follows through."

"Vanessa, you can't say a word."

"My lips are sealed." She mimed zipping up her mouth and throwing away the key. "See? This is so exciting!"

Should I trust her? I'd already told so many lies it was hard to keep up with the truth. What would Emmy do? Dammit, I should have kept my earpiece in twenty-four seven. This was what happened when I allowed myself to get distracted. When I let feelings get in the way of my job. Vanessa was still staring at me, her mouth slightly open. I had to trust her, didn't I? If I kept prevaricating, I'd only dig myself into a deeper hole.

"It's the Rosenbergs."

"The *Rosenbergs*? But...but they're good people."

"There may be others involved too."

"Why? What have they done? No, no, they can't

have done *anything*. They wouldn't."

"We think they've stolen some paintings."

"Paintings? They've got hundreds of paintings here. Why would they steal more?"

"These are expensive paintings. Masterpieces. *The Shepherd's Watch* got lifted during a charity dinner last month, and we think they might have taken it. They were there."

Vanessa gaped at me for a full twenty seconds, and then her eyes hardened. "So? I bet other people were there too. Are you investigating all of them?"

"The painting was passed to a man posing as a waiter, and we tailed him all the way to the school gates."

"There must have been a mistake. Your people probably followed the wrong car or something."

"That's what I'm here to find out."

What a bloody mess. My first undercover job and I'd screwed it up totally. Why hadn't I hidden the damn chocolates? I knew Vanessa had a sweet tooth.

"So you're trying to get the Rosenbergs sent to prison, and when you don't find any evidence, then you'll just disappear?" Vanessa folded her arms. "Is that why you're spending so much time with Asher? Because he's a Rosenberg?"

"No! I like Asher. I really do."

"That's even worse. You're going to break his heart."

"I know." And quite possibly, I'd break my own heart in the process too. I slumped onto the bed. "That's the worst part of this."

"What about me? I thought we were friends. Is that all an act too?"

"It's not an act. And at this rate, I'll be here until the end of the school year anyway."

"So you *haven't* found anything? I'm not surprised."

"Neither am I. This isn't a regular gang of thieves. They use the postal service to communicate, for crying out loud. They're stuck in the Stone Age."

"The postal service? How do you even know?"

"From a... Well, I guess you'd call him an informant." Yes, we'd kind of kidnapped Marshall, but he *was* informing us of stuff, so the description still fit. "The gang sends instructions out to their minions by mail, telling them to steal paintings. Like a work order. Do this, do that... The letters come from all over the place, though, so we can't track them down through those."

Vanessa stopped waving her arms and froze in much the same way as I had earlier. Was it me or had she paled a shade or two?

"Letters? Oh my gosh." Her turn to collapse onto her bed. "What do they say? The letters? Tell me."

"I haven't actually seen one myself. Why?"

Her voice dropped to a whisper. "I think I might have."

"Might have what?"

"Seen one."

"Huh?"

"A couple of years ago. We have a letter-writing club that meets on Tuesday evenings, but I haven't been for weeks because we've been hanging out, and... anyway, we write to people. Like, people we don't know. Seniors in residential homes, and kids in hospitals, that sort of thing. Sometimes we send pictures or little gifts, and we collect all the cards into a big box. Mostly we mail them from Shadow Falls, but if we go home, or on vacation, we each take a handful and mail them from someplace else. Because then people get surprise letters and cards from all over the world, see? And some enthusiasts collect the stamps too. What do you call them? Phlebotomists?"

Why was she asking me? "I've got no bloody idea."

Vanessa already had her phone in her hand, checking. "Philatelists. They're philatelists."

I needed to get this back on track. "And you think somebody in the club was sending these letters?"

"Not somebody. Mrs. Austen. Saul Rosenberg's assistant? She organises everything."

Was Vanessa serious? The Rosenbergs were using schoolkids as unwitting accomplices?

"What makes you say that?"

"When I used to spend vacations at home, I took letters back to California to mail. And one time, I accidentally spilled coffee on an envelope. So I figured I'd just take the contents out, put the stuff in a fresh envelope, stick on a new stamp, and send it. I remember hunting for a stamp while my mom and her boyfriend were yelling at each other in the next room."

"And?"

"And they split up real soon after."

"I mean what happened with the letter?"

"Oh, yeah. It was weird. There was a card with photos of three paintings stuck on the front. And inside, it said something like 'Confirmed at 900.'"

"That *is* weird. But why do you think that has anything to do with this investigation? I'm not saying it doesn't, but..."

"Because the paintings on the front were all stolen a

month later. I recognised them on the news. And I thought it was weird, but they were all in the same gallery, so I figured maybe someone bought a cheap card from the gift shop."

"And why do you think Mrs. Austen was involved?"

"Because it was her handwriting on the inside. She always writes her nines really odd, like g's, so it looked like 'Confirmed at goo.' Did I participate in an art theft? What if I did? What if it was my fault? I didn't know!"

"You did nothing wrong. Nobody knew, not even the FBI."

"The FBI? You work for the FBI?"

"No, their investigation's separate. I need to call my boss, okay? Please, please can you keep your mouth shut about this?"

"What'll happen? If the Rosenbergs go to jail, what'll happen to the school? To us? I don't have anywhere else to go."

And neither did Asher.

"I'm sure they'll just get some new teachers." At least, I hoped so. The Rosenbergs did seem integral to the running of Shadow Falls Academy. "Ones who aren't criminals."

"But what about our exams? Our grades? If we have a whole new set of teachers, they won't know us. They won't know the school. We can't—"

I grabbed Vanessa's waving hands. "You can. People have died because of these thefts. More people will die if the Rosenbergs aren't stopped."

"But..." A tear rolled down Vanessa's cheek. "I hate this. *Hate* it. I wish I'd never tried to eat those damn chocolates."

You and me both.

"Will you please stay quiet? Just for a short while?"

Vanessa took a deep breath. Her bottom lip quivered. "I won't say anything. But you have to tell me what's going on, okay? I can't afford to mess up my education."

"I'll do my best. I promise."

Now what? The job was in danger of going to shit, and I had to call Emmy, but I didn't particularly fancy doing it in front of Vanessa. So I changed into running gear, shinned down the tree, and headed up the hill to Asher's shed. That seemed like the safest place for a private conversation. Apart from a new spiderweb in the doorway, it was exactly as we'd left it.

"Hi, it's Sky."

"Afternoon, sleepyhead. Good night, was it? Tired?"

I knew exactly what she was thinking. "It wasn't like that. I fell asleep on Asher's sofa while we were watching a movie."

"Sure, okay. You're eighteen—just be careful."

"I'm trying, but there's been a slight technical hitch."

Emmy's voice changed. The playfulness went out of it. "What kind of technical hitch?"

"Vanessa knows why I'm here now. She found the chocolate bugs when she got peckish, and once she started asking questions, it turned out she actually had some information."

"What information?"

I told Emmy about the letters, and she gave a low whistle. "That's cold. Roping the kids in to act as mules? Cunning, but cold."

"I'm so, so sorry Vanessa found out. She says she won't tell."

"It's called recruitment, Sky. We all do it. That's literally how every intelligence agency in the world operates. The execution could use a little work in your case, but the end result is that we have new information we didn't have before. The brevity of the wording she described fits with what Marshall told us, by the way."

"So we've got another name?"

"Seems that way. Can you get a bug under that woman's desk?"

"I'll try."

"Take your time. Things are heading in the right direction, and we don't want any screw-ups because you're rushing."

"Rune leaves on Monday."

"We'll cover for her. We have enough science experts at Blackwood."

"How much longer do you think I'll be here?"

"How long is a piece of string? Don't you have classes to go to?"

"First period starts in fifteen minutes."

"Then get your ass there. Check in later with an update, and I'll tell Nate to find a better hiding place for his bugs. Fucking chocolates. What if Vanessa broke a tooth?"

Yet again, it seemed I'd gotten away with a mistake, but I couldn't continue making them. There was only so much shit that could slide off me. Sooner or later, it would start sticking. I only hoped it wouldn't stick to Asher and Vanessa too.

CHAPTER 34 - SKY

AFTER THE DRAMA of Friday morning, the rest of the day was somewhat of an anticlimax. Rune talked me through my classes, and I felt a pang of sorrow when she signed off in the evening. I'd miss her voice when she left. She cracked jokes and told me stories from her own lessons. Ryder was quieter, and Sofia was a lunatic.

I spent the evening with Asher again, although I did go to his apartment via Mrs. Austen's desk with one of the chocolate bugs. Vanessa seemed almost disappointed when I told her I was fine doing the spy stuff, as she called it, on my own.

Things were a lot more relaxed between Asher and me that night. No difficult conversations, just popcorn, ice cream, and a reasonably good movie. I got a kiss on the forehead, and I was back in my bed by one a.m., which meant I got six hours' sleep before the shit hit the fan again the next morning. And for once, it wasn't my fault.

I trooped downstairs a few minutes after seven with Vanessa in tow, only to find a group of girls clustered around a sofa in the living room. Not the Britneys, thank goodness—they'd been keeping a low profile since the shart incident—but one of them was crying.

"What happened?" I asked.

"Hillary's crush is in the hospital," a brunette explained. "She's devastated."

"Was there an accident?" I hadn't heard an ambulance, but Asher had turned the volume on the TV up loud to cover the sound of our conversation. Linton Hall had thin walls. He'd already faced questions about our laughter the other night, and he'd had to pretend he was watching a stand-up show.

"No!" a redhead said. "It was totally deliberate."

"What was deliberate?"

"Celebgossip.com says a masked man broke into his mansion in Malibu and cut off his you-know-what. Then made him eat it!"

"What? Whose house?"

"Brock Keaton's, of course. Hillary's been in love with him forever."

A chill ran through me. Actually, it was more of an iceberg, and it ploughed into my stomach.

"Somebody broke into Brock Keaton's house and cut off his..."

"His penis," the brunette whispered. "Why would anyone do such a thing?"

I had a fairly good idea. If I'd had to write a list of who I thought might have done it, that list would've had precisely one name on it. Personal time, my ass. I didn't know whether to kiss his feet or yell at him.

Instead, I traipsed back up the hill to Asher's shed and dialled. This time, Rafael picked up.

"Good vacation?" I asked.

"It was...satisfying."

"Let me guess—you went to LA?"

"I don't think we need to go into the details."

"Why didn't you tell me? And how did you even

know it was him?"

"Tell you what?"

"You're an asshole, you know that?"

"Yes."

"I sent you twenty messages, and you didn't reply to any of them."

"Black said everything was under control."

"That's not the point."

Rafael's voice softened. Just a tiny bit, but it was there. "I'll call next time."

Next time? Good grief. But a little of the fight went out of me. Rafael had cut my rapist's fetid dick off, and if Hillary and her friends were to be believed, he'd also made Brock eat the sorry remains. That motherfucker wouldn't be able to hurt another girl the way he'd hurt me.

"Thank you," I whispered. "For everything."

"How's the job going?"

"Nate hid the latest batch of bugs in a box of chocolates and my roommate tried to eat them, but apart from that..."

A rare laugh from Rafael. "I'll see you when you get back."

"See ya."

Aaaaand he was gone.

As I walked back down the hill, I tried to sort through the muddle of thoughts in my head. Asher. Rafael. The case. Vanessa. How was Lenny? I missed life at Riverley and its brutal simplicity.

Everything was jumbled.

Which was perhaps why I almost missed him. Almost, but not quite. The waiter from the Grove walked towards me pushing a wheelbarrow, this time dressed in the black cargo pants and maroon polo shirt worn by all the groundsmen. I still had my phone in my hand, and I managed to snap a photo of him.

"You're not meant to be out here alone," he said as we passed. Thankfully, there was no spark of recognition in his eyes.

"Sorry. I was with my friend, but she got ahead."

"Stay together next time."

I felt like punching the air. All the pieces were finally falling into place.

CHAPTER 35 - SKY

SUNDAY AFTERNOON, AND the clouds were heavy with rain. I was counting down the minutes until it would be dark enough for me to sneak out of New Hall and into Asher's apartment, which would hopefully be sooner rather than later because everything was grey, grey, grey. Miss Brooks was on guard downstairs again, and this time she'd brought her cello. The strains of a haunting tune drifted up the stairs, and it would have been quite lovely if anyone but that old bag had been playing it.

The day had been pretty much a write-off. Half of the teachers were in—unusual for a Sunday—which meant I was shit out of luck when it came to planting bugs. I'd dragged myself out for a run this morning, careful to avoid the waiter-slash-art-thief, and I'd shocked myself by actually doing my biology homework.

My phone pinged with a message from Vanessa. She'd spent the morning trying to convince me that we should snoop around the art department just in case anyone had hidden a hot painting there, which seemed quite unlikely, and in the end, I'd begged Asher to call her and insist they work on the song they were writing together. That had bought me an hour of peace, but it seemed it wasn't to last.

Vanessa: Come over! We're in the creepy music room in the west wing.

Me: Can't. Teachers everywhere and I'm not allowed near Asher.

Vanessa: He says they're all going to some meeting. It'll be dead quiet.

A meeting? My synapses fired. What kind of a meeting? A regular staff meeting, or could it be the special meeting that Saul and Dr. Merritt were discussing the other day? We'd confirmed it *was* Dr. Merrit now. Who told Asher about the meeting? Did he have any more information?

Me: Which is the creepy music room?

The whole damn school was creepy. That description didn't narrow it down much.

Vanessa: Asher says you went there before with him.

Me: Five minutes.

I stuffed in an earpiece, told Ryder I was going to the main building, and slid down the tree trunk. The heavens opened the moment I hit the ground, and by the time I hauled open the back door, I was soaked through to my knickers. Bloody brilliant. I wasn't exactly vain, but I didn't particularly want Asher to see me looking like a drowned rat. A roll of thunder rumbled overhead, and I almost missed the footsteps coming in my direction. Crap! I ducked into an alcove seconds before Dr. Merritt ambled past. So much for everyone being in a meeting. Well, I wasn't going back to my room, not in that storm. I'd wait it out.

My shoes squelched all the way to the music room, and I was still dripping when I pushed the door open. Asher and Vanessa both stopped mid-note and stared.

"What happened?" Vanessa asked.

I gestured to the window just as a bolt of lightning lit up the grounds. "Hello? It's pissing down out there."

Asher pulled his sweater over his head. "Here, put this on."

"I'm fine, honestly. I'll dry out faster without it. I can't stay long, anyway—there are still teachers around out there."

"Nobody ever comes in here," Vanessa told me, shuddering. "It's meant to be haunted."

"Really? Has anyone ever seen a ghost?"

"Hayley Blankfeld swears she followed a shadowy figure along the hallway, and she heard the piano playing, but when she opened the door, there was nobody in here."

"Doesn't bother me," Asher said. "It means nobody ever uses this room, and the piano's the best in the building."

"I just don't want us to get caught together again. You said there was a meeting?"

"Yeah, some planning session for the next theatre production. Uncle Saul wants me to go for dinner with the clan afterwards." He grimaced. "Sorry."

Dammit, false alarm. But perhaps if I stuck around, I could sneak in another bug or two.

"Sounds fun."

"I'll probably get another lecture on my career path. Did I tell you that Uncle Ezra wants me to be a concert pianist?" Asher began bashing out "Bohemian Rhapsody" and singing too. Badly. "What d'ya think?"

"I need earplugs."

Vanessa elbowed him. "Play it properly. He really is good."

"Okay, okay."

She was right. Asher really was good. In so many ways including, it turned out, on the piano. Vanessa joined in singing, and it was like having my own private concert. Although I did feel a little like dead wood in their company—at school, I'd managed to play about three notes on the recorder, and I usually got those in the wrong order.

"Play something else."

The bugs could wait for a few minutes. I'd have happily listened to Asher and Vanessa all night.

"Do you want to hear the song we've been working on?" Vanessa asked.

"I'd love to."

I leaned against the wall by the door, and the lights went out. Vanessa gave a shriek.

"What happened?" she yelped.

"Sorry, that was just me. I hit the light switch by accident. No biggie." I turned the lights on again. "No ghost either."

"I'm so jumpy tonight. I think it's the storm."

As if on cue, another fork of lightning snaked across the sky, illuminating the driving rain. I hoped it didn't get my tree. I'd be in the shit if that happened.

"Ready?" Asher asked, and he didn't give Vanessa a chance to answer before he started playing. She opened her mouth to sing, but before she got a note out, I heard a *click* from the bookcase next to me.

"Wait!"

"What?" she asked.

"I heard a noise."

"The ghost?"

"Not the freaking ghost."

No, it was worse. The bookcase was moving, sliding slowly to the left to reveal a yawning hole in the wall. Asher was at my side in an instant.

"What the hell...?"

I pulled out my phone. Why didn't it have any service? At least the flashlight function was still working, and I shone it into the hole. Rough wooden stairs led downwards, far enough that I couldn't see the bottom. My heart raced, and I forced myself to breathe slowly. Emmy wouldn't hyperventilate. Could we finally have found the Master's lair? I mean, Emmy and Black kept all sorts of goodies in their basement, didn't they? And this passage didn't appear anywhere on our schematics. Alaric had checked out the main part of the cellar on my interview day, and he said there was nothing there but dust and junk.

"Do you think...?" Vanessa asked.

"I don't know. Maybe."

Asher gave us a curious look. "What are you two talking about?"

Oh, fuck. How did a girl tell the guy she was really starting to like that she suspected his family of stealing millions of dollars' worth of famous artworks?

She didn't. She stalled.

"Could we perhaps discuss this later?"

"Sky..."

I turned away for a moment.

"Ryder?" I whispered. No answer. Where was he? I stuck a finger into my ear to check the widget was turned on, and it came away wet. Ah, crap. The fucking thing had probably short-circuited.

Right. Okay. *Take deep breaths and think this through.* I needed to take a look in that cellar, but first

I had to let Blackwood know what I was doing.

"Vanessa, I'm just gonna run back to our room and
—"

The door started closing. Shit, shit, shit! Could we open it again? Maybe, maybe not. I had no idea why it had opened in the first place. I only had a split second to make a decision, and my gut took over.

"Sky, no!" Vanessa squeaked.

The bookcase closed behind me, leaving only darkness. Pitch bloody black.

"Sky?" Asher whispered in my ear, and I nearly had a heart attack.

"Why the hell did you follow me?"

"Because I care about you and I didn't want you getting trapped in a dark cellar on your own?"

"Oh."

"Why on earth did *you* come in here?"

"Temporary insanity?"

It wasn't just the paintings that were missing; I'd lost my damn mind as well. I felt Asher turn around, and his ass bumped mine.

"No kidding. I can't find a handle or a catch or anything."

"Hold on..."

I turned the flashlight on again, but the back of the bookcase was made of smooth wood. There was nothing to grip hold of and nothing to turn or pull. Now what? We didn't have a lot of choice, did we? We'd have to go down the stairs.

"Do you have your phone?" I asked.

"I left it on the piano."

Brilliant. "I've got about a quarter of my battery left."

"So let's get out of here. I'll go first."

"No, you won't. I take responsibility for my bad decisions."

At the bottom, a passage curved to the right. I ran a hand over the wall—it seemed to be carved from rock, and when I looked up, the roof was curved rather than flat. What was this place? An old water channel someone had happened across? Or a man-made hidey-hole? Whatever it was, it went on for what seemed like miles. A maze. A catacomb. Smaller passages led off to the sides, and I half expected to walk around a bend and find a pile of old bones. Somewhere, something was dripping, and the whole place felt damp.

"Is that a light up ahead?" Asher whispered.

I shut off my phone, and sure enough, the faintest glimmer showed, highlighting the outline of an arch. Turn back? Press on? How the hell were we gonna get out of this wretched place? I hadn't seen anything that looked like an exit yet.

Asher reached out and squeezed my hand. "Should we keep going?"

"We don't have a choice."

Forward we crept, and the air felt warmer here. Drier. The darkness was disorientating, but I was almost certain we were going uphill.

Finally, the passage emptied out into a cavern, forty feet long at a guess. And this... This was no catacomb. It had a parquet fucking floor, and a twinkling chandelier hung from the ceiling. The rows of wooden benches arranged on either side reminded me of church pews, all facing what looked like an ornamental wardrobe. What was in it? Other chambers led off the main room, some with doors and some without.

"This is creepy as fuck," Asher said.

My sentiments exactly.

"Surely one of these doors has to be an exit?"

We hugged the wall as we scurried through the cavern, trying each door in turn. The lights were on, so somebody was home, but where were they? The place made the hairs on the back of my neck stand on end.

And then we found it. Or rather, we found them. I eased a door open to reveal rows of slim wooden crates stacked neatly in size order. I'd seen crates like that before, twice in fact. Once in the boot of Beth's car when I stole it, and once when she picked up the Picasso and brought it to Riverley. They were the kind of protective crates that valuable paintings were shipped in. And there had to be at least a hundred of them. I tiptoed closer. Each crate had a name written on the side in black marker. *Madonna and Child with Angel.* I presumed it didn't mean the singer. *Garden of Eden by Night. The Shepherd's Watch.* I ran to the other end of the row, to the larger paintings. Where was she? Was she here?

The Girl with the Emerald Ring.

Holy fuck, they still had her!

My moment of elation was short-lived, however. The *snick* of a semi-automatic being cocked sent my head whipping around, and my stomach dropped to the polished floor when I saw Saul Rosenberg standing in the doorway.

"Step away from there."

Asher swivelled too. I didn't take my eyes off the gun, but I heard the confusion in his voice.

"Uncle, what are you doing? Why do you have a gun?"

"For protection."

"Against what?"

"Against people who stick their noses where they don't belong."

"We're just lost, okay? We found a door hidden behind a bookcase, and then it closed behind us. Can you tell us how to get out of here? And put the damn gun down. We're not burglars."

"I'm afraid it's not that simple."

No, it wasn't. I'd seen too much.

"What *is* this place?" Asher asked, still refreshingly naïve.

Saul motioned at me with the gun. "Out. Slowly. You too, Asher."

He wasn't going to let us go. Not me, anyway. His eyes betrayed him. They were hard and calculating, two steely orbs that watched me carefully as I made my way to the door. Okay, I could do this. I'd practised a thousand times with Rafael. Once I was close enough, I could grab the pistol and clonk him over the head with it. I'd nearly given Rafael a concussion once; dealing with a middle-aged schoolteacher should be child's play. Asher obviously didn't have a clue what was going on, and I felt shitty about that, but I couldn't stop to explain.

We closed the distance. Ten feet, eight, six...

I sprang. Grabbed the pistol. Blocked out Saul's howl of pain as his finger twisted in the trigger guard, but the bloody thing got jammed at the knuckle when I tried to wrench the gun out of his hand. I was about to go in with a left-handed uppercut when a bullet whistled over my head. The *bang* left my ears ringing.

"Get back, or the next one goes through your

brain."

I raised my hands slowly. My old friend the waiter had joined the party, and he didn't look as if he wanted to celebrate. Asher hadn't moved. Hardly surprising when the scuffle had lasted five seconds at most.

"I knew you were trouble when I saw you in the forest."

"And I knew you were trouble when I saw you hightail it out of the Grove's parking lot." Oh, that startled him. "Got careless, didn't you?"

Saul rolled to his hands and knees, coughing. "Get her out of here."

"Where should we put her, boss?"

"Confiscate her phone and put her in the storage closet beside the Holy Ark." The what? "That bitch broke my finger."

"What about him?" The waiter jerked his head towards Asher.

"Him too."

Half a dozen others had appeared in the doorway, and I recognised Dr. Merritt and the track coach among them. One man I could deal with, two or three even, but not eight when at least two of them had guns.

"Uncle?" Asher's voice rose in panic. "What's going on?"

"Get them both out of here *right now*."

Chapter 36 - Sky

OUR PRISON WAS more of a room than a closet, but nonetheless, we were stuck in there. I'd tripped up the step as they dragged me inside, and my knee ached like fuck. I let the pain spur me on.

Pool noodles, lane markers, deflated beach balls, wetsuits, a baseball glove, an old set of scuba apparatus... Nearly all water-related. If I had to guess, I'd say the room was a storage area for the swimming pool, which meant we were around four hundred yards north of the main building. Even if a miracle happened and Team Blackwood did show up, hunting for me would be like looking for hay in a needle stack. Almost impossible and with a high likelihood of blood being shed. Why couldn't we have been near the sports field? A hockey stick might actually have come in useful.

"Sky, what's happening?" Asher asked.

I threw a paddleboard aside and hit pay dirt. Another door! But where did it go? I tested it with my shoulder. Solid.

"Come over here and help me."

"What the fuck is going on?"

"We need to break down this door."

"Why?"

"Because your uncle is a criminal, and he's going to kill me and possibly you as well if we don't get out of here."

"You're gonna have to explain that statement."

"He was waving a gun at me. How much more of an explanation do you need?"

"He probably thought we were burglars. And you attacked him first."

"Okay, fine. That room we were in? I'd say it housed a good proportion of all the famous paintings that have gone missing over the past, oh, four or five decades."

"And you know this how?"

"Because..." I took a deep breath. "Because I was sent here to search for them."

I kept my eyes on the door. Not because I thought it might suddenly open, although that would have been nice, but because I couldn't bring myself to face Asher.

"You... I... So, what are you? An undercover cop?"

"A private investigator."

"You're a... How old are you?"

"Eighteen. This is my first job, and aren't I doing great at it?"

"Hell." I knew if I turned around, I'd find Asher's hand scrubbing at his hair, but my feet stayed where they were. "You lied to me."

"I didn't tell you the whole truth."

"Bullshit. You lied. Your parents—are they even your parents?"

"No."

"I can't believe this. I told you secrets I've never told anyone."

"I did the same."

"Did you? Really? Or was it just an act?"

"No! It wasn't like that. Everything that I said happened to me, it happened. I grew up on the fucking streets, Asher. My real dad beat me. Is that what you want to hear? Does that make you feel better?"

"Better? *Better?* The only thing that would make me feel better right now is flying back to San Diego and never seeing you or this place again."

"Then could you please help me with this door?"

"Fine." He muttered curses under his breath, but he did at least line up next to me. "*Fine.* On three."

"One... Two... Three."

Ow, fuck, that hurt. Pain radiated through my shoulder, and the door didn't budge an inch. Asher gave it a kick for good measure, then hopped a bit.

"It's solid," he groaned.

"Yeah, I'd noticed."

"Do we try again?"

"And break the other shoulder too? Sure, why not?"

Bloody hell. This time, the pain was hotter. More intense. That sturdy old piece of oak was probably laughing at us. There was no give whatsoever in the wood, and not a millimetre of light showed around the edge. I guessed at a bolt top and bottom, the same as the door to the cavern. I'd heard them shoot home when the men locked us inside.

"We're not trying a third time," I said.

"Gotta agree with that." A pause. "You really think there're stolen paintings in all of those boxes?"

"Yup."

"Why? Why would Saul take them?"

"It's a long, long story, but there are various reasons. At first, it was retribution for crimes committed during the Holocaust. Then simply for the money. And lately, he's been using them to buy favours."

Asher sat down on a plastic container and covered his face with his hands. "I fell for all this bullshit. Yours and theirs. How do I even know who's telling the truth now?"

I crouched in front of him. "I've got no reason to lie anymore."

"And it's not just me you lied to. What about Vanessa? She thinks you're her friend."

"Uh, she knows why I'm here. And she *is* my friend."

"She *knows*?"

"She helped me to put some of the clues together."

"So it's just me who's the schmuck?"

"How could I have told you? What would you have said? Even after Saul pointed a gun in my face, you still thought it might have been a mistake."

Silence.

I reached out and took Asher's hand, and my heart stuttered when he flinched.

"Whatever else happens here, everything between us was real. You have to understand that. I really fucking like you, Asher Martinez."

Hammering on the door made us both jump, and somebody yelled instructions. Saul? The waiter?

"Stay back, both of you. We're armed."

We stood as the bolts thunked back, and the door slowly swung towards us. The waiter. He was turning out to be a real pain in the ass.

"You, come with us."

He motioned with the gun in his hand, and I took a step forward.

"Not you. Him."

Asher didn't move. "I'm not leaving without her."

"Get out this door, or I'll shoot her right now."

"Just go," I whispered. "I'll be okay."

Although I had no freaking clue how. This was possibly the worst situation I'd ever been in.

"But—"

"Go!"

As soon as the door closed behind them, I ran forward and pressed my ear to the wood. Where were they taking him? Which direction?

"Take him to Saul," the waiter said. "He wants a word."

"And her?" somebody asked.

"Saul wants to keep the bitch as leverage for now, and he'll most likely have questions for her."

"So we'll dispose of her later? Because we'll have to prepare for that."

"Then prepare," the waiter snapped. "I need some fucking Tylenol."

Chapter 37 - Emmy

"WE NEED TO go in for a closer look," Alaric said. "It's time."

"How?" Nate asked. "I'm not doing jail time for paedophilia."

"I'm talking about going undercover."

"As what?"

"Schoolgirls?" I suggested, twirling my hair. "Me, Dan, and Sofia? From the back, we'd look the part. Just don't ask us to turn around and show off our wrinkles. Or do maths."

Sofia was sitting on my lap, and I had my hand on her thigh. I was ninety percent sure Black knew I was only doing it to annoy him, and I was one hundred percent sure I didn't care. When he scowled, I let my fingers creep higher. Sofia just giggled. I had an inkling she was edging towards one of her manic phases again, but that sure beat her being miserable.

We'd all congregated at the rented house near Shadow Falls this evening. The little clues Sky had been finding... It felt as if this was building up to something bigger. And I might have been snarky about it, but I did agree with Alaric. We needed to go into the school for a closer look.

"Beth and I could visit Sky," he said. "Say we're checking up on her."

And what would they do? Wander around the gardens again?

"Maybe I'll go and have a mooch," I murmured, half to myself.

"When?"

"No time like the present."

"We're in the middle of a storm."

"Perfect. Everyone else'll be tucked up inside, watching TV."

"I'll come with you," Black offered.

"Ace. Then if there's lightning, it'll hit you first." Another scowl. This was almost like a sport, and I'd scored twenty-seven points already today. I reached out a foot and nudged Ryder. "What's Sky doing? Is she busy with that dude?"

Now Rafael scowled too. Interesting. Did it run in the family?

"She's gone quiet. The last thing she said was that she was heading over to the main building. Probably took an opportunity to sneak around."

"Can you ask her?"

"Hey, Sky. Whatcha doing?" His forehead creased into a frown. "She's not answering."

"Perhaps she can't," Alaric said. "Are there people about?"

"I can't hear any voices."

A tiny bud of concern formed in my gut. "I'll try texting her. Maybe the storm screwed with the comms? Could that happen?"

"Thunderstorms can cause disturbances in the partially ionised plasma of the ionosphere and distort radio signals."

"Is that a yes? I didn't understand anything you just

said."

"It's a yes, but it would be more of an intermittent crackle, not total silence."

Two minutes passed, but Sky didn't answer. I began to get a bad, bad feeling about this.

"I'm going over there."

"Wait." Ryder held up a hand. "There's something coming through on one of the bugs." His frown deepened. "This...this is odd."

"Put it on speaker."

Ryder switched it over, and yes, there were some crackles, but the words were clear.

"Hey... Is this...? Hi? Is this working? I have no idea... Sky people? Dammit! Uh, if you can hear me, my name's Vanessa, and I'm Sky's roommate." More static. "...went into a cellar with Asher. Like, we found this secret door in the music room? Behind a bookcase? And now it's closed, and I can't open it again. And I heard... I don't know... I think maybe it was a gunshot? But muffled, like, far away? Hello? Hello?"

Fuckety fuck. I was already strapping on my weapons before Vanessa finished speaking, and when I looked around the room, I saw everyone else was too. Guns, knives, Nate was stuffing a bunch of explosive charges into a backpack, and Sofia had enough shit in syringes to off an entire Death Row.

"Go ahead with Alaric," Black said softly into my ear. "I'll follow on behind."

"Why? What are you planning?"

He was up to something, I knew it.

"Just do as you're told for once, Diamond."

"Asshole."

Yet another scowl. Make that twenty-eight points.

CHAPTER 38 - SKY

I PACED THE storage room, the stray baseball bat I'd found hidden among the pool noodles resting on my shoulder. If anyone came through that door, I was taking their fucking head off.

But that still didn't solve the wider problem. There were more of them than me, and while I might get one or even two of those assholes, they'd defeat me in the end. What else could I find in this hellhole?

I rummaged through boxes and baskets, tossing aside musty swimwear and a puckered inflatable shark. A handy plastic sign informed me the pool was ten feet deep with a cheery *Warning: Danger of Death.*

Now they mentioned it. Bit late.

Something scraped my skin, and I didn't know whether to swear or sing the hallelujah chorus. A rusty screwdriver! I could put that through someone's eye, or possibly, just possibly... I could lever out the hinge pins on the door to the cavern. They were on my side, and even down here, everything was well oiled. The waiter seemed to have a maintenance fetish.

But again, that didn't entirely solve the problem. The cavern was positively buzzing now, judging by the number of voices I could hear. I'd be walking out into a firing squad. Unless I managed to create some sort of distraction...

I nudged the plastic drum Asher had been sitting on with my foot. There were two of them, side by side. How heavy were they? Perhaps I could toss them out the door first and Saul's men would waste all their ammunition the way they did in the movies? On second thoughts... No, they weighed about a ton each. What did they have in them? Lead? No, hydrochloric acid and chlorine bleach.

Acid and chlorine... Acid and chlorine... Who had mentioned those recently? Dr. Merritt?

No.

No!

Sofia.

Sofia, the crazy lunatic bitch. Mix the acid and chlorine disinfectant together, and you'd get chlorine gas. Voila. I could gas those fuckers out. The only problem? I'd probably end up dying myself. How long could I hold my breath? Long enough to get back through the passages? Back to the library? If I did make it, how the hell would I open that door? There had to be a handle somewhere.

Didn't there?

I'd have given the gas thing a go if it hadn't been for Asher. Risking my own life was one thing, but his as well? I'd fucked him over enough already. And Saul might kill me, but he wouldn't kill his own nephew.

Would he?

Saul didn't seem all that fond of Asher. Whereas I really was. More than fond of Asher, in fact, and I'd hurt him badly. Why, oh why, had I gone into that bloody cellar? That was the worst decision I'd made since I left the Academy nightclub with Brock bloody Keaton. *The Academy...* I'd have laughed at the irony if the situation weren't so serious. *Fuck my damn life.* I wanted to make Saul eat his own balls—if he had any, that was. He didn't seem to do much of his own dirty work. Did Ezra know what his brother was involved with? The younger Rosenberg seemed meeker, sometimes bumbling, but he ran the damn school. Would he miss a bazillion bucks in stolen paintings being stored right under his nose?

So many questions, so few answers.

There had to be some way out of this. *There had to be.* I was eighteen years old, and I'd only just started living, really living. I'd finally found my tribe. My family. I couldn't lose them now.

Breathe, Sky. Keep breathing. A lightbulb pinged in my brain. *Keep breathing.*

What if? What if...?

CHAPTER 39 - SKY

I WEDGED ONE end of the *Danger of Death* sign under the door, then stuck two pool noodles under the other end to form a rudimentary funnel. Did it matter which chemical I poured first? I hoped not, but I had a fifty-fifty chance, which was a whole lot better than zero. I hefted a drum onto one knee and began tipping it. Colourless liquid splashed onto the sign and ran under the door. How much was I meant to use? All of it? Perhaps I should have paid more attention to Sofia's ramblings.

Glug, glug, glug. The hydrochloric acid didn't smell of much, but I sincerely hoped nobody splashed through the puddle before I got to the good bit. Finally, the last dregs ran out of the drum, and I tilted the bleach in the same way. Yuck. That stank.

The first shout came a minute later. A confused, "What's that smell?" followed by footsteps. Time to get ready. I crouched down and fastened the buoyancy control device around my chest. I didn't need to use it, but I'd strapped the scuba tank onto the back, which made it a lot easier to carry. The cylinder had fifty bar of air left in it, about a quarter full—not great, but if I didn't exert myself too much, it should be enough to get me out of there. I put the matching mask on to protect my eyes and nose and tucked a spare into the BCD's pocket. Okay. Ready. I picked up the baseball bat and waited.

Waited.

Waited.

It wasn't long until the bolts shot back, *clunk, clunk*, one after the other. Somebody coughed. Muttered, "You little bitch." Saul? Or the waiter again? That seemed like something either of them might say. I stood to the left and waited for the door to open wide enough that I could see who was on the other side, and once I'd confirmed it wasn't Asher, I let fly with the bat. The waiter's skull caved like an eggshell. There was surprisingly little blood.

During my training, I'd wondered how it would feel to kill a man. I always knew I'd have to do it someday. But now that I'd popped my cherry, so to speak, I felt nothing. Nothing at all. A man's actions determined his fate, and he'd deserved it.

But where was Asher? Had Saul taken his nephew with him? The chamber was deserted, a soupy cloud of yellow gas making everything look blurry. Running feet sounded in the distance.

I took out my regulator and nearly choked when I opened my mouth to yell.

"Asher!"

Please answer. Please.

A shout came back, the voice unmistakable.

"In here!"

In where? The shout had come from my right, and I ran towards the sound. Those swines. Those utter bollocking fucktwizzling cuntwaffles. They'd left Asher with one hand cuffed to a wooden railing in a small room that looked like a shrine crossed with an office, all shiny wood and carvings and weird little statues. He had his eyes screwed shut and his shirt over his mouth, and anger burned through me like red-hot lava because his family, his own flesh and blood, had left him there to die.

I fumbled the spare diving mask over his head, and when he opened his eyes, I stuffed the backup regulator into his mouth and removed my own for a second.

"Breathe slowly. We don't have much air. Do you understand?"

He nodded, eyes wide, then ducked as I picked up a stone figure that might have been a saint or a sinner and swung it like I was aiming at Saul Rosenberg's head. The railing splintered, and I tugged the handcuff free, then grabbed my bat again. Asher hesitated, and I hauled him towards the door, pausing to check the cavern was clear before we exited.

Don't fucking stop.

But when I tried to run towards the exit, towards the music room, Asher pulled me in the other direction. No, no, no. I knew where I was going. I shook my head, but still he wanted to head the other way.

He spat out his regulator. "Uphill. Go uphill. Chlorine gas...heavier than air. Sinks."

It did? Sofia had failed to mention that little snippet of information. But now that I thought about it, the air near the ceiling did look clearer. I followed Asher, and we set off at a slow, stumbling jog, leaving the light behind as we got farther along the highest passage. The waiter had taken my cell phone, so we had no way of lighting the path. How much air did we have left? I had no idea. I couldn't see the gauge.

All I could do was keep walking. Keep breathing.

Until I couldn't breathe anymore. I tried to inhale, and there was nothing but a horrible sucking sensation, as if someone was trying to pull out my lungs. Asher's fingernails digging into my palm told me he was experiencing the same. The air was still hazy, and I tried to quell my panic as I undid the clips on the BCD and let it fall to the floor. Losing that weight was a relief, at least. It had to weigh twenty pounds, and my thigh muscles were burning.

"Keep going," I gasped.

Asher didn't answer, but he did start walking again, which I took as a good sign. What wasn't a good sign? The wall of rock I bumped into thirty seconds later.

I clawed at the edges of the passage, but it was a dead end. Where had we gone wrong? We didn't have time to go back and find a different route, and when I gave in and took a breath, the air was acrid, pungent with the stink of chlorine.

"Over here," Asher told me, and he guided my hand to something sticking out of the rock. Smooth metal, cold, cylindrical... The rung of a ladder! I swarmed up it until my head hit the ceiling. Asher was right behind, and his arms wrapped around me, his body moulded to mine as we both gulped in the cleaner air at the top.

"You okay?" he asked.

"Bloody marvellous." I sucked in another lungful of sweet, sweet oxygen. "Alive, so there's that."

"I thought I was dead. They left me there. Uncle Saul left me there."

I heard the torment in his voice, the hollow agony at being betrayed by two people close to him on the same day. I couldn't change the past, but I wanted to give him a future.

"Me too. So at least he won't be looking for us."

"How are we gonna get out of here?"

"Hold me steady?"

His arms tightened, and I reached mine up. Nobody built a ladder that didn't go anywhere, and when I'd hit my head, it had been a *clonk* rather than a *crack*. The ceiling above us was wooden. A trapdoor. I climbed up a rung and shoved. There was a metallic clatter as something above fell over, and the panel flipped open with a heavy *thunk*. I stuck my head through the hole, and a creature skittered over my face. I'd never been so grateful to see a spider in my life.

The shed. We were in the old toolshed. A momentary spasm rippled through me as I thought of the time we'd spent there before. Those bittersweet moments when Asher had started opening up to me. When he'd peeled away the first layer of armour he wore and given me a glimpse into his soul.

I offered a hand and helped him out of the dungeon. "We need to get off the campus. Even if Saul and his buddies aren't looking for us, they're still around."

Asher patted his pockets. "I've still got my car key. Let's go."

Hand in hand, we started down the path in the rain. There wasn't much of a moon, but every so often, a flash of lightning helped to guide us. And so did the noise. As we got closer to the main building, I heard high-pitched ringing plus the squeals of several hundred panicked students. They were milling around everywhere, and I noticed Deandra standing at the side of the basketball court on her own. Such a shame.

"What's happening?" I muttered, half to myself.

"Somebody's set off the fire alarm."

Who? Why? Had the chlorine gas triggered it somehow? Whatever the reason, I didn't want to stick around to find out. I broke into a run. We could use the confusion to our advantage and escape. Blackwood's rented house was only a few miles away, and if we got there, we'd be safe.

"Holy shit. *This* is your car?"

Asher had stopped beside a vintage muscle car, dark metallic blue with white stripes over the bonnet. It should have been in a movie, not a school parking lot.

"A 1967 Ford Mustang Fastback. I restored it myself."

Okay, he was right. His talents were wasted at school. But while the car looked beautiful and the roar of the engine was music to my ears, I didn't have time to stop and admire it because Asher suddenly hunched forward over the steering wheel.

"What? What's wrong?"

"See that Mercedes going down the driveway?"

"Yeah?"

"That's Uncle Saul's car."

Well, shit.

"Are you sure?"

"I know cars, Chem. What do you want to do?"

Duh. "Go after him."

CHAPTER 40 - EMMY

OKAY, WHO SET off the fire alarm?

Shadow Falls Academy had eight music rooms, two of which were on the ground floor. Only the one in the west wing had bookcases, so by process of elimination, we had to be in the right place. One minute, Nate was trying to work out which bookcase to blow off the wall, and the next, bells were ringing. Fucking smoke detectors. Maybe one of the kids was burning their stash? We'd worn DEA windbreakers for fun, battered down the front door, and marched straight through the building. The handful of students we'd come across had leapt out of our way when Alaric barked that we were there acting on a tip-off.

"Just blow them all," Ana said. "We have enough charges, *da*?"

Then the shelves nearest to me began to move.

"Quiet!"

Everyone caught the urgency in my voice, and it took mere seconds for them to stack up either side of the widening doorway. Someone dimmed the lights. What the fuck was that stink? I wrinkled my nose. A cross between a swimming pool and one of Sofia's science experiments? Ah, chlorine gas. I glanced over at her and saw she was putting goggles on, then she cut her hand across her throat. Message received. Bad shit.

Standard operating procedure meant we all carried lightweight goggles in our pockets, and I followed suit, breathing shallowly. Sofia was the expert at this. If and when we needed to leave, she'd tell us.

A shadowy figure stepped through the opening, and Rafael lived up to his nickname—Quicksilver—and grabbed him around the throat. I saw the silhouette of a gun pressed to the man's temple. The second suspect went to Ana, the third to Alaric. Black had finally turned up, and he snagged a fourth. We waited another thirty seconds, but nobody else appeared. I turned the lights up again and wedged the piano stool into the gap in case the bookcase decided to slide back. Fia was already throwing the windows open.

Who had we caught?

Well, well, well... Ezra Rosenberg. I recognised Sky's chemistry teacher as well, plus the track coach and a member of the kitchen staff. As I watched, Rafael fished a revolver out of Ezra's waistband and stuck it into his own. There was a contingent of Americans who wanted to arm schoolteachers, but I wasn't sure this was quite what they had in mind. Hmm, where to start? In situations like this, I always went straight for the big dog. Ezra almost doubled over when I kicked him in the nuts, and I say "almost" because Rafael soon snapped him upright again.

"Where's Sky?"

That grunt wasn't really an answer.

"Blonde, my height, kind of mouthy?"

Vomiting didn't help either. I stepped to the side so it didn't splash on my shoes and tsk-tsk-tsked.

"Would it help if I shot you in the kneecap?"

"I-i-in the cellar."

"Whereabouts in the cellar?"

"A h-hundred yards? Two hundred? F-f-follow the passage. She's locked in a room."

Two hundred yards? Fuck, that was a big cellar.

"And where's your brother?"

"I don't know."

"Was he down there?"

Ezra managed a nod.

"Is there another exit?"

No answer, but Ezra's eyes gave him away. There *was* another exit.

"Where?"

Silence. Obstinate silence. I booted him in the shin, hard, and he sagged in Rafael's arms as he fainted. Ah, fuck. Why did bad guys have such low pain thresholds?

"Where did all this gas come from?" I asked the next asshole.

"I-I don't know."

I was pretty good at holding my breath, but I didn't fancy searching a massive cellar without a respirator, especially if there were other gun-toting miscreants skulking around down there. We'd have to go slowly, and chlorine gas was nasty stuff. When it came into contact with the moist tissues of your eyes, your throat, your lungs, it produced acid that ate away at the surfaces. It wasn't great for your skin either. I'd need to shower as soon as I got out of here.

But first, we had a problem to solve. Luckily, someone out there had done us a favour. Above the jangling din of the fire alarm, I heard sirens. Fire trucks. And they'd have breathing equipment on board.

"Get these fuckers secured and move them to another room. We need to borrow gear and search the cellar. Fia, you take Rosenberg. See what else you can get out of him."

If four people stayed above ground with the prisoners, that left six of us to venture underground. Actually, make that five.

"Where's Silver?"

Ryder was trussing up Ezra now, flex cuffs on the fucker's arms and ankles and duct tape everywhere else. He jerked his head towards the door.

"He went to check the Rosenberg residence."

For fuck's sake. I tried raising Rafael on the radio, but I only got a crackle in response. Bloody storm.

"He can take care of himself," Black said.

"Yes, I know, but rescuing Sky is our most pressing problem right now. We need all hands on deck. Time's ticking."

"He's gone to look for Saul. Ten bucks says there's an exit at the house."

"Fine." I had to concede that did make a certain amount of sense, and there was a chance Saul could have taken Sky with him if she was incapacitated. "Let's get the kit we need."

We didn't bother to ask the firefighters if we could use their stuff. Thankfully, they were too busy herding running students and trying to work out where the fire was to even notice us rummaging through the trucks. My coat was too big, and Black's was a little tight across the shoulders, but the breathing apparatus worked just fine.

The gas was still thick as we descended into the bowels of the school, and the place sure lived up to its name. Dark, shadowy, ghouls hid in every corner. Ezra Rosenberg hadn't been kidding about the distance either—the passages went on for what seemed like miles. I was impressed. It put the arrangement of tunnels underneath Riverley to shame. But we'd done ours with an excavator, and here it looked as if a small army had carved the maze out of the limestone rock a million years ago, so I guess they'd had a head start. Fifty yards in, I tripped over a body. When I flipped her over with my foot, I recognised Saul Rosenberg's assistant. Ah, well. Saved me a job later.

We carried on.

What was this place? Through the haze, the passage opened into a cavern. Some pretentious prick had even installed a fucking chandelier.

"Is this a church?" I asked. "Are those pews?"

"A synagogue," Xav told me. "That closet looks like the *Aron Kodesh*."

"The what?"

"The Holy Ark. The place where they keep the Torah scrolls. My people have been persecuted all their lives. Some decided it would be safer to worship underground."

"Literally underground?"

"In this case, it appears so."

No, in this case it appeared they'd lost their faith entirely. The Holy Ark and most of the pews were covered in a thick layer of dust and the odd cobweb. Nobody had worshipped there recently, that much was clear.

"Do they all keep stolen shit in a side room too?" Ana asked. "These are paintings, yes?"

I ran over to take a look. Holy hell, again quite literally. I read the scribbles on the first crate. *Hieronymus Bosch—The Last Judgement*. There had to be over a hundred wooden boxes in that room, most of them slim and flat enough for paintings. The Master wasn't just a thief, he was a bloody hoarder. But the paintings weren't the priority tonight.

"Sky isn't in here. Keep looking."

"I found the source of the chlorine," Sofia said from across the room. "And this dead guy has two phones in his pocket. Is one of them Sky's?"

It was—she had a picture of my cat as her screensaver and the "I'm Sunshine with a chance of Hurricane" sticker on the back came courtesy of Bradley. The dead guy on the floor could have been Sky's handiwork too, but where the hell was she?

"Clump of long blonde hair caught on the door frame over here," Dan called. "Might be Sky's."

"Get after her."

I was about to follow, but movement by the passage from the music room caught my eye. The enemy? I got my gun up, then lowered it just as quickly. It was Black. Better late than never, but what did he have in his hands? The gas cloud shifted in a draught, and I got a clearer look.

That cunning, conniving, devious motherfucker. I had to hand it to him. That was slick. Real slick. As soon as the remainder of the team disappeared through the far doorway, he stepped forward.

"Put them in there," I told him, pointing to the side room Ana had found.

He didn't hesitate, just strode inside and stacked his offerings with the rest of the loot. One wooden box and one aluminium briefcase.

"You kept the pay-off all this time?"

"Thought it might come in useful one day."

"I don't know whether to kiss you or kill you."

"If you don't do the first, you might as well do the second."

I stared at him for a beat, considering. I'd told Black to fix things for Alaric and he had, but Sky was still missing, and if anything had happened to her...

Black could wait. I turned and ran after the others.

CHAPTER 41 - SKY

"HAVE YOU GOT your seat belt on?" Asher asked.

No, but I did it up pretty damned quickly as he accelerated after Saul. The Mustang was fitted with six-point belts—the kind you got in racing cars—and it went like a rocket. What the hell did it have under the bonnet?

"How fast does this thing go?"

"It's not about the top speed, Chem. I'll never reach that. It's about the acceleration."

"So how fast does it accelerate?"

"My best eighth-mile pass is four point eight seconds at a hundred and fifty-three miles per hour. She's got a thousand and forty-five horsepower from the engine alone, but another seven hundred when you add the nitrous."

"What does that even mean?"

"It means she's high-maintenance. Now do you see where most of my money went?"

Until that point, we'd been keeping Saul's Mercedes in sight, but now Asher flipped a switch on the dash and the car shot forward as if a giant foot had kicked it. In an instant, my head was jammed back against the seat and we were kissing Saul's rear bumper. Asher flashed the headlights.

"Just saying hi. You wanted to catch him? Well,

we've caught him."

"Okay, so I'm not sure I totally thought this through." I didn't have a phone and neither did Asher. We couldn't call for help. "The last chase I was in was a lot slower."

At least I had gas money this time. I'd started carrying fifty bucks in my back pocket, just in case.

"The *last* chase?" Asher shook his head. "I really don't know you at all, do I?"

No, but at least this time when he said it, he didn't sound quite so pissed.

"We can do a Q and A session later if you like, but for the moment, do you have any ideas?"

"Yeah."

"Care to elaborate?"

"When we were in that cellar, before the gas came, Saul gave me a choice. He said it was time to decide between my family and my stupid infatuation. 'Think with your head,'" Asher mimicked. "'Not your dick. If you're not with us, you're against us.'"

"And I was the stupid infatuation?"

"So Saul thought." What did *that* mean? "Then he told me he'd given my mother the same ultimatum, and she'd made the wrong decision. He pushed her away. Made her life hell. And he thought he'd do the same to me."

"I'd give you a hug if you didn't hate my guts and if we weren't going at..." I leaned over to see the speedometer. "At a hundred and freaking ten miles an hour."

"You want to slow down?"

"I wouldn't mind."

Smoothly, so smoothly, Asher inched forward and

gave Saul's bumper the tiniest nudge, and we shot past as the Mercedes began to fishtail wildly. I twisted in time to see it career into a tree and disappear into the darkness.

"Now we can slow down."

My breath came in pants as the car drew to a halt. Did that just happen? Did Asher really just run his uncle off the road?

"That? *That* was your plan?"

"I might regret it in the morning, but right now..." He shrugged. "I'm good. Prison won't be any worse than that fucking school."

"Prison?" I fumbled to undo my seat belt. "No way."

"What are you doing, Sky?" he shouted as I slammed the car door. "Where are you going?"

"I'm going to check he's definitely dead."

Dead men told no tales. And if Saul *was* still breathing? I'd finish the fucking job.

Saul, it turned out, hadn't bothered to buckle up. The way his brain had splattered across the crazed windscreen reminded me of a Jackson Pollock painting. An expensive mess. But hopefully one that could be written off as an accident rather than the artist's intention. The storm... A wet road...

Twigs cracked as Asher scrambled down the slope behind me.

"Don't look," I told him. "You don't need to see this."

"Is he...?"

"Yup. Does your car have much damage?"

Had he looked?

"Barely a scratch. It'll polish out."

Of course he'd looked. I backtracked to the rear of the Mercedes, and there were so many dings and dents from its trip through the trees that I wasn't sure an extra one would matter. The road was quiet. No witnesses. Was there anything else we needed to consider? Something niggled me about this picture, but I couldn't put my finger on what.

Then it hit me.

Why was the passenger door open?

For the second time that night, the *snick* of a gun being cocked made my stomach clench.

Oh, fuck.

Who was left? Ezra? Dr. Merritt? I turned slowly, catching sight of the expression on Asher's face as I did so. The Mustang's headlights were shining down on us, and he'd gone absolutely white.

"Grandma?" he whispered.

A grey-haired lady came into view, and the pistol she gripped with both hands was almost as big as she was. But it didn't waver.

"Stay where you are, both of you. Hands in the air." She tutted as we complied. "I'm disappointed in you, Asher. I thought you were different."

"D-different?"

"You've taken after your mother. Let the devil bewitch you."

Bloody hell, this whole family was nuts.

"What are you talking about?" Asher asked.

"I had plans. Without Mina's influence hanging over you, I'd hoped that in time you'd join us in the family business."

"You...wanted me to become a teacher?"

She just laughed. "The *other* family business."

"The paintings?" he whispered.

The laugh turned into a cackle. "See? You're not as dim as Ezra thought. Ezra..." She shook her head. "What a disappointment he turned out to be."

"You're criminals. Why the hell would you think *I* wanted to get involved?"

"Because this is your chance to do lasting good. Do you have any idea how many works of art were looted during the Second World War? Over half a million, and a hundred thousand of those are still missing. Scores were killed for their faith and for their treasures. And the people who hold those artifacts now, who hang them on their walls and show them off to their friends, they know where they came from. And still they won't give them up. Somebody needs to right the wrongs of the past."

"By...creating more wrongs?"

"In San Diego, you didn't mind breaking the rules. The car races on the freeway. All those women you serviced for money."

"You... You..."

"Of course I knew," she snapped. "I've had a private investigator keeping tabs on you from the moment you could walk."

This was bad. Really bad. The old bat was clearly psycho, but also smart. And then I got it. *She* was the original Master. And she'd still been behind the scenes, pulling the strings the entire time.

"So now what? What's going to happen to us?"

"The girl's got to go, of course."

She gestured to me with the gun in an offhand

manner. If I'd been ten feet closer, maybe I could have made a grab for it, but I was just too far away.

"When she came to Shadow Falls, you changed," Grandma continued. "Stopped coming to dinner, neglected your family. She's got a demon living inside her, the same as your father did, and demons need to be exorcised. But you, Asher... I haven't quite made up my mind. You're weak, but perhaps your soul can still be salvaged. Saul wasn't perfect—that boy was too greedy for his own good—but with the proper guidance, he achieved great things. And family is family."

"So you want me to come with you? To help you?"

"To serve me. No matter what Saul called himself, I'm still the Master."

Yup, absolutely batshit crazy. And also still pointing a gun at me.

Asher inched closer. "We'd move away?"

"Thanks to your little whore, we don't have much choice. I have money. We can start again."

He glanced at me, and I saw the distress in his eyes. The sorrow. And something else... An apology? Why? He wouldn't seriously go with the insane bitch, would he? Sure, he'd had a few transgressions, but the idea of him embarking on a life of crime was laughable.

But then his gaze flicked towards the gun, and I realised. I realised what he planned to do.

"Asher, no," I choked out.

"I'm sorry, Chem." He looked away. "Grandma, we should go. The cops will be coming."

He closed the gap as she levelled the gun at me, and everything moved in slow motion. Her finger tightened on the trigger. Asher sprang forward. An almighty *bang* tore through the air, and blood sprayed far enough to splash my face.

"No!"

I barely recognised my own scream. Asher and his grandma had landed in a heap, and I clawed at him. If she'd missed his head, missed his vital organs... Fuck, I couldn't even call an ambulance. Was he still alive? He groaned as I rolled him over, and I desperately tried to remember facts from the introductory first aid course Emmy had sent me on at Blackwood's headquarters. I needed to stop the bleeding. Where was the wound? Asher was covered in blood, red and sticky with its distinctive coppery smell.

"Don't leave me. Life won't be the same without you driving me crazy, you asshole. Don't you dare fucking leave me!"

Then hands pulled me away, and I struggled and slapped because I needed to help Asher. I had a belt. I could make a tourniquet. Drag him to the car, drive him to the hospital.

"Let me go!"

"Sky!" Someone slapped me hard, and my mind cleared enough to think.

"Rafael?"

"Focus. He'll live. She won't."

He turned me back to face Asher, just in time for me to see him sit up. He was okay? I blinked and realised half of his grandma's head was gone. Little pieces of cauliflower-brain were dotted all through the grass. Holy fuck. Rafael had gone for the apricot, and he hadn't missed.

The sound of car doors slamming on the road above jarred me closer to reality. Who was it? Rafael didn't seem concerned by the new arrivals, and I took that as a good sign.

"Fuck me. You made one hell of a mess tonight, Malone."

Emmy was there. I almost cried with relief.

"Somebody bring blankets," she shouted. "Either of you injured?"

"I'm not sure. I'm okay, but Asher..." He tried to get to his feet, and I grabbed his hand. "Are you hurt?"

"I don't think so."

"Your eyes?" Emmy asked. "Your throats? Lungs?"

"We had scuba gear."

"Bet that was a sight. C'mon, get your arses in the car. We've got a hell of a lot of clean-up to do on this one."

"In Asher's car? Where should we go?"

"In Dan's car. We'll sort out the rest."

A blanket was wrapped around my shoulders, and somebody nudged me towards the road. I grabbed Asher's hand, now minus the dangling cuffs, and he came along too.

CHAPTER 42 - EMMY

IT WAS ALMOST five o'clock in the morning when we arrived back at Riverley. I'd sent Dan and Sofia on ahead with Sky and Asher, and the pair of them were sleeping peacefully now. Fia might or might not have had a hand in that. Ezra was in jail along with his buddies, and Vanessa was back in her room with instructions to keep her mouth shut. She was the one who'd set off the alarm. When Sky and Asher hadn't come back, she'd set fire to a wastebasket in one of the A-block bathrooms, figuring that the fear of smoke inhalation would get any bad guys out of the cellar so her friends could leave too. I'd speak to her properly tomorrow.

For now, we'd handed the scene over to the FBI. They were busy clashing with the fire department as they pulled all manner of stolen paintings out of the Rosenbergs' lair. Alaric and Nate were still there, keeping an eye on things. Well, Nate was in the music room, nosing around the bookcase. The lock appeared to be musical. When Sky turned the light switch on and off, she'd woken it up. It then "listened" for a set period of time, and when Asher played a particular combination of notes on the piano, it triggered the door to open. The unit itself was crude, Nate said. As if it had been cobbled together for a student project and then repurposed. Quite possibly it had.

I'd hung around with Alaric until they rescued *Emerald*. She'd caused so much trouble, yet I'd never seen her in the flesh before. Had it been worth the wait? Not really. I could quite cheerfully have barbecued the smug bitch by that point, but the relief on Alaric's face made all the effort worth it.

What *was* worth the wait? Driving Asher's car back from Shadow Falls. That beast was sweet. A gas guzzler, but boy could it go. Now I needed to buy a Mustang. And more gin. I added ice to a glass and poured myself another G&T from the wet bar in the corner of my living room. Did this count as late drinking or early drinking? I wasn't sure, but I came to the conclusion I didn't care.

"Diamond?"

Black appeared in the doorway, and I knew what he wanted. My forgiveness. The past three months had been brutal on everyone, not least him. Yes, he'd deserved it, but I still hated to see him looking so tired.

And what was the outcome? I'd spent the trip back turning things over in my mind. When I wasn't blowing past other cars, that was.

Alaric had suffered the most from Black's deceit. But if the original handover had gone smoothly, he'd never have met Bethany. And she was far better for him than I could ever have been. He was totally head over heels for her. And he had Rune. If not for *Emerald*'s curse, she'd be either dead or turning tricks in a Thai whorehouse. I'd never have met Sky, and she wouldn't have met Asher. Where was *that* relationship going? The jury was still out, but she seemed to like him.

And then there was Sirius. Alaric would have

stagnated at the FBI, but I wasn't sure he'd have had the guts to set out on his own without that initial push. New Alaric was more relaxed. His smiles came easier. Plus he had Ravi and Judd and Naz, although Judd was still an asshole. I had a feeling they'd all be pretty busy once word that *Emerald* and the pay-off had been found got out. In Shadow Falls, Black had taken charge of the scene, called in favours, contained the fallout, and talked up Sirius's involvement in the hunt. Alaric's reputation had been restored.

Yes, I forgave Black.

And I liked to think he'd learned his lesson.

"I've missed you," I said simply, and he understood. I was in his arms before I could blink.

And naked before I could take a breath. How the hell had he gotten my clothes off so fast?

Ah. A switchblade.

He leaned his forehead against mine. "I'm sorry. For everything I did wrong."

"Don't hurt me again," I said. Then I sighed and dropped to my knees. "Because the pink vibrating dildo Bradley came up with is no match for the real thing."

And it played the hallelujah freaking chorus when I came. No kidding. I'd tensed up so fucking fast I fired that monster right across the bed.

Black snarled his disgust at my battery-operated boyfriend, and like magic, he started to harden under my fingers. We weren't going to make it anywhere near the bedroom, were we? I was glad Sofia had slipped our house guests a little something-something because we'd have had awkward questions to answer otherwise. I got Black's belt open and his fly too, and then I took his cock into my mouth. Breakfast of champions.

"Fuck, Emmy," he groaned when my lips got within shouting distance of the base.

I let him go with a quiet *pop*. "Thought you'd never ask."

"What do you want? Top? Bottom? Against the wall?"

"Yes."

I noticed he didn't suggest heading for the sofa. Bending me over the back was an old favourite of his, but our couch-related activities hadn't ended too well last time. This morning, he carried me over to the sheepskin rug in front of the fireplace and laid me down. It was white, so the cum stains wouldn't show, but I was paranoid about it getting crispy underfoot and we'd replaced it three times already.

But I soon forgot the rug when he slid inside. I'd missed this, I'd missed *him*, so fucking much.

"I love you, Chuck," I whispered in his ear. "Don't you bloody forget it."

"Trust me, I won't. You've made your point, Diamond, and I learn from my mistakes."

Chapter 43 - Sky

"AFTERNOON."

EMMY WAS sitting at the kitchen table when I stumbled through the doorway. My body felt heavy. Stiff. I'd never experienced tiredness quite like it.

"Hey, boss."

The news was on the TV in the corner, and when I saw a picture of *Spirit* on the screen, I paused to listen. Emmy turned the volume up.

"The art world is celebrating today after a huge cache of stolen treasures was found at a private school in northern Virginia. Among the works found were *The Shepherd's Watch*, taken recently in dramatic fashion during a charity event, and a piece believed to have been painted by Leonardo da Vinci. A source has indicated that Astinov's masterpiece *Spirit of the Lake* was also present at the scene, and it's unclear what this means because that particular painting is believed to be hanging in the Stiller Collection in Miami. More to come on that later. And in other news, police are no further forward in identifying the man who attacked pop sensation Brock Keaton in his Malibu home last week."

Emmy pressed the mute button, thank goodness.

"How's Asher?" she asked.

"I haven't spoken to him yet. I wanted to talk to you

first."

She took a sip of coffee. "Yeah, I suppose we could do with a debrief."

"I'm sorry for the mess. I don't really know what else to say."

"Eh, it wasn't that messy. They got rid of the chlorine gas with big fans in the end. The tunnels went all over the place. One came out in the chemistry teacher's office, another under Linton Hall, plus there was one in the cellar at the Rosenbergs' house."

"What about the bodies?"

"There were only half a dozen."

Black materialised and sat next to Emmy. As in, *right* next to Emmy, and then he wrapped an arm around her. She leaned into him. Okay, this was new.

"Nobody knows how the chemical spillage occurred, and Rafael shot Tovah Rosenberg with Ezra's gun after the accident. Timelines get confused."

"But there'll be an investigation. Won't there?"

Emmy waggled her head from side to side and did air quotes, Dr. Evil-style. "'Investigation.'"

"Huh?"

"People owed Black favours. And besides, if they looked into the details too closely, they'd have to admit they screwed up with Alaric eight years ago. The cops found *Emerald*'s original pay-off in the cellar last night. Guess the Rosenbergs took it after all."

She stared at me over the rim of her coffee cup, daring me to disagree. No way was I about to do that.

"Right. Good thing that turned up."

"Isn't it? Of course, Ezra Rosenberg's screaming for a lawyer, but it's a slam-dunk case. The whole damn family was involved. The ledgers in the room where

Saul tried to gas Asher have all the details, although Ezra swears the whole thing was Saul's and his mother's idea and he wanted out. The FBI's up to a hundred and thirty stolen works of art and still counting. Lucky we acted when we did—*The Shepherd* was due to leave in two days."

"What'll happen to the school?"

"Not sure yet. I expect somebody'll appoint a new headmaster and staff to replace the Rosenbergs and their accomplices, but the authorities are still trying to work out who all of them are, so it won't be instantaneous."

"I'm worried about Vanessa. She helped me through this, school and everything. I couldn't have done it without her."

"We'll make sure Vanessa's okay."

"And I'm also worried about Asher. I was wondering... You said that if I pass my probation, then I'll get paid three hundred thousand quid, and I know I'm only halfway through and I might fail, but if I could even have a small bit of the money, then I want to give it to him. He's got nothing now. Well, he's got his car, but I'm pretty sure he likes that more than he likes me, so..."

"No," Black said.

My stomach dropped. "No?"

"You've earned that money. It's yours. We'll take care of Asher separately."

"He needs to graduate to get an inheritance from his father, and I'm not sure if you know, but he isn't great at reading and writing."

"Understood. We can pay for him to board somewhere. Or he can stay here for a while and go to a local school. Or you can get a place together. There are options."

"Really? You'd let him stay here?"

"Between the two main houses and the guest house, we've got twenty-six bedrooms. I'm sure we can squeeze him in somewhere."

Was that an attempt at humour from Black? I pinched myself to check I wasn't dreaming. Nope, it bloody hurt. Okay then. In truth, I wasn't sure Asher would be keen on staying at Riverley, but at that moment, I realised how much I wanted him to.

"I need to see how he is."

"Good idea," Emmy said. "Take him a coffee. We can have a proper chat later. Four o'clock?"

"Okay."

"And Sky?"

"What?"

She broke into a smile. "You didn't do bad out there."

The talk with Emmy had gone a hell of a lot better than I thought it would, but would a heart-to-heart with Asher be as easy? I was thinking not. He'd stayed in the room next to mine last night, and when I got upstairs, I knocked on his door.

"It's Sky. Are you awake?"

A mumbled answer came back. "I'm not sure."

"Can I come in?"

The door swung open and Asher stood before me in a pair of pyjama pants, rubbing his eyes. His hair was mussed, and I tried not to stare at his chest, but it was quite nice as chests went. Not stacked like Rafael's, but athletic.

"What time is it?" Asher asked.

"A quarter to one."

"I feel like I've been hit by an eighteen-wheeler."

I held out a steaming mug. "Would this help?"

"Thanks. I was hoping everything that happened at the academy was a nightmare, but if that were the case, I guess I wouldn't be here, would I?"

"I'm so sorry."

He opened the door wider. "We probably need to talk."

"We do."

I stepped inside his room. Should I sit down? I didn't want to assume that was a good idea, so I leaned against the wall instead.

"Sky... *Is* your name Sky?"

"Sky Malone. I don't have a middle name."

"First question, Sky. What is this place?"

"The Riverley estate. It belongs to my boss and her husband."

"It's a private home?"

"Yes."

Asher looked around the room, his gaze pausing on the window. Emmy's horse was running around like an idiot in a far-off pasture.

"It's..."

"Wow?" I suggested.

He nodded. "I don't... I can't... What I did last night..."

"You said you might regret it this morning."

"But I don't. That's the thing—I don't. When the room started filling with gas, Uncle Saul knew it was poisonous. Dr. Merritt yelled at him to leave, and I begged him to let me go, but he stood in the doorway, and he looked back at me, and he shrugged. He fucking shrugged. And then he left."

"I understand."

I really did. If ten-year-old me could have smashed my father into a tree, I'd have done it.

"And Grandma... I'd never seen that side of her before. Never. She was gonna kill you, Sky. I saw it in her eyes."

"I know. I saw it too."

"Who...? What...?"

"Somebody I work with. He followed us from the school."

Emmy told me Rafael had seen us leaving and jumped into his SUV. When he caught up, Asher and I were already down at Saul's car, and Rafael had crept through the trees and watched. And waited. And listened. And that creeped me out more than a little bit because I'd had no clue he was there. Not even a hint. He was just one more shadow among the trees until he fired the round that had killed Tovah Rosenberg.

"She kept saying we were family, but when it came to making a choice, I wanted you to live, not her."

"Or you."

"Or me." He cleared his throat. "When I was lying there on the ground, you said... You said..."

I remembered, and boy was this awkward. "That life wouldn't be the same without you?"

"Did you mean it?"

I couldn't look at him, because what if he broke my heart? In so many ways, I was a coward.

"I did. At least, I'm pretty sure I did because I've never felt this way about anyone before, so I've got no point of reference and—"

"Sky?"

"Yes?"

"Stop talking." Asher took both of my hands in his. "Last night, I learned who my friends were."

Then he kissed me—properly—for only the third time, and I knew we'd make it through this. Blackwood had our backs, and we'd get through it together.

My life was still a mess, but now I had friends, a proper home, and a job that challenged me in ways I'd never thought possible. And I also had two men. One who would kill for me, and another who'd die for me.

What more could a girl ask for?

Speaking of men, one of them had gone missing in action. Rafael had found me at the rented house last night and checked I was okay, but I'd barely seen him since. And I needed to thank him. If he hadn't been such a sneaky bastard, either me or Asher would be dead right now. Quite possibly both of us. Rafael had also shown up at the debrief in the afternoon, but Rune was getting ready to leave for England with Alaric and Beth right afterwards, and by the time I'd finished saying goodbye to her, Rafael had vanished again. His Navigator had gone from the parking area by the stables, and when I borrowed a car and drove to his house, he wasn't there. My text went unanswered.

"Has anyone seen Rafael?" I asked the group hanging around in the kitchen at Riverley Hall. Mrs. Fairfax had set up a buffet for dinner, and the gannets had descended. "He's not here, and he's not at home."

"We drove past him," Hallie said, breaking off from her discussion about a new case. Something about a cussing parrot. "He was heading towards Richmond."

"Richmond? Any idea which part?"

Was he working tonight?

"Probably he's going to his apartment," her friend Mercy said.

His...apartment?

"But he has a house. Right here."

"And an apartment in the same building as us," Hallie said. "You didn't know? It's on the third floor, but he doesn't go there much."

"Just with girls," Mercy added. "But he never stays the night. Sometimes we find them wandering in the hallway the next morning."

Hallie giggled. "One looked so sad I took her for breakfast."

Rafael had a fuck pad in town? That made me feel... Actually, I wasn't sure how it made me feel. I suppose I shouldn't have been surprised because I knew he was no saint. It stood to reason that he had to get his kicks somehow. Then I recalled the tiny stab of jealousy that had knifed me between the ribs when I thought he took random hook-ups to his half-finished farmhouse, and I smiled inside. Why? Because *I* was the girl he invited into his real home, and when I passed out on his sofa, he stuck around to make me coffee the morning after.

"Wow. Guess I'll catch up with him tomorrow, then."

"Want to meet up for dinner later in the week?" Hallie asked. "We've missed you."

"Yeah. I think I'd like that."

I dished up food onto plates, covered them with tinfoil, and schlepped the whole lot back to Little Riverley. Asher didn't need to deal with a big crowd tonight. Emmy had suggested a few quiet days, no pressure, just chilling out of the way while the mayhem at Shadow Falls finished unravelling. We'd both need to speak to the police, but Emmy's lawyer would be running interference. I wasn't worried. Alaric said the guy was a shark, and I had the whole of Blackwood on my side.

"Dinner and a movie?" I asked as I walked into the living room.

"Don't you have to jump through a window first?"

"I can do that if you want."

"I almost puked every time you leapt that gap between the wall and the dorm." Asher stretched out an arm along the back of the sofa. "How about you just sit down instead?"

"Sounds good to me."

Snuggling up to Asher was my favourite way to spend an evening, but as the glass-and-chrome grandfather clock in the hallway struck midnight, I tucked a blanket over him and tiptoed outside, past the Mustang and over to Emmy's Corvette. I'd lifted the key from her pocket earlier, after the debrief. Sometimes, just sometimes, I thought I might be able to live up to the expectations she had of me.

For the third time in two days, I heard the quiet *snick* of a pistol being cocked, but this time, I wasn't worried.

"Don't shoot; it's me."

Rafael stalked towards me in jeans and a half-done-up shirt. Shoes, but no socks.

"You set off my perimeter alarm."

Oops. "I do hope I didn't interrupt anything."

His scowl told me all I needed to know. But he was still polite. When he waved me towards the front door, I walked in front of him, careful to skirt around the pile of bricks beside the porch. A glimmer of light came from the barn to the back, and I nodded towards it.

"We never did go bowling."

He turned off the alarm and locked the door behind us. "You came over in the middle of the night because you want to go bowling?"

"No, I came over because I never got the chance to thank you properly, and I didn't want to leave it any longer."

"It was nothing."

"It was everything. If you hadn't—"

"Stop. Don't dwell on what didn't happen. I've told you this before. Learn from your mistakes, but don't relive them."

"I'm trying to do that, but it's hard."

Rafael walked around me, focused with laser intensity. He didn't touch me, not once, but it felt as though he were undressing me with his eyes. I wanted to cover parts of myself with my hands, but it would have been pointless against his X-ray vision. What was he doing?

"Where's your weapon?" he asked.

Oh. Shit.

"Uh..."

"If you'd stopped to pick up a gun yesterday, I wouldn't have had to decorate your boyfriend with his grandmother's brains."

"Stopped where? I was—"

"There were three Blackwood cars parked within

spitting distance of Martinez's Mustang. One of them was mine, and they were all loaded with enough shit to start a war. You need to be more aware of your surroundings."

"Weren't they locked?"

"Break a fucking window, Sky. Think."

It hurt, but Rafael spoke the truth. I hadn't seen the bigger picture.

"Right."

"But apart from that, you did well."

Coming from him, those words were the equivalent of a standing ovation. I followed as he walked into the kitchen and took a bottle of Scotch out of his drinks cabinet. He didn't bother with ice as he sloshed a generous measure into a glass.

"Drink?" he asked.

"I'm driving."

He poured the Scotch down his throat, slammed the glass onto the counter, and levelled his gaze at me. I didn't look away, and he barked out an unexpected laugh.

"What?" I asked.

After a second, he slowly extended a hand. "Fuck it. Let's go bowling."

"Now?"

One shoulder twitched in a shrug.

Fuck it indeed. I took Rafael's hand, and we walked out to the old barn.

CHAPTER 44 - ALARIC

SEPTEMBER SIXTEENTH, AND Alaric had been on edge all day. Almost a week had passed since the showdown at Shadow Falls Academy, and things were finally getting back to normal. Or as normal as things could be in the new post-*Emerald* world.

Rune had gone back to school, and yesterday, Alaric had returned to the US with Beth for meetings. The phone had been ringing off the hook this week with new enquiries now that Alaric's name had been taken off the blacklist. Old contacts were calling, and at this rate, Sirius would be turning away work. Alaric might even be able to toss a few contracts in Emmy's direction as thanks for the jobs she'd given him when the firm was in its infancy. Outside of Judd, Ravi, and Naz, she was the one person who'd believed in him all these years.

He'd always love her, but not the same way he loved Beth.

Beth. He'd liked her as soon as he met her, even when he thought she was working against him, but nothing had prepared him for what he'd find when he scratched through her prim and proper exterior. Fifty shades of filth hidden under demure little suits and sky-high stilettos. They'd finally achieved one of his life goals on the flight back to the US, and when they'd both squeezed out of the tiny bathroom at forty thousand feet and a grey-haired lady had shaken her head and tutted, Beth had just giggled. Then given him a handjob in first class.

His perfect woman, and she wasn't a bad PA either. Sirius's office had never been so organised.

All of which meant he was keeping her. Permanently. Two months, twenty-nine days, and twenty-three hours ago, she'd agreed that three months was an appropriate length of time to wait for a proposal. He had an hour left to wait. The ring was in his pocket, dinner was in the oven, and there was a bottle of champagne on ice. Hell, he'd even arranged both of her wedding gifts. Was he nervous? No. She'd practically said yes already. Gift number two? *That* made him edgy. She'd said she wanted it, but did she really?

"Ready to eat?" he called up the stairs.

"Five minutes. I'm just changing my clothes."

Alaric almost asked if she needed a hand, especially with her shoes. She loved fancy high-heeled pumps, and so did he. On her, not himself, obviously—he'd break an ankle if he tried to walk in those things. But that could wait until later. The salmon en croûte would burn if he got distracted. Mrs. Fairfax had said to give it exactly forty minutes, not a moment longer. He had it on the table by the time Beth walked down the stairs, laid out beside steamed vegetables and a bottle of chilled white wine.

"You look beautiful," he said when she finally appeared. Not that she didn't always, but she rarely wore four-inch Louboutins for a quiet dinner at home.

"So do you. Handsome. I mean handsome."

Alaric pulled out her seat and poured her wine. He'd never lived with a woman before, but it was worth the wait. Getting up in the mornings was so much easier these days.

"I hear Killian Marshall went home this afternoon," Beth said.

"He did."

Strangely, Alaric had become quite fond of the man over the last few weeks, despite their difficult start. Marshall kept his mouth shut regarding the precise details of his illicit dealings, but they'd had some interesting discussions about art in general and art theft in particular over late-night glasses of Scotch. Alaric liked to think they'd stay in touch.

"Do you think he'll go straight?"

"Yes. I actually do."

"What about Hugo Pemberton?"

That was a trickier question. He was still handling stolen paintings, undoubtedly, but after some serious contemplation, Alaric was inclined to agree with Marshall over him. Better for the world's missing treasures to be kept in tip-top condition until they were eventually found than for Sirius to turn a relatively harmless old man over to the police. Besides, they had someone monitoring him. Gemma was still working at the gallery by day and staying at Judd's place in London by night.

"Reckon we'll leave him alone for the moment as well."

"I can't pretend that I'm not still a teensy bit annoyed that he fired me, but I think that's the right decision. And I suppose, really, I should thank him. I wouldn't be here otherwise."

"Strange how things turned out, isn't it? For everyone."

"I'm so glad Vanessa has a place at a new school. Sky and Asher both seem fond of her, and I wouldn't wish another year at Shadow Falls on anyone. Apart from perhaps that Deandra girl. From what Sky's said, she seems ghastly."

"Karma moves in mysterious ways."

When it became clear the academy would be closed for a month at least while the FBI dug into the backgrounds of all the staff and decontaminated the cellar, Black had pulled yet more strings and gotten Vanessa accepted at his old school. Rybridge Prep counted the current president among its alumni, and its reputation was second to none. Vanessa would be boarding, but Alaric had a feeling they'd be seeing a lot of her at Riverley on the weekends.

He nodded at Beth's plate. "How's the salmon?"

"Very—"

Beeping cut her off mid-sentence, and Alaric tensed. It was time. He'd been waiting for this moment for three long months. He fished his phone out of his jacket pocket to shut off the noise, only to find it wasn't his alarm ringing. When he looked up, Beth was tapping away at her phone screen.

"Sorry about that." She swallowed hard. "I don't know if you remember, but three months ago—"

Now Alaric's alarm went off, and what could he do but laugh?

"You beat me to it. Seems great minds think alike."

"You *did* remember?"

"I was hardly going to forget."

"Sorry. It's just that being married to Piers for so

long... He forgot every birthday and every anniversary. Anyhow, enough about him." She smiled brightly and fumbled a gold band out of her cleavage. "I bought you a ring and everything."

Alaric slipped a velvet box out of his pocket. "As I said: great minds. Give me your hand, Beth. In marriage and in life."

"But of course."

Thank goodness for that. The ring fit perfectly, the same way Beth fit him.

"An emerald?" she asked.

"I thought it was appropriate."

She slid her ring onto his finger, and that was it— they were both officially off the market. Alaric abandoned all thoughts of dinner, walked around the table, and kissed his girl stupid to seal the deal.

"So..." she said once they came up for air. "What's an appropriate length of time to wait between engagement and marriage?"

"Five minutes?"

"Be serious."

"I am. I'll fly you to Vegas right now if you want."

"Ugh, no. I'm not getting married in Vegas. That's so tacky."

"Don't say that to Emmy or Black. They got married there. Twice."

"My lips are sealed."

"They'd better not be. I have big plans for tonight."

Beth's eyes widened, and she put on that breathy voice that made him hard every time.

"Precisely how big are we talking?"

"Eight inches?"

"I think it's closer to nine."

The champagne could wait. Alaric scooped Beth up in his arms and carried her out of the dining room.

"Bedroom? Or do you want to bend over my desk ag —"

Bzzzzzzzzzz.

Who the hell was at the gates? Emmy was under strict instructions to keep her crew away from Hillside House tonight, and the other members of Team Sirius were in England. Nobody else even knew where he lived now.

"Get rid of them," Beth mumbled. "Please."

"I will."

It was probably canvassers, or someone trying to sell him a new religion, but he picked up a gun just in case. You never could be too careful. And there were still three paintings missing from the Becker Museum. Were they all cursed? Very likely, because when Alaric checked the screen on the entry phone, the sight before him was worse than he'd ever imagined. He'd rather have faced a hit squad.

"Oh, shit."

"What? Who is it?"

"My parents."

"Your parents? I thought you didn't speak to them anymore?"

"I don't."

Not for eight years, anyway. Not since they'd found him guilty of all charges and cut him off. He was tempted to leave them outside in the rain, but he knew his father too well—if Bancroft McLain had decided he wanted to talk to his son, then they'd be talking, sooner or later. Best to get it over with.

Beth kissed him softly on the cheek. "Whatever you

decide, I'll support you."

"I should probably find out what they want."

"Shall I wait upstairs?"

"No, stay." His father would be less likely to act like an arse with another woman around. And they might need a mediator. "If you're okay with that. They might be rude."

"I spent half a lifetime pretending to be nice to my parents' friends. I'm used to it."

Reluctantly, Alaric buzzed the gates open, and his father's Bentley pulled up outside the front door. Way to spoil a great evening.

Beth stayed polite as the elder McLains checked her over. Fortunately, she looked like exactly the type of girl they'd want him to marry, which led to a bemused smile from his mother. Lavinia McLain hadn't been fond of Emmy at all.

"Mom, Dad, meet Beth. Beth, these are my parents, Bancroft and Lavinia McLain."

Cue handshakes and polite noises.

"Tea or coffee?" Beth offered. "Water? Something stronger?"

A glass of Scotch would have gone down well, but Alaric kept his mouth shut.

"No need," Alaric's father said. "We won't be staying long."

Good. Alaric got straight to the point. "Why are you here?"

His parents looked at each other, and then his mother deferred to his father, the same way she always did.

"We saw the news."

"Am I supposed to be impressed?"

"They finally found that money."

"They did."

Blackwood's and Sirius's names had both been kept out of the media. The people who mattered knew, but publicly, the FBI got the credit.

"I hear you had a hand in it."

So his father still had ears in the right places.

"Somebody had to keep looking."

Another glance between his parents, and finally his mother spoke.

"We shouldn't have doubted you all those years ago. We've come to apologise."

Well, well, well. Miracles did happen. "It's a little late for that."

His father took over again. "I understand why you would feel that way. We can't turn back the clock, but we wanted to make amends." He drew a slim envelope out of his pocket and placed it on the hall table. "We'll just leave this here."

Alaric's mother glanced at Beth again, and suddenly she smiled. "You two are engaged?"

He nodded and took Beth's hand. "We are."

"Congratulations. That's lovely, isn't it, Bancroft?"

"You've done well for yourself, son." His gaze flitted around the large hallway, assessing, and then came back to Beth. "Very well."

"I know."

Technically, the house still belonged to Emmy, but one day Alaric hoped to buy it from her. If Sirius kept growing, he'd manage it.

"So... We'll be going then."

Alaric didn't bother to stop them. Why should he? Even before the *Emerald* incident, they hadn't made things easy for him, and when he'd needed their support, they'd turned their backs.

"I'll buzz you out."

Once the gates had closed behind them, Beth sank onto the ornamental couch Bradley had put in the hallway. He'd just shown up one day, directed two men where to place it, declared it looked "fandabidozi," and scurried out again. Eight years, and he hadn't changed a bit.

"That was weird," Beth said. "Are you okay?"

"That's the closest my father's ever come to apologising for anything."

"Perhaps he could give my father lessons. What's in the envelope?"

"No idea."

Alaric tore it open and found some sort of legal document, folded into three. McLain Family Trust, blah, blah, blah, from this date, blah, blah, blah, authorised signatories, blah, blah, blah.

"It seems as if they've unrevoked access to my trust fund."

"Really? How much is in there? Not that I care or anything," she hastened to add. "I'm just nosy."

Alaric knew she didn't care. Beth wasn't in this relationship for the money. When she'd fallen in love with him, he'd been camping out on friends' couches, for pity's sake.

"About five million bucks, give or take." And if his parents had relented, he'd inherit ten times that someday. "Guess we can build those stables you want now."

He tossed the document back onto the table. He didn't much care about the cash either. Wealth wasn't important to him, not anymore. Integrity was important. Friends were important. And Beth? She was vital.

He picked her up again, bridal-style, and carried her towards the stairs.

"Now, where were we?"

She whispered in his ear, and a grin spread across his face. They could drink the champagne for breakfast.

Chapter 45 - Sky

HOW THINGS COULD change in a month. Asher was enrolled at the Summit Academy in Richmond, a school that specialised in teaching students with dyslexia and related learning differences. When he'd gotten accepted, I'd seen the way relief warred with apprehension, but his worries had dissipated now. Yesterday, I'd caught him reading a book voluntarily, an actual paperback, and I'd be forever thankful to Black for greasing the wheels to get Asher a place there.

While he drove himself to school each day, I went back to training. Asher didn't love the career I'd chosen, and he didn't seem particularly keen on Rafael either, but he understood why I did it, and he supported me. When I crawled back home in the evenings, he'd be waiting with dinner or a movie or a massage. He *was* pretty damn good with his hands.

Emmy was taking advantage of his hands too. She'd bought—in Asher's words—a Deandra of a Mustang. Pretty on the outside, and an absolute bitch on the inside. While I worked late in the evenings, he tinkered in the garage with Emmy's new toy and his own beautiful beast. He hadn't let me drive it yet, but one day...

We'd even been on vacation together, albeit a very short one. A quick hop over to England because Emmy had business there and I wanted to see Lenny. His treatment was going well, but some of his addictions were so deeply ingrained that the medical staff thought he'd benefit from a longer stay. Probably because Emmy was paying the Abbey Clinic a bloody fortune, but Lenny seemed happy there, and most importantly, he was alive.

When I went to visit him, I found him in the lounge, playing chess with the woman I was fairly sure gave birth to Emmy. When he saw me arrive, he broke out in a huge grin and ran over to give me a hug.

"Sky!" He picked me up with strength he never used to have and spun me around. "I've missed you."

"The doctor said we can go out for lunch. How d'you fancy a Maccy D's?"

Because I was dying for one. Toby had been feeding me lean meat and pulses and vegetables all month, and while I appreciated his concern for my well-being, my scrawny arse craved Chicken McNuggets and a milkshake.

"Yeah, all right."

It'd been ages since we'd had a proper catch-up. For the first time in years, Lenny looked healthy—shiny hair, clear skin, breath that didn't smell like a badger's armpit—and that alone made slogging my guts out for Emmy worth it.

"How's rehab?" I asked.

"Different to how I thought it'd be. We do a lot of talking. A *lot*. And they dig up shit that I wanted to forget, like stuff from before the two of us ever met, and it's hard. But sometimes getting it out there makes me feel lighter, ya know? 'Cause then there's less crap left inside."

"I guess that makes sense. Are the people nice?"

"Yeah. Fussy sometimes, but nice." He leaned forward over the table and whispered, "I've even got a girlfriend. She's older than me, but still really hot."

A momentary panic seized me. "Not the woman you were playing chess with?"

"Julie? You told me to get to know her."

"Yes, but—"

"Chill, sis. It's not Julie. Her name's Debra. She ended up using some heavy shit after she got divorced, but she's clean now."

"How much older is she?"

"Like, five years? She's easy to talk to."

Thank goodness. "So, uh, congratulations." Then curiosity got the better of me. "What's Julie like?"

"Julie's a bitch. Smart, but a real bitch. And sneaky. She knows how to manipulate all the staff, and she kicks off if she doesn't get her own way."

None of that really surprised me. Genetics at work, eh?

"Just be careful around her. I'll come back as soon as I can, okay?"

"I'm cool, Sky. Don't worry about me."

I didn't, not anymore. A weight had been lifted when I returned to Emmy's London home and Asher. We were going to the West End tonight for dinner and a show. You know, normal things that normal people did? I couldn't wait.

Back in Virginia, my sleeping arrangements had changed too. The comfiest place to watch a movie in the evening was in my bed because Bradley had bought a fucking massive TV for my room, and when I fell asleep halfway through, it meant I didn't have to wake up and move in the middle of the night.

And when Asher started watching movies with me, he couldn't be arsed to get up either.

In the mornings, we'd wake up all squashed together, and his chest made a nice pillow. He didn't seem to mind me using it. Then when my alarm blared, he'd stroke my hair for a minute before I stumbled into the bathroom and he went back to sleep for another hour.

We were comfortable with each other. Sharing a bed was easier than not sharing a bed.

Sometimes, we shared a bathroom too, which led to an awkward moment when I went to take a shower and he'd just got out of it and we both stood there naked for a good ten seconds, staring at each other with steam billowing around. I was getting to be quite proud of my body by that point. I didn't have Emmy's abs yet, but I had curves in all the right places and muscles too. And Asher didn't have anything to be ashamed of either. He checked me out, and I checked him out. And then we simply went about our business. I got into the shower, and he wrapped a towel around his waist and brushed his teeth, and neither of us made a fuss about anything. Being with Asher was easy.

From time to time, I'd prop myself up on one elbow and watch him sleep. Wonder what might have happened if Brock Keaton hadn't screwed me up and the rich ladies of San Diego hadn't done the same to Asher. *Could* sex be enjoyable? Emmy and Black certainly seemed to think so, and I suspected they were getting plenty of it now. Last Tuesday, I'd snuck down to the kitchen for a midnight snack only to be greeted by the sight of Black's ass clenching as he thrust against the fridge with Emmy's legs wrapped around his waist.

I'd decided that perhaps I wasn't so hungry after all, and now I kept a stash of snacks in my closet.

I was craving a Mars Bar when I woke up early one Sunday with Asher curved around me like a deformed banana. As usual, we'd fallen asleep in the middle of a mediocre movie, except this morning, the TV remote had got wedged between us. I reached behind myself to get rid of it, only to realise it wasn't the TV remote at all.

Oh, shit.

I froze as Asher stirred groggily.

"Sky?"

"I'm sorry!"

He reached between us as well.

"Hmm. Guess that thing does still work. Don't you have work today?"

"Rafael's away for a couple of days, and Emmy said I could have a lie-in."

Mainly, I suspected, because *she* wanted a lie-in.

"Good." Asher snuggled against me again.

"Don't you need to do something about that... thing?"

"It'll go down by itself."

"Will it?"

"I'd rather stay here with you than give myself a handjob in the bathroom." He nuzzled between my shoulder blades. "And if it's a choice between you and sex, that's the easiest decision I'll ever have to make."

"What if..." I took a deep breath. "What if you could

have both?"

"But I thought you didn't want..."

"Lately, I've been thinking that maybe I should try. But only if you want to." I twisted to face him. "I'd rather have you than sex as well."

"But you want to try it?"

"Perhaps I should find out what all the fuss is about? One day. Possibly."

"Possibly? Where consent's concerned, 'possibly' doesn't cut it, Chem."

"That works both ways. I'd never push you into anything you didn't want to do."

"Once upon a time, I enjoyed sex. And lately, *I've* been thinking I wouldn't mind trying it again. But not on a 'possibly.'"

"How about a 'yes'?"

"Are you sure?"

I nodded before I could change my mind.

"Okay." His turn to take a deep breath. "Now?"

"Might as well get it over with."

I lay on my back, opened my legs, and screwed my eyes shut. Would it hurt? It couldn't be worse than a gym session with Rafael, surely?

Laughter wasn't the reaction I'd hoped for. I cracked one eyelid open. "What?"

"That's not how this works, Chem."

"Yes, it is. You might not have listened in those biology lessons, but I did."

Sort of.

"That's just mechanics, gorgeous. Close your eyes again. Relax. This is one place where I don't take shortcuts."

I expected a bit of prodding, which was mostly what

I remembered from Brock, so the barely-there whisper of Asher's lips over my collarbone was a surprise. Quite a nice one, though. He followed up with the tip of his tongue, and a shiver ran through me.

"Okay?" he asked.

"Mmm-hmm."

He went over every damn inch of me like that, from my forehead to my toes. *My toes.* Who knew my feet were so sensitive? Certainly not me, although I'd have needed to be a contortionist to find out. Every so often, Asher would work his way up my body and raise my head with one hand, tangling his fingers in my hair while he kissed me breathless. If I tried to open my eyes, he told me to close them again.

Then he started using his teeth, little nips and teases that made me jolt off the bed. That magic tongue swirled around each nipple in turn, and I arched up to meet him.

"You're so damn beautiful," he whispered, and his breath danced across the damp trails, cool above the fire burning under my skin.

I didn't flinch when he parted my knees wide, but I did let out a long moan when he finally buried his head between my legs. By then, I was a mess of sweat and fuck knew what else, but he didn't seem to care. He added his fingers to the mix, and then my whole world exploded. Detonated like C-4, only I might well have been louder.

Holy fuck.

"*This* is what I've been missing?" Something twitched inside me, but when I looked down, it was only Asher's fingers. "Oh."

"Just the start, gorgeous."

"There's more?"

"There is, but I need to find a condom. I should've thought of it before."

"I... Uh, there's one in my bag. Fake Dad gave it to me the day we got called into the principal's office."

Asher chuckled. "I'll take your fake family over my real family any day."

A little fishing around, and we were ready to go. The feeling of apprehension was back, but not nearly so strong. Asher wouldn't hurt me. I knew that.

"So, do you go on top? Do I go on top? How does this work?"

He kept his voice soft. Gentle. "Lie on your side."

"My side?"

He lay down next to me and hooked my top leg over his hip. "That's it. If you feel uncomfortable at any time, all you have to do is roll away." His smile calmed my nerves. "I'm gonna stretch you. It might be uncomfortable your first time."

"It's not—"

A tiny edge came into Asher's voice. "It *is*. What that monster did to you doesn't count."

It wasn't only me that Brock's actions had affected, was it? Indirectly, he'd hurt Asher too. Rafael was a fucking hero. Albeit a hero with a weakness. He was absolutely shit at ten-pin bowling, and I'd never ever let him forget it.

I closed my eyes again, and this time, there was no mistaking what slid into me. I'd expected it to feel like someone hammering a salami through a mouse hole because that was the experience I'd carried with me for years, but Asher's efforts were more like steel sliding over satin. Only once I felt the tickle of hair against my bits did I realise he was all the way in.

He feathered fluttery kisses over my cheeks, and although I could never say it to his face, I knew now why women had paid the big bucks for his services. The man was a wizard.

And that was how I felt *before* he started to move.

I didn't get the whole fireworks thing again, but I did feel a crazy deep connection, one that intensified with every thrust. And when he came with a quiet groan and his heat spread through me, I wrapped every limb around him and then the tears came. Tears of relief. Tears of happiness. I wasn't as broken as I'd always thought.

"Don't cry, Sky. What's wrong?"

"These are good tears, okay? Just don't tell anyone or they'll think I'm a pussy."

He kissed my forehead, then rolled me on top of him.

"Your secrets are always safe with me."

CHAPTER 46 - ALARIC

BETH HAD ONE request for the wedding. She wanted to ride Chaucer down the aisle, and Alaric was only too happy to accommodate her because he knew how much she loved that horse.

Which meant they'd initially planned on having a small wedding in England. Just the two of them and Rune, plus Ravi as best man and Judd and Naz as witnesses. Alaric invited Sky and Emmy too, and although having your ex at your wedding might have been considered odd, Beth understood why he wanted the two women there. If it weren't for that pair, he and Beth would never have ended up together.

But then someone—Beth suspected a busybody from the livery yard—told Beth's family that they were getting hitched, and suddenly they were being bombarded with so many orders and instructions that Beth informed her mother they were getting married in America and slammed the phone down.

Alaric didn't mind. It was easier to fly the horse to Virginia than deal with his soon-to-be in-laws.

The downside was that Bradley took over, but at least he didn't try to invite five hundred people and draw up a contract to have the photos featured in a national magazine the way Beth's mother had. And Emmy did her best to keep Bradley under control. She also agreed to let them hold the ceremony at Riverley, which wasn't Alaric's first choice of venue, but Beth loved the little sun temple thing in the corner of the west lawn, and who was he to disagree?

Originally, Beth's parents had planned to make the trip to Virginia, but last week her sister, Priscilla, had announced she was divorcing her new husband to marry Beth's ex, and Mr. and Mrs. Stafford-Lyons cancelled to deal with the fallout. Was Beth upset by the news? No, she'd laughed her pretty head off.

The wedding had grown a little—thirty or so people and their plus-ones, or in Judd's case plus-two because he'd decided he was bringing not only Gemma but Nada or whatever her name was as well. Both women were still living in his house, along with Nada's baby daughter. Nada had also borrowed his surname four months ago, and so far, she didn't appear to have given it back. Even the baby had a passport naming her as Indamira Millais-Scott. Alaric wasn't quite sure what was going on there, but he did know that he was in no position to judge, especially in light of his plans for tonight.

"Everybody, take your places," Bradley instructed. "We need to get this show on the road." He closed his eyes, crossed his fingers, and tilted his head heavenwards. "Please don't let the horse poop in the aisle."

Alaric and Ravi walked slowly towards the sun temple. The little domed building looked centuries old, a relic from another civilisation, but it hadn't been there eight years ago. Bradley had planted a grand piano beside it, and Asher was tinkling away on the keys.

"Thanks for doing this," Alaric said to Ravi. "It means a lot."

"Beth's your unicorn." Ravi smiled the smile that had drawn Alaric in on the night they first met. "Maybe one day, you'll return the favour."

"I'd like to think so."

The officiant took his position under the rose arch, and the guests took their seats. Emmy stood to the side, waiting to hold Chaucer once Beth had ridden down the aisle.

And there they were. His two girls. Beth in a cream satin dress astride her gleaming bay horse with Rune walking alongside. The younger McLain had skipped school to play bridesmaid, but her headmistress didn't mind because Rune had studied half the syllabus by herself during summer break anyway.

At the sun temple, Beth slid off Chaucer into Alaric's arms, and it was all he could do to make himself let go while Rune rearranged the bottom of the dress. He folded back Beth's veil and looked into those beautiful blue eyes. Was he nervous? No, just happy.

"Dearly beloved, we are gathered here today in the sight of—"

Frantic neighing interrupted the officiant, and it wasn't coming from Chaucer. Emmy's horse wasn't the culprit either—for once, Stan-slash-Satan was grazing peacefully in the distance. Suddenly, a white streak rounded the corner of the house, followed by a sprinting cowgirl waving her arms. Oh, fuck. Alaric stared in horror as the runaway horse bore down on them. Guests were already scattering, and half of them had guns in their hands.

"Don't shoot!" he yelled. "Don't anybody shoot!"

Beth's mouth dropped open as the grey horse skidded to a halt in front of her, ribbons of pristine turf curling from under his hooves.

"Polo?"

The one and only. Beth had his name tattooed over her heart, right above Alaric's. The ink was still fresh on the latter—she'd revealed that surprise two weeks ago when he got home after signing yet another new contract on behalf of Sirius, the sly little minx.

Now Polo nuzzled her, leaving a streak of yellow goop up the front of her dress.

"Oh my gosh, it's him. It's really him."

Alaric, the vows, the entire wedding was forgotten as Beth hugged her old horse. It had taken Sirius months to find that nag. None of the transfer-of-ownership records for that breed registry were computerised, and Ravi had spent three nights going through filing cabinets in the dark while Judd kept watch outside the building. Hartsfield Napoleon II, also known as Polo, had been renamed Ghost of the Ages and sold as an eventer to a teenager in Belgium. After she'd fallen off a number of times, he'd bounced around the world and, as far as Naz could ascertain, eventually ended up in Ohio. Frickin' Ohio. Emmy had gone to Columbus with Alaric because he didn't know one end of an equine from the other, and she'd concluded it was the right horse. By then, Polo was festering in a field, having refused to go over a single fence with his latest owner, and Alaric bought him for a song. The horse just gnashed his teeth as the deal was concluded. Harriet, a new friend who happened to own a horse farm, had picked him up and hidden him until today. She'd been only too happy to help after Alaric promised her the fifty-thousand-dollar reward that came from returning *Emerald* to the Becker Museum.

"It was meant to be a surprise," Alaric muttered.

"Oh, it is. It definitely is. My goodness, he's got so fat. And his coat's much lighter."

By then, Beth had mascara streaked all down her face, and Alaric's black suit was covered in white horse hair.

"Happy wedding day, my sweet."

Beth clapped her hands to her cheeks. "The wedding! I'm so sorry."

At least Alaric knew where he stood in terms of his soon-to-be wife's affections. Luckily, she had enough love to go around. A red-faced Harriet moved Polo to the side to stand with Chaucer, and Alaric finally had his Mrs. McLain.

And an hour later, he had her again, this time bent over the saddle rack in the Riverley tack room, still in her wedding dress. Alaric had learned his lesson from Beth's sister and locked the door while he fucked his new wife harder, harder, until she screamed not only his name but several obscenities she'd never utter in public.

Four months ago, on the day they got together, they'd confessed their darkest fantasies to each other. Three each. A wish list of filth to work their way through. Alaric's items were all checked off, but he still owed one to Beth. Tonight he'd pay up. She just didn't know it yet. No, she sat patiently with her legs spread while Alaric cleaned up the mess he'd made, and then they staggered outside so she could feed carrots to her horses.

"This is the best gift ever."

"Let's see if you still say that tomorrow," Alaric murmured.

"Sorry?"

"Never mind."

The reception—or the after-party, as Bradley insisted on calling it—would have been fun on any other day. Good wine, good food, good friends. But tonight, Alaric couldn't wait to escape. He finally got his wish as darkness fell and the limo he'd hired pulled up near the rear terrace. Tonight, they'd be staying at Hillside House. Emmy and Black had offered their private island for a honeymoon, but Alaric had arranged the flights for the following week, first to Lorelei Cay and then on to Italy to visit the vineyard he part-owned. Having just got Polo back, Alaric didn't think Beth would thank him if he tore her away for a vacation right afterwards. Next summer, they planned to take a month off and drive Route 66 with Rune— their first proper trip as a family. Alaric looked forward to the future now. The past was the past, and there the bad memories would stay.

Tonight, Rune was staying at Riverley, and she rushed over to give them both a hug. She wasn't quite back to her old self after *Emerald* did her worst, but she was heading in the right direction thanks to a good therapist and the school she loved. Plus she seemed to be getting along well with Sky, despite their vastly different personalities. Alaric wasn't sure whether that was a good thing or a bad thing.

"See you tomorrow," she said. "Love you both."

"Love you too, sweetheart."

Beth ran off to the stables to say a last goodbye to the horses, and Emmy sidled up to Alaric and straightened his jacket.

"I'm glad you got your girl."

"So am I." He removed the envelope she'd surreptitiously slipped into his inside pocket. "What's this?"

"The deed to your house."

"What? You can't..."

"Just did. Now sod off and make your wife happy."

She didn't look back as she took Black's arm and walked past Rafael into Riverley Hall. Typical Emmy. Kind yet bitchy at the same time. Alaric was still chuckling softly when Beth's arm wrapped around his waist.

"What's so funny?"

"Nothing. Let's go home."

They climbed into the back seat of the limo, but rather than gliding straight down the driveway, it made a pit stop at the front of the house. Ravi slipped out of the shadows and climbed into the car with them.

Beth's face was an adorable mask of confusion.

"What's going on?"

"You had three wishes, sweetheart."

It took her a few moments, but she finally understood.

"Oh!"

If she balked, Ravi would leave. He and Alaric had discussed this at length, and Ravi was up for a little experimentation if Beth was.

But Beth didn't balk. The look of shock faded, and her eyes gleamed.

"Oh..."

Alaric leaned forward and tapped on the privacy screen. The limo moved off. He lifted Beth's dress, pushing the layers of silk and lace up to her waist, and ran his hand along her thigh. Ravi mirrored him on the other side.

"Ohhhhh…"

Chapter 47 - Emmy

I HUGGED THE darkness at the edge of the window, watching the scene on the driveway below.

"Why did Ravi just get into the limo with Alaric and Beth?"

Black flicked one spaghetti strap off my shoulder.

"I'll give you three guesses," he said. "'Three' being the operative word."

Oh my freaking fuck. Those dirty fuckers! Alaric, yeah, it didn't surprise me, or Ravi either, but Beth? She'd always seemed so prim.

"That's an, uh, interesting development."

Black's filthy laugh vibrated against my ear as one hand crept up my thigh.

"That's one way of putting it. And speaking of interesting developments, did you see the look on Rafael's face as we walked inside?"

Yeah, I had, and it'd been weird. A cross between anger and sorrow.

"It was kind of...intense. I've never seen it before."

"I have."

"Really?"

"In the mirror, every time you got a new boyfriend and I kicked myself for not having the guts to tell you how I felt."

I closed my eyes and replayed the scene on the

terrace. I'd gotten good at that over the years. Each party I went to, I took mental snapshots and stitched them all together in my head. Who had been in Rafael's field of vision? Dan and Ethan, Harriet and Stéphane, Bradley, two waiters, Asher and... Oh, fuck.

"Sky?"

"It's going to be a fun few years."

"Bloody hell."

"How do you feel about a pool?"

"No. No way. You're not running a pool on Sky and Rafael."

"So we'll just keep this to ourselves?"

Too damn right. "Yes, we'll keep this to ourselves."

BONUS CHAPTER

From time to time, I like to write extra bits that go with my novels. These are FREE to members of my reader group.

If you'd like to find out what happened when Rafael met Brock Keaton, you can get a bonus chapter by following this link:

www.elise-noble.com/sh4dows

WHAT'S NEXT?

My next book will be *A Vampire in Vegas*, the first book in the Planes series...

When nightclub hostess Genevieve Pelletier finds singer Serenity Strange's body in a storeroom at Club Dead, the search begins to find her killer...but it won't be easy. The list of suspects is longer than the line of beautiful people waiting to get in.

Detective Jack Callaghan has earned a reputation for solving the unsolvable, but this case may be beyond even his formidable skills. The deeper he digs, the darker the trail gets. Serenity's death is just the tip of the blood-soaked iceberg.

Can Jack and Vee solve the murder? Or will they end up on the killer's hitlist?

For more details: www.elise-noble.com/vampire

The next Blackwood Security novel will be Hallie's story, *Pretties in Pink...*

Five years ago, Mila Carmody disappeared from her bed, and that was just the beginning. Six little girls, swallowed by darkness, never to be seen alive again. For Micah Ganaway, it might be the end. Arrested for child abduction, he's already been tried in the court of public opinion and found guilty. The lead detective assures him the trial is just a formality.

But private investigator Hallie Chastain isn't so sure. On paper, Ganaway makes a good suspect, but in person... Well, that's a different matter.

For more details: www.elise-noble.com/pink

If you enjoyed *When the Shadows Fall*, please consider leaving a review.

For an author, every review is incredibly important. Not only do they make us feel warm and fuzzy inside, readers consider them when making their decision whether or not to buy a book. Even a line saying you enjoyed the book or what your favourite part was helps a lot.

Want to Stalk Me?

For updates on my new releases, giveaways, and other random stuff, you can sign up for my newsletter on my website:
www.elise-noble.com

Facebook:
www.facebook.com/EliseNobleAuthor

Twitter: @EliseANoble

Instagram: @elise_noble

If you're on Facebook, you may also like to join Team Blackwood for exclusive giveaways, sneak previews, and book-related chat. Be the first to find out about new stories, and you might even see your name or one of your ideas make it into print!

And if you'd like to read my books for FREE, you can also find details of how to join my advance review team.

Would you like to join Team Blackwood?

www.elise-noble.com/team-blackwood

END OF BOOK STUFF

All good things come to an end, and this is the end of Alaric's trilogy, although he'll still pop up from time to time in other books. But it's just the beginning of Sky's story. She'll be around for a while :) Asher and Rafael? They'll be back too, and we'll see how things go...

When I wrote Shadows, there was a bit of an academy trend happening in the book world, mainly bully romances, but I find those a bit of an oxymoron so I thought it would be fun to write my own book set in a school but with a dude who isn't an asshole. Shadows was the result.

Over 650,000 works of art were looted by the Nazis, and many of them are still missing. In 2013, a billion dollars worth of art was discovered in the Munich apartment of Cornelius Gurlitt, the son of a WWII art dealer who bought some paintings at knock-down prices from Jews fleeing the Nazi regime and just plain stole others. Picasso, Matisse, Renoir... He had pieces by them all. Hildebrand Gurlitt double-crossed everyone—both the Nazis and his fellow Jews. Yes, he saved valuable paintings from being destroyed, even while acting as an official art buyer for Hitler, but in the end, he was corrupted by money and kept many of the treasures for himself.

Cornelius, by his own account, felt it was his duty to

protect the paintings as his father had done, from thieves, from the authorities, and from their original owners. German restitution laws relating to looted art are complex, and few pieces get returned, even though many are believed to be sitting in the dusty backrooms of the country's museums. All things considered, it doesn't seem outrageous that a civic-minded soul might take matters into their own hands and start righting old wrongs, but like Hildebrand, Saul Rosenberg got suckered in by greed and started down a dark path...

Next up in the Blackwood Security series will be Hallie's story. Remember Mila Carmody, the kidnapped girl mentioned in Black is My Heart? Well, it's time to find out what happened to her...

But in the meantime, we're stepping over to the supernatural side with the fifth instalment of the Electi series—*Judged*—plus two linked books set in the same world. Time for me to carry on writing...

Elise :)

OTHER BOOKS BY ELISE NOBLE

The Blackwood Security Series
For the Love of Animals (Nate & Carmen - prequel)
Black is My Heart (Diamond & Snow - prequel)
Pitch Black
Into the Black
Forever Black
Gold Rush
Gray is My Heart
Neon (novella)
Out of the Blue
Ultraviolet
Glitter (novella)
Red Alert
White Hot
Sphere (novella)
The Scarlet Affair
Spirit (novella)
Quicksilver
The Girl with the Emerald Ring
Red After Dark
When the Shadows Fall
Pretties in Pink (TBA)

The Blackwood Elements Series
Oxygen

Lithium
Carbon
Rhodium
Platinum
Lead
Copper
Bronze
Nickel
Hydrogen (TBA)

The Blackwood UK Series
Joker in the Pack
Cherry on Top (novella)
Roses are Dead
Shallow Graves
Indigo Rain
Pass the Parcel (TBA)

Blackwood Casefiles
Stolen Hearts
Burning Love (TBA)

Blackstone House
Hard Lines (2021)
Hard Tide (TBA)

The Electi Series
Cursed
Spooked
Possessed
Demented
Judged (2021)

The Planes Series
A Vampire in Vegas (2021)

The Trouble Series
Trouble in Paradise
Nothing but Trouble
24 Hours of Trouble

Standalone
Life
Coco du Ciel (2021)
Twisted (short stories)
A Very Happy Christmas (novella)

Books with clean versions available (no swearing and no on-the-page sex)
Pitch Black
Into the Black
Forever Black
Gold Rush
Gray is My Heart

Audiobooks
Black is My Heart (Diamond & Snow - prequel)
Pitch Black
Into the Black
Forever Black
Gold Rush
Gray is My Heart